Cindi Myers is the author of more than fifty novels. When she's not crafting new romance plots, she enjoys skiing, gardening, cooking, crafting and daydreaming. A lover of small-town life, she lives with her husband and two spoiled dogs in the Colorado mountains.

Delores Fossen, a *USA TODAY* bestselling author, has sold over fifty novels, with millions of copies of her books in print worldwide. She's received a Booksellers' Best Award and an RT Reviewers' Choice Best Book Award. She was also a finalist for a prestigious RITA® Award. You can contact the author through her website at www.deloresfossen.com.

D0756065

9030 00005 8769 2

Also by Cindi Myers

Also by Delores Fossen

Discover more at millsandboon.co.uk

STRANDED WITH THE SUSPECT

CINDI MYERS

LAWMAN FROM HER PAST

DELORES FOSSEN

MILLS & BOON

First Published in Great Britain 2018
by Mills & Boon, an imprint of HarperCollins*Publishers*
1 London Bridge Street, London, SE1 9GF

Stranded With The Suspect © 2018 Cynthia Myers
Lawman From Her Past © 2018 Delores Fossen

ISBN: 978-0-263-26563-7

39-0318

MIX
Paper from
responsible sources
FSC™ C007454

This book is produced from independently certified FSC™ paper to ensure responsible forest management.

For more information visit: www.harpercollins.co.uk/green

Printed and bound in Spain
by CPI, Barcelona

STRANDED WITH THE SUSPECT

CINDI MYERS

For Deann

Chapter One

"I'm sorry, we don't have any messages for you, Ms. Daniels. I promise to put any calls or other communications through to your room at once. Is there anything else I can do for you?" The desk clerk at the Brown Palace Hotel smiled as she spoke, as if she really was concerned that Andi have everything she needed.

"No. Thank you." Andi tried to return the smile, but it wasn't something she was used to doing anymore. The past year hadn't given her much to smile about.

"Did you enjoy your visit to our spa this morning?" the clerk asked, after a quick glance at her computer screen, which no doubt showed every spa treatment, room service meal and other amenity Andi had enjoyed during her stay at one of Denver's oldest luxury hotels.

"Yes, it was lovely." Everything about the Brown Palace was lovely, from the richly patterned carpet beneath her feet to the stained-glass skylights in the main lobby. Towering fresh flower arrangements and elegant artwork shared space with photographs of the many celebrated personages who had stayed at the hotel, from the Beatles to US presidents. But none of it impressed

Andi. For one thing, she had seen it all too many times before, when she stayed here with her father, Senator Pete Matheson.

That seemed a lifetime ago. Now all of this—the opulence and grand sense of history—wasn't her world anymore. She craved simplicity over elegance, reality more than comfort. This felt so phony.

"If you need anything at all, please let me know, Ms. Daniels," the clerk said.

Andi nodded and turned from the desk. Her name wasn't even Daniels—it was Matheson. But Daniel Metwater had thought it amusing to register her under a variant of his Christian name when he had brought her here three days ago. He was supposed to have contacted her before now, to let her know he was coming to get her and take her home.

She reached up and put her hand over the pendant at her neck, the rose-cut diamond in the old-fashioned gold setting a comforting weight at the base of her throat. Daniel didn't know that she had taken it before she left to come to Denver, but after all, he had promised it to her baby, so why shouldn't she have it now? If he asked about it when he arrived, she would tell him she had been keeping it safe for him. He might not be pleased with that explanation at first, but he would come around. Daniel wanted her to be happy.

She waited for the elevator, her ankles swollen, feet hurting. Absently, she rubbed at the bulge of her abdomen, the baby kicking inside her. She tried to imagine what the little one looked like right now, recalling pictures in the tattered copy of *What to Expect When*

You're Expecting that one of the women in camp had loaned her. She had no idea if she was carrying a boy or a girl. It didn't matter—she would be happy with either. Part of her was anxious for the child's arrival. Another part of her wanted to put it off as long as possible. She hadn't seen a doctor since the public clinic had confirmed her pregnancy months ago, so she had no idea of her due date. But the other women in camp had assured her that the baby would come out when it was ready, and that she would be ready then, also.

Since she wasn't ready for the birth, the baby must not be either, which was reassuring in a way. She didn't want to have her child alone in this city that no longer felt familiar to her. She wanted to be back in the camp in the wilderness in southwest Colorado, with the women attending her and the men waiting outside, chanting for her and the baby's health.

"Ms. Matheson? Andi Matheson?"

She turned toward the speaker before she could stop herself. A lean, athletic man with a blond goatee smiled at her. "So good to see you again," he said, with just a hint of a foreign accent. Austrian? Russian?

"I… I'm sorry. You must have me confused with someone else." She turned to face the elevator once more, but she could feel his eyes on her.

He stepped closer, brushing against her arm. "Oh, but I am sure I am right. I would never forget such a beautiful woman."

She said nothing, teeth clenched, willing the elevator doors to open so she could make her escape.

"You are living with the evangelist, Daniel Metwater, now, are you not?" the man asked.

Daniel wasn't an evangelist. Not in the sense most people used the word. He was a prophet and a teacher.

The man touched her arm. "I would very much like to meet your boyfriend. Perhaps you could arrange it, no?"

She jerked away. The gilded doors of the elevator opened and she hurried inside. The man started to follow, but a dark-haired man shoved him out of the way and slipped in after her, immediately hitting the button to close the doors. "What floor?" he asked, his back to her.

"Fourteenth," she said, still shaken from the encounter with the blond.

He pressed the button for fourteen, then turned to face her. She gasped as she recognized his face, and pressed her back against the railing on the inside of the elevator car. "What are you doing here?" she asked.

The vertical line between his dark brows deepened as he frowned at her. "I'm not going to hurt you," he said.

She wasn't afraid of him. Not exactly. Officer Simon Woolridge wore his disdain of her and the other members of the family she belonged to on his face for all to see, especially his contempt for the man who led them, their Prophet, Daniel Metwater, but he had never given Andi reason to be afraid of him. He had never tried to befriend her the way some of the members of his organization, the Ranger Brigade, had. After a lifetime of dealing with frauds and posers, she could appreciate that kind of honesty.

"Why are you here?" she asked again. "Is something wrong? Has something happened to the Prophet?"

The elevator door opened and Simon touched her elbow. "Let's go to your room, where we can talk."

He walked beside her to her room at the end of the hall, a tall, commanding presence at her right elbow. She was used to seeing him in uniform, but today he wore jeans and a black Western shirt that emphasized his broad shoulders and narrow waist. The clothes made him seem less familiar and more...intriguing. She hadn't bothered to look much past the uniform before, but now she was aware of him as a man most women would give a second—or a third—look to. He waited while she slipped her card key from her purse, slid it in the lock and opened the door. Then he followed her inside.

She braced herself for him to make a disparaging remark about her luxurious suite, a sharp contrast to the tent she had been living in since she had joined Daniel Metwater and his followers five months previously. But he only gave the room a cursory glance before turning to her. "How are you feeling?" he asked.

The question caught her off guard. "I'm fine," she said automatically.

His gaze swept over her, his dark eyes intense, making her want to cover herself, even though she was fully dressed. He reminded her of a sleek cat, preparing to pounce on its prey. "You look pale," he said. "Your ankles are swollen and you keep arching your back, as if it hurts."

She put a hand to her lower back, which did ache, as

did her swollen feet. She didn't know whether to be flattered he had noticed so much in such a short time, or to be unnerved by his scrutiny. "I'm fine," she said again.

"You're a lousy liar. Who was the man you were talking to by the elevator downstairs?"

"I don't know."

"He acted as if he knew you."

Yes. And that had been unsettling. "He knew who I was," she said. "He called me by my name—my real name."

"I heard him ask about Metwater."

"Yes. He wanted to meet him. Maybe he was simply a fan." Yes, that was probably it. The Prophet attracted many followers wherever he went.

Simon turned away from her to prowl the room like a restless predator. "Metwater must be doing pretty well siphoning money off his followers," he said. "If he can afford to hide you away here."

There was the cynicism she had been expecting. "I'm not hiding," she said. "And the Prophet has money of his own. He inherited it from his father."

Simon paused in his circuit of the room and looked back at her. "Then why does he need your money?"

Andi didn't answer.

"You signed the agreement, didn't you?" Simon asked. "The one that gives Daniel Metwater all your assets— now and in the future, as long as you remain with him."

"The money goes to the Family," she said. "We pool our resources so that no one has more than anyone else."

"The money goes into Daniel Metwater's personal bank account. I have the records, if you don't believe me."

The Rangers had no business looking into the private affairs of the Prophet, though of course, they thought their badges gave them the right. "He decides the best use of the funds for the Family," she said.

"I guess this week, stashing you in a suite in the Brown Palace was the best use of the funds."

Again, she said nothing. He had obviously made up his mind. And what business was it of his how the Family spent their money? She opened her mouth to ask him, but he cut her off.

"Whose idea was it to come here?" he asked her.

"The Prophet's."

"He wanted you here so that you couldn't tell us anything we could use against him," Simon said. "But it's too late for that now. We already have everything we need to put him away."

"Are you saying you arrested him?" She tried to keep the alarm out of her voice, but failed. For months, the Rangers had been harassing Daniel Metwater and his followers. The Family, as they called themselves, got the blame for every crime that occurred on the public lands the Ranger Brigade patrolled.

"When was the last time you heard from him?" Simon asked.

"I haven't heard anything from him since he brought me here three days ago," she said. "Why? Where is he? What have you done to him?"

"We haven't done anything. We don't know where he is." Simon's eyes met hers, black and hard as coal. "I was hoping you did."

She shook her head and sank onto the sofa, fearful

her legs would no longer support her. "What's happened? Why are you looking for him?"

"We found your friend Starfall's baby."

"Hunter!" Fear clogged her throat. Her tentmate's child had disappeared from camp two days before Metwater drove Andi to Denver. Starfall had accused the Prophet of taking her child, but Andi knew that couldn't be true. "Is he okay? Where was he?"

"He's fine. He was with a couple of guys named Smith. Two brothers. Sound familiar?"

She shook her head, relief flooding her. "Then you know Daniel didn't take Hunter," she said. "Why are you still looking for him when you know he's innocent?"

"The Smith brothers told us Daniel Metwater paid them to take Starfall's baby," Simon said. "Metwater said he wanted to teach her a lesson."

Andi shook her head. "No. He wouldn't do something like that."

"Then why did he kidnap Starfall and try to kill her? He tried to kill Ethan Reynolds, the Ranger who was trying to help her, too."

"You're lying. The Prophet would never do anything like that. He promotes peace."

Simon stood over her, his shadow falling across her face, his bulk making her feel even smaller. "Why are you defending him?" he demanded. "What has he done for you but take your money and sleep with other women?"

She cringed at the words. "He's trying to teach me not to be possessive." Wanting the Prophet of their people all to herself was her personal failing, one she struggled with.

"A truly good man wouldn't treat you this way," Simon said, his voice gentler. "He would cherish you and protect you, not lie to you and use you."

"You don't know what you're talking about."

His expression hardened. "Maybe not. But I know you're in danger if you don't get away from him."

"Danger?" The word shocked her out of her despair. She sat up straighter. "What kind of danger?"

"Daniel Metwater is running for his life right now. Every law enforcement agency in the country is hunting for him," Simon said. "He knows sooner or later we're going to catch him. When we do, he doesn't want you around to testify against him."

"I would never testify against him," she said, horrified at the idea.

"You're not married to him. You can be compelled to tell what you know."

"But I don't know anything."

"I think you do," Simon said. "You're closer to Daniel Metwater than anyone. You may not realize the significance of the information, but it's something big enough that he took care to hide you away here, under an assumed name."

"If that's true and he's so terrible, why didn't he just kill me?" she asked. "That's apparently the kind of man you think he is."

Simon's expression didn't change. "He has to keep you alive until your twenty-fifth birthday, when your trust comes under your control. If you die after that, the money all goes to Daniel Metwater—am I right?"

He was, though she had no intention of confirming this. "The Prophet would never harm me," she said.

"I'll bet Starfall thought the same thing, until he beat her and stole her baby."

Andi pressed her hands against her belly, feeling the child shift inside her. "You need to leave," she said.

"I'll go for now," he said. "But I won't be far away." He headed toward the door. "I have a feeling Metwater is going to come back for you, and when he does, he'll find me waiting."

He left, closing the door firmly behind him. She stared after him, rage and fear and sickness swirling through her. Simon Woolridge was a horrible man. How could he make such terrible accusations against a man who spoke words of peace and caring? Daniel Metwater had saved her, and so many others.

Simon was a hard, abrasive cop who had no concern for her or her feelings.

But Daniel Metwater, despite all his goodness, had lied to her more than once. As far as she knew, Simon had never lied to her, even when telling the truth hurt.

Chapter Two

Simon prowled the hallway outside Andi's room, immune to the appeal of well-upholstered chairs and elegant chandeliers. He viewed the hotel like a battleground, noting positions from which to mount an offensive, and the many places a fugitive might hide.

His conversation with Andi hadn't gone as he had hoped. He had meant to come down hard on her, to insist that she come with him to a shelter or another place of safety. But one look at her beautiful, weary face had melted his resolve. Maybe it was better for her and her baby if she stayed here, where she would at least be comfortable. He would guard her and wait.

Metwater was going to come for her; Simon was sure of it. The man preached poverty and the simple life to his followers, but he had used the very people who depended on him to amass assets in excess of sixty-eight million dollars. And that was only the accounts Simon had managed to locate. There was probably more stashed elsewhere.

But he was a fugitive on the run now, his bank accounts frozen and unavailable to him. He would need money to leave the country, to run out of the reach of US law. Andi had money, and Metwater could be confident she would give it to him. All he had to do was get to her. A different type of man might have gotten by on wits and cunning alone, but Metwater was used to paying his way out of trouble.

He was the son of a man who had made a fortune manufacturing plastics in Chicago. He had a twin brother, David, who had reportedly embezzled hundreds of thousands of dollars from the family business before Metwater Senior's death. Without his dad to reign him in, David had really gone off the rails, racking up gambling debts, dabbling in the drug trade and getting in deep with the Russian mob. He had died under mysterious circumstances, supposedly killed by organized crime members he had tried to double-cross.

Meanwhile, Daniel kept on managing the family business, serving on the boards of various charities and cleaning up the mess his brother made. David's death, he told the press, cut him deeply, to the point where he sold the family business and took to the road, preaching peace and poverty to a growing list of followers, who eventually followed him to the public lands of Colorado, where they set up camp in the Rangers' jurisdiction.

The good twin and the bad twin. A classic cliché. Simon didn't buy it. He figured Daniel had been every bit as corrupt as his twin, but managed to hide it better. Nobody was the saint the press made Daniel out to be.

Simon knew a few real saints—nuns who lived real vows of poverty and worked to save children in border-town slums, doctors who used their own money to fund clinics for the indigent, police officers who faced down corruption and paid the ultimate price when they were assassinated for refusing to look the other way.

But Simon was no saint. Working for Immigration and Customs Enforcement, he had sent widows and orphans back to uncertain futures and poverty because they had the bad luck to be born on the wrong side of the border. He didn't believe in mercy for those who broke the law, and he had little patience for whiners and weaklings.

And he knew there was a special place in hell for men like Daniel Metwater, who took advantage of the lost and lonely.

Beautiful Andi Matheson was a little of both. She had the kind of ethereal beauty that drew the eye. The first time Simon had seen the blonde there in Metwater's camp, he had a hard time not staring. She had been born into privilege and by all accounts was a spoiled socialite who had never been denied anything—all reasons enough for him to dislike her, which he had been prepared to do.

Then he had looked into those sapphire eyes, and the hurt and fear in them had hit him like a sucker punch. Stripped of her beauty-queen gowns and protected privilege, he had seen her for the lost, struggling soul she was. From that moment on, Simon had appointed himself Andi's guardian. Which is why he patrolled the hallways and public areas of the hotel, alert to anything that might signal danger.

He was torn between the desire to station himself outside Andi's door, and the need to find and question the man who had spoken to her at the elevator. Simon sensed a threat from that man. If he could deal with the stranger, then he could focus on Metwater.

In the hotel bar, The Ship Tavern, he spotted a familiar blond head—the man who had approached Andi outside the elevators. He entered the bar and was immediately engulfed by a wave of noise—a dozen conversations rising over the blare of two TVs and the clink of glasses. The gleam of brass—brass railings, brass light fixtures, brass ornaments on the wall—caught and reflected back the light from old-fashioned ship's lanterns and faceted chandeliers. Simon squeezed past a shapely brunette in a sequined cocktail gown. She smiled warmly and looked him up and down. "Hi, handsome," she breathed.

He ignored her and continued on until he reached the bar, and eased in beside the blond man, who immediately turned to see who had joined him. Simon nodded in greeting. The blond returned the nod, and gave no indication that he recognized Simon. "What can I get you?" the bartender asked.

"Fat Tire," Simon said. When the bartender had walked away, Simon turned once more to the blond. "I saw you talking to Andi Matheson earlier," he said. He seldom wasted time with subtlety. In his experience, a direct confrontation was more likely to catch people off guard.

The blond tensed, one hand slipping inside his jacket. "Who are you?"

"Are you going to shoot me right here in this bar because I made a simple remark?" Simon kept his voice even as he turned to accept the beer from the bartender, who flicked a glance at the blond.

The blond brought his hand back out in the open and nodded to the bartender. "My friend thinks he's so funny," he said, his English very good, but definitely with a hint of a Russian accent.

The blond waited until the bartender had walked away before he spoke again, keeping his hands outside his coat. "Who are you?" he asked again.

"I'm a friend of Ms. Matheson's," Simon said. "Who are you?"

"You're the man in the elevator." Understanding lit his eyes.

"Who are you and what do you want with her?" Simon asked.

"I am also a friend."

"That's not what she says. She says she never saw you before."

"She doesn't remember." He sipped his drink— something dark and thick in a small glass. "It was at a party, with a lot of people."

"When? Where?"

"Why are you so interested?"

"It's my business to be interested."

The blond studied Simon more closely. He tensed again, eyes narrowed. "You're a cop," he said.

Simon didn't deny or confirm, but met the blond's glare with a hard look of his own.

"I don't like cops," the blond said.

"I don't like people who bother Ms. Matheson. She said you asked her about Daniel Metwater."

The blond contemplated the liquid in the glass. "Her boyfriend. He's putting her up here, isn't he?"

"What makes you think that?"

"I have a connection at the front desk." He cut his eyes to Simon, his expression wary. "Are you after her for something—or is it Metwater you want?"

"Right now, I'm interested in you."

"I'm a man having a drink in a public bar." He drained his glass and set it down on the bar with a hard *thunk*. He pulled a heavy gold money clip from his pocket, peeled off a twenty and laid it on the bar. "Good night."

"Leave Ms. Matheson alone," Simon said.

"Watch your back," the blond said softly, but loud enough for Simon to hear.

Simon started after him, only to be blocked by a group of men and women who pushed toward the bar. By the time he got free, he reached the door just in time to see the blond pushing through the glass doors of the hotel lobby to the street.

Simon returned to the bar and paid for his beer, then walked back into the lobby. A quick scan satisfied him that the blond hadn't returned. But Simon had added the Russian to the short list of people who might be a danger to Andi.

He made his way back to the fourteenth floor and the room two doors down from Andi's. His bosses were going to scream when they got the bill for the suite, but it couldn't be helped. If Daniel Metwater—or the Russian—tried to get to Andi, they would have to get past Simon first.

SIMON'S VISIT HAD banished all hope Andi had of resting. Not that she had been sleeping much lately anyway. She missed having other women around to talk to—that had been one of the best things about joining the Family. An only child, she had never realized how comforting it could be to have other women around you—sisters who understood your concerns and were always willing to listen or offer advice. Casual acquaintances you didn't live with could never understand you as well as family. A check of the clock showed it was only eight thirty, so she dialed the number for her former tentmate at the Family's camp, Starfall. She would have to remember to call her Michelle, now that she had left the group and decided to go by her birth name once more.

"Hello?" Michelle answered.

"Hi. It's Andi."

"What do you want?" Michelle's voice wasn't exactly angry, but it wasn't friendly either.

Andi grimaced. She had forgotten that the two of them had argued the last time they had spoken. "I heard they found Hunter safe," she said. "I wanted to tell you how glad I am about that." Michelle must have been half-crazy with worry when her little boy disappeared.

"No thanks to Daniel Metwater," Michelle said. "He was the one who hired the guys who kidnapped him. And then Metwater tried to kill me. He tried to kill Ethan too."

So it was true. Not that Andi had really doubted Simon's words. "I heard," she said. "I'm sorry."

"Who told you about it? You're not with Metwater now, are you?"

"No, no. I haven't seen or spoken to him. Simon Woolridge told me. He's one of the officers with the Ranger Brigade."

"I know Simon. When did you talk to him?"

"A little while ago. He came to Denver—I guess he's hoping he'll catch the Prophet when he comes to pick me up at the hotel. But I don't think he's coming. Why would he risk it?"

"Besides the fact that he thinks he can get away with anything?" Michelle asked.

"Why did he try to kill you?" Andi asked. "Why would he want to kidnap Hunter? None of that makes sense to me."

"I don't know," Michelle said. "Most of what he said didn't make sense—but Ethan thinks it's because I know something that could get him into trouble."

"Ethan is the officer who was helping you?" Andi asked.

"Yes. He's been great." Michelle's voice softened, her tone almost wistful. "I can't believe how great he's been."

"What does he think you know that could hurt the Prophet?" Andi asked.

"I wish I knew what it was—I'd shout it from the rooftops."

"Simon says he thinks I must know something that could hurt Daniel, too," Andi said. "That's why he hid me away here in Denver."

"So, what do you know?"

"Nothing. I swear. I can't think of anything."

"You spent the most time with him and were closest

to him," Michelle said. "I'll bet you saw a lot of things you shouldn't have."

"No." In spite of all the time they'd spent together, she really didn't know much at all about Daniel Metwater. He had kept her ignorant, changing the subject whenever she asked about the past or his plans for the future, or even what he did in the hours she wasn't with him. She knew only what he wanted her to know, and that wasn't anything beyond his public image as a sincere, wise teacher and leader.

"Stay away from him, Andi," Michelle said. "He wants people to think he's good and has their best interests at heart, but that's not true."

"I'll be careful," Andi said.

"Stick with Simon," Michelle said. "The Rangers had Metwater figured out a long time ago. I wish now we had listened to them."

"It's a little strange, hearing you, of all people, talking about trusting the cops," Andi said. The Prophet had always taught that law enforcement officers were not their friends, and Michelle, who had apparently had her share of run-ins with the police, had agreed wholeheartedly with this assessment.

Michelle laughed. "And now I'm in love with one. I can hardly believe it myself."

"I'm glad things are working out so well for you," Andi said, ignoring the stab of jealousy that lanced through her. Michelle sounded so happy. As if she lived in some alternate universe different from the one Andi occupied. It didn't even seem possible to be that happy in her world.

"Take care of yourself," Michelle said. "And keep in touch. Let me know when your baby is born."

"I will." They said goodbye and Andi hung up the phone. She had hoped talking to a friend would soothe her, but the conversation had only reinforced the reasons she had to be worried and afraid. All this emotional upheaval couldn't be good for the baby. She needed to find a way to stay calm.

She phoned room service and ordered a cup of warm milk. That had been her mother's remedy when Andi struggled to get to sleep as a girl. She set down the phone, tears pricking her eyes at the memory of her mother. Cancer had taken her almost ten years ago. Everything had changed after that—Andi's father had become more focused on his political career, more concerned with power and prestige than with his daughter, except when she could be an asset to his image.

If her mother had lived, maybe things would have been different. Maybe Andi wouldn't have fallen for her father's bodyguard—a man who turned out to be married. Already pregnant, Andi had discovered the bodyguard's deception and her father's corruption. Wanting to escape the dishonesty and shallowness of her life, she had found solace in the teachings of Daniel Metwater. She was sure he was a man she could respect and love, and she hated men like Simon Woolridge for making her doubt her beliefs.

Now Michelle was telling her Simon was right, and she didn't know what to think. Had her judgment really been so poor? Or was Daniel Metwater extremely gifted in deceiving people?

A knock on the door disturbed her thoughts, and she checked the peephole and recognized the livery of the hotel staff. Relieved, she opened the door, only to find herself shoved backward into the room.

Daniel Metwater tossed the tray with the cup of milk aside and grabbed Andi by the wrists. "We don't have much time," he said. "We have to get out of here."

Chapter Three

Simon paced the length of the hotel room, too unsettled to sit still. When he had booked the room, he had imagined using it as a base to keep an eye on Andi's suite, but the layout was all wrong. He couldn't see her door clearly from here, and the walls were too thick, the carpeting too plush, for him to hear anyone approaching.

Under other circumstances, he could have worked with hotel security to set up a surveillance camera to monitor her door. But that kind of thing took warrants—and it took time. Time Simon didn't have.

Metwater was running, and he was desperate. Maybe he would leave town, or even leave the country and forget about Andi altogether, but Simon didn't think so. For one thing, he didn't have the resources he would need to make a getaway. For another, he had already proven he didn't like loose ends or unfinished business. He had hidden Andi away here—or thought he had—when the Rangers began closing in. He didn't want the cops talking to her.

And Metwater would know that Andi's twenty-fifth birthday was only a few days away. Once her trust—

several million dollars—passed to her, he could use his power over her to control the funds. A man as greedy as Metwater wouldn't want to pass up the opportunity to have that kind of money.

Simon had the Russian to consider too. He had seen the man leave the hotel, but he could have easily circled around and come back in through another entrance. Though the man hadn't directly threatened Andi, Simon couldn't shake the feeling that he was a danger to her.

Not on my watch, Simon thought, and stepped back into the hallway. He could station himself outside Andi's doorway as a guard, but Metwater would see him and avoid approaching. That might keep Andi safe, but it wouldn't trap Metwater. Simon wanted to stop the Prophet before he hurt anyone else. That meant staying hidden and getting the jump on him when he did approach.

He scanned the hallway, his gaze coming to rest on a recess that housed a decorative plant. A real plant, he noted as he squeezed in behind it, not a silk one. The space was cramped and uncomfortable, but he settled in as best he could, gun drawn, eyes focused on the doorway to Andi's room and the hallway leading up to it.

The events of the past two days dragged at him—the rescue of Hunter Munson, the search for Michelle and Ethan, their safe return and then the long drive to Denver to get to Andi before Metwater could reach her. He fought sleep by focusing on the Russian. Where did he fit into the picture? Metwater's twin brother had supposedly been murdered—rather, assassinated—by the *Bratva,* the Russian mob, though the Chicago police had never found enough evidence to formally charge anyone with the crime. The case was still open.

When Russians had shown up in Black Canyon of the Gunnison National Park and two people associated with them had ended up dead, Daniel Metwater had panicked and demanded protection from the Ranger Brigade, though he would never say why he thought the Russians were after him. The Russians turned out to be part of a smuggling ring that was trying to move into the park, and not after Metwater at all, but the cool, sophisticated mask of the Prophet had slipped for those few days, allowing Simon to see how frightened he really was.

Did he know the blond Russian was asking about him—possibly looking for him? Or was the man, as he had said, merely someone who had met Andi before who wanted to renew the acquaintance? After all, she was a very attractive woman—her pregnancy didn't detract at all from her beauty.

The elevator opened and a man in hotel livery stepped out, carrying a tray. He moved past Simon without noticing him, head down, a bored employee on the late shift, with hours to go before he got off work. He approached the door and knocked, and after a moment it opened and he stepped inside.

Simon waited. One minute. Two. How long did it take to deliver a tray, collect the tip and leave? His heart started racing, anxiety knotting his stomach. Something about the waiter wasn't right. Something about the way he walked was a little too familiar. His blood went cold as he realized why.

He exploded from behind the plant and raced for Andi's room, praying he wasn't already too late.

GONE WAS THE SERENE, confident Prophet who had mesmerized Andi so. The man before her was unshaven and dirty beneath the clean clothes he must have taken from the real room service waiter, his hair greasy and smelling of sweat. She tried to pull out of his grasp. "Let go, you're hurting me!" she protested.

He released her, but his attitude didn't soften. "Call for a taxi. Tell the driver to meet you across the street, in front of the bank. What have you got that I can wear? And I need a scarf for my hair. I'll be your sister, visiting from Grand Junction."

"Daniel, wait! What's going on?"

"You're going to help me get out of here, that's what's going on," he said.

"What about Starfall, and that cop—Ethan? And Starfall's baby, Hunter? Did you really try to hurt them?" She hadn't meant to say anything about any of that, but the words tumbled out. Simon and Michelle had planted all these doubts in her head and she needed the Prophet to allay her fears.

"Who have you been talking to?" He turned on her, rage contorting his face, and before she could draw back he hit her, hard, snapping her head back and leaving her cheek stinging.

She gasped, tears filling her eyes. No one had ever hit her before—no one. "Shut up and get moving," Metwater said. "Or I'll make you wish you'd obeyed me when you had the chance."

He turned back toward the door, but it burst open. Simon Woolridge didn't hesitate; he hit Metwater hard, dropping him to his knees. He pulled flexi-cuffs from his belt and reached for the Prophet's wrist. "Daniel Metwater, you are under arrest."

Metwater shook his head and rose up with a roar, shoving Simon backward. Andi screamed.

"Get out of here!" Simon shouted at her. "Go to the lobby, where you'll be safe."

"No." She couldn't leave him. For that matter, she couldn't leave the Prophet. She had to stay and see how this played out.

Metwater lunged at Simon, swinging hard. Simon dodged the punch, but crashed into an end table, sending it toppling. The Tiffany-style lamp that had been sitting on it slid to the floor and shattered into a kaleidoscope of bright shards. Andi screamed again and looked around for anything she could use to defend herself. Simon staggered to his feet, reaching for the gun in the holster at his side. A vision of him shooting the Prophet filled her head. "No!" she sobbed, and started toward him.

He turned at the sound of her voice, which gave Metwater the opening he needed to grab Simon's arm, trying to get at the weapon. "Don't kill him!" Andi pleaded, not even sure which man she was defending now.

The men reeled away from her, grappling, and crashed into a second table, sending more fragile ornaments cascading to the floor. Glass crunched under her feet as she backed away. She spotted the telephone on the table at the end of the sofa. She should call someone. Not the police—they were looking for Daniel. But the front desk? Housekeeping, to clean up the mess?

Fighting back hysterical laughter, she reached for the phone, just as someone pounded on the door. "Hotel security!" boomed a man's voice. "What's going on in there?"

Daniel Metwater jerked his head toward the door. "Don't open it," he growled.

"Open the door!" Simon ordered.

"If you don't open up in five seconds, we're coming in!" the voice on the other side said.

Andi started toward the door. She had taken only two steps when Metwater rushed past her. She reeled away from him, but he scarcely noticed. He jerked open the door and, as two uniformed men rushed in, he ran past them and down the hall.

Simon tried to run after Metwater, but the two men who had just entered the room held him back. "What's going on here?" the first man, tall and broad-shouldered, demanded.

Simon, whose shirt was half out of his jeans and who was bleeding from his mouth, still managed to look dignified as he presented his credentials. "Agent Simon Woolridge, Ranger Brigade," he said. "The man who ran out of here is Daniel Metwater, a wanted fugitive." He tried to move past them again, but the men—who were dressed in the uniforms of hotel security—held him fast.

The first guard studied Simon's credentials for a long

moment before returning them to Simon. "What's your fugitive doing in this hotel?" he asked.

"Probably getting away," Simon said, as he tucked the leather folder back into his pocket. He shoved past the two guards, who let him go this time. He rushed out the door, footsteps pounding down the hall.

"Ma'am, are you all right?" asked the second security guard, who was short but muscular.

She nodded, and pushed her hair out of her face. "I... I'm fine," she managed.

"We had a report of screams and crashing," said the second man. "Sounds of a struggle." He surveyed the broken glass and overturned tables. "Can you tell us what happened?"

She shook her head. What exactly *had* happened? Had the Prophet really hit her? Had he really threatened her? The violence was so unlike him. He would never want to hurt her, would he? "He burst in here, and he was terribly upset," she began. "He's desperate, I think. And afraid..."

Simon stepped into the room once more, breathing hard. "He got away," he said. "We'll need to block all the entrances and conduct a search of the entire hotel."

The two guards blinked at him. "We don't have the authority to do something like that," the first man said.

"Don't you need a warrant or something?" the second man asked.

"Do you want to wait until he kills one of your guests before you do more than stand around twiddling your thumbs?" Simon snapped.

"I don't really think the Prophet would kill anyone," Andi protested.

"He could have killed you," Simon said. His eyes met hers, searing her with their anger. He turned back toward the security guards and she started to protest, but a sharp cry out of her own mouth cut off her words.

She cradled her abdomen and tried to brace herself against the sharp pain that tore through her. As she blinked back tears, she realized the three men were staring at her. Simon was the first to reach her side. "What is it?" he asked. "What's wrong?"

She shook her head. "I'm fine. Just…gas or something."

"She needs a doctor," Simon said, helping her to the sofa.

"We have a physician on call." The older security guard pulled out his phone and punched in some numbers.

"No. I'll be fi—" But another sharp pain cut off the words. Andi closed her eyes. She couldn't be going into labor. Not now. Not when so much was unsettled.

Simon took hold of her ankles and swung her feet up onto the sofa. "Lie back and close your eyes," he said. "Breathe deeply and try to relax." He had removed her shoes and was rubbing her feet. She ought to object, but it felt so good she couldn't force the words past her lips.

"What about your felon?" one of the security guards asked.

"His name is Daniel Metwater," Simon said. "Thirty-two years old. Six foot two inches, one-hundred sixty-five pounds, curly dark hair and eyes. Contact the police and alert the rest of your staff, but if you see him, don't try to deal with him yourself. He's dangerous and may be armed. But he has enough of a head start that he's probably already left the hotel."

"We'll get someone up here to clean up this mess once the doctor is done," one of the men said.

"It can wait until morning," Simon said. "I don't want any more strangers in here than necessary."

Andi kept her eyes closed and let herself drift. Simon's hands were warm, his fingers strong and soothing. Where had he learned to give a foot massage like that? As he dug his thumb into her aching arch, she had to bite back a moan. She may even have fallen asleep.

She wasn't sure how much time had passed when someone squeezed her hand. "Hello, Ms. Daniels," said a smooth, lightly accented voice. "I'm Dr. Johar. I understand you've been experiencing some discomfort."

She opened her eyes and stared into the face of a handsome, brown-skinned man. She looked past him, searching for Simon. "Where's Simon?" she asked.

"He's in the hallway, talking to the local cops." The older security guard stepped forward.

The police. They would be after Daniel. He wouldn't stand a chance now. She struggled into a sitting position. "I'm fine now," she said, hoping the words were true. She needed to talk to Simon, to plead with him not to be too hard on Daniel. Yes, he had hit her, but it must have been because he was out of his mind with fear. Ordinarily, he would never do anything like that.

Then Simon's face came into view, hovering over the doctor's left shoulder. "She had at least two moments of pain that were strong enough to make her cry out," Simon said. "I did what I could to help her relax."

"Are you her husband?" the doctor asked as he felt for Andi's pulse. "Or boyfriend?"

Andi waited to see how he would answer. "No," he said and turned away. "I'm a cop."

"Perhaps you would like to step away and give us a little privacy," the doctor said. "Ms. Daniels, would it be all right with you if I examined you? I want to check on your baby."

Andi consented, and with less embarrassment and discomfort than she would have thought possible, the doctor made a thorough examination. When she was dressed and seated upright once more, he gave her a reassuring smile. "Everything looks good," he said. "You are not yet in labor, though you are effaced two centimeters."

Her face must have betrayed her confusion, because he added, "Your body is preparing for the upcoming delivery. The baby is shifting into position for birth and your cervix is getting thinner."

"How long before the baby is born?" she asked.

"I take it this is your first child?"

She nodded.

"It could be a couple of weeks or a few days."

"What was the pain?" she asked.

He glanced around the room, at the overturned tables and broken glass, at Simon standing by the window, his back to them. "The person who telephoned me said there had been an altercation. I assume the person who did this—" He nodded to indicate the mess "—is gone now?"

"Yes," she said. Daniel was gone, though she wondered if Simon was right, and he would return.

"The pain was probably a stress reaction. A particularly sharp kick, a tension in the muscles." The doctor shrugged. "What matters now is that you don't worry about it, and try to get some rest." He patted her hand. "You are young and strong and everything looks as it should be. When is your due date?"

"I'm not sure," she said.

He raised one eyebrow, but didn't comment, merely stood there. Simon turned toward them. "How is she?" he asked, though Andi was certain he had been eavesdropping on their conversation.

"She is fine," the doctor said. "All she needs is rest and no stress."

"Would you mind waiting with her here for a few minutes?" Simon asked.

"For a few moments," the doctor agreed.

Simon left the room. The doctor looked down at Andi once more. "This cop—he is a friend of yours?"

"Not exactly," she said. She was sure the doctor was curious, but she refused to elaborate—not that she could have found words to explain the bizarre situation in which she had suddenly found herself.

Simon returned in less than five minutes, carrying a black backpack. "Thank you," he said to the doctor. "You can go now."

As soon as the door shut behind the doctor, Andi sat up. "What happened to the Prophet?" she asked.

"He got away," Simon said. "But the Denver police are looking for him. And hotel security will be watching for him."

"When you find him, promise you won't hurt him," she said.

He glared at her. "He didn't have any problem hurting you."

She flinched at the anger in his voice. "He's terrified. He's never been in a situation like this before," she said. "I'm sure when he calms down he'll cooperate."

"Save your breath," Simon said. "No matter how much you want to believe it, Daniel Metwater isn't the saint he's been pretending to be. My guess is this isn't his first run-in with the law."

Was Simon right? How much did she know about the Prophet, really? But he had always been so gentle and kind to her. She couldn't make the crazed, angry man who had confronted her tonight fit with her previous experience with him. "What are you doing?" she asked as Simon set the backpack on the floor at the end of the sofa.

"I'm staying here tonight."

"You can't do that."

"I can and I will."

"I don't want you here," she protested.

"Maybe not, but you need me."

She swallowed down the fear his words kindled in her. "He left," she said. "He won't come back."

"You don't really believe that, do you?" He sat on the sofa, only a few inches from her feet. "He won't give up that easily, and when he returns, you'll be glad I'm here. What did he say to you while he was here?"

"He wanted my help to get out of here. He planned to dress up in some of my clothes and pretend to be my sister."

"Did you refuse to help him? Is that what set him off?"

She put a hand to her cheek, remembering the sting of the slap. "I asked him about Michelle and Hunter. I asked if it was true that he tried to hurt them. He became very angry and slapped me. Why would he do that? He's never done anything like that before."

"He knows we're closing in on him," Simon said. "I think he's trying to destroy everyone who could provide evidence against him."

"But what do I know that could possibly hurt him?" she asked.

Simon regarded her coolly. "You've lived with him how long now? About six months?"

"Five."

"You're closer to him than anyone else."

They were the same words Michelle had used. But they weren't true. "He isn't really close to anyone."

Simon angled toward her, one arm along the back of the sofa. Weariness pulled at his eyes, and the dark shadow of beard showed along his jaw. If he had driven from Montrose this morning, that meant he had been up for hours. "Help me understand," he said. "What is it about Metwater that attracted you? Why leave everything to live in the middle of nowhere with him?

Seems to me you had it pretty good before you hooked up with him."

"That's because people like you think money solves everything," she said. "My life was shallow and meaningless before I met the Prophet and heard him talk about what really matters."

"And what is that?" he asked.

"Living in community. Being close to nature. Focusing on things of real worth, not merely those of monetary value."

She braced herself, prepared for him to mock her, but he only nodded his head thoughtfully. "Those things are certainly important," he said. "The problem with Metwater's approach is that his idea of community is to live apart and isolated. He didn't contribute to society, he only took from it. He liked to pass himself off as a giver, but really, he's just a user. He used you."

She hugged her arms across her chest and glared at him. "You're one to talk," she said. "You don't care about me. You only want evidence for your case."

His expression hardened. "You're right. I want to build a case that will put Daniel Metwater away for years. He's the worst kind of criminal—he pretends to care about people, then he takes advantage of the most vulnerable."

"You're wrong! You haven't seen how he's helped so many people. He's helped addicts quit drugs and ex-convicts go straight."

"Yeah? At what price? He takes everything they have and makes them believe they need him to survive."

"Maybe they do," she said. "Not everyone is capable of living in normal society."

"Then that's sadder still," he said.

She turned away from him, not wanting him to read the confusion and hurt in her eyes. She wasn't an idiot. She recognized that some of what he said was true. But why couldn't he see that the good Daniel had done outweighed the bad? Yes, he had struck her, but that was only one more sign of how afraid and desperate he was. She couldn't wrap her mind around the idea that he was a violent man.

Simon stood. "Try to get some sleep," he said. "Tomorrow, we're headed back to Montrose."

"You can go," she said. "I'm staying here."

"You don't have a say in the matter," Simon said. "As of now, you're officially in protective custody."

Chapter Four

Simon shifted on the hotel suite sofa, unable to get comfortable. Not that he was expecting to sleep—he had his gun on the coffee table within easy reach, ready in case Daniel Metwater returned. Though the local police and hotel security were looking for the Prophet, Simon didn't have confidence that they would find him. The two patrolmen who had responded to the hotel security call earlier had treated the incident as a domestic dispute between a woman and her boyfriend. They hadn't taken Simon's assertion that Daniel Metwater was a dangerous fugitive seriously.

But Simon knew better. Now that Michelle Munson—Starfall—and her child were out of his reach in a safe house elsewhere in the state, Metwater was focused on Andi Matheson. He only had to get hold of her and keep her alive two more days, until her twenty-fifth birthday, and he would have everything he wanted—her money and her permanent silence after he killed her.

Simon had stretched the truth a little when he told Andi she was in protective custody. He couldn't force her to accept his protection, but it was the only way he could think of to make sure she was safe.

She refused to see the danger. Even after he had struck her, she still thought of Daniel Metwater as a prophet who only wanted to do good. Metwater had spent a lot of money cultivating that image, but Simon knew scum when he saw it. His line of work put him on a first-name basis with the worst of the worst—coyotes who took every dime a poor laborer ever made, then abandoned him and his family to die in the desert far from home. Men who promised to protect a young girl and find her a good job across the border, only to sell her into slavery in an illegal brothel in the city. Metwater was no better than those kind of abusers. He had managed to make Andi believe the best she deserved from him was to be one of many women he slept with, privileged to work as his unpaid secretary and be at his beck and call.

Maybe the other men in her life—her father and the man who was the father of her unborn child—had made her think she didn't deserve to be treated better. They were both dead now, and as far as Simon could determine, no great loss there.

If he had a woman like Andi in his life, he would treat her with the care she deserved. He would make her his partner, not his servant, and protect her with his own life, if necessary.

Not that he'd ever have anyone like Andi. She was used to men with money and power and sophistication. Simon had none of those things. He was a hard man who spent his life doing hard, sometimes ugly things. Some-body had to do the things he did, but Andi deserved better. She deserved someone as good as she was.

He sighed and closed his eyes once more, willing himself to rest. He had done everything he knew to protect her. He had done what he could to make it tougher for Metwater to get to Andi.

But not impossible. That small room for doubt was what made every cop's job a walk along a razor's edge. There was always some aspect of the situation he couldn't see, some action he couldn't plan for.

The phone at his belt vibrated. He withdrew it and frowned at the unfamiliar number. "Hello?" he answered, speaking softly so as not to wake Andi in the next room.

"Officer Woolridge? This is Owen Pogue—one of the security guards here at the hotel."

Simon sat up. "Yes? What is it?"

"This might not be connected to the man you're looking for, but one of the housekeeping staff was assaulted on the third floor about half an hour ago. Whoever did it came up behind her, threw a blanket over her and shoved her into one of the supply closets. He didn't really hurt her, but he took her keys."

Simon was on his feet, headed for the door. "Did she get a look at the man?"

"No, sir. He surprised her. Do you think it's your guy?"

"It could be. You still have the photo I sent you?"

"Yes, sir. I shared it with everyone on staff—not many people this time of night. The housekeeper was the only one on duty in her department."

"Did you call the police?"

Pogue hesitated. "Did you?" Simon demanded.

"I let them know we had had an incident. But management doesn't like a police presence here. It upsets the guests. I told them we had everything under control."

Simon ground his teeth together, holding back a flood of curses. "Put someone at every exit, watching for him," he said.

"Sir, I only have three people in my department tonight, and the hotel has half a dozen entrances."

Simon didn't even waste his breath swearing. "Do the best you can," he said. "He may have already left, but the fact that he has a set of keys makes me think not. He's probably hiding somewhere in the hotel. It would be better if we could search the rooms."

"We could never do that without a warrant," Pogue said. "Management would fight it, for sure. The guests would throw a fit, especially since, at this time of night, it would mean getting most of them out of bed."

Simon knew Pogue was right. He was an out-of-town cop chasing a man wanted for out-of-town crimes. No Denver judge was going to agree to kick a bunch of wealthy, and in some cases famous, people out of their posh hotel rooms in the middle of the night for a random search. Bottom line—Simon was pretty much on his own with this one. "Let me know if anything else happens that doesn't feel right to you," he said, and ended the call.

He walked to the bedroom and tried the door. Not locked. Was it because Andi didn't see him as a threat?

More likely, she had been too exhausted and upset to think of setting the lock.

She had made a mound of blankets on one side of the king-size bed, illuminated by the glow of the digital clock. Simon stood in the doorway for a long moment, watching the gentle rise and fall of her body, listening to the soft sigh of her breathing. The room smelled of her perfume—something floral and expensive, and a luxury she apparently hadn't given up when she had moved to the wilderness. He had smelled it before, on his visits to camp.

After assuring himself she was sleeping well, he slipped across the room to the door that connected this suite with the one next to it, allowing the two apartments to be opened into one larger unit. He verified that the deadbolt was turned and the safety chain in place. Even if Metwater had a master key that would allow him to get into the room next door, he wouldn't be able to come through here.

He was moving back toward the door when the woman in the bed stirred. "What are you doing?" she asked, her voice clear and calm—not the voice of someone who had just awakened.

"I was checking the door lock."

"Why?"

He hesitated. No sense explaining about the maid and the missing keys and his suspicion that Metwater was still in the hotel. Why frighten her? "I'm obsessive about locks," he said instead.

"You would be," she said, and rolled over, her back to him.

The retort almost made him smile. He liked that she didn't take him too seriously. He returned to his place on the sofa and lay back down, eyes open, waiting.

ANDI SHIFTED POSITION in the big, overly soft bed for the dozenth time, her mind as restless as her body. She had slept only briefly, awakening to the feel of someone watching her. She had realized right away it was Simon. The tall, edgy cop didn't frighten her, though his refusal to see any good in the Prophet frustrated her, and the accusations he made against a man she loved confused her.

His words stuck in her head—what he had said about Daniel stealing not only people's possessions, but their independence. To someone like Simon, autonomy probably seemed like something valuable, but Andi wasn't so sure.

She had never really been on her own. As her father's daughter, she had been protected and watched over, scrutinized even, by photographers and gossip columnists and hangers-on who coveted her beauty or her money or her power—none of which she could claim any control over. The beauty was a trick of genetics she had been born with, and the money and power belonged to her father, not her. She had been pampered and educated, groomed for a life as the wife of another rich man or politician like her father. She had never questioned her upbringing or desired a particular career. She had accepted everything she received as her due.

And then she had discovered she was going to have a baby, and something inside of her shifted. She had glimpsed a different kind of future, one as wife to the man she loved, mother to a little girl or boy. But the man she had given herself to hadn't loved her—not really. He already had a wife and family. Discovering that had shocked all the love out of her—though maybe her feelings hadn't really been love, but instead the self-deception of someone who wanted so badly to be valued for herself and not merely for her looks or her name or her money.

The Prophet had promised to give her that value. He told her she was special—and he had made her feel special. He didn't flatter her beauty or measure her wealth or talk about her power. He simply looked into her eyes and told her he loved her.

And she had believed him. Now this cop was telling her different, and she wanted to deny his lies. Except something deep inside her told her that maybe he wasn't lying. That maybe she was the one deceiving herself.

Her cell phone buzzed, and she fished it out from under the pillow and answered it. "Hello?" she whispered.

"Are you all right, Asteria?" The Prophet's voice was soothing, full of concern, addressing her by the name he had given her—a name for a goddess, he had said. Her heart beat faster at the sound of it.

"I'm worried about you," she said.

"I'll be all right," he said. "Good is stronger than evil. Haven't I always told you that?"

"Yes." But what was evil? Was Simon evil? She couldn't see it.

"I need you to help me," the Prophet said.

"Yes. Of course."

"I know that cop is watching you, but you don't need to be afraid of him."

"I'm not afraid." She had never been afraid of Simon, though she couldn't say why.

"Because you're good, and your goodness makes you strong," Daniel said.

She waited, not sure how to answer this.

"I need you to do one small thing for me," he said. "But don't let the cop see."

"All right."

"Go to the door that connects your bedroom to the one next door, and open the deadlock and slide back the chain."

She looked toward the door, the one Simon had checked.

"Can you do that?" Metwater asked.

"Yes. But why?"

"Don't worry about the why. 'Only obey and all good will come to you.'" The words were from a chant he had taught them. One she always found especially calming.

"Only obey, and all good will come to me," she repeated.

"That's right."

"What do I do after I open the locks?" she asked.

"Wait."

He ended the call, and she slid the phone back under her pillow. Then, listening for any movement from the seating area, she tiptoed to the connecting door and carefully turned the knob for the deadbolt, then slid back the chain. It rattled against the doorframe and she froze, heart pounding, not daring to breathe. But she heard nothing from the other room.

She went to the bathroom, then returned to the bed to wait.

She didn't have to wait long. She felt rather than heard a shift in the air as the door connecting her suite to the one next door eased open. A shadow filled the doorway, and then Daniel was beside her, kneeling on the bed, his lips brushing hers with a soft kiss. She reached up to put her arms around him, but he gently pushed her away.

He put his lips against her ear and spoke so softly that she had to strain to make out the words. "I couldn't leave without you," he said. "I risked everything to come back and be with you. Do you understand?"

"Yes." The answer was automatic, but not exactly truthful. Why would he risk capture to be with her? "It's too dangerous for you here," she whispered.

"Not with you by my side. You'll protect me." He brought his hand up to caress her shoulder, then moved toward her breast, going still when his fingers brushed the locket pendant. "What is this?" he asked, pulling it from beneath her gown, the chain tightening around her throat.

"It…it's the necklace you told me you would give my baby," she said. "I know I shouldn't have taken it without permission, but I wanted it to help me feel close to you while we were so far apart."

She braced herself against his anger, but instead, he kissed her cheek. "Bless you," he said. "I knew you were my good luck charm." He reached for her hand

and she shied away, remembering when he had struck her not an hour before.

"It's all right," he said soothingly. "I would never let any harm come to you."

This time she let him take her hand. As much as experience told her not to trust him, her memories of how good things had once been between them beguiled her into cooperating.

"Come on," he urged. "We have to hurry."

"Where are we going?" she asked.

"A safe place. I promise."

The bed creaked as she shoved herself into a sitting position on the side, and stretched out her feet to find her shoes.

Metwater pulled her roughly up while she was still searching, and she made an involuntary cry of protest.

The bedroom door opened, spilling light into the room. Simon stood in the doorway. "Andi, are you all right?" he asked.

Before she could answer, Metwater clapped his hand over her mouth and pulled her tight against him. Something stung her throat and she gave another cry. Light flooded the room, and Metwater's voice filled the silence. "Drop the gun, or I swear I'll cut her throat and she'll bleed to death right here."

Chapter Five

Time slowed, every sense magnified as the two men faced off. The blade of the knife glinted in the glow of the crystal chandelier overhead. A single crimson jewel of blood slid down Andi's pale neck. Simon focused on the strong beat of her pulse at the base of her throat, and his own heart matched its rhythm.

"Drop your gun," Metwater ordered.

Simon crouched and laid the weapon on the carpet, Andi's gaze fixed on him.

"The other one, too," Metwater said. "In the ankle holster."

Simon complied, then straightened. He glanced toward the connecting door, which stood partially open. He should have stationed Pogue or one of his men there.

"What are you looking at?" Metwater shifted and Andi gasped, a fresh bead of blood forming.

Simon looked into Metwater's eyes. Gone was the handsome, arrogant man so assured of getting away with whatever he wanted. He didn't have an army of followers and lawyers protecting him now. It was only him against Simon. Metwater had the woman and the knife, which he thought gave him the advantage.

Simon shifted his gaze back to the door. "Pogue, now!" he shouted, and dropped to the floor.

Metwater jerked toward the door. Andi's scream bounced off the walls in the small room as Simon scooped up his Glock and fired. But in trying to make sure he didn't hit the woman, he caught Metwater in the shoulder.

Not a killing shot. But enough to make him drop the knife. Simon aimed again as Metwater lurched from the bed toward the door.

Andi's screams changed pitch, interspersed with sobbing. "I'm bleeding to death!"

If Simon pursued Metwater, he could probably catch him, but at what cost?

He moved toward the bed, where Andi sat, clutching her throat, the sheets and her gown stained crimson. He pulled out his phone and dialed 911 as he crossed the room. He identified himself and explained the situation as succinctly as possible.

"Yes, sir. I'm dispatching an ambulance. Please stay on the line."

But he had already hung up and pocketed the phone. Andi stared at him, eyes huge in her pale face, hands clutched to her throat. She was still conscious—that was a good sign. "Let me take a look," Simon said. He took both her hands in his and gently tugged them toward her lap.

She resisted. "It's all right," he said. "I promise I won't hurt you."

She lowered her hands, and he studied the two six-inch long slashes where blood was already beginning to clot. Relief flooded him. "The cuts are shallow," he said. "You'll be sore, but you shouldn't even have a scar once they heal."

"But there's so much blood." She looked down at her hands.

"You have a lot of blood vessels in your head and neck," he said. "But he didn't sever any arteries. The ambulance is on its way to check you over and make sure everything is okay."

Tears welled in her eyes. "He tried to kill me," she said. "Why?"

He could go over the old arguments about why Metwater wanted her dead, but now wasn't the time. "I won't let him hurt you again," he said.

"Where is he now?"

"He ran. But he won't get far."

"You shot him." He couldn't tell if the idea frightened or comforted her.

"I did. That will slow him down. He'll have to get help, and when he does, we'll bring him in."

He had already gotten through to a supervisor at the Denver Police Department. He hoped this second attack would shock them into real action. They were sending over a senior officer, and soon every cop in the city would be looking for the man who had tried to kill a young woman at the Brown Palace. Simon would try to keep Andi's name out of the news, but the information was bound to leak eventually.

Andi Matheson had been one of the beautiful people

who had been a fixture at every prominent social function in Denver and DC. Her disappearance five months ago, and subsequent reports that she had become Daniel Metwater's most devoted follower, had kept the interest in her alive. News that she had resurfaced—and that she had been almost killed by the man she had given up pretty much everything for—would be enough to send the media into a frenzy.

He pulled out his phone and called Pogue. "An ambulance and the Denver Police are on their way over," he said. "Direct them to Ms. Daniels's suite."

"Is she okay? What happened?"

"Metwater came back. She's frightened, but she'll be okay."

"Where is he now?"

"I don't know. But he's wounded and he's got a knife."

"I'll let my men know."

The room phone rang, the bell loud and jarring. Simon answered it. "Ms. Daniels?" The woman on the other end sounded unsure.

"This is Officer Woolridge. I'm with Ms. Daniels."

"This is Cami at the front desk. There's an ambulance here, and two police officers."

"Send them up."

Five minutes later, the room was full of people— three EMTs, two police officers, Pogue and another man who said he was with hotel management. Simon started to move away from the bed, but Andi grabbed his hand. "Don't leave me!" she pleaded.

"I won't go far," he said. "But I need to let the EMTs examine you."

One of the emergency medical technicians moved in alongside Simon. "It'll be all right, ma'am," he said. "You'll feel a lot better once we get this checked out and cleaned up."

Simon stepped back, and a wiry black man in uniform tapped him on the shoulder. "You Simon Woolridge?" he asked.

"I'm with Immigration and Customs Enforcement." Simon showed his badge.

"Sergeant Tyson Daley." Sergeant Daley glanced at the bed, where two EMTs were bent over Andi. "She an illegal?"

"I'm on special assignment with the Ranger Brigade, working out of Black Canyon of the Gunnison National Park. We're a federal task force focused on crime on public lands."

"You're a few hundred miles out of your territory, aren't you?" Daley asked.

"I came to Denver to apprehend a fugitive, Daniel Metwater," Simon said. "He's the one who cut her."

"We had a report of a domestic dispute here earlier," Daley said. "This the same guy?"

"It is. He must have hidden in the hotel until he saw his chance to get at her again."

"Tell me what happened," Daley said.

"I shot him—got him in the shoulder, I think."

Daley didn't look happy about this news. "So now we're looking for a wounded crazy guy with a knife. What do you want him for, anyway?"

"Kidnapping and attempted murder, for starters. But he may be connected to several other crimes."

Daley pulled out a tablet computer. "Okay. Let me get some particulars and we'll put out an APB and alert the local hospitals and emergency clinics. I'm gonna need a statement from you and from Ms. Daniels."

Simon didn't bother telling him he would have to wait for his statement. As soon as Simon was satisfied that Andi was safe, he was going to follow Metwater's trail himself. While he wouldn't be upset if the locals caught up with the Prophet before he hurt anyone else, Simon wanted the satisfaction of being the one to track him down.

He gave Daley the information he needed, then excused himself. "I need to call in to my commander," he said.

Though it was after two in the morning, Commander Graham Ellison of the Ranger Brigade answered on the fourth ring. "Ellison."

"It's Simon. I'm here with Andi Matheson at the Brown Palace in Denver. Metwater tried to get to her. I wounded him, but he got away."

"I'm listening." Simon pictured the commander moving from his bedroom to his home office, transitioning from family man to cop. "Tell me everything."

Simon summed up all that had happened since he had arrived in Denver. "I'm going after Metwater," he concluded. "But first I need to make sure Andi is safe."

"Do you think she's still a target?" Graham asked.

"Yes," Simon said. "He's going to come back for her."

"Then stay with her," the commander ordered. "Be ready when he comes back."

"Yes, sir."

"We obtained a warrant and searched his motor home," the commander said. "The team is still sorting through everything we found—a number of items that apparently belonged to his brother, as well as items from the family business in Chicago."

"Anything that links him directly to a crime?" Simon asked. He wanted everything they could find to throw at Metwater in court, so that he would stay behind bars for a very long time.

"Not yet," Ellison said. "Michelle Munson says he has a necklace that belonged to her sister—the one she thinks David Metwater murdered—but we haven't located it. We're still looking though."

"What about the rest of his followers?"

"A few are still in camp, but most of them have moved out—back to family or old hangouts. We have a census and asked them to provide contact information. A couple had outstanding warrants, and we turned them over to the Montrose sheriff's office."

"Any clue where Metwater would go to hide?" Simon asked. "Any other property he owns? Friends? Relatives?"

"We haven't found anything like that yet, but we're looking. I'll keep you posted."

"Something else you could look into for me," Simon said. "There's a Russian guy, midthirties, blond with a goatee. He approached Andi in the hotel lobby last night—called her by her real name and pretended they had met at some social function a while back. She swears she had never seen him before. He was asking about Metwater."

"If he's Russian, he won't be a friend of Metwater's," the commander said.

"That's what I'm thinking."

"I'll see what we can find out about him."

Simon ended the call, and one of the EMTs approached. "The wounds aren't severe, but she's had quite a shock," the tech said. "With her advanced pregnancy, we'd like to take her in to the hospital to be monitored overnight."

Simon glanced over the man's shoulder and found Andi's gaze fixed on him. "What does she think of the idea?"

"She doesn't want to go, but she's worried about the baby. She said she would consent if it was all right with you."

"Tell her I'll come with her."

"That would be great."

"Tell her I won't leave her." Not until he knew she was safe. Metwater wouldn't give up yet. Andi Matheson wasn't the kind of woman a man left behind.

VICTOR KRAYEV SAT in his rental car across the street from the Brown Palace Hotel, cell phone clamped to his ear. "I had to leave the hotel," he said. "There's a cop in there who's watching Andi Matheson. He started questioning me, and I figured I'd better lay low for a while."

"Why is he watching her?" the man on the other end of the line asked. He was the one who had hired Victor for this job, and for many others.

"Maybe the same reason I'm here—he wants Metwater."

"He can wait in line."

"When we get through with Metwater, there won't be anything left for the police," Victor said.

"Did you talk to the woman?"

"I approached her in the lobby. I pretended we had met before, at a party. She seemed upset that I knew her real name—she's registered at the hotel under an alias—Daniels."

"Metwater probably thought of that. He believes he's so clever."

"I asked her about Metwater, but the cop interfered before she could answer. I'm sure she's in contact with him though. Metwater made the reservation at the hotel and personally delivered her here. And she's going to have his kid any day now. Not to mention she's loaded. If he's planning on skipping town, my bet is he's going to take her with him."

"Do whatever it takes to get him. And the key. We must have that key."

"I know my job. I haven't failed you yet, have I?"

"Don't let this be the first time."

He ended the call and tucked the phone back inside his jacket. The lights from the hotel cast a golden glow over the warm brown stone of the facade, though many of the rooms were dark and only a few people came and went from the lobby. Daniel Metwater wasn't one of them.

Flashing lights distracted him, and he turned to see an ambulance approaching. It pulled up to the hotel, followed by two Denver Police cars. Victor sat forward, straining for a better look.

Then he dug out his phone and dialed the hotel number. "Welcome to the Brown Palace Hotel and Spa. This is Cami. How may I—"

"Cami, it's Vince. How are you doing, beautiful?"

"Oh, Vince. Hi." Her voice took on a girlish flutter. "I'm good. How are you?"

"I'm good, gorgeous. I just drove by on my way downtown and saw the cop cars and an ambulance. What's going on over there?"

"Oh, um, well. I'm not sure I'm supposed to say."

"Aw come on. Who am I gonna tell? I just want to know if it's safe to come back and see you again."

"Oh, I'm sure it's safe." She lowered her voice. "I had to move away from the desk. I guess the cops are here because there was a fight upstairs. It happens sometimes. Word is some woman got cut."

"What woman? Do you know her name?"

"I'm sure I'm not supposed to say that." Her tone was teasing. Flirtatious.

He mirrored it. "How about if I guess and you tell me if I'm right?" he asked. "Was it Ms. Daniels, up on the fourteenth floor?"

She gasped. "How did you know?"

He hadn't known. But since Andi Matheson was the only occupant of the hotel he cared about, hers was the only name he had to throw out there. "Lucky guess," he said. "Is she going to be all right? Do they know who cut her?"

"I don't know who did it, but I guess he got away, because I overheard security talking with one of the cops about looking for him. But I don't know any more than that. Honestly, I don't."

"There's another man there," Victor said. "A plain-clothes cop. Dark hair and eyes. He's wearing jeans and a black shirt. What's his name?"

"Do you mean Mr. Woolridge? He has the room two doors down from Ms. Daniels. Is he really a cop?"

"That's him," Victor said. "I thought I recognized him—an old friend I haven't seen in a long while. I'll have to say hello to him next time I'm at the hotel."

"When will that be?" Cami asked. "When will I see you again?"

He cringed at the whine in her voice. "Soon," he said. "You don't think I could stay away from you long, do you?"

She giggled. "I have to go now," she said. "Call me back in an hour or two, after the commotion has died down."

"Sure thing, darling." He ended the call. Cami wouldn't be hearing from Vince again, but she didn't have to know that. Victor would keep an eye on the ambulance, and on its occupant. He would bet gold that Daniel Metwater was the one who had cut Andi. Maybe she had given him grief about the trouble he was in, or she didn't want to leave her cushy hotel. He had cut her, but something or someone had interrupted him—the cop Victor had met in the bar?

Maybe, but Metwater wasn't one to leave a job unfinished. He would be back. And when he showed up, Victor would be there. The man owed a debt, and Victor fully intended to collect.

Chapter Six

Andi woke to soft pink light reflected off walls the color of clouds at sunset. Lime-sherbet tinted sheets covered her, and the gentle beeping of a monitor and low murmur of distant voices provided soothing background sounds that threatened to lull her back to sleep. Then she swallowed, and the ache at her throat reminded her of everything that had happened last night. Heart pounding, she looked around and spotted Simon, slumped in a chair beside the bed, asleep.

He needed a shave, as evidenced by the suggestion of a dark beard along his jaw, and his shirt was rumpled, his hair uncombed. He looked dangerous, but seeing him there calmed her. As she studied him, he stirred and opened his eyes. "How are you feeling?" he asked, his voice rough from sleep.

"A little sore, but okay." Better than she would have expected. She smoothed the sheets over her belly. "The doctors said everything checked out okay. I guess I was lucky."

He made a noise she took for assent, and stretched.

"What time is it?" she asked, looking for, but not finding, a clock.

"Morning."

"Have you been here all night?" The thought touched her.

"I didn't want to leave you."

"What happened to the Prophet?" she asked. "Did you find him?"

"Not yet. But every cop in the state is looking for him. He won't get away."

"I won't be safe until you capture him." Saying the words made her feel heavy with sadness.

"No. But we will capture him."

She looked away, trying to process this thought. It was what she wanted—Daniel Metwater locked away so he could never hurt her again. But she had a hard time reconciling the man who had hurt her—the one she was so afraid of now—with the man she had followed and adored for the past seven months.

She slid her hand up to clutch the necklace. Daniel hadn't minded that she had taken it. Was that because it was evidence he had been involved in a crime, and now that she had it, he thought the police couldn't link it to him? Michelle had talked about a necklace that belonged to her sister, who had died of an overdose in David Metwater's apartment. But maybe the sister had given it to David, and that was why Daniel, as his brother's heir, had it.

Andi shook her head. It was all so confusing.

The door to the room opened and a slender man in green scrubs hurried in. "Ms. Daniels, how are you feeling this morning?" he asked. "I'm Dr. Ogilvie. I saw you last night."

"I'm fine," she said. "Very well, thank you."

Dr. Ogilvie studied the array of machines and nodded, apparently satisfied. "As I said last night, keeping you for observation was just a precaution. No worries. As soon as I sign the discharge papers, you're free to go, though you'll want to take it easy and avoid stress." He looked at Simon when he spoke the last words.

"I'll take care of her," Simon said.

The doctor opened his mouth as if to say more, but his gaze shifted to the gun at Simon's side and he pressed his lips together, silent.

The doctor was scarcely out the door when a nurse bustled in, long braids gathered in a ponytail atop her head. "I'm here to unhook you from all the monitors and help you get dressed," she said. She scowled at Simon. "You can go get coffee down the hall while we're busy. You look as if you need it."

As Simon left the room, Andi resisted the urge to call after him. She had never been one to startle at shadows before, so she wasn't going to start now.

"He wouldn't budge from your side all night," the nurse said as she began disconnecting tubes and switching off machines. "Sat in that chair all night and glared at anyone who came near you. I've seen overprotective husbands before, but he beats them all. Must be the cop thing."

Andi let the words flow over her, not bothering to correct the woman's assumption that Simon was her husband. If she had had someone to protect her so fiercely all along, maybe she wouldn't be in such a fix now.

The nurse pressed a bandage over the small hole where the IV needle had been inserted. "All untethered now," she said. "Your clothes are in the little cabinet in the bathroom. You can shower if you like. Do you need any help?"

"No, thank you."

"There's a call button in the bathroom if you need anything, or your husband can always help you."

She hurried away, and Andi shuffled to the bathroom, the idea of Simon helping her undress—and shower—sending a not-unpleasant flutter of arousal through her. Where had that come from?

By the time she emerged from the bathroom twenty minutes later, freshly showered and wearing the slacks, top and boots that Simon or someone must have fetched from her hotel room, she felt much more alert and ready to face whatever lay ahead.

Simon was sitting in the chair by her bed. He handed her a cup of coffee. "If you don't drink coffee, or you're not supposed to have it, I can get something else," he said. "Tea or milk or juice."

"Coffee's good." She sipped from the cup. The coffee was heavily laced with cream and sugar—just the way she liked it. She had tried to limit her caffeine during her pregnancy, but she couldn't give it up altogether.

Simon looked around the room. "Do you have anything to take with you?"

The gown she had arrived in had been stained with blood—she shuddered at the memory. In any case, it had been discarded and quickly exchanged for a hospital smock. She shook her head. "No. What will we do now?"

"We'll go back to the hotel for the rest of your things," he said. "But then we need to leave." He opened a closet and pulled out a full-length faux-mink coat. "Put this on. It's cold out. Weather forecasters are predicting snow."

The Prophet had given her that coat. It screamed expense and privilege, and now it made her skin crawl to wear it.

"Come on." Simon held it out. "You need to stay warm."

She swallowed hard and nodded. He was right, and it was just a coat. *Things don't matter*, the Prophet had preached. She had believed him, even when his actions contradicted the words. He wore expensive designer clothing and insisted on the best accommodations when he traveled, even when some of his followers lived in patched-together tents and trailers. How was it the contradictions hadn't bothered her before?

She put on the coat and walked beside Simon to the elevator. "I don't see how you walk in those heels," he said, looking down at her stiletto boots. "But they were the only shoes I could find to bring up here."

"I'm used to them," she said. "And they're the only shoes I brought with me. I really didn't think I would be staying in Denver that long."

They stopped in front of the elevator and he hit the down button. "Where are we going now?" she asked.

"I'm taking you back to Montrose, to a safe house."

She started to protest that she wanted to go home, but

it wasn't as if she could go back to the Family's camp—if there was even a camp left. Her father was in prison and her baby's father was dead. She had no close relatives. She had the money and resources to live on her own, but not the will—at least not right now.

"Is the rest of the Family still in our camp?" she asked.

"A few. Without Metwater there, most of them have gone back to their families, or to their old lives."

"He was what held us together," she said.

"Doesn't say much for a belief system if it all depends on one man, does it?" he said.

She glared at him. "Whatever you think of the man—whatever he is now—he did a lot of good," she said. "I won't stop believing that."

"If that makes you happy, I'm not going to stop you," he said. "But as far as I can tell, nothing he said was original. He was just good at plagiarizing."

"Are you always so cynical?" she asked.

"Yes."

"You don't believe there's good in the world?"

"There's good," he said. "But the real saints in this world do good things instead of merely talking about them." He took her arm. "Let's go. I want to get on the road before the traffic gets heavy."

Someone had cleaned her room at the Brown Palace, removing the broken glass and bloodied sheets, polishing the furniture and freshening the flowers, even replacing the broken lamp with one that looked identical. "Pack what you'll need for a few nights in one bag," Simon said as he crossed the room to look out the window at the downtown scene below. "Anything else we'll ask the front desk to send on to Montrose."

"I only brought one bag with me." At his surprised look, she laughed. "I'm not a spoiled socialite anymore," she said. "If nothing else, the Prophet taught me to travel light."

"There's something else you've learned since being with him," Simon said, his expression serious once more. "Something he doesn't want you to tell the rest of the world. If we can figure out what that is, it could be the key to stopping him."

"If I knew, I promise I would tell you," she said. "But until he turned against me, I never knew anything bad about him."

"Keep thinking," Simon said. "You know something, and I'd like to find out what it is before he tries to kill you again."

She froze, one hand on the doorknob to the bedroom. "He's on the run," she said. "He knows you're looking for him. He won't risk trying to get at me again."

"A smart man wouldn't do that, no. But a desperate man would. And from what I've seen, Daniel Metwater is a very desperate man."

"Are you trying to frighten me?" she asked.

"I'm being honest with you. Would you rather I told you pretty lies?"

His eyes met hers, and the steadiness of his gaze made her feel less shaky. "No," she said. "I've been lied to enough in my life." Maybe an honest man—even one who didn't spare her feelings—was worth sticking with, at least for a while.

BY THE TIME they left the hotel, low clouds had blanketed the area, blotting out the sun. The air had the cold, heavy feeling of imminent snow. At least Andi wouldn't have to worry about keeping warm in that coat of hers. Simon pulled his sheepskin-lined jacket out of the back of his cruiser, along with leather gloves, ready for whatever the weather brought.

Andi wasn't a chatterbox, that was for sure, which was fine by Simon. He had a reputation as not much of a talker himself. He preferred action to words, most of the time anyway. He glanced over at his passenger as they waited at a red light, trying to gauge her mood. Not nervous or afraid. He would have said she was calm, even.

So far, he had been pretty impressed with her, something he hadn't expected. She looked delicate and weak, but when push came to shove, she had nerves of steel. She had been threatened, cut, examined by strangers and betrayed by her lover, yet she hadn't wilted or whined or complained. She was struggling with her emotions—he hadn't missed the moments of troubled silence or brief tears—but she was keeping it together.

The light changed and he turned right onto a side street, drove two blocks, then made another right. "What are you doing?" Andi asked.

He made another right. "I'm driving," he said.

"That's the second time we've passed that car wash," she said, nodding to the Sudzy Ride sign.

"I'm making sure we aren't being followed. Nice to know you're paying attention."

"I'm not as dumb as I look."

"I never thought you were dumb." Naive, misled and too trusting, but not dumb.

"Then you don't believe the stereotype?"

He headed up the entrance ramp to Interstate 70. "And what is the stereotype?"

"That blondes are dumb. That beautiful women aren't serious or smart. That rich women only care about shopping." She waved her hand. "I'm familiar with all the assumptions."

"Did you try to prove them wrong?" he asked.

"I studied botany at Brown," she said. "My father told everyone I was learning to grow roses and arrange flowers. He thought it was more suitable than telling people I was interested in science."

"What century was he living in again?"

"Oh, he was positively Victorian. But he wasn't alone. Plenty of rich men want wives who look good, do good and keep their mouths shut. He couldn't imagine why I wasn't excited about the prospect."

"Is your mother that type?" he asked.

"She wasn't. But she married my father before he had money. And she died when I was fifteen."

"I lost mine when I was sixteen," he said. This confession—the intimacy of it—surprised him. He never talked about his family.

"Mine died of cancer," she said. "What happened to yours?"

"She was murdered."

He regretted the words as soon as they were out of his mouth. Andi looked stricken. "How horrible!"

He cleared his throat, as much to buy time to measure his words as to rein in his emotions. "She was a nurse, volunteering at a center for pregnant teens. One of the girls' boyfriends broke into the place, high on drugs. He killed his girlfriend, and then he killed my mom." He still remembered the grayness of the days after that—the darkness of every room, and the hollowness of every conversation, as if the black void left by her absence was taking over the world.

"She sounds like a very good person," Andi said.

"She was."

"And your father?" she asked. "What was he like?"

"He was a cop."

"Like you."

"Not like me. He was a city cop. A street cop. He made a difference in people's lives every day." Simon couldn't say that about his own work. His dad had relationships with the people on his beat. Simon's interactions with both suspects and victims were usually brief.

"Is he still working?"

"He was killed in the line of duty." Set up to take a fall by corrupt bosses he had stood up against, but no sense going into that. An investigation had revealed the truth, and he had been awarded a medal, posthumously. Simon had the medal in a drawer somewhere at home. He couldn't bear to throw it away, but he didn't keep it where he would see it often—a reminder of how the system had failed his father, coming through only when it was too late.

"At least he's someone you can be proud of," Andi said. "Not like my father.'

"Have you had any contact with your father since

he went to prison?" Simon asked. Pete Matheson had pleaded guilty to killing Special Agent Frank Asher and was currently serving time in a federal prison near Denver.

"No." Her voice was clipped, and cold enough to send a chill through Simon.

"Has he tried to get in touch with you?"

"I don't know. And I don't care."

But the tears that roughened her words told Simon she did care. He reached out and took her hand. "If you ever do want to see him, I can help arrange that," he said. "And if you don't, that's okay too."

She pulled away from him and wrapped her arm across her belly. "I don't know what I want," she said softly. "Just for all of this to be over. I want to be somewhere quiet, where I can focus on my baby and not think about anything else."

"I'm working on that," he said. "Just hang on a little longer."

She pulled the coat more tightly around her and didn't say anything for a few miles. When sleet began to hit the windows, she turned toward him once more. "I guess winter has finally decided to show up," she said.

The tension in Simon's chest eased at the words. She didn't sound so upset anymore. He wouldn't have blamed her if she had decided to sulk in her misery for a while, but she was stronger than that, and he appreciated it more than he could say. Funny—he wasn't someone who especially liked talking to people, but he was finding that he enjoyed his conversations with her. "It would have been pretty miserable, camped in the woods all winter," he said. "We can get a lot of snow in that country."

"The Prophet talked about heading south for the winter," she said. "Maybe Mexico." She shifted toward him. "Maybe that's where he's gone now. He said he had friends down there." She frowned. "Well, not exactly friends. He said he had 'connections.'"

"I'll mention it to my commander next time I talk to him," Simon said. "He'll check it out. Is there any place else he mentioned—another house he owned or friends he might turn to for help?"

She shook her head. "None of us talked about our lives before we came to the Family," she said. She had tried a few times to bring up the past, but Daniel had always deflected her attempts to unburden herself, and he had revealed very little of his own history—nothing, she realized now, that hadn't already been written in news stories about him. "The whole point was to start over, with a clean slate. To focus on the present and the future, not the past."

"Kind of makes me wonder what he had in his past that he didn't want to talk about," Simon said.

"Don't tell me you don't have things in your past, things you did or said, that it hurts to remember," she spoke softly. "Choices you made that you wish you could take back."

"Of course I do. Everyone does. But I try to learn from them, not pretend they never happened."

"Not everyone can do that."

"So all that time you spent with him, and he never talked about his past?" Simon asked.

"Not really."

"What about his family?"

"He said his father was a cold man who was only interested in work and money. Greed drove all his decisions and he judged everyone by how much they owned."

"Sounds like he brought his son up to follow in his footsteps," Simon said. "Between his family's wealth and what he was acquiring from his followers, he's put together a considerable fortune." A fortune he couldn't access, since authorities had frozen his accounts.

"Yes, he liked money, but it was never his main focus," she said. "I'm sure of that. If it had been, he would have lived in a mansion, instead of a motor home. With his looks and charisma, he could have been one of those TV evangelists."

"So why didn't he do that?" Simon asked. "Why hide out with a small group of followers in the wilderness?"

"Because he believed that was the way to spiritual purity." She said the words without a hint of sarcasm or irony.

"Or maybe he wanted to keep a low profile because he was afraid of the wrong kind of attention," Simon said. "From what I recall, he was a little paranoid about the Russian mafia."

"Because they killed his brother," Andi said. "David's death affected him deeply."

"David Metwater was suspected of double-crossing his killers," Simon said. "He gambled, did drugs and stole from the family business. He was living the kind of life that pretty much guaranteed he would come to a bad end."

"He was Daniel's twin," Andi said. "His identical twin. It didn't matter that he was living a terrible life. Daniel said they were two halves of a whole. David's death left a void that could never be filled."

"It's a good story," Simon said. "But something tells me there's more to it than that. First, he goes after Michelle Munson—Starfall—because he finds out she's got a scrapbook full of articles about him and his brother. She wants a necklace that belonged to the sister she thought David Metwater murdered. Daniel Metwater would rather kidnap her baby, and try to kill her and a cop, rather than hand over that locket or let us get a good look at that scrapbook. And now he's gone after you."

Andi put a hand to her chest. "When he came to me last night, he said we were meant to be together."

Simon tightened his grip on the steering wheel. It shouldn't matter, but hearing her sound so lovesick over a man like Metwater caused him physical pain. "Do you believe that?" he asked.

"No." She pulled the coat more tightly around her, though he had turned the heater up to high. "He's not the kind of man who could ever be devoted to one person. I knew that from the first. I told myself it was because he had so many followers to care for, and higher things to focus on."

"Do you still believe that?"

The look on her face was pure misery. "No. I think he's just another man who thinks the world owes him everything."

Simon winced. He was no expert on women, but he

figured now was a good time to stop talking. He focused instead on the traffic creeping out of town, west toward the mountains. The sleet had turned to snow, and was beginning to stick to the browned grass along the roadside.

He exited the freeway onto a county road. The weather would have I-70 traffic slowed to a crawl, so this rural route would probably be faster. "I remember traveling this way once with my mother when I was about twelve," Andi said, apparently having decided that, even though he was a man, he was worth talking to.

"Where were you headed?" Simon asked.

"My uncle has a cabin in South Park." She smiled. "The real South Park—the one the show was named after."

"Just a mother-daughter getaway?"

"Not exactly," she said. "At the time I didn't realize it, but looking back, I think she and my father had had an argument of some kind and she wanted to get away for a few days, so she took me to stay at the cabin. It was all a novelty to me—a woodstove for heating and cooking, a hand pump for water and a little log outhouse. We hiked and fished and roasted marshmallows over a campfire." She smiled. "Living with the Family reminded me of those times."

"When was the last time you were there?" Simon asked.

Her smile faded. "About six months before my mother died. My uncle still has it, but he only uses it for a few weeks during hunting season. Maybe I'll go back one day." She rubbed her belly. "I'd like to show it to my son or daughter."

The baby. Something else for him to worry about.

The doctors had said she could deliver any time now. "How are you feeling?" he asked.

"I need to use the bathroom."

He spotted a sign for a gas station up ahead and signaled to pull in. The snow was heavier now, fat white flakes clumping on the windshield and clinging to the branches of the evergreens that lined the road.

"Take your time," Simon said as Andi climbed out of the cruiser. "I'm going to fill up while we're here."

After he filled the tank, he pulled into a parking spot near the door and went inside. He bought coffee, then lingered by the hot plate. When Andi came out of the restroom, he'd ask her if she wanted anything.

"It's nasty out there," the man behind the counter said. Simon judged him to be in his fifties, his hair in a long silver braid down his back, fastened with multiple rubber bands.

"Mmm." Simon turned back toward the restrooms, not interested in small talk.

"They're saying it's going to get worse before it gets better," the clerk said.

Simon suppressed a sigh. Now if he didn't talk to the guy, he would call even more attention to himself. He would be that rude guy who was too snotty to make conversation. "That's pretty much what they always say, isn't it?" he said.

The man laughed. "You're right about that. Where you headed?"

"Breckenridge," Simon said. The popular ski town was the opposite direction of where he intended to travel.

"They'll be excited to see snow this early," the clerk said. "Not enough to ski on yet, but it's coming."

Andi emerged from the ladies' room and moved toward Simon. He realized he was staring again—something he did too often when he was around her—and made himself look away. "Do you want something?" he asked, holding up his coffee cup.

She looked around, grabbed a granola bar and handed it to him, then added a package of nuts. "I get hungry," she said, a little defensively. "I'm eating for two."

"I imagine you do." He should have thought of that before now. He added a second pack of nuts. "So do I, and I'm only eating for one."

He paid for their purchases, and the clerk slid his change across the counter. "You folks have a good time in Breck," he said.

"In Breck?" Andi asked when they were in the car. "What did he mean by that?"

"He asked where we were going, and I told him Breckenridge."

"Why did you lie?"

"In case someone comes along after us and asks where we were headed."

"You mean Daniel. You shot him. He's probably in the hospital somewhere. You don't really think he'll come after us."

"I don't see any reason to take chances."

His phone rang, and he checked the display. A Denver number. "Hello?"

"Sergeant Daley, Denver Police. Is this Simon Woolridge?"

"Speaking."

"I've got an update for you on your fugitive."

"I've got you on speakerphone with Ms. Daniels, in my car. Do you have Daniel Metwater in custody?"

"Not such good news as that. He sought treatment at an emergency clinic near downtown, using a fake ID. He had an Oklahoma driver's license in the name of David Michaels. The clinic treated him, then phoned us to report the gunshot wound. That's when they found out he was wanted. He ran out a back door before they could stop him."

"Any idea what he's driving?" Simon asked, making a quick check of the other vehicles in the gas station parking lot.

"No," Daley said. "In any case, he's probably ditched it and stolen something else. Easy enough to do—first real cold spell and everybody leaves their car idling while they run into the convenience store to grab a cup of coffee or pay for their gas. Anyway, I thought you'd want to know he's still in the area. And we're looking for him."

"Thanks."

Simon ended the call and turned to Andi. She looked pale but resolute. "I heard everything," she said. "He's coming after us, isn't he?"

"That's what we have to assume." He shifted the cruiser into gear. "But he's not going to stop us. Not if I can help it."

Chapter Seven

Victor drummed his fingers on the steering wheel as he inched his car forward in the bumper-to-bumper traffic. The heavier the snowfall, the slower the traffic crawled, until they were hardly moving at all. This was Colorado—people here were supposed to know how to drive in this weather. He ground his teeth in frustration, pain throbbing behind his eyes.

Between trailing the ambulance to the hospital and getting an update on Andi's condition, staking out the hospital parking lot, then following her and Officer Woolridge back to the hotel, he had grabbed only a few hours of sleep in the front seat of his rental car.

He had stolen this one only an hour before, just in case Woolridge had somehow figured out his identity— or one of his many aliases. The traffic and weather made tailing the cop more difficult. He had thought he would have a chance to grab Andi when they stopped for gas, but Woolridge stayed too close to her.

On the seat beside him, his phone rang. It was the sound of an old-fashioned phone, the kind almost no one seemed to own anymore. He glanced at the screen, wanting to ignore the caller, but the number belonged to a man who could not be ignored. He picked up the phone and swiped his finger across the screen. "What?"

"What's this about Metwater being shot?" The boss sounded annoyed, but then, he always sounded disgruntled. Life irritated him. "Did you shoot him?"

"What are you talking about?" Victor swerved to avoid rear-ending the car in front of him, which had slammed on its brakes.

"We have a contact in the Denver PD. They said Metwater was shot last night. Not dead. Wounded."

Victor grunted. "Where did this shooting take place?"

"The Brown Palace Hotel. I thought you had the place staked out."

"I did." How had he missed Metwater? He knew the answer to that one—because the cop, Woolridge—had blocked him. "He was there for the woman," Victor said. "He tried to cut her throat. I knew I was right."

"Is she dead?"

"No. I'm following her right now."

"Why are you following her? You should be going after Metwater."

"He'll come back for her."

"Or he'll be smart and head for Mexico."

"When was he ever smart?"

"If you were smarter, you'd have him by now."

Victor ground his teeth together until his jaw ached. "I'll get him," he said. "He's going to come back for her. She has everything he needs. She's rich and he needs money to get out of the country."

"He has money. He has a million dollars that belongs to me."

"I don't think he does have it—not where he can get to it. If he did, he would have used it by now."

"No, he doesn't have it," the boss agreed. "I have men watching the bank where he keeps it. He hasn't come to get it. He hasn't sent anyone else with the key either."

"Then that means he doesn't have the key," Victor said. "Or he knows you're watching the bank."

"He doesn't know. The men I put on the job are very good. They're invisible."

"Then he doesn't have the key. He needs the key to get to the money."

"Then where is the key? The cops tore his place apart. They haven't come for the money either, so they don't have it. Or if they do, they don't know what it's connected to."

Victor squinted through the thick cascade of snow collecting on the hood of his car. "Maybe the woman has the key. Maybe that's why he's so anxious to get to her."

"Then get the woman—and get the key. And get Metwater."

"I'm following her right now," Victor said. "I'm going to get her, and I'll make sure Metwater knows it. He'll come after her."

"How are you going to get her? Didn't you say she has a cop protecting her?"

"You don't think I can handle one lousy cop?"

"All I've heard from you so far is a lot of talk. I want action. I want Metwater. I want him dead. And I want the million dollars he stole."

"You'll have him. Dead. And you'll have the key." He ended the call and clutched the steering wheel with both hands, squinting through the thick snowfall. The more he thought about it, the more it made sense to him that Andi Matheson had the key to the safe-deposit box where Metwater had stashed the stolen money. The Prophet had sent her away not to safeguard her, but to keep the cops from getting their hands on the key and the money. Metwater had planned all along to meet up with her, collect the cash and get out of town. But the cops had been one step ahead of him.

And Victor was one step behind. But he wouldn't stay behind. He would catch up with the woman and force her to give him the key. Then, when Metwater showed up, he wasn't just going to kill the lying cheat, he was going to make him suffer. Payback for all the trouble Victor was going to now.

ANDI STARED OUT the windshield at the curtains of white flakes coming down, obscuring the road. "Is it even safe to drive in this?" she asked.

"We're fine," Simon said. "As long as the road stays open, I can drive."

"I guess cops are trained in things like that," she said. "Driving in adverse conditions."

"Not really," he said. "But I grew up in Colorado. I know how to drive in snow."

"I grew up here too, but I'm not crazy enough to take my car out in this."

"I guess I am."

He was teasing her—she got that now. He had a very

dry sense of humor that some people probably didn't appreciate, but she liked that he didn't joke around and try to humor her. Her father and his friends had been like that—making light when she tried to discuss serious matters with them. Too often, it came across as either patronizing or shallow. Simon wasn't either of those things.

She looked out the window again. "At least no one is going very fast," she said. The line of cars crept along on the snow-covered highway, brake lights barely visible in the whiteout.

Simon glanced in the rearview mirror. "It makes it easier to spot someone following us," he said.

"I don't see how Daniel could find us," she said. "He was running away from that clinic when we were leaving the Brown Palace."

"He probably guessed that we were headed back to Montrose," Simon said. "I should have thought of that and taken a different route."

She looked around them at the cars on either side, behind and ahead of them, drivers hunched over the steering wheel, peering through the blizzard. No one even glanced her way. "Well, I don't see anyone following us," she said.

"I do," he said.

She froze in the act of reaching for her cup. "Who?"

"Don't look," he said. "But there's a white Kia two cars back. He's been with us since the gas station."

"Just because he's traveling in the same direction as we are doesn't mean he's following us." She fought the urge to look back over her shoulder. "Is it Daniel?"

"I can't tell." Simon checked his mirrors again. "I'm pretty sure it's a man, but beyond that, he's too far back and the snow is too heavy for me to make a positive ID."

"What are you going to do?" she asked.

"Wait a while, see if I can figure out what he's up to."

"What do you mean 'what he's up to'?"

"If he's simply following to see where we go, that's not much of a threat. If he's going to try to intercept us—to get to you and maybe to kill me—then I'll need to try to stop him before he acts."

"How can you possibly know what he's going to do before he does it?"

"I can see how aggressively he tries to keep up with us, what kind of maneuvering he does." He nodded ahead of them. "Once we head up toward Kenosha Pass, the traffic will thin. It will be tougher for him to keep other cars between us. The weather won't allow him to get too far back, or he'll risk losing us. He'll have to show his hand."

Snow crunched under their tires as they wound their way up a series of switchbacks toward the pass. Towering evergreens draped in snow crowded in on either side of the highway, and a few log cabins, smoke puffing from their chimneys, were visible in the distance. The windshield wipers beat steadily, clearing snow from the windshield even as it piled up on the road.

The road widened and Simon pulled to the right, slowing the cruiser. A truck passed them, and then the white Kia. Andi stared at the driver. "That's not Daniel," she said, the tension in her chest easing. "His hair's too light, and that guy had a beard."

Simon scowled. "Maybe I was wrong. Or maybe Metwater has an accomplice."

"Or maybe he's a stranger who was never following us at all."

Simon sped up again. "Are you sure you didn't recognize him?"

She wanted to lie, to tell him she had never seen the man before in her life. But he had been right when he said she was a lousy liar. "He looked familiar to me," she said. "Though I can't think of where I've seen him. But that still doesn't mean he was following us."

"I never got a good look at him. Or his license plate. Snow was covering it, though the cop in me wonders if that was intentional."

"You don't trust anyone, do you?" she asked.

"I'm in a profession that teaches you not to trust."

They reached the top of the pass. Eighteen wheelers were parked on either side of the summit, drivers adjusting chains, or maybe just waiting out the worst of the storm. They started down the long curve that descended into the high-altitude expanse of open prairie known as South Park. Brake lights shone crimson ahead of them, then the vehicle they were following suddenly swerved sideways, and came to rest straddling the road just where it narrowed to two lanes again.

"What is he doing?" Andi asked, as the driver's door opened and a figure raced to the side of the road.

Simon braked, the cruiser fishtailing wildly on the icy road. Andi screamed as the cruiser slid into the side of the stopped Kia, the tortured scream of twisted metal mingling with her own high-pitched cries.

Chapter Eight

Pain exploded in Simon's nose, Andi's screams filling his ears as he tried in vain to see what was going on. The screams stopped—which sent panic through him. He fought to push aside the mass of the airbag, which had expanded on impact and crashed directly into his nose, which was now streaming blood. "Andi!" he shouted. "Are you all right?"

He groped to his right and came into contact with something soft—her shoulder. "I'm okay," she said.

"The baby?"

"The baby's okay too."

The airbags began to deflate. Simon pushed his aside, then shoved Andi's out of the way as well. "Are you sure you're okay?" he asked, resisting the temptation to examine her for broken bones.

"I'm fine. Really."

She did look fine, calmer than he would have thought. "Your nose is bleeding," she said.

He touched his nose and winced. He felt along the ridge. "I don't think it's broken," he said. "Just bruised. Better than a broken head if the airbag hadn't inflated."

"Right."

"Wait here," he said, unfastening his seat belt.

Andi gripped his arm. "What are you doing?"

"I'm going after him." He stepped from the cruiser and almost fell, feet sliding on the ice and snow that caked the road. Daylight was fading fast, the snow still coming down in a curtain, piling up on the shoulders of his coat and clinging to his eyelashes. He saw no sign of the driver of the Kia. A faint trail up the side of the road, heading into an empty field, might have been made by him, but the snow was filling it in fast. Running after him would mean leaving Andi alone. Maybe that was what the man wanted. Maybe there was someone in another car waiting to grab her as soon as Simon was out of sight.

Bracing himself on the side of the cruiser, he made his way to the front and surveyed the damage. The pipe grille guard welded to the front of the vehicle had protected it from the worst of the damage. One headlight was broken and the license plate dangled by a single screw, but other than that, it looked okay. The engine still ran, though the air bags would have to be replaced.

The Kia hadn't fared so well. The impact had sent it sliding toward the ditch, its side caved in, windshield shattered. It sat, halfway in the northbound lane, canted onto the passenger side. A quick check showed no one inside—no luggage or papers or anything to identify the driver, though he had left the keys dangling in the ignition. The swirl of red-and-blue lights reflected on the snow, and Simon turned to see a county sheriff's SUV creeping toward them. The window rolled down and a young, clean-shaven deputy looked out. "What happened?" he asked.

"The Kia slid to a stop in the middle of the road." Simon indicated the wrecked car. "I couldn't stop on the ice. The driver bailed out just before I plowed into him."

"Where's the driver now?" the deputy asked.

"I don't know." Simon started walking back toward the cruiser.

The deputy pulled alongside him and squinted at the emblem on the driver's door. "The Ranger Brigade," he said. "What the heck is that?"

"It's a multiagency task force based in Black Canyon of the Gunnison National Park," Simon said. "We deal with crime on public lands."

The deputy nodded. "I think I've heard of you guys. That case in the spring with the FBI agent who was murdered by that senator?"

"That was us," Simon said. He glanced toward the cruiser. Andi sat quietly, smart enough to wait in the vehicle. He hoped she hadn't heard the deputy's comment. The FBI agent had been the father of her baby, the senator her father. The whole thing had been a nasty business, and she had been caught in the middle.

"Is your passenger okay?" the deputy asked.

"Shaken up, but fine," Simon said.

"What about you? Is that blood on your coat?"

"Busted my nose when the airbag deployed. I'm okay." In the cold, the bleeding had stopped quickly.

"Your vehicle looks okay to drive," the deputy said. "But that Kia is totaled." He left the lights going and climbed out of the car. "We'd better look for the driver.

He gets lost out here, and he could freeze to death before morning."

Simon made no comment. He had a feeling the driver had someone waiting to pick him up—perhaps up the hill at the top of the pass. Maybe he had hoped to grab Andi in the confusion after the wreck, but the arrival of the county cop had scared him off.

"Do you have a description for me?" the deputy asked.

Simon shook his head. "I never got a good look at him, with all the snow."

"Guess I'd better see some ID from you," the deputy said.

Simon showed his badge, and braced himself for the inevitable question, which the deputy asked next. "What brings you to our side of the divide, Agent Woolridge?"

"I'm following up on a case."

The deputy glanced at Andi. They were close enough now that he could clearly see she was pregnant. He was going to ask about her next, and Simon wasn't in the mood to explain. "It's cold out," he said. "I'd like to get the young lady to someplace safe for the night, and take my car to a repair shop."

The deputy glanced behind them, up the pass. "Denver would be the best bet to get those airbags replaced, but you won't be going there tonight," he said.

"Why not?" Simon asked.

"The pass is closed. You were probably the last vehicle through before we put the gate down." He gestured ahead of them. "It's socked in on both sides of the pass. Ground blizzards can ice up the road, and we get people sliding off left and right. Better for every-body to close it."

"We can't spend the night here," Simon said. Alone, he wouldn't have cared so much, but Andi couldn't spend the night sitting up in a freezing car.

The deputy scratched his chin. "You can try to make it to Fairplay. We'll have a wrecker here in a bit to get this Kia out of the way, and you can follow him."

"It doesn't look like we have much choice."

"Pull your vehicle over to the side there and put on your flashers. I'll radio for some help."

Simon climbed into the cruiser and put it into gear. "What's going on?" Andi asked.

"The road behind us is closed now. We're going to wait here for a wrecker that's coming to deal with the Kia, then we'll follow it to Fairplay, a little town up ahead." He had passed through Fairplay a few times on his way to and from Denver, but he didn't remember much about it, except that it was small and not close to much else. "Are you warm enough?" Simon asked. She had the coat pulled tightly around her. "I can turn up the heater."

"I'm fine. The coat isn't my style, but it's warm."

"What do you mean, it's not your style?"

"Daniel bought it for me. He thought it was what I should wear."

"But you don't like it."

She shrugged. "It's too flashy and conspicuous. I hate standing out."

"I don't think a woman like you can help standing out."

"If I'm supposed to be flattered by a comment like that, I'm not." There was no missing the chill in her words.

Strike out for Simon. He leaned his head back and closed his eyes, fatigue dragging at him. He hadn't slept more than a few hours in the past twenty-four, and that had been sitting up in the chair in Andi's hospital room. As soon as he had Andi safely settled for the night, he was going to pass out.

He must have dozed off for a few minutes, because he jerked awake to a loud, beeping noise and had to hit the wipers to clear the windshield of snow. A massive orange snowplow was crawling down the road toward them, followed by a wrecker, lights strobing. "The deputy must have called the snowplow too," he said. "Good thinking."

"You must be exhausted," Andi said. "I hope we can find a hotel room in Fairplay."

"We'll find something." If he had to drain his bank account to bribe someone to give them a room, he would do it.

The wrecker winched the Kia up onto the flatbed while the plow turned around. Simon pulled his cruiser in behind them, and they headed south at a crawl. Even with the plow scraping the road surface and spreading sand, the trip was treacherous. Whirlwinds of snow swirled in front of the cruiser, rocking the vehicle and obscuring the way ahead. Simon hunched over the steering wheel, gripping it until his knuckles ached, focused on the dull red glow of the wrecker's taillights and hoping the driver didn't slide off the pavement, taking Simon with him. Beside him, Andi was rigid, and absolutely silent.

After what seemed like an hour, but was probably only twenty minutes, the wrecker signaled a right turn. The wind had died and the road was less icy. Simon followed him onto the main street of Fairplay, Colorado. Through the curtain of snow, he could just make out the lighted signs of the businesses along the town's main street—a real estate office, bank, liquor store and taxidermist.

"That was horrible," Andi said. "I thought we would slide off the road—and maybe off the side of a mountain—at any minute."

"I knew we'd be fine," Simon lied.

"What do we do now?" she asked.

He spotted a large lit-up sign. The red letters spelled out *Hotel*. "I think we get a couple of rooms for the night."

THE FOOTE HOTEL reminded Andi of a grandmother's house—if her grandmother had gone for moose heads, bear skins and cozy, flowered furniture. A string of cowbells on the door announced their arrival as she and Simon stepped into a wood-floored front room. Heat from the fire blazing on a stone hearth blasted them—she was so tired she could have stretched out on one of the chintz-covered sofas and fallen asleep with only her coat for a coverlet.

A tired-looking, genial-faced man looked up from behind a counter. "Nasty night out," he said.

"Do you have any rooms?" Simon asked.

"We've got one room left. Grandpa Foote. It has two beds and a private bath. The rate includes a full breakfast in the morning."

"We'll take it." Simon pulled out his wallet and handed over some bills.

"Where you folks from?" the man asked.

"Denver," Simon said. "Apparently, the road closed behind us."

"You're lucky you made it through." He handed over Simon's change and an old-fashioned key on a brass fob. "The room is at the end of the hall on the left. If you need anything, I'm Mike, the manager."

"It's such a charming hotel." Andi slid her hand along the back of a polished oak rocker. "Has it been here a long time?"

"Since the thirties," Mike said. "Some people say we're haunted, if you're interested in that kind of thing."

"Haunted?" Andi gaped at him, sure he must be teasing her.

"People say they've seen Grandpa Foote rocking in that chair there. And there's a young man who supposedly walks around upstairs, but personally, I don't believe in ghosts."

"I don't either," Andi said, but she moved her hand away from the back of the rocker.

"Is there any place close we can get some dinner?" Simon asked.

The hotel manager glanced over at Andi. She must have looked as bad as she felt. "I've got some lasagna left over from a dinner I catered," Mike said. "I can fix plates for you, eight dollars each."

"That sounds wonderful," Andi said before Simon could answer. "Thank you."

"You go on up and I'll bring it up to you," Mike said.

Simon went out to fetch their bags. "Where are you headed?" Mike asked.

"Breckenridge," Andi said.

"With snow like this, the ski resort will be opening soon," Mike said. "Could be the earliest opening in a while."

"Do you ski?" Andi asked, more to be polite than because she was interested.

"Over a hundred and thirty days last year," Mike said.

Simon returned and led the way up the wooden stairs, which creaked loudly as they made their way up. Each room had a name as well as a number—School House, China Jane, Nature. Grandpa Foote, at the end of the hall, featured two iron bedsteads covered with patchwork quilts, a rocking chair and a bathroom with an old-fashioned white cast-iron tub on claw feet.

Andi stared at the rocking chair. "Do you believe in ghosts?" she asked.

"No." He set down their bags and shed his coat. "But I believe they probably make a good marketing hook for tourists. Do you want to change clothes or anything before we eat?"

"A hot bath sounds so good," Andi said, hugging her arms across her chest.

"Go ahead," he said. "I'll let you know when the food gets here."

She felt self-conscious, undressing with Simon just

on the other side of the door. He was still the cop who had harassed the people she cared about for the past months—but she was beginning to see other sides to him. The memory of waking up in the hospital to find him by her side stirred something in her. He made her feel vulnerable in a way she hadn't allowed herself to feel since her mother's death. As much as she had cared for Daniel, their relationship had always been about him—what she could do for him, what he needed from her.

Simon was different. He didn't seem to expect anything of her, and seemed more concerned for her comfort than his own.

She stepped into the warm bath water, sighing as it flowed over her body. She smoothed her hands over the taut mound of her belly, smiling as the baby shifted at her touch. This little life inside her had transformed her, from a woman whose whole identity was defined by her looks and her position in society, to someone who scarcely ever thought about such things. She hadn't looked in a full-length mirror in months. Her body had changed, but her way of thinking had changed, also. All the things that used to matter to her—clothes and shopping and parties—felt silly and empty now. The most important thing was providing a good, safe life for her child.

She thought she had found that safety with the Prophet, but obviously she had been wrong. She touched the necklace, the rough surface of the diamond and the smooth warmth of the gold. She had lied when she had told Daniel she took it as a way to feel closer to him. She had taken it because she was angry with him for cheating on her with other women. She looked at the necklace as payment for the grief he had put her through. Part of her had even been disappointed that he hadn't been more upset by her theft of the piece. He had actually seemed happy for her to have it.

She slid her hand up to her throat, and touched the rough lines where the knife had cut her. It seemed so unreal—a terrible nightmare. That a man she had loved could do such a thing…a chill ran through her in spite of the heat from the bathwater.

From there her mind drifted to the Kia driver who had followed them. He had looked so familiar to her, but she couldn't place him. Who did she know who was blond with a beard? Not a beard, exactly—more like a goatee.

The image of the man by the elevator in the Brown Palace, the one with the Russian accent, made her sit upright, water sloshing over the side of the tub. But why had he been following them?

When she emerged from the bathroom, dressed in a loose gown and robe, Simon indicated a tray that sat on an old-fashioned wooden chest of drawers. "Mike just brought up the food," he said.

Her stomach cramped with hunger. "I'm starving." She started to lift the tray, but Simon intercepted her.

"Sit in the rocker," he said. "I'll bring it to you."

"You don't have to wait on me," she protested.

"I do," he said. "Otherwise, my mother might come back to haunt me. She was a Southern belle from Atlanta and believed in old-fashioned manners."

She smiled at the idea of this stoic, rather severe lawman being schooled by his mother to say *Yes, ma'am* and hold open doors. She settled into the rocker and he brought a plate to her. The aroma of the lasagna made her mouth water, and she feared her own manners suffered as she devoured it, as well as the salad and bread that accompanied it.

Hunger sated, she looked across at Simon. Head down, his shoulders drooped, as if they carried a burden that was too heavy. She should tell him that she thought the driver of the Kia had been the Russian, but what could he do about that now? It would only make him worry. He might even try to go out in the storm to search for the man. She would tell him tomorrow, after they had both had a chance to rest. "Why don't you take a bath now and I'll carry the dishes down," she said.

"I can take them down," he said, starting to rise.

"No, please." She stood and added his plate to hers on the tray. "I'd like to stretch my legs, after sitting in the car all day."

"I should go with you," he said.

"Oh please," she said. "Who's going to bother me here? With the snow and the roads closed, no one can reach us here—if they could even find us. And you'll feel better after a bath. It will take the chill off."

"All right." He rubbed the back of his neck. "The hot water would feel good."

He went into the bathroom, and she gathered the dishes on the tray and headed downstairs. She found Mike in the kitchen. "Dinner was delicious," she said, as he hurried to take the tray from her. "Thanks so much. I wasn't looking forward to going back out in that storm."

"Glad you enjoyed it." He carried the dishes to the sink at the back of the kitchen, and she followed him a few steps inside. "If you need anything else, let me know," he said. "I remember when my wife was expecting our kids, she would get hungry a lot."

"I do that too." She smiled, relaxed for the first time in a long while.

"When are you due?" he asked.

"I have another couple of weeks, I think," she said. The doctor had told her the baby could be born any time now, but she didn't want to worry this nice man. And she felt fine. A little awkward and uncomfortable, maybe, but she had felt that for months.

"Tough time to travel," Mike said. "Do you have family in Breckenridge?"

The question puzzled her, then she remembered that she and Simon were supposed to be on their way to Breckenridge. If she lied and said yes, she had family there, Mike might ask their names, and that would lead to a whole other mess of lies. "No. Simon has business there and we didn't want to be apart, with my due date so close." That sounded better—all sweet and romantic, even.

"I remember when my first was born, I felt that way too," he said. "I didn't want to let my wife out of my sight."

She swallowed past the sudden tightness in her throat. If only someone really felt that way about her. It sounded so nice. Instead of someone who loved her watching over her every move, she was being stalked by a man who wanted to do her harm.

The bells on the front door jangled and Mike looked in that direction. "I'd better go see who that is," he said.

"Is it all right if I make tea?" she asked, indicating the tea and coffee service on the table just outside the door.

"Help yourself," he said, and moved past her into the front room.

She selected a tea bag and filled a mug with hot water, then stood waiting for it to brew before she added sugar.

"Do you have a room for the night?" The familiar voice, with its softly accented tones—definitely Russian—sent a chill through her.

"Sorry, but we're full," Mike said.

"I don't require anything fancy," the voice said. "My car broke down, and I hitchhiked into town. The other places I asked said they were full too."

Scarcely daring to breathe, Andi tiptoed to the door that separated the dining area from the front room and peered out. The blond with the goatee who had addressed her by name at the Brown Palace stood across from Mike. He wore a stocking cap and a dark blue ski jacket, but it was the same man, she was sure.

"I can let you sleep on the sofa," Mike said, indicating the chintz-upholstered furniture in front of the fireplace. "That's the best I can do."

"I would be so grateful. Do you have a restroom I could use?"

"Right over there." Mike pointed to the men's room.

As soon as the blond closed the door to the men's room behind him, Andi left the dining room and headed for the stairs.

"Did you change your mind about tea?" Mike called after her.

"Yes. Thank you," she said, and all but ran up the stairs to the room at the end of the hall. She shoved her key into the lock with shaking hands and pushed open the door.

Simon emerged from the bathroom, bare chested, toweling his hair. "Everything okay?" he asked.

She sank onto the bed, her wobbly legs unable to support her. "There's a man d...downstairs," she managed to stammer. "He just came in. I'm sure he's the man who was talking to me at the Brown Palace—the one by the elevator who knew my name."

"You're sure it's the same man?" Simon asked.

She nodded. "He has an accent—Russian, I think."

Simon sat beside her, not touching her, but his presence so close steadied her. "I'm wondering now if he was the man in the Kia," she said. "I think I recognized him."

"It might have been him," Simon said. "Did he see you?"

"I don't think so. I was in the kitchen. I overheard him talking to Mike, then I peeked around the door. It was definitely him."

"What did he say?"

"He said he wrecked his car and had to hitchhike to the hotel. He looked pretty cold, but not too frozen. Mike told him he could sleep on the sofa by the fire, since all the rooms are full. He went into the restroom and I hurried up here."

She gripped Simon's arm. "What are we going to do? We can't leave without him seeing us, and where would we go in all this snow?" Her throat tightened and she fought down panic. When they had left Denver, she had thought they were safe. Instead, they had ended up in a worse predicament. "We're trapped here—with a man who probably wants to kill us."

Chapter Nine

Simon's first instinct was to hustle Andi into the car and drive to safety, but common sense overruled that impulse. They were both too exhausted to go anywhere that night, and in this weather he was as likely to drive off the side of a mountain as to reach his destination safely. He reached for his shirt. "I'm going downstairs to check him out," he said. "Lock the door behind me and don't let anyone in."

"All right." Andi's lower lip trembled, but she steadied herself. "Be careful."

"Always."

He finished dressing, then tucked his pistol in the waistband of his pants and covered it with a loose shirt. Only a pale glow guided him as he descended the stairs. The kitchen and dining areas, as well as the check-in counter, were dark and there was no sign of Mike. A fire blazed in the hearth, and a lone man sat on one of the sofas facing the fire. He turned to look at Simon.

"I didn't expect to find anyone else up," Simon said.

The man rose from his seat, the light from the fire

throwing his face half in shadow, giving it a sinister cast. "What are you doing here?" he asked.

Simon moved closer to the man he had confronted in the Ship Tavern bar—was it really only last night? It felt like ages had passed. "I'm spending the night here out of the snow," he said. "What are you doing here?"

"The same." He couldn't see the man's face well enough to read his expression in the dim light. "The manager is allowing me to stay down here tonight," he said.

"You've been following me," Simon said.

"I understand paranoia is one of the first signs that one is losing his grip on reality," the Russian said.

"You were driving the Kia that caused us to crash," Simon said.

"I don't know what you're talking about." He glanced up the stairs. "Is Miss Matheson with you?"

"Why do you want to know?"

He shrugged, an overly casual gesture that didn't fool Simon. "It would be good to say hello to an old friend."

"She doesn't want to talk to you."

"How is it your business who she talks to?"

Simon brushed back the tail of his shirt to reveal the gun in its holster and the badge clipped to his belt. "Agent Simon Woolridge. And you are?"

"You may call me Victor."

"Is that your real name?"

Again, the casual shrug.

"Leave Ms. Matheson alone."

"I think you and I are interested in the same person, and it isn't Miss Matheson," Victor said. "I am looking for Metwater. I think you are too."

"Do you know where he is?" Simon asked.

"No. But I think he will come for Miss Matheson. You think so too. That is why you are here."

Simon didn't deny or confirm this. "When I find Daniel Metwater, I'm going to arrest him," he said.

"Not if I find him first."

"I could arrest you for interfering with police business."

"Unlike my homeland, this is a free country," Victor said. "You may not like my being here, but I haven't broken any laws. You can't arrest me."

"Leave Andi Matheson alone," Simon said again.

Victor sat back down, and stretched his arms over his head. "I am tired. I would like to sleep now," he said.

"I'll see you in the morning," Simon said.

"Good night," Victor said. He lay back and closed his eyes.

Simon waited a moment, then turned and started up the stairs. At the landing, he looked back, not surprised to find that Victor had raised his head and was staring after him.

Upstairs, he knocked softly on the door to his room. "Andi, it's me, Simon," he said.

Something scraped across the floor, then the lock turned. The door opened and Andi stood, one hand on the back of a straight wooden chair. Simon sent her a questioning look.

"I shoved the chair under the knob after you left," she said. "I figured it would make it harder for anyone to get in."

"I don't think Victor will make any moves tonight,"

Simon said. He shut the door behind him and turned the lock.

"Is that his name? Victor? How do you know?" She followed him across the room.

Simon removed his gun and laid it on the bedside table. "I introduced myself, and he told me his name is Victor," he said. "I don't know if it's his real name—probably not."

"You talked to him? What did he say?"

"As little as possible." He sat on the side of the bed and began removing his shoes. "I let him know I was onto him, that he was to leave you alone or there would be consequences."

"Consequences?"

"I promised to protect you, and I will. By doing whatever that requires."

He didn't look up, but he could feel her eyes on him. She had a way of looking at him that made him feel stripped bare, as if she could see past any front he put up and tell what he was really thinking. It was both unnerving and oddly freeing, as if he didn't have to pretend anything with her, because there was no point.

The bed springs creaked as she sat on the other bed across from him. "Maybe it's just a coincidence that he's here," she said.

"He made you uneasy at the Brown Palace," Simon said. "He knew your real name."

"Maybe I really did meet him somewhere before," she said. "I went to a lot of public functions with my father. So many that I lost track of them all. I could have very easily met him and forgotten."

"He said he was looking for Metwater." He hadn't intended to reveal this to her, but saw no point in hiding the information now.

Her eyes widened. "Why is he looking for him?"

"I don't know. But when I told him I intended to arrest Metwater, he said that wouldn't happen if he got to him first."

"Does that mean he's going kill him?" Her lower lip trembled.

"Maybe. Or maybe he's going to help him get away." Simon didn't think so, but he had been trained to look at every possibility in a case.

"I doubt that," she said. "Daniel didn't like Russians. He was a little afraid of them, even. I always assumed it was because the Russian mob killed his brother."

Simon stifled a yawn. "I'm not going to worry about it now," he said. "He's downstairs, we're up here and no one is going anywhere tonight. The best we can do is try to get some sleep."

Andi glanced over her shoulder, toward the door. He stood and checked the lock, then positioned the chair back under the knob. "I won't let anyone get to you," he said, before returning to the bed closest to the door.

THOUGH HER BODY ached with exhaustion, Andi lay awake in the darkness, every creak of a floorboard setting her heart thumping. In the bed across from her, Simon slept, his breathing deep and even. He must truly believe they were in no danger, to sleep so soundly. Yet her mind refused to let go of her fear. What did the Russian—Victor—want? Was he really the man in the Kia? Was his name even Victor? Why had he followed them?

So many questions, and no answers.

Seeking distraction, she focused on Simon. Having seen him in camp many times, she thought she had him figured out. He was a tough, by-the-book cop, prejudiced against Daniel Metwater and all his followers, quick to judge and loath to compromise. He was sarcastic, impatient and stubborn.

Having spent most of the last twenty-four hours in his company, she now knew that he was all those things, but also much more. He had shown her nothing but kindness. He had a dry, subtle sense of humor and a compassion that ran deep. He was honest to a fault, and she believed she could trust him with her life.

Beneath his cool, brittle exterior, she sensed a man who judged himself as harshly as he judged others—a man wary of relationships who had nevertheless revealed things to her she sensed he had not revealed to his coworkers or others he called friends.

She was drawn to him, in a way she had not been drawn to any other man. Though not physically imposing, he had a lean, athletic grace that stirred her. Sometimes when his dark eyes met hers, she felt swoony as a lovesick teen—and aroused as only a mature woman could be.

She felt safe with Simon. Not merely physically safe, but free to be fully herself without judgment. Though he had said more than once that he thought she was beautiful, she sensed he looked beyond surface beauty, to something deeper. He had seen her pale from fear, hollow-eyed from lack of sleep, swollen from pregnancy, with uncombed hair and no makeup, yet none of that made any difference to him. He had touched her just as gently, held her with just as much strength.

Did he know how strongly she was attracted to him? How much she wanted to feel his arms around her just now, to explore the hard plane of his chest with her hands, to trace the lines of muscle in his arms and shoulders?

Clearly, she had found something to distract her from worries over her safety, but now she was anything but sleepy. Not that she expected Simon to do anything about her aroused state, but if she could only lie beside him, she thought she would be able to relax enough to go to sleep. Maybe he would appreciate the company as well. Or, exhausted as he must be, he might not even wake up.

Carefully, she folded back the blankets and sat, wincing as the iron bedstead creaked. She tiptoed across to the bed where Simon slept, the bare wood floors cold against the bottoms of her feet, and lifted the covers, then eased herself in beside him.

He immediately rolled over to face her. She lay on her back, scarcely daring to breathe. Any second now, she half expected him to cry out in alarm, or to send her back to her own bed.

When he spoke, his voice was quiet, nothing like that of a man who had been in a deep sleep. "Andi, what are you doing here?" he asked.

"I couldn't sleep," she said.

He waited, saying nothing.

Tentatively, she reached out and touched his side. He was naked from the waist up, wearing only a pair of boxers. "I thought I would feel safer if I was closer to you."

He rolled toward her and put one arm around her, pulling her to him. She turned on her side, spooning against him. His arm rested under the curve of her belly. "Is that better?" he asked, his breath soft against her neck.

"Yes. It's wonderful." She settled more firmly against him, a breathy cry escaping her as his arousal poked against her bottom.

"Sorry," he muttered, and tried to shift away.

"Don't be." She pressed more firmly against him. When he didn't move away again, she took his hand and brought it up to cup her breast.

He shaped his hand to her and pressed his head against her shoulder. "Have I done that lousy a job of hiding my feelings for you?" he asked.

Her heart sped up. "You have feelings for me?"

"Since the first day I saw you."

"I didn't know," she said. "I was afraid you would think I was being foolish. Or worse—manipulative."

He pressed himself more fully against her. "I deal with a lot of manipulative people in my job. You don't strike me as one of them."

He didn't mention Daniel's name, but he didn't have to. The more time Andi spent apart from the Prophet, the more she saw how he had played her, how he played all his followers. He was very good at figuring out what they needed and giving it to them. He had recognized how lonely and lost she had been, and had given her companionship and direction.

It was as if Daniel had put her in a trance from which she was only now awakening. "No, I'm not trying to manipulate you," she said. "I only want to be with you. Tonight."

When he didn't respond, she reached back and took the hard length of his arousal in her hand. The soft hiss of his breath through his teeth encouraged her. She began to stroke him, gently at first, then with more firmness.

Simon's hand on her wrist stilled her. "You don't have to do this," he said.

"Oh, but I want to," she said. She rolled over to face him, and brought her lips to his.

He didn't hesitate to respond, his lips firm and caressing. He kissed her gently at first, as if gauging how far she would let him go. When she responded eagerly, he pressed more, teasing apart her lips with his tongue, angling his head to deepen the kiss, setting every nerve ending buzzing with awareness of him.

Her lips still pressed to his, she began stroking him once more. This time, he didn't stop her, but began fondling her breasts, the nipples beading at his touch. "Is this all right?" he asked.

"More than all right," she gasped. She licked her palm, then grasped him once more. He bent to draw one nipple into his mouth through the thin fabric of her gown and she moaned, need thundering through her, her muscles tightening, aching for more.

She started to slide down the length of him, but he pulled her up again. "Just your hands this time," he said.

"Yes," she whispered. She wanted that closeness too,

that face-to-face, body-to-body contact—that feeling of being held and carried along with your lover to completion.

She began to caress him again, sliding her fingers down to fondle his balls, varying the pressure and speed of her movements. He buried his face against her neck, his breathing increasing, until he was panting. She wrapped her free arm around him, pulling him against her until she could feel the pounding of his heart. She matched her breathing to his, her own desire winding tighter as he neared his release.

When he came, she cried out as well, and he gripped her tightly to him, kissing her neck, her face and finally her lips, a deep, drugging kiss that left her light-headed and breathless.

He leaned over her and pulled a handful of tissues from the box on the bedside table and cleaned himself. She lay on her side, her head on his chest, listening to the steady beat of his heart. She fully expected him to go to sleep now, as exhausted as he had been earlier. And that was all right. Maybe they would find another time for him to return the favor.

But Simon had other ideas. He tossed the tissues in the trash, then traced his hand along the curve of her body, slipping down lower, until his fingers probed at her entrance.

"Oh!" She let out a cry of both delight and surprise as he slid one finger into her.

"Your turn," he said, and kissed her cheek.

"You don't have—" But the protest died on her lips as he began to stroke and fondle, sliding in and out of her, teasing her with his fingers and thumb. She clung to him, gripping his back as desire shuddered through her. She sighed and gasped, unable to keep quiet as the urgency built. He kissed her lips, then along her jaw, hesitating a moment when he reached the diamond necklace, before moving on to her breasts, sucking and teasing her aching nipples until she was half-blind with need.

She came hard, bucking against him, shutting her eyes tightly and riding the wave of pleasure that rocked her. Simon's hand and mouth stilled and he held her, cradling her against him, strong arms wrapping around her. She kept her eyes closed, breathing in the scent of him, reveling in the pleasure of being surrounded by him, her senses overtaken by Simon.

Eventually, he shifted, pulling his arm from beneath her. She sat up. "Going back to your own bed?" he asked. Was she imagining the disappointment in his voice?

"No, I'm only going to the bathroom."

She returned shortly and slid beneath the covers beside him once more.

"Your feet are cold," he said, as she pressed them against his warm legs.

She smiled, then laughed.

"What's so funny?" he asked.

"Nothing." She couldn't tell him she had laughed because it was such an old married couple comment— or at least it seemed like one to her. In her admittedly limited experience, new lovers never complained about anything, intent on making the best impression. Only long acquaintance made people comfortable enough to voice objections.

But Simon wasn't like that. He never held back his honest opinion. Though neither did he move away from her and her cold feet. She settled her back more firmly against him, his arm draped over her ribs once again. "Good night," she said softly.

He slid his hand up and took hold of the necklace. "I didn't notice this before," he said. "Where did you get it?"

She stiffened, groping for some lie that would satisfy him. But she couldn't move from being so intimate with him to lying. "It's Daniel's," she said. "I...well, I took it from him."

"Can I take a closer look?"

"I guess so."

He sat and leaned over her to switch on the lamp on the nightstand. "It looks old," he said.

"I think it might be." She had to hold herself back from wrapping her hand around the pendant, trying to hide it.

"It looks like the one Michelle Munson described— the one she said belonged to her foster sister."

"Yes. I guess it might be. I thought maybe Cass gave it to David, Daniel's brother, and that Daniel inherited it when David was killed. But if it really was Michelle's sister's, I'll give it back to her."

His gaze shifted from the necklace to her eyes. "Why did you take it?" he asked.

"I was angry with him for sending me away. I saw it when I was going through his motor home, gathering things to take with me, and I just took it. I wanted to get back at him, I guess. But it didn't work."

"What do you mean?"

"He saw the necklace when he grabbed me in the hotel room last night. He actually seemed happy that I had it. He said I was his good luck charm."

Simon grasped the pendant. "Michelle said her sister's necklace was a locket. That means it opens, right?"

"Right. But I don't think this one opens. There are no hinges, and I don't see a catch." About that time the front of the pendant sprang open. "Oh!" she cried. "How did you do that?"

"There's a hidden catch along the side," he said. "See, there's a shallow compartment here." He leaned closer. "There's a key." He held up a flat brass key, notched along one side.

"It's an odd-looking key," she said. "It doesn't look like it fits a door or a car."

"I think it's a safe-deposit box key," Simon said. "Did Metwater ever mention a safe-deposit box?"

She shook her head. "No."

Simon fit the key back in the locket and closed it. "Maybe he didn't know about it. It might belong to his brother. Or to Michelle's sister."

"We can ask her when we see her again," she said. "Whenever that is."

"Tomorrow," Simon said. "I plan on taking you to the same safe house where she and her son are staying."

She lay back, weariness dragging at her. "That would be good." There were too many unanswered questions in her life right now.

Chapter Ten

Victor lay awake long after the hotel had fallen silent. The clock on the mantle struck a doleful midnight, and he rose and began to pace. The old wood floors creaked beneath his feet and odd drafts swirled in his wake, setting the pages of magazines fluttering and the leaves of potted plants rustling. He added wood to the fire and the blaze roared to life, sparks spiraling up the chimney, the logs popping and crackling. He should have been exhausted, after hours in the cold, trudging miles through the snow before he was able to flag down a passing county truck, the driver astonished to find anyone out on the closed road. By the time he had reached the Foote Hotel, he had been half-frozen and aching for bed.

But his encounter with Simon Woolridge had energized him. He had had no idea Woolridge and Andi were here when he chose this place to stay the night. He just needed a room for one night, and this was the only place he could find. This had worked out great because it saved him having to look for her, but he had to figure out how to get the cop out of the picture so that he could get to Andi. Soon after that, Metwater and the key to a million dollars would be his.

He moved to the kitchen, ignoring the employees-only sign on the door, and headed for the massive commercial refrigerator. He needed fuel for his body and his mind. He opened the door and found a pan half full of lasagna, which he ate with his hands, red sauce staining his fingers and running into his goatee. He grinned at the idea, and grabbed a pint of milk to wash down the culinary carnage. Finished with his meal, he left the empty dish in the sink and washed his face and hands, dripping water on the floor.

He returned to the front room and the crackling fire, and listened for any sound of movement overhead. Wind moaned outside and the old house creaked, but he could detect no sign of life from the occupants of the bedrooms overhead. Behind the front desk, he found an old-fashioned registrar. Apparently the bookkeeping at the Foote Hotel was as antiquated as the furnishings. He flipped to that day's date and found the neat inscription, "Mr. and Mrs. Simon Woolridge." Mr. and Mrs., was it? Another attempt to hide Ms. Matheson's identity? Probably. A woman who would hook up with Metwater didn't strike him as the law-and-order type.

The Woolridges were in the Grandpa Foote room, which the fire plan on the wall showed him was at the very end of the hall. He studied the layout of the hotel with a critical eye. To get to that room from here, he would have to climb the stairs—which creaked. He knew because he had spent the early evening listening to the treads protest loudly with almost every footfall as the various guests made their way up to bed. Then, once he had surmounted the obstacle of the stairs, he would have to traverse a long hallway, which also transmitted the sound of every footstep in amplified clarity. At this time of night, most of the guests would probably wake at his approach, and it was pretty much a given that Woolridge, the wary cop, would as well.

The fire plan indicated every exit in red letters—including one at either end of the long upstairs hallway. Each of these doors opened to an outside balcony, with steps leading down to the street. The doors were probably locked at night, but a survey of the keys stored in a drawer beneath the register revealed one marked Outer Doors. He pocketed this one, then found the key labeled Grandpa Foote and took it as well. Adrenaline buzzing in his brain like good vodka, he moved to the sofa and extracted his pistol from his coat and checked that it was fully loaded. Holding it at the ready in his right hand, he eased open the front door and walked around the side of the building until he came to the stairs that led up to the balcony at the end of the hallway nearest Simon and Andi's room.

These steps were newer and quieter than the ones inside, and the night wind helped hide the sound of his approach. He opened the door with his key, closed it behind him and tiptoed a short five steps to the door marked Grandpa Foote.

An ear to the door revealed the muted rumble of soft snoring. He eased the gun into his coat pocket and pulled out a knife. He would cut Woolridge's throat while he slept, and threaten Andi with the same if she didn't come with him quietly.

The key slid smoothly into the lock, and the knob turned soundlessly. But when he tried to push open the door, it refused to budge. He pushed harder and heard the scrape of wood on wood, and then a woman's startled cry.

Hastily, he retreated toward the deeper shadows near the exit. The door to the room across the hall from Woolridge's opened, and a woman's pale face peeked out. "I told you," she whispered, staring directly at him. She looked over her shoulder, back into the room. "It's the ghost of Grandpa Foote. I told you I felt his presence. I knew he would materialize tonight."

While her face was turned away from him, he darted to the exit and out onto the porch again. He would give the two ghost hunters time to settle down before he tried again. Obviously, Woolridge had barricaded the door from the inside. Victor needed to find a way to draw him out. Then he could slip in and grab Andi.

His thoughts shifted to the fire plan, picturing the layout of the hotel once more in his mind. He could see the red exit signs marked on the little hand-drawn map. But there had been other red letters too, those marking fire alarms—one at each end of the hallway.

He glanced inside and spotted the alarm on the wall. A check of the door across the hall from Grandpa Foote—a room marked as Mountain Man—showed the door shut tight. The ghost hunters had once more retired. Wasting no time, Victor opened the door, moved to the alarm, jerked open the cover and pulled down the handle. An ear-splitting mechanical shriek filled the hallway as he retreated outside once more.

The door to Mountain Man was the first one to open. "The ghost set off the alarm," a stout woman with short curly hair announced to no one in particular. "I saw him."

No one paid her any attention. The alarm continued to shriek, and soon other guests joined the ghostbusters in the hallway, milling around in pajamas and robes and hastily donned coats and slippers. At last the door to Grandpa Foote opened and Simon emerged.

"What's going on?" he shouted above the murmur of the other guests and the blare of the alarm.

"The ghost set off the fire alarm," the curly-haired woman said.

"I think I smell smoke," another woman added.

"We'd better get out of here," a man said, his hands on the shoulders of a petite woman in a Wonder Woman nightshirt. "A place this old could go up in a flash."

This started an exodus toward the stairs. Victor took advantage of the commotion to slip inside, keeping to the shadows along the wall. With Simon's back still to him, he moved into Grandpa Foote and shut the door behind him.

SIMON PUSHED HIS WAY through the crowd in the hallway, trying to assess the situation as the fire alarm echoed in the enclosed space. Up and down the hall, doors stood open and people milled about. If the building really had been on fire, half of them would be toast by now, but Simon didn't smell any smoke. For that reason alone, he had suggested Andi stay in the room while he checked things out. No sense in her going out in the cold if she didn't have to.

"Did anyone call nine-one-one?" someone asked as the guests crowded onto the stairs.

"Did anyone call Mike?" Simon asked.

"I did," someone else said. "He's on his way."

The fact that the alarm was sounding, but none of the hotel's smoke alarms were going off, made Simon suspect deliberate mischief rather than an actual blaze. He located the alarm on the wall, the door open and the handle forced down. "I don't think there's a fire!" he shouted to be heard above the commotion. "Someone pulled the fire alarm. Probably a kid who thinks he's funny." He recalled doing the same when he was a young teen—and being grounded for a month afterward when his father found out. He tried to shove the handle back up, hoping to shut off the deafening clamor, but it refused to budge.

"The ghost set that off." A woman stopped at his shoulder and scowled at him. "I saw him."

Whatever she had seen, Simon was sure it wasn't a ghost. "What did he look like?" he asked.

"He had white hair and a white beard," she said. "I'm sure it was Grandpa Foote."

"We should go." A man took her arm and tried to move her toward the door, but she stood her ground.

"There's no fire," she said. "The ghost of Grandpa Foote is playing tricks."

Blond hair could look white in the semidarkness, Simon thought. And hadn't Andi described Victor's goatee as a beard earlier? Cold sweat drenched him as he looked around for the Russian, who was nowhere to be seen in the milling crowd. Cursing himself for leaving Andi, he rushed back to his room.

The door swung open easily at his touch, and he stared into the empty room. Andi's robe lay in a silken puddle by the bed, as if she had been interrupted in the act of putting it on. Cursing himself for a fool, Simon raced outside again. "Andi!" he shouted.

Half a dozen heads turned toward him, their faces blank. "Has anyone seen a very pregnant woman?" he asked. "Blonde, in a white nightgown?"

Mutely, they all shook their heads. He spotted the woman who had told him about the ghost. "This ghost, have you seen him again?" he asked.

She shook her head. "No. He probably won't show himself again tonight. He got what he wanted—everyone up and in a turmoil. He'll be happy now. For a while, at least. That's how the spirits are."

When Simon found Victor, he was going to make him very, very unhappy.

ANDI WAS GETTING really tired of men grabbing her and trying to drag her off. First Daniel, and now this Victor guy. She was going to have to start arming herself or something. But honestly, she had been expecting Simon when the door to her room opened, not the Russian. Before she could even scream, Victor had clamped one hand over her mouth, wrapped the other arm across her chest and dragged her backward into the hall and out the door. She could hardly breathe, he was squeezing her so tightly.

And now she was freezing, the rough boards of the porch icy against her bare feet, an arctic wind cutting through her thin nightgown. The night was pitch-black, with no moon and certainly no streetlights to illuminate the scene. A few people had emerged from the hotel to the street below, but they were oblivious to what was happening right over their heads. There was no way this was going to end well for her, and she had her baby to think of too.

Years ago, she had taken a women's self-defense seminar at her university. About a hundred young women had gathered in a gymnasium while a pair of burly guys demonstrated a dozen ways to fight back against an attacker. Then the women had paired up and practiced a few of the moves, with a lot of giggling and not a great deal of finesse. Andi struggled to remember any of those moves now. Wasn't there something about gouging eyes or trying to break his nose?

She reached up and raked her nails across Victor's face, which only earned a punch to the side of her head that made her ears ring. But it also made her even angrier, and instinct took over from her faulty memory as she kicked her heel back to land firmly between Victor's legs.

The results were both instant and highly gratifying. He let out a strangled moan, released her and dropped to his knees, hands covering his crotch. She stumbled down the stairs and into the street, where she collided with Mike, who was hurrying down the sidewalk toward the hotel. "Hey, there." He steadied her with both hands. "What's going on?"

She shook her head. Explaining now would take too much breath. "Have you seen Simon?" she asked.

"No. I just got here."

She followed Mike inside, to a front room full of other guests. The blare of the fire alarm wasn't as loud down here, the raised voices of the guests almost drowning it out. Mike ignored their questions and marched past them up the stairs, Andi behind him.

They met Simon at the top of the staircase. He was fully dressed, including his coat, his dark brows drawn together in a forbidding expression. "I tried to shut off the fire alarm, but no luck," he said to Mike as he moved down the stairs. Then he spotted Andi and stopped. "Are you all right?" he asked.

She nodded, and started past him. He touched her arm, gently, the slightest brush of his fingers. "Victor?" he asked.

She nodded. "I don't know where he is now. I don't care."

"I thought he had kidnapped you," Simon said.

"He tried, but I got away."

"How?"

She frowned at him. "I'm a lot tougher than I look. But right now, I'm freezing. I need to get dressed."

"I'll be up in a minute."

She continued upstairs after Mike, while Simon started down again. He was probably going to look for Victor, though she was sure by now he would be gone.

There were too many people around at this point for him to attempt to grab her again.

Upstairs, Mike disabled the alarm. "What idiot set this off?" he asked.

"It was the ghost of Grandpa Foote," said the curly-haired woman from the room across the hall, a fuzzy brown robe belted around her solid figure. "I saw him. He was hovering over there, next to his room." She pointed to Andi and Simon's room, the one labeled Grandpa Foote. "Then he moved over and pulled the alarm."

"Why would a ghost pull a fire alarm?" Andi asked.

"They like to cause trouble," the woman said. "Especially for people who are occupying the places they once occupied." She turned back to Mike. "You should consider doing something to appease him. Maybe hang his portrait downstairs in a place of honor or something."

"Thanks for the advice," Mike said. He waited until she and her husband had retreated to their room and shut the door before he turned to Andi. "Any idea who actually did this?"

"I think it was Victor," she said. "The man you let sleep on the sofa. I think I saw him up here right after it happened."

Mike's shoulders slumped. "That's what I get for being a nice guy. Well, as my dad always said, 'No good deed goes unpunished.'" He glanced down at her bare feet. "You must be freezing. You should go back to bed."

She returned to her room, taking care to lock the door behind her, and fix the chair back in place. She was pulling on socks when someone knocked. "It's me," Simon said.

She tugged up the last sock, tightened the belt on her robe then went to let him in. He was still scowling, and the wind had tousled his hair. She resisted the urge to smooth it back into place. "No sign of him," he said, moving past her and taking off his coat.

She fitted the chair back under the doorknob then sat down on the side of the bed again, pulling the blankets around to cover her knees. Simon paced in front of her. "I should have realized it was a trick to draw me away," he said. "I never should have left you alone."

"I'm not going to accept an apology for something that wasn't your fault." She caught his hand as he passed, and he stopped and met her gaze. "If you had insisted I come with you, instead of leaving me behind in the room, maybe he would have shot you or stabbed you, and then dragged me away anyway. As it is, I'm okay."

He sat beside her, still holding her hand. "What happened?" he asked.

"He came in the room, grabbed me and dragged me out onto the porch. I kicked him where it hurts, he let me go and I ran. I hope he's still hurting."

Simon glanced at the clock. "It's only two thirty. You should try to get some sleep."

"Only if you'll try to sleep too."

He shook his head and started to rise, but she tugged him down beside her once more. "You're not going to help anyone by staying awake until you're dead on your feet," she said. "He's not going to come back here tonight, but if he does, we can set up something so we'll hear him."

"Like what?" he asked.

She looked around the room, and spotted the old-fashioned bowl and pitcher on the dresser. "We'll put those china dishes, plus the glasses from the bathroom, on the chair in front of the door," she said. "If anyone tries to shove it open, they'll fall to the floor and break—or at least make enough noise to wake us."

Simon considered the idea, then nodded. "It's primitive, but effective." He stood and carried the dresser set to the chair, then retrieved the glasses from the bathroom and balanced them so that any movement of the door would send them crashing down. Then he lay beside Andi, still fully clothed.

"Are you going to undress?" she asked.

"No." He reached up and switched off the bedside lamp. "Go to sleep," he said. "I'll be right here."

Were there any more comforting words in the English language?

And was there anyone more stubborn than this lawman? Andi closed her eyes and settled against the solid, reassuring wall of his back. She had proved tonight that she could defend herself when she had to, but she liked knowing she had this gentle man on her side, a man who was determined to protect her at any cost.

Chapter Eleven

Simon woke with a start, the first gray light seeping beneath the window shade. The memory of where he was—and why—filled him. He turned his head to look at Andi, who lay curled on her side next to him. He clenched his hands into fists, resisting the urge to reach out and touch her, not wanting to wake her. The erotic tenderness of the night before had been so incredible—the kind of experience that changed a person on some level he couldn't name. How was it possible to feel so close to a person he had known for such a short time?

True, they had been acquainted with each other for months. He had interviewed her in connection with various cases, and studied her as Daniel Metwater's closest follower and perhaps the key to unraveling the mystery of the Prophet.

But all the while, he had been trying, unsuccessfully apparently, to hide his attraction to her. Something about this quiet, beautiful woman drew him in.

He had had relationships with women before, dating one for as long as two years. But he wasn't one to open himself up to other people. His long-time girlfriend had left him because she said she was tired of feeling shut out. It wasn't that he had deliberately excluded her, but he had always been a man who kept his thoughts and feelings to himself.

Somehow, being with Andi was easier. When he did talk, she listened, but he never sensed that she wanted more. The fact that she had made the first move toward intimacy thrilled him.

The rest of the night hadn't been quite so wonderful, of course. When he had realized Victor had gotten to Andi, he had been equal parts enraged and terrified. He had underestimated the Russian's daring, and it had almost cost him everything. He wouldn't make that mistake again.

Andi stirred and opened her eyes. Her lips curved in a sleepy, sexy smile that he felt right in his groin. "Good morning," she said.

"How did you sleep?" he asked.

"Better than I would have thought possible." She rolled onto her back and stretched, her breasts thrusting upward in a way that left him dry mouthed. "How about you? Did you sleep at all after we came back to bed?"

"Some." Trying to sleep fully dressed—which included his bulletproof vest—wasn't the easiest of propositions. "I dozed a bit."

Her smile faded. "I'd scold you about being so stubborn, but I know it wouldn't do any good," she said. "So it's your own fault if you're miserable now."

"Not all of last night was miserable," he said. He rolled over to face her and propped himself up on one elbow.

Her smile returned, her cheeks flushed pink and eyes sparkling. "No, I'd say the first part of the night was pretty wonderful."

"Only *pretty* wonderful?" He tried to look hurt. "My pride is wounded."

"I'm leaving room for even more spectacular revelations in the future." She smoothed her hand down his arm, eyes heavy-lidded with desire.

He tried to smile at her teasing tone, but he had a hard time pretending there would be any future for the two of them. He couldn't imagine two people from more different worlds, and in any case, today duty had to come before his personal desires. "You're very tempting," he said. "But we really need to get back on the road."

She dropped her hand and sighed. "Somehow, I knew you'd say that."

He sat up on the side of the bed and looked over his shoulder at her. "How are you feeling?" he asked.

"You mean, am I in labor yet?"

"That's not what I asked."

"No, but it's what people usually mean when they ask me that question these days. I know I look like I'm going to pop any minute, but not today, I don't think."

"I promise, that's not what I meant," he said.

"Then maybe you mean, how do I feel about what happened last night?" She sat up also, her body angled toward him, close enough that he could feel her warmth, smell the lingering aroma of her perfume. "I feel wonderful." She met his gaze with a challenge in her eyes. "How are you feeling?"

Conflicted. Not the answer she wanted to hear, or

that he would give her. On one hand, this gorgeous woman he had been attracted to for months was apparently attracted to him too. On the other hand, she was a crime victim he was charged with protecting, as well as a very pregnant mother-to-be. His job was to get her to safety, not to indulge in his desire to make love to her as often as possible. And was it even safe to have sex when she was so close to delivering? What if he sent her into labor?

"I'm feeling like I'm a pretty lucky man right now," he said, and kissed her cheek. "And as much as I'd like to stay here in bed with you all day, I think we really do need to get up and get on the road."

She closed her eyes and sighed. "I know. How's the weather out there this morning?"

He walked to the window and pulled up the blinds. Ice rimmed each pane, forming a crystalline frame for the scene outside. Sunlight sparkled on six inches of snow that dressed the trees and fence rails, and covered the mud and dirt—a clean, fresh blanket over the peaceful landscape. "It's beautiful out," he said. "Clear skies and hopefully clear roads."

She threw back the covers on her side of the bed. "I'm starving, but that probably doesn't surprise you."

"Mike promised a full breakfast."

At only a little past seven o'clock, the dining room was empty except for a young woman with curly black hair, who greeted them with a smile. "Sit wherever you like," she said. "We have breakfast burritos this morning, and some fresh banana bread."

There was also cereal, fruit, cottage cheese and half a

dozen different breads and baked goods. And coffee—strong, hot coffee served in thick white mugs. Simon and Andi filled cups and plates and moved to a table by the windows.

From this seat, Simon could see into the living room. The sofa was empty, the fire cold. The front door opened and Mike entered, wearing cargo shorts, snow boots and a flannel shirt. He dumped a load of firewood on the hearth and began building a fire.

Simon was halfway through his burrito when the manager entered the dining room. "Good morning," he said.

"Morning." Simon nodded toward the sofa. "I see our Russian friend never came back."

"After the stunt he pulled, he had better not show his face around here again." Mike jerked a thumb toward the kitchen. "He apparently decided to raid the refrigerator and left a mess. If he ever has the nerve to show his face around here again, I'll be filing charges."

"I hope none of us ever see him again," Andi said. She leaned closer to Simon and lowered her voice. "Where do you think he went?"

"He probably stole a car and is lying low for the time being." He took a sip of coffee.

"But you think he'll be back."

"He wants something you have," he said. "Or, more likely, he wants to get to Metwater through you."

"Daniel has no idea where I am right now," she said. "How could he?"

"You're probably right." But he couldn't shake the

feeling—call it a lawman's sixth sense—that they hadn't seen the last of Daniel Metwater.

Andi finished off her burrito and pushed the plate away. "Oh, I'm feeling much better now. That was so good."

"We should get going as soon as we can," he said, finishing up his own burrito. "Get on the road before the weather changes."

She pushed back her chair. "I didn't really unpack last night, so it's just a matter of collecting our things."

"I'll go up and get them," he said. "You stay here with Mike. Have another muffin or something."

"I just might do that."

He took the stairs two at a time, pulling out his cell phone as he climbed. Despite the early hour, he wanted to check in with the commander before he hit the road again. He wasn't surprised when Agent Graham Ellison answered on the second ring. Sometimes Simon wondered if the commander ever slept. "I guess this means you survived the night," he said.

"Yes, sir," Simon said. He unlocked their room and pushed open the door. "We ran into a blizzard south of Conifer and got into an accident—which I suspect may be deliberate." He explained about the Kia following them and the driver running off into the storm.

"Any idea who it was?" Graham asked.

"I'm pretty sure it was the Russian I told you about yesterday. He introduced himself as Victor, though I suspect that's not his real name. He showed up here after we checked in last night and talked the manager into letting him sleep on the sofa. After midnight, he pulled the fire alarm and when everyone came out of their rooms to investigate, he saw his chance and tried to kidnap Andi Matheson. She managed to fight him off and he fled. But I have a feeling he'll be back."

"What does he want with Ms. Matheson?" Graham asked.

"No idea. Maybe he thinks he can get to Metwater through her. Any word on the fugitive prophet?"

"Nothing. The trail's gone cold, though we're pretty sure he hasn't left the country. We've been watching the borders closely. What did you say this Russian is calling himself?"

"Victor. No last name."

"Wait a minute. I think I have something for you." A brief silence, and then the commander returned to the phone. "I think this is your guy—Victor Krayev. Thirty-five. He's from Moscow, but has been in the United States for the last decade. He's a suspected *Bratva* assassin. He was the first suspect in the murder of David Metwater, but Chicago police were never able to come up with enough evidence to pin the charge on him—if they could have even found him. He apparently moves around a lot, and keeps a low profile."

"Interesting. Is he after Daniel Metwater now? Why?"

"Find the answers to those questions, and you might find him," Graham said.

"He probably figures she's his best link to Metwater, especially since Daniel's trail has gone cold."

"Has she told you anything that implicates Metwater in a crime?"

"Not yet. But she must know something. I don't see any other reason for him to pursue her so doggedly."

"He's going to need money to get out of the country, and Andi is his best source," Graham said.

"And tomorrow she turns twenty-five, and gets access to millions of dollars," Simon said. "Which Metwater probably thinks she'll be happy to hand over to him."

"You don't think she will?"

"I think the events of the past few days have opened her eyes a lot about Daniel Metwater." He hoped so. He didn't like to think the intimacy the two of them had shared had been a sham—and that Andi still loved the man who had cheated, lied and tried to kill her.

"It could be as simple as him believing she betrayed him by coming over to our side, and he wants retribution."

"Maybe. Either way, I don't think he would give up now. He'll keep coming after her until we stop him."

"How is she doing?"

"Good." *Great. She's the most amazing woman I've ever met.*

"She's not giving you a hard time, then? Still defending Metwater?"

"No. She's starting to realize how he used her." He hoped that was true, anyway.

"Get her to the shelter," Graham said. "It will be easier to keep her safe there."

"That's the plan for today. Oh, and two other things—Andi says Metwater has connections in Mexico. He may try to head there. And she has the locket that Michelle Munson said belonged to her sister. The one that disappeared the day she died."

"How did Andi get a hold of it?" Graham asked.

"She stole it from Metwater." Thinking about it made him smile. "She was angry at him for sending her away and I guess she wanted to get back at him, so she took it."

"Risky move, considering what he's shown of his temper."

"She says he knows she has it. I guess he found out the first time he attacked her at the Brown Palace. But he wasn't upset. He actually seemed happy about it."

"She could be lying."

"I don't think so, sir. And another thing—there's a key inside the locket. It looks like a safe-deposit box key. Andi didn't know it was there."

"Does Andi know what the key is to?"

"She says not."

Another long silence. Simon tensed. "Sir?"

"I trust your judgment," Graham said. "But be careful."

"Yes, sir."

"All right. I expect to see you in a few hours, then."

"Yes, sir."

He ended the call and finished packing the bags, then carried them downstairs, where he found Andi by the front desk, talking to Mike. "Leaving so soon?" the manager asked.

"We need to get going." Simon laid the key on the desk. "Thanks for everything."

"I was telling Mike about my uncle's cabin," Andi said. "He actually knows where it is."

"Sure I do," Mike said. "It's only a few miles from here, up the road to Wilson Pass. I think his kids still come up there in the summers. One of them—Frankie maybe—had me do some repairs up there last fall."

"Frankie is Uncle Doug's oldest son," Andi said. She looked sad. "I haven't seen any of them in years."

"Maybe you can have a reunion up here sometime," Mike said.

"We'd better get going." Simon touched Andi's arm.

She nodded. "Yes, we'd better."

"Drive safe," Mike said. "Weather reports are predicting more snow this afternoon."

"We'll be careful."

The icy wind hit them like a slap when they stepped onto the sidewalk outside the hotel. "Brrr." Andi pulled her coat tightly around her and headed for the cruiser. Simon stowed their bags in the back, then started the engine and stepped out again to scrape ice from the windshield. He kept alert for any sign of Victor, but at this time of morning the streets were almost deserted. Maybe their Russian friend had found a ride out of town.

"So much for the sun," Andi said as Simon turned onto the highway leading out of town. She leaned forward to peer out the windshield at the gunmetal gray sky. "I think the weatherman was wrong about it waiting until this afternoon to snow again."

"As long as the road stays open, we'll get through," Simon said. Even if Monarch Pass was closed, they could go around. The trip would take longer, but this time he wasn't stopping unless he was forced to.

Andi sat back. "I can't believe Mike knew about my uncle's cabin."

"I guess it's not so strange," Simon said. "Fairplay is a small town."

"I wish I could see it again," she said. She turned toward him, the unasked question plain on her face.

"We don't have time to take a detour," he said. "Especially not with the weather threatening to turn on us."

"I know. I'm just feeling nostalgic because of the baby, I guess." She faced forward once more, hands on her abdomen.

"Maybe you can get back over here when things have settled down more," he said. Why did he feel so rotten for not being able to take her to see her uncle's cabin, even though he knew pushing on was the right thing to do?

"Yes, I should do that," she said. "I'd like for you to see it."

Did that mean she was thinking about a future for the two of them? He pushed the thought away. Once Andi Matheson settled back into her real life of wealth and privilege, he couldn't see her continuing a relationship with a lowly cop.

"What's that light on the dash?" Andi asked.

He glanced down at the orange light at the bottom of the control panel. "Tire sensor," he said. "Sometimes when it's really cold it comes on. I'll check the pressures next time we stop for gas."

"Amazing how smart cars are these days," she said. "All anyone in camp had were old beaters, so I'd forgotten about all the new technology."

"Yeah, it's useful, but it can be annoying too." He slowed for an icy spot in the road, and the cruiser swerved. Simon frowned. Something didn't feel quite right here. "I'm going to pull over and check the tires," he said. "Just in case something is wrong."

He pulled to the shoulder and waited for a car to pass before he got out and walked around the vehicle. Andi lowered the passenger window and looked out. "Everything okay?" she asked.

Simon stared down at the right rear tire. It was definitely low, and deflating quickly. "We've got a flat," he said.

"Did you run over a nail or something?" Andi asked.

"Maybe," he said. "Or maybe Victor wanted to slow us down. I should have thought of that and checked before we left the hotel." He opened the back door and retrieved his coat. "I'll have to change it. It will only take a few minutes. Stay in the car, where it's warm."

He walked around to the back to retrieve the spare and the tire tools. Another car approached, slowing. Maybe a Good Samaritan offering to help. Simon looked up to wave the guy off and had half a second to register Victor's grim face in the driver's seat before the gun the Russian held fired.

The impact of the bullet in his chest knocked him backward. He sank to his knees in the snow, Andi's screams echoing in the still, cold air.

Chapter Twelve

The image of Simon being shoved against the cruiser by the impact of the bullet and his body slumping to the ground paralyzed Andi. "Simon!" she screamed, fumbling for her seat belt, her numb fingers refusing to work. She could no longer see him, the image of him falling flashing over and over in her head.

She looked down, cursing the stubborn safety restraint. She had to get out of here. She had to help Simon.

The passenger door of the cruiser opened and someone grabbed her arm. She stared up into the face of Victor, who leaned over and hit the button to release the safety belt. "Get out," he ordered, and pulled her from the car.

"No!" She tried to resist, but he held her in an iron grip. Her boots slipped on the icy ground as he pulled her toward a battered blue sedan parked behind the cruiser on the shoulder of the road. "What about Simon?" she asked, looking back and trying to see the other side of the cruiser, where Simon had fallen.

"He can't help you now," Victor said. He opened the

sedan's passenger door and shoved her inside. "He's dead."

A sob escaped her at the words. She fought against the tears. "He's not dead," she said. "You're only trying to frighten me."

Victor climbed into the driver's seat and slammed the door. "I shot him in the chest," he said. "I saw the bullet hit. I saw him fall. Dead." He pulled onto the pavement and made a sharp U-turn, throwing her against the door of the car. She groped for her seat belt and fastened it.

"Don't try anything," he said, showing her the gun he still held in his right hand. "I've killed women before. I don't have a problem with it."

She believed him, but that wouldn't stop her from fighting back any way she could. "Why did you shoot Simon?" she asked. "Who are you? What do you want with me?"

"You ask too many questions." He glanced in the rearview mirror and signaled a turn back onto Fairplay's main street.

She grabbed hold of the dash to steady herself as he made the sharp turn. The car was an older model, the dash faded and stained, the upholstery ripped. And it reeked of cigarette smoke. It must have been easy to steal, or maybe he thought no one would miss such a heap. "Do you work for Daniel?" she asked. "Did he send you after me?"

Victor laughed, openmouthed, showing yellowed teeth. "That would be a good one, me working for Metwater." He glanced at her, the menace in his eyes making her ice-cold, in spite of the fur coat. "I need to talk to your lover. I am taking you so that he will have no choice but to come to me."

"What do you want to talk to him about?"

"Again with the questions." He shook his head.

"Maybe I already know what you want to know, and I can save you time and trouble," she said.

"I want to talk to him about his brother. What do you know about David Metwater?"

The question surprised her. "Nothing. I never met him. And Daniel never talked about him. Or hardly ever."

"Don't you think that's odd—that he didn't talk about his twin—his identical twin—that he was so close to?"

"It was too painful for him," she said. "His brother's death affected him deeply. It made him change the whole course of his life."

"Yes, it did, didn't it? And you don't find that odd also—for a man to turn his back on wealth and privilege, to go hide in the middle of nowhere, with a band of loyal followers—people he could depend on to do anything to protect him?"

"Losing his brother made him reevaluate the shallow existence he had been living and retreat to the wilderness, seeking spiritual purity." Daniel had said those words so often she could repeat them by rote—but did she really believe them anymore? Where was the spiritual purity in cheating on her and lying to her and stealing—yes, she could finally admit the truth in Simon's accusations—he had stolen money and other property that belonged to his followers. Daniel had said a lot of good things, but how many of his own words did he really believe?

The look Victor gave her was equal parts pity and disgust. "I see he has fooled you, the same way he fooled so many others."

Yes, she had been a fool. But she was determined to be smarter in the future. "If it's money you want, I can give that to you," she said. "I have money."

"Do you have a million dollars?"

She gasped. "Daniel won't give you a million dollars. He doesn't have that kind of money."

"He has that and more." He slowed to allow a group of schoolchildren to cross the street. The pavement gleamed wetly, the same dull gray as the sky overhead, in which no hint of blue showed. He held the gun low now, out of sight of passersby, but still aimed toward her so that a bullet would cut through her. "What about a key?" he asked. "Did your prophet ever give you a key?"

"What kind of key?"

"A safe-deposit box key. Small, and made of brass."

Like the key inside the locket. "No," she said, hoping the lie didn't show. "He never gave me anything like that."

"What kind of things did he give you?"

"He gave me this coat." But not the necklace. Daniel hadn't given her that—she had taken it.

He stared at the coat, as if he might see through it. The truck behind them honked its horn and Victor pressed down on the gas, sending them shooting forward. "Where are we going?" Andi asked, as the truck sped up and passed them.

"We are going to Breckenridge. That cop told everyone that's where you were going—though it obviously wasn't true, since you headed out of town in the opposite direction. But Metwater will have heard this is your destination, so he will try to follow you there. I want to make it easy for him to find you."

"What makes you think he will bother to come looking for me?" she asked. "I'm not the only woman he sleeps with, you know."

"Ah. So you are aware he is unfaithful. And yet you still love him. How touching."

She bit her lip to keep from denying that she loved Daniel. She wondered now if her feelings for him had ever been real love.

"Your prophet needs money," Victor said. "The police have frozen his bank accounts, and if he has the key I'm looking for, he won't be able to use it. You are a rich woman. He will come to you for money."

And tomorrow, on her twenty-fifth birthday, she would be even richer. Daniel knew this. He had even talked about taking her to Mexico or the Bahamas to celebrate—not that she wanted to be anywhere near a beach and bikinis right now. Since she had agreed that all she possessed belonged to the Family—to Daniel— they had both assumed that once she gained control of the trust, the money would become one of the group's assets also. Daniel probably still believed that. He surely wouldn't be able to fathom that a woman who had made such a fool of herself over him for so long would come to see him in a different light.

He wasn't going to touch another cent of her money if she could help it.

"Besides—you are the only woman who is about to have his baby," Victor said. "A man will go to great lengths to keep his child."

She wouldn't tell him that Daniel wasn't the father of her child—that he had no special ties to her baby, even though he had always claimed he wanted to raise the baby as his own. He had claimed a lot of things that she was learning were not true. But if she revealed the truth to Victor, he might not see her as valuable to him anymore. He might decide to kill her, the way he had murdered Simon.

Simon. The memory of him, slumped on the ground, so still, sent a physical pain through her. When she had first met him, back in camp with the Family, she had hated him. She had thought him a cold, unfeeling lawman who only wanted to persecute her and her friends. But she had been so wrong! These past few days, he had treated her with so much kindness. He had been strong, yet gentle, serious, yet surprisingly funny, too.

He had been her friend, and her lover, and the knowledge that he was gone now was almost too much to bear.

PAIN RADIATED FROM Simon's chest, and he had to fight for breath. He struggled back to consciousness, aware of the cold ground beneath him, the hard metal of the car against his head. Gritting his teeth against the throbbing in his chest, he shoved to his feet, then dared to look down at the hole in his coat and shirt—at the deep indentation in his bulletproof vest where the bullet that had struck him was still lodged.

He put his hand over the area, feeling the bullet and the torn fabric, but no blood. The vest had done its job. He was bruised, but not bleeding. He had had the wind knocked out of him by the force of the impact, but he was still alive.

Andi! Concern for her galvanized him. He spun around and stared at the open cruiser door, and the empty passenger seat. Footprints in the snow told the story of her leaving in another car—but not alone. A clear image of Victor firing the gun stayed with him. But he had never gotten a good look at the vehicle he had been driving—the one that had taken Andi away.

He examined the tracks left by both the driver and the car. Victor had headed back toward Fairplay. Simon would start there.

Ignoring the dull ache in his chest, he returned to his cruiser and stared down at the flat tire. Victor had probably slashed it last night or this morning, then simply waited for Simon and Andi to drive away and followed them, knowing they would eventually have to stop. With a heavy groan, he knelt in the snow and began changing the tire.

Fifteen minutes later, he had the spare in place and had verified that none of the other tires were damaged. He headed back toward Fairplay, watching the roadside for any sign that a car had turned around. Victor may have been trying to fool anyone following into thinking he was going one way, when he intended to go another.

But who would be following him? He probably

thought Simon was dead. He hadn't bothered to fire a second shot or to make sure his quarry was mortally injured—he had been too intent on kidnapping Andi and leaving. That was a mistake Simon would make sure he paid for.

He slowed for the light at the turnoff to Fairplay. Which direction had Victor traveled? If he was working with Metwater, he might have headed back to Denver to meet up with the Prophet. Even if he wasn't working with Metwater, Denver offered more places to hide and more opportunities to move on to other cities, states or countries.

The light turned green and Simon accelerated forward. He had no idea how much time had passed between the shooting and when he had recovered his senses, but it couldn't be very long. Then he had to include the time he had spent changing the tire. Whatever that added up to, Victor had a good head start. Simon was tempted to use his lights and siren to pass the few vehicles on the road, but he didn't want to give Victor warning that he was following. Better to run silent and travel as fast as he dared.

Which wasn't that fast, considering the road was still coated with ice in places. He passed through the desolate stretch of country where he and Andi had almost been stranded yesterday. The wind had whipped the snow into waves in the empty fields, and ice glinted on the barbed wire fencing. A coyote trotted across the highway ahead, disappearing in the clumps of trees along a creek.

Red brake lights glowed ahead and Simon slowed,

then stopped. He was last in a line of about eight vehicles, with no oncoming traffic. Frustrated by the delay, he turned on his flashers and pulled into the opposing lane and made his way to the head of the line. He stared into each vehicle he passed, but none of them held a blond Russian or a beautiful pregnant woman.

At the head of the line, a Park County Sheriff's deputy had his cruiser positioned across both lanes, blocking traffic. Just past him, a jackknifed semi truck lay on its side at the bottom of the pass. Simon stopped his cruiser and got out. The deputy—not the one who had helped Simon the day before—nodded in greeting. "When did this happen?" Simon asked.

"About five minutes ago," the deputy said. "Fortunately, nobody's hurt. Driver got out okay." He nodded to the side of the road, where a man in a shearling-lined denim jacket stood, hands in pockets, frowning at the disabled truck.

Simon looked beyond the truck, to the empty northbound lane. If Victor had come this way, he was out of Simon's reach now. "Looks like you've got everything under control," he said.

"Just waiting on the wrecker, but it will be a while," the deputy said. "They said they have to get someone from Denver. If I were you, I'd try another route."

"Thanks, I'll do that." He returned to his cruiser, drove past the growing line of waiting traffic, then pulled over to the shoulder and took out his phone.

Sergeant Daley answered promptly. "What's up, Woolridge?" he asked. "But before you ask—no, we haven't found Metwater yet. He's gone off the radar."

"I've got a different problem now. A guy who may or may not be working with Metwater—a Russian who goes by the name Victor Krayev—has kidnapped Andi—Ms. Daniels." He gave Daley the descriptions of both Andi and Victor.

"We'll put out an APB," Daley said. "Got a description of a vehicle they might be traveling in?"

"Unfortunately, no. I never got a good look."

"Got the jump on you, did he?"

"He shot me. Knocked the wind out of me, but my vest did its job."

"Ouch. Knew a guy that happened to—he ended up with a bruised liver. But considering the alternative…"

"Yeah," Simon said. "I think my guy is headed for Denver, but I don't know for sure. I'm stuck in Fairplay, with the road closed. I'm going to try going around through Breckenridge, but it will take longer."

"Don't bother," Daley said. "Interstate 70 is shut down too. Better to hunker down and wait out the weather. I'll let you know if we get any leads."

"Thanks." He ended the call, then immediately phoned Ranger Headquarters.

Randall Knightbridge answered. "Hey, Simon! We thought maybe you'd decided to run off to Bermuda or something."

"Bermuda would be nice, considering the weather here," he said, frowning at the lowering clouds that promised more snow.

"Nice and sunny here," Randall said. "But I hear the other side of the Divide is getting hammered."

"Is the commander in? I need to speak to him."

"Hang on a sec."

A moment later Graham picked up the phone. "What's the latest?" he asked.

Simon gave him as brief a report as he dared. "Are you all right?" Graham asked.

"I'm fine." He rubbed his chest, which was bruised and sore, but nothing a couple of aspirin and a good night's sleep wouldn't help. "I don't know about Andi. I don't know what Victor wants with her. And I'm stuck here with the roads closed and more snow coming."

"You don't know for sure he went to Denver," Graham said. "And while we can't rule out that he might be working with Metwater, we have nothing that tells us he is. So where else could he have gone?"

"Anywhere." Simon looked around him at the empty landscape. Two-lane dirt tracks led off from the paved road to remote ranches and national forest land. Maybe Victor had a hideout somewhere along one of those roads.

"Where did he think you were headed?" Graham asked.

"I've been telling people we were going to Breckenridge. I thought it would throw him off track."

"Then it's possible he headed there. Maybe because he thinks Metwater will be there too."

"Maybe." Simon shifted the car into gear. "One thing, at least—I can get to Breck from here. I'm going to check it out." And hope he wasn't already too late.

Chapter Thirteen

Though Andi kept her body still, her mind raced as they left Fairplay behind and climbed above tree line on the icy two-lane road. All color seemed bleached from the landscape of white snow, gray sky and black asphalt. The desolate country drove home how alone she was now. If she was going to survive, she had to come up with a plan on her own. She couldn't count on help from anyone else.

She glanced at the man in the driver's seat. Victor was young, good-looking and confident, like so many men she had known. Daniel had certainly fit that mold, but as much as his looks and confidence had drawn her in, she knew he had underestimated her. He'd mistaken her calm for passivity, her gentleness for weakness. Victor had made the same mistake. He hadn't bothered to tie her up because, hey, what was a pregnant woman going to do to him? Especially when he was holding a gun on her. She couldn't fight him in her condition, and it wasn't as if she was going to run away.

Not only did men like Victor and Daniel see her as weak, they saw her as disposable. Interchangeable. They would use her as long as it suited their purpose, then put her aside—or worse. She didn't trust her chances with either one of them now. She couldn't forget the feel of that knife Daniel had held to her throat.

Traffic slowed as they approached the small community of Alma, with its clusters of vacation cabins and false-fronted stores along the highway. "Some tourist afraid to drive on ice," Victor muttered as they joined a line of cars crawling through town. He pounded the steering wheel. "Pull over and park, you idiot!" he said.

Focused as he was on the cars ahead, he wasn't looking at Andi. He probably wasn't even thinking about her. She reached around and carefully undid her seat belt, holding it in place with her left hand so that he wouldn't notice it was loose. With her right hand, she thumbed the lock open and gripped the door release. The car rolled to a stop and she said a quick prayer, then shoved open the door and stumbled out.

Victor's shout pursued her as she shuffled across the snow toward the first building she saw—a log cabin on the side of the road, children's toys scattered across the snowy front yard. Brakes squealed and more shouts rose, but she ignored them and pounded on the door. "Please let me in!" she pleaded. "I need help!"

The door opened and a short woman with a mass of curly red hair answered. "I need to call the police," Andi said. "Please help me." She was crying now, her nose running, her hair falling in her eyes.

"What's going on?" A man appeared behind the woman—a very tall, very broad man with a long black beard down to the middle of his chest.

"Call the police," Andi said. "A man is trying to kidnap me."

"My wife and I were just having a little fight." Victor's hand closed around Andi's upper arm, pulling her away from the door.

Andi turned to look at Victor. He was smiling, but his eyes flashed with violence. He had driven the car halfway into the yard of the cabin. It sat now, both doors open, engine running. "No!" she protested, and tried to pull away.

"She's moody because of the baby," Victor said, and yanked harder on her arm.

"Let her go."

The big bear of a man stepped in front of Victor, glaring at him. "Let her go and leave. She doesn't want to go with you."

Victor stared up at him. Andi wondered if he would pull out his gun and shoot the man, the way he had shot Simon. Had she made a mistake, involving innocent people in her troubles?

"I'm calling the police." The woman behind the man held up a cell phone, then punched in three numbers— Andi assumed nine-one-one.

"All right, I'm leaving." Victor released her and backed away, hands in the air. "Andi, when you've calmed down, you know how to reach me," he said.

The bearded man might have been able to tackle and hold Victor, but Andi didn't want to risk the gun making an appearance, so she said nothing and let him leave. The woman put her arm around Andi's shoulder. "Come inside and get warm. The sheriff is sending someone over."

"Thank you," Andi said, her voice catching. "Thank you so much."

"I got his license plate number," the bearded man said. He nodded to Andi. "Did he hurt you?"

"No…only frightened me." She hugged herself, pulling the coat more tightly around her, but was still unable to get warm.

"You're shaking," the woman said. She led Andi to a sofa near a glowing wood stove. "Sit down here. I was heating up some soup for our lunch. Would you like some? And maybe a cup of hot tea?"

"Yes, that would be wonderful." Andi sat, hoping the shaking would subside soon.

"I'll get the soup and tea," the man said. "You stay here with her." He left the room, his slippers making a shuffling noise on the wood floor.

The woman sat beside Andi and began rubbing her back. "I'm Carrie, and my husband is Lyle," she said.

"I'm Andi."

"Are you okay?" Carrie asked. "Is the baby okay?"

Would she ever really be okay again? Simon was dead, she'd been betrayed by Daniel, her father was in prison and her baby's father was dead…she shook her head. "I'm fine. I'm just…a little overwhelmed."

Carrie glanced back toward the door. "Was that your husband? Or boyfriend?"

Andi shook her head. "It's a long story, but he isn't either of those things."

Lyle returned, carrying a tray with a bowl of soup, a

spoon and napkin and a mug with a tea bag floating in hot water. Andi looked at the food and tears came to her eyes—not because she was so hungry and it looked so good, though both of those things were true, but because it represented so much kindness from two strangers.

Pull yourself together, she told herself. *You have to stay strong.*

"Thank you so much," she said again, and accepted the bowl of soup Carrie handed her.

"Don't let me keep you from your own lunch," she said.

"It can wait." Lyle settled into a worn brown leather recliner across from her and continued to study her. "You're not from around here, are you?"

She shook her head and sipped the soup—vegetable, and not from a can. Delicious. "I'm from near Montrose." That was as close to a home as she had had in a while.

A knock on the door interrupted them. Carrie left to answer it and returned a moment later with a Park County Sheriff's deputy. "This is Andi, and she's the reason I called," Carrie said. "A man was trying to make her go with him and she didn't want to go."

The officer came to stand in front of Andi. "Deputy Paul Chasen," he said, handing her a card. "Tell me what happened."

Andi set aside the half-finished bowl of soup, picked up the cup of tea and sipped it cautiously. It smelled of cinnamon and apples and tasted of honey. "My name is Andi Matheson," she said. "I was traveling to Montrose with Agent Simon Woolridge, a member of the

Ranger Brigade, operating out of Black Canyon of the Gunnison National Park. Our car had a flat and when Simon—Agent Woolridge—got out to look at it, a man I know only as Victor drove up, shot Simon in the chest, pulled me out of the car and took me with him."

"That's the man you ran away from?" Lyle asked. "A guy who shot a cop?"

"Where did this shooting occur, and when?" Deputy Chasen asked.

"Less than half an hour ago, just outside of Fairplay, on Highway 285." She swallowed another knot of tears. "I'm sure the cruiser is still there. And Simon's body."

Chasen pulled out his phone and relayed this information to someone on the other end, watching Andi carefully the whole time. When he was done, he pocketed the phone once more. "There is no vehicle on the side of the road, and no body," he said. "Why don't you try again—and with the truth this time."

"Everything I said is true!" Andi protested. "There was a shot, Simon slumped to the ground, then Victor dragged me away and said he was taking me to Breckenridge. When we came through town another car was holding up traffic. We rolled to a stop, I bailed out of the car and came here for help."

"I have the license plate number for the car the guy was driving," Lyle said. "And he was being rough with her, trying to drag her away."

"Give me the number." Chasen called it in. This time when he hung up, he looked less severe. "The car was stolen from a guy in Fairplay this morning," he said. "But we still haven't had any report of a body. That's a busy stretch of highway, even in this weather. Some-body would have reported it by now."

"I don't understand," Andi said. "I saw him fall. There was a hole in his chest." She swallowed hard, fighting nausea as she relived the horror of that moment.

"Is there anyone else who can confirm your story?" he asked.

"The Ranger Brigade can confirm part of it," she said.

It took a few minutes, but the deputy was able to get a number for the Ranger Brigade from information and made the call. "I've got a woman named Andi Matheson here who claims she was kidnapped by someone named Victor, who killed one of your guys, Simon Woolridge."

He listened a moment, then held out the phone for Andi. "He wants to talk to you."

"Andi?" The voice was one she recognized as be-longing to the Ranger Brigade commander.

"He killed Simon," she said. "I saw it happen. I'm so sorry." Then the tears she had been holding back for so long refused to be kept inside any longer. She sobbed into the phone, the pain too much to bear.

"Andi, listen to me!" The commander's voice was kind, but firm. "Simon isn't dead!"

She sniffed, and Carrie stuffed tissues into her hand. Andi dabbed at her nose. "Why do you say that?" she asked. "I saw him fall."

"He was wearing a bulletproof vest," the commander said. "It's part of the uniform. The impact knocked the breath out of him. He called just a little while ago and told me everything. He's all right, and he's looking for you."

Tears flowed again, but this time they were tears of relief. "Tell him I'm right here, waiting," she said.

SIMON HAD ALMOST reached the little town of Alma when he got the call about Andi. Five minutes later, he was standing on the doorstep of the house where she had sought refuge. The bearded man who answered the door sized him up, gaze lingering on the hole in the breast of Simon's coat. He stepped back and motioned behind him. "She's in here," he said.

Andi tried to stand to greet him, but almost lost her balance. A short, redheaded woman put her arm around her and urged her to sit back down. She sat, but reached up to Simon, tears streaming down her face. His throat tightened as her arms came around him. "I'm okay," he said, patting her back. "I'm okay."

She wouldn't release her hold on him, so he ended up seated on the sofa next to her. A sheriff's deputy approached. "Paul Chasen," he said, offering his hand.

"Simon Woolridge." The two men shook. "The guy you're looking for was driving a car he jacked in Fairplay this morning," Chasen said. "My guess is he'll ditch it at the first opportunity and steal another. But he'll probably have to wait until he gets to Breckenridge to do it. There's not much between here and there."

Simon nodded. His first instinct was to take off after Victor, but Andi was his priority now. "I need to get Andi to Montrose," he said. Until she was safe, he couldn't leave her.

"She needs somewhere quiet and away from this stress." The redheaded woman who sat on the other side of Andi spoke. "She could have this baby any minute now, and she shouldn't be chasing lunatics all over the country."

"We've got a safe place waiting for her," Simon said. He removed Andi's arm from around him, though he continued to hold her hand. "Are you ready to go?" he asked.

"I just need to use the ladies' room," she said.

"I'll pack some food for the road," the redhead said. "It's a long way to Montrose."

"The weather isn't looking too good," Chasen said. "You'd better get going before Monarch Pass gets socked in. From there you should be okay. The roads on the other side of the divide are still reporting clear."

"This weather has been chasing us the whole trip," Simon said.

He stood. Chasen studied the tear in Simon's coat. "You really took a direct hit and got away unhurt?" he asked.

"Knocked the wind out of me," Simon said. "A few bruises." He fingered the hole in his jacket. "I'll need a new coat. And I guess a new vest."

Chasen shook his head. "They tell you about stuff like that in training, but you always wonder."

Andi returned to the room, the redhead right behind her. She handed Simon a shopping bag. "There's water and juice and some sandwiches and stuff in there." She looked at Andi. "I remember with my two, I was always hungry."

"Thank you." Andi hugged the woman, and then the bearded man, and shook hands with Chasen. "Thank you so much for everything," she said.

"Yes. Thanks," Simon echoed. "I don't want to think about what might have happened if you had refused to help Andi."

"We never would have turned her away," the woman said. "You two take care."

They set out again. Neither of them said anything for a while.

"I'm glad you're okay," Simon said finally.

"I'm so relieved you weren't hurt," Andi said at the same moment.

He glanced at her and she smiled. He returned the grin. "Nothing like coming back from the dead to give a man a new perspective," he said. Then he sobered. "I'm sorry I couldn't keep Victor from getting to you."

"If you hadn't been knocked senseless, he might have realized you were still alive and shot you in the head," she said. "I'm just glad I got away."

"How did you get away?" he asked. "No one ever said."

"I waited until the car slowed to almost a stop, then I unlocked the door, opened it and got out. He hadn't bothered to tie me up or anything because, hey, what was a pregnant woman going to do?"

"He might have shot you." A shiver ran through him at the thought.

"I thought about that, but he was focused on driving. I just hoped that if I was quick enough, he wouldn't have time to fire, not without losing control of the car."

"You took a big risk," Simon said.

"I had to get away from him. There was something in his eyes that was just so cold." She rubbed her arms, as if warding off a chill.

"Did he say what he was going to do to you?" Simon asked. "Why he wanted you?"

"He wanted to use me as bait to get to Daniel." She shifted toward him, her voice rising with indignation. "He thought I was the Prophet's great love or something, and he said if Daniel wouldn't come to rescue me, he would come for his child." She rubbed her hand across her belly. "I didn't tell him Daniel isn't my baby's father—or that he doesn't care two cents about me anymore."

"So Victor isn't working with Metwater," Simon said.

"No. But he wants to lure Daniel to him. He wants to talk to him about his brother. But he wouldn't say why."

"Word was David Metwater was in deep to the *Bratva*," Simon said. "Maybe they expect Daniel to pay his brother's debts."

"Maybe so. Victor said Daniel was hiding out in the wilderness, and maybe there was something to that. I know he was afraid of the men who killed his brother—and who can blame him for that?"

"So we know why Victor wanted you, but we still don't know why Metwater is so set on getting you back," Simon said.

"I think I might know." She fingered the locket, feeling the shape of the diamond through the fine knitwork of her sweater. "Victor said Daniel had a key—a safe-deposit box key. Victor asked me if I had the key. I'm pretty sure he said the box it was to contained a million dollars."

"The key in that locket is a safe-deposit box key," Simon said.

"I know." She fished the locket from beneath her sweater and felt along the side for the catch. The front sprang open and she worked her fingernail underneath the key, which was wedged tightly in the locket's small interior hollow. "There's no bank name on it," she said. "Just a number." She squinted to read it. "Nine, six, two."

"That would be the box number, I'm guessing," Simon said. "I think it's pretty standard not to have any other identifying information on them."

"Would a million dollars fit in a safe-deposit box?" she asked.

"If the money is in large bills," he said. "I think you can rent some fairly large boxes."

"Then why does Daniel need my money if he already has a million stashed away?" she asked.

"If it's a million he—or his brother—stole from the Russian mob, the money is probably too hot for him to touch," Simon said. "And then there's the whole greed angle. If one million is good, three or four are even better."

"To think I almost let him take everything from me," she said. "I can't believe I was so stupid."

"You were trusting," he said. "You wanted to believe in something good. Don't beat yourself up about it."

She took his hand. "Thank you for saying that. I hope I've learned something from this whole experience."

What could he say to that? *You're welcome* was lame, as if he had done some great thing for her. "You were strong enough to risk running away from Victor, where you weren't sure what you had to run to," he said. "Remember that."

She nodded and released his hand. Silence settled around them once more. It wasn't a strained silence, but one of contentment to be with each other without speaking. Snow began to fall more heavily, fat white flakes that clung to the windshield wipers and frosted the road signs. Simon's chest ached, but all he could do was try to ignore it.

They passed through the small towns of Johnson Village and Poncha Springs and made the turn up toward Monarch Pass, but as they approached the bottom of the pass, Simon saw the sign he had been half expecting, but dreading.

"The pass is closed," Andi said, as Simon pulled the cruiser to the shoulder.

He didn't answer, but pulled up a road report on his phone. "Cochetopa Pass is open," he said. "We can go around." The road that direction was narrow and winding, and would add hours to their trip, but he didn't see any alternative.

"Oh, Simon." She imbued those two words with all the frustration and dread he felt. "That will take hours. I don't think I can do it."

"We don't really have any choice," he said. "I need to get you to Montrose, where you'll be safe."

"We do have a choice," she said. "We can turn

around and go to my uncle's cabin. It isn't far. We can spend the night there, rest and wait out the weather."

"I don't know,' he said.

"We'll be safe there. We have food. There's a wood-stove and you can build a fire." She took his hand again. "All I want is one night in the place where I always felt most at home. One night alone, with you."

He stared at the snow, which looked for all the world as if someone were shaking out the entire contents of a feather bed factory over their heads. He could drive all the way around to Cochetopa Pass, only to find it was closed by then as well. He and Andi were both exhausted, cold, and hurting—the kind of condition in which people made mistakes. His goal was to make sure she was safe, and her uncle's cabin seemed as secure— maybe more so—than any safe house. "All right," he said. "One night."

One night alone together. If nothing else, he knew it was something he would remember for the rest of his life.

Chapter Fourteen

On the drive to the cabin, Andi sat forward in the seat, clutching the dashboard, heart racing with equal parts anticipation and dread. She had lost so much in the past few years that she half expected to find the cabin had been razed, or that the cozy retreat she had so cherished had morphed into a dismal shack.

When the cabin finally came into view, she let out a cry of relief, almost bouncing up and down with joy. "That's it," she said. "Turn in here." The single-story log building was almost hidden in a forest of pine and fir, its steeply pitched metal roof streaked with rust. The same redwood Adirondack chairs Andi remembered from previous visits flanked the front door, even if the once-cheerful red of the door was now faded to a muted brick.

Simon bumped down the rutted driveway and parked at the bottom of the front steps. Andi popped her seat belt and had the door open before he had even come to a complete stop. "He always kept the key around here," she said, moving around to the side of the cabin, where a massive pine tree stood next to the old-fashioned outhouse. Reaching up, she felt for the nail, and the single key hanging there. Triumphant, she snagged the key and held it aloft.

Simon motioned for her to lead the way up the steps and across the porch. She fitted the key in the lock and pushed open the door. The weak light that filtered through the windows showed a room that served as kitchen, dining and living room, with a three-burner gas stove, a propane refrigerator, sink, square wooden table with four chairs, a sagging couch and armchair and a woodstove set against the back wall.

"That door leads to the bedroom," Andi said, pointing to the open door on the west wall. "And the ladder in the corner goes up to a loft. That's where I always slept. What do you think?"

Simon nodded. "It looks good. We should be all right here."

Not a ringing endorsement, but she would take it. She went to the table and lifted off the chimney of a glass kerosene lantern, turned up the wick and lit it with a match from the box that sat beside the lamp. Two more lamps fit into sconces on the walls. They cast a golden glow that dispelled some of the gloom.

"I should start a fire," Simon said, going over to the stove.

"There's a woodpile around back," Andi said. She bustled around, pulling things out of cabinets, wiping down the table with a rag. Being here energized her. She felt sure of herself here, and safe in a way she couldn't have felt on the road.

Simon left and returned a moment later with an armful of wood. "I'll start the fire, then get our things from the cruiser," he said. "Then I might check in with the Denver cops, see if they have anything new for me." He had called the commander and informed him of their change of plans when they had stopped for gas and a few more groceries on their way back through Johnson Village.

"Unless things have changed, you won't have a cell phone signal here," Andi said.

He scowled, something he did all too often, she thought. She didn't sense any real anger behind his curmudgeonly expressions though. She thought of them as a kind of habit, or a shield to make other people keep their distance. She had done something similar when she played the role of haughty socialite. That part of her life seemed like years ago now.

"I don't like being out of touch," he said as he arranged kindling inside the woodstove.

"It's only one night." She stood beside him and watched him work. "I know it probably seems strange to you, but I like being where it feels like no one else can reach us."

"As long as you don't decide to go into labor tonight."

She laughed. "I don't think it's a matter of deciding," she said. "But don't worry—I feel great." All the terror and despair from earlier in the day had yielded to a kind of euphoria. Simon was alive. She was alive. They were safe.

And they were together. Whatever they had between them—whatever she sensed was building—seemed too tenuous to last outside the crazy situation they found themselves in, yet her feelings for him overshadowed her doubts. Maybe this caring cop wouldn't want to waste time with her once he had delivered her into someone else's oversight, but right now, with circumstances forcing them together, she was going to hold on to whatever he was willing to give her.

"I think that's going to do it," he said as flames licked up the side of the logs in the stove. He made sure the flue was open, shut the stove door and dusted his hands on his pants. "I'll get the groceries and the luggage."

By the time he returned, she had lit the stove and put a kettle on to boil. "We have tea or instant coffee," she said, studying the supply of staples in the cupboard. "Or the water Carrie sent with us."

"Coffee is fine." He removed his coat and hung it on a peg by the door. Then he unpacked the food while she got out cups and plates. "Your friend Carrie must have thought we were going to Montrose by way of Texas," he said as he surveyed the sandwiches, fruit, chips and cookies in the bags.

"She wanted to make sure we didn't go hungry," Andi said. "She seemed like the nurturing type. Good thing too. Not everyone would let a crazed, weeping woman into her home."

"I guess we both have had our share of luck today," he said.

They sat down to lunch with coffee for him and tea for her. The simple food tasted so good, and not merely because of her increased appetite. Eating a meal in a place you wanted to be, with someone you wanted to be with, was the best seasoning.

The meal done, Simon pushed his chair back. "You should rest," he said. "I'll have a look around outside so I don't disturb you."

"First, I want to have a look at your chest." She had seen the bullet strike him, had watched him fall. Until she saw his wound—or lack of it—she couldn't quite accept that he was really all right.

"There's nothing to look at," he said.

"How do you know? Have you undressed and examined the wound?"

"There hasn't been time for that."

"There's time now." She pushed back her chair and stood. "There's even a first aid kit in the closet if we need it."

"You're not going to take no for an answer, are you?"

"No, I'm not."

He moved to the sofa and she followed. He removed his gun belt and draped it over the back of the sofa, then unbuttoned his shirt and slid out of it. The Kevlar vest was a bulky, black shield over his torso, the place the bullet had hit barely visible as a small tear in the fabric.

He hesitated a moment, then took off the vest, muscles bunching with the movement. "Oh, Simon," she breathed, when she saw the angry purple bruising across his sternum.

He looked down at himself and winced.

"Does it hurt?" she asked.

"A little."

She brushed her fingertips across his shoulder, then bent and kissed the bruise, the gentlest flutter of her lips that nevertheless made him draw in a sharp breath. "I'm sorry," she said, and tried to move back, but he pulled her to him once more.

"That wasn't a sound of complaint," he said, eyes dark with passion.

The need within her—a different kind of hunger that had lain just beneath the surface all day—surged inside her. She wrapped her arms around him and kissed him, all of her longing and wanting and waiting telegraphed in the meeting of their lips.

"You're the most amazing woman I've ever met," he said, stroking her cheek, as if he needed to touch her to reassure himself she was real.

"Come to bed with me," she urged. "I want you to make love to me."

"I want that too," he said. "But are you sure? With the baby?"

"We may have to make a few…accommodations… for the baby, but you can't hurt it. And I think it would do us both good."

His answer was to kiss her again, the burn of his day-old beard against her face a reminder that this was no fantasy, but achingly real—and for now, at least, so right.

SIMON FOLLOWED ANDI to the bedroom, where they were confronted by the unmade bed. "There should be linens in the closet," she said, crossing the room to a narrow door. He watched her move, with the careful, heavy walk of the very pregnant. There was still time to stop this—to turn around and walk out of the room and out of the house. He could shovel snow or chop wood or find some way to work off his lust.

But then she turned and smiled at him—as if he was the only man she had ever wanted, and he knew he wouldn't leave unless she ordered him away. He reached to take the stack of sheets from her, and his fingertips brushed the underside of her breast. It was as if she had a direct connection to his groin, pulling the tension there tighter.

They made the bed together, then she turned her back to him and began to undress. He watched, mesmerized, as she stripped, revealing full, heavy breasts and the taut, rounded mound of her abdomen. She was so obviously, intensely female and his every response felt heightened.

She looked over her shoulder at him. "Well?" she said, with a pointed look at his trousers.

He stripped quickly, leaving his clothes where they fell on the floor, and moved in behind her, caressing her curves, kissing the soft roundness of her shoulder and the satiny skin of her throat, holding the weight of her breasts in his hands and wishing, not for the first time, that he had had a part in making the child inside her.

She cupped his face in her hands and kissed him fiercely, eyes dark with need, breathing rapid. "I don't want to wait anymore," she said.

"No," he agreed.

She knelt on the bed and he positioned himself behind her, hands cradling her hips, her rounded belly. "Hey, what's this?" he asked, running his thumb over the tattoo of a pink rosebud on the curve of her bottom.

She looked back at him and grinned. "That's my little secret."

"Mine now too," he said. He moved his hands around to the front, massaging her breasts.

"Yes, that feels so good," she said. She closed her eyes and arched her back. "Yes."

She was ready for him, and he eased into her slowly, alert to any sign of resistance. There was none, and when she tightened around him he went a little senseless. He cradled her in his arms, wrapped over her and around her and in her. When he moved his hand lower to fondle her, she moaned and thrust back hard against him, her uninhibited passion fueling his own desire. But he held himself back, focusing on her, on teasing and pleasing her, drawing out her pleasure as well as his own.

She moved easily beneath him, setting the pace, thrusting back against him, then rocking forward, eyes closed, a half smile curving her lips as she lost herself in some private pleasure. Watching her fueled his own arousal, and he indulged himself in the pleasure of exploring her body, running his hands over her breasts, tracing the curve of her back with his lips. The tension building in her moved into his body as well, until he was holding his breath, balanced on the edge of his own release, waiting for her.

She came with a loud cry, convulsing in his arms, the intensity of the moment stripping him of the last of his control and he followed her over the edge, rocking against her until he was spent and breathless, every pain and doubt and coherent thought momentarily banished.

Afterward they slept, the sated, cocooned sleep of those who had found safe harbor in each other's arms. When Simon woke it was almost dark, only a thin gray light coming through the windows. He eased out of bed and, still naked, went to build up the fire, which had burned down to coals. He found another blanket in the closet and draped it over Andi's sleeping form, then carried his clothes into the living room and dressed.

Outside, the snow had stopped falling, though a thick white blanket lay over the landscape, softening hard edges and hiding details of the world outdoors. Simon walked around the house, assessing its defensive position. Not that he expected to have to hold off intruders, but his training was too ingrained to ignore.

He shoveled a path to the outhouse, then decided to park the cruiser out of sight, around the back of the house. The smoke from the stovepipe and lights in the windows made it evident the cabin was occupied, but he didn't have to advertise by whom. On his way back up to the house he met Andi, on her way back from the outhouse. "Going somewhere?" she asked.

"Not without you." He gathered her close. "How about some supper?"

"You really know the way to my heart."

They decided to eat in front of the fire. He insisted she sit on the sofa while he heated soup and served it on a tray. She sighed. "This is so nice," she said.

"Yeah, it is." It couldn't last—she was still in danger, and he still needed to get her to a safe house and set to work finding and stopping not only Daniel Metwater, but Victor Krayev. But he would try to set that aside for a few more hours, and focus on enjoying this night with her.

"Tell me about the rosebud," he said. "How did you end up with a tattoo on your backside?"

She laughed. "I got it on a dare. Silly, I guess, but it made me feel rebellious and brave. I know to everyone else it looked like I had the perfect life—looks, money and social prestige. But the one thing I didn't have was freedom. Someone was always watching me—either my father, to make sure I wasn't doing anything to tarnish his reputation, or the bodyguards he hired to protect me, or the press who reported on our every move."

"So you got a tattoo."

She laughed again—a lilting cascade of notes that did crazy things to his insides. "I know, right? No drugs, sex or rock and roll for me. I got a tattoo of a flower where most people will never see it." She shrugged. "I was a good kid, I guess. But in the end, I could never be good enough. I could never live up to my dad's idea of what I should be."

"I know what that's like," he said.

She put a comforting hand on his knee. "Did your father expect you to be a police officer like him? Surely he would be proud of you now."

"I'll never be the cop he was," Simon said. He could never be as genuinely *good* as his father—and his mother and uncles and aunts—had been. They had all devoted their lives to serving others. Simon had been cut from a different mold. He had realized it when he was still young, and he was sure everyone else could see it. He had come from a family of saints, and he was the bad apple of the bunch.

"You're the best cop I've ever known." She squeezed his knee and leaned toward him, her tone teasing. "At least you don't have any tattoos, do you? Or did I miss something?"

He shook his head. "No tattoos."

"Why not?" she asked. "You don't believe in them?"

"I like being different."

"You like being contrary." She nodded.

"All right, that too."

"At least you didn't get one and then regret it," she said. "I know people who have done that."

"So do I." He yawned. The warm fire and easy company had relaxed him completely. Andi was right—they had both needed this break from the constant stress of the past few days.

"Daniel had a tattoo he was ashamed of," she said. "He almost always kept it covered."

All lethargy vanished at this revelation. He looked at her intently. "I saw him dancing around the fire in little more than a loincloth," he said. "I don't remember any tattoo."

"It was on his biceps." She indicated a spot on the outside of her left arm. "A lion with devil horns, mouth open in a roar, blood dripping from its fangs." She shuddered. "Pretty gruesome. He told me he hated it, and wished he had never gotten it."

Simon and his fellow Rangers had been studying Daniel Metwater intently for months, but he was sure none of them knew anything about a tattoo. "How do you cover up something like that?" he asked. "Makeup?"

She shook her head. "He had this elastic sleeve. It was flesh colored and really thin, but opaque. He could pull it on like an armband. You could hardly see it. For the bonfires, he would wear these tribal armbands over it and no one could tell. I probably would never have known about it if I hadn't walked in on him getting dressed one night, before he put on the sleeve."

"How did he react when you saw it?" Simon asked.

"He was angry, but then he calmed down and apologized. He said he was just so ashamed of the ink—that he didn't think it set a good example for his followers. He asked me to promise to never say anything about it to anyone." She made a face. "I guess I just broke that promise."

"When a guy puts a knife to your throat and threatens to kill you, I think it negates any promises you made to him," Simon said.

"I guess so." She shifted to stare into the fire, seemingly lost in thought. Was she thinking of Daniel Metwater, trying to reconcile her love for him with all he had done to her? A black mood settled over Simon at the thought. She deserved so much better than Metwater, but when had love ever had anything to do with merit?

"I've been thinking a lot lately about all the things I could have done differently in my life." She let out a heavy sigh. "I guess the prospect of being a mother has me reassessing everything, but especially my bad choices."

"You trusted people who betrayed you," Simon said. "Beating yourself up over that won't do any good."

"Oh, I know that." She turned to him, her eyes clear and calm. "But I want to make better choices in the future. And I want to do what I can to make up for past mistakes." She took his hand, her grip warm and firm. "Were you serious when you said you could help me get in touch with my dad?"

"If that's what you want, yes."

"I don't know what I want. But…he's the only family I have. And I miss him." She shook her head. "I don't miss the man he was the last few years—driven by ambition and greed—but the father he was when I was younger, before my mother died. What he did—killing Frank—was horrible. But I think, in a twisted kind of way, he believed he was protecting me."

"You could write to him," Simon said. "Then if that goes okay, you could arrange to visit him—though seeing him in prison will be tough. Emotionally, I mean."

She nodded. "A letter would be a good start. Maybe writing down how I feel about everything that has happened would be good for both of us."

He studied the soft curve of her cheek, the silky fall of her hair—she looked impossibly young and innocent, yet she had already seen enough tragedy for a lifetime, and it hadn't broken her. "You're amazing," he said.

She blinked. "Why do you say that?"

"Because you've been through so much, and you're still so good."

She laughed. "There are plenty of people out there who wouldn't agree with you on that."

"I don't care what they think."

Something flared in her eyes—passion or joy—and she leaned forward and kissed him gently on the cheek. "Then I don't care, either."

He pulled her close, and the moment might have evolved into another round of lovemaking, if she hadn't had to stifle a yawn. "Sorry. I don't know why I'm so sleepy."

"I think we're both still catching up from the past few days," Simon said. He stood and offered her a hand. "Come on. Let's go to bed. Tomorrow will be another full day." He hoped it was the day the Rangers captured Daniel Metwater and Victor.

She wrapped her arms around him and kissed him on the lips. "You're too good to me," she said.

"I'm not that good," he said. Though she certainly made him want to be better.

She smiled and took his hand. "I'll be the judge of that, Officer."

ANDI WOKE WHILE it was still dark, the room cold, though she was warm under the heavy quilts. Her heart pounded, as if she had been running—or awakened in the middle of a nightmare. What had her feeling so panicked? She couldn't remember.

She reached out a hand and felt Simon's solid, warm bulk at her side. Reassurance filled her, and she snuggled back down under the covers and closed her eyes.

Thump! She opened her eyes, heart racing once more. What was that sound?

Creeeak. She tried to tell herself the noise was

merely the old cabin settling, but instinct told her otherwise. It was as if the air around her had shifted—she was sure there was someone else in the cabin.

"Simon!" She put her mouth next to his ear, her whisper urgent. "Wake up!"

"Mmm." He rolled over and reached for her.

She pushed against his chest. "Wake up! Someone is in the cabin."

He lay still, tensed. There was a sound like something scraping against the floor. Simon sat, pushing back the covers. He took his gun from the nightstand. "Stay here," he said. Then he slipped out of the room.

Chapter Fifteen

Simon eased the door to the bedroom shut behind him, careful not to make a sound. Then he stood still for several minutes, forcing his breathing to slow.

And he listened. His ears strained to hear anything other than the pounding of his own heart.

Scrape. The sound of something being dragged across the floor—not in the cabin itself, but outside, on the front porch. It was a sound effect out of a horror movie, and all the more chilling in real life. Slowly, carefully placing each step, Simon moved toward the front window.

Moonlight illuminated a black-and-white world of snow and shadows. Far to the right of the cabin, in the darkness cast by the building itself, a vehicle hunched—an SUV of some sort, tall and boxy. Footsteps clearly showed in the snow, leading from the vehicle and up the front steps to disappear in the deeper shadows of the porch.

The scraping noise came again—someone prying at the front window, just on the other side of where Simon stood. He moved to the door, hand on the knob. Opening it would probably make enough racket to announce his presence—though he could still likely catch whoever was out there off guard. If the cabin had a back door, he might try to go out that way and sneak up behind the person on the porch, but the only way out the back was through the bedroom window.

The scraping continued, followed by a grunt and a wrenching sound as the intruder succeeded in forcing up the window. Time for Simon to make his move. He started to step forward, when a second shadow emerged from the trees at the edge of the driveway. It skirted past the front of the house without stopping, moving swiftly behind the building and out of sight. The figure at the window gave no indication that he had noticed the newcomer. Was this an accomplice, heading around to cover the back of the house?

This definitely complicated things. It was two against one now, and too much distance separated the intruders for Simon to take them both out at once. He would have to eliminate them one at a time. And he'd need to move quickly.

He eased open the front door and stepped out onto the porch. "Freeze!" he shouted, aiming both his gun and his flashlight at the shadowy figure.

Daniel Metwater squinted into the light, one hand to his eyes to shield them. He fired the pistol he carried in his other hand, the bullets tearing into the wood of the door frame as Simon dove for cover behind the firewood stacked at the end of the porch.

ANDI HUDDLED IN BED, covers pulled tightly around her, as the sharp report of bullets shattered the midnight silence. She strained her ears, listening for cries, but heard nothing more. Moonlight poured through the window to her left, illuminating the room's sparse contents. Her gaze fixed on the bulletproof vest that hung from the bedpost. She should have insisted that Simon put it on before he left the bedroom.

She should have asked him to give her a gun too, so that she could help defend them. She hated sitting here, helpless.

All this fretting over what she should have done wasn't going to help anyone. She eased out of bed and pulled the fur coat over her gown, then sat on the side of the bed to pull on the boots. Maybe they weren't the most practical footwear for evading bad guys in the wilderness, but they were the only shoes she had with her, and they were warm.

She winced and rubbed at her lower back, trying to ease the cramp that tightened her muscles. The Braxton Hicks contractions she had been experiencing on and off for the last two months had started up again. Another sign her body was getting ready to deliver her baby, the women in camp had assured her.

Wait a while longer, little one, she said silently, sending a message to the infant in her womb. *Mommy isn't ready just yet.*

She stood and tiptoed to the bedroom door. Simon had ordered her to stay put, but she had to find out what was going on.

Another blast of gunfire shook the cabin and she stifled a cry, heart pounding painfully. Frantic, she looked around for anything to use as a weapon. Her mind flashed on the old toolbox her uncle kept under the kitchen sink. There would be something in there— a hammer or a big wrench or something she could use to strike out at an attacker. Something to make her feel less helpless.

She eased the door open farther and prepared to move into the front room as more shots sounded from the front of the house, coupled with the noise of shattering glass behind her. Disoriented, she turned and stared at the broken glass scattered across the bed and the floor. Had someone shot out the window? Then she saw the rock, as big as a man's head, that rested in the middle of the bed.

Right about where she had been sitting only moments before.

A man's head and shoulders appeared in the window, and then Victor hoisted himself up over the sill. Andi turned to flee, but he was on her faster than she would have thought possible, his hands holding her roughly.

"You're not going anywhere," he said, his lips brushing the top of her head. "You're mine now, and this time, I'm not going to let you get away."

FROM BEHIND THE WOODPILE, Simon returned fire, but his shot went wide as Metwater retreated around the corner of the house. Metwater's accomplice would have been alerted by now. Simon thought if he hadn't heard Simon's shout, anyone within a mile would have heard those shots. He hoped Andi had the sense to stay put in the bedroom and not go investigating. He glanced over his shoulder, to make sure no one was moving in behind him, then turned back toward where Metwater had disappeared. "Give up!" he called. "I won't let you leave here alive."

Metwater's answer was another volley of shots into the woodpile, sending chunks of wood flying. Simon crouched there, his face pressed against the rough logs, the smell of pine mingling with the sting of cordite. He cursed his choice of cover. He should have retreated into the cabin, where he would be closer to Andi. As long as Metwater had ammo, it didn't matter if he actually hit Simon or not. All he had to do was keep him pinned here while his accomplice got whatever he was after.

It didn't take a genius to figure out what that might be. Andi was the only thing in the cabin worth having. Now she would pay for Simon's poor judgment.

The best he could hope for was to keep Metwater distracted and look for an opening to get to him. "How did you find us?" he called.

"Asteria used to talk about this cabin," Metwater said, using the name he had given Andi. "She even talked about bringing me here to visit someday. I knew she wouldn't get this close without stopping by."

"Why are you here?" Simon asked. "What do you want?"

"I want Asteria."

"Why?"

"She has something that belongs to me."

"What's that?" Was he talking about the necklace, or the key inside it or something else entirely?

"I'm tired of talking. Send her out and I'll let you go."

"Never." He emphasized his point by aiming where he thought Metwater's head might be and firing.

"He's not the one you need to deal with now." The Russian's accent revealed his identity even before Simon turned to see him step from the side of the house. He had one arm around Andi, who was wrapped in the fur coat, wearing her boots. At least Victor had allowed her to dress before bringing her out in the cold.

In the other hand, Victor held a small pistol, the barrel of it pressed to Andi's temple. "Either of you make a move, I'll kill her," he said. "Now throw out your guns."

"Go ahead and shoot her," Metwater said. "It will save me the trouble."

Andi flinched. Victor pulled her more tightly against him. "Now the question I ask myself is—are you serious, or are you bluffing?" he said. Andi didn't make a sound, though her gaze remained fixed on Simon, pleading, her face paper white in the moonlight, eyes huge and dark.

Sweat slicked Simon's hand as he tightened his grip on his gun.

"Don't even think about it, Officer," Victor barked. "Drop your weapon. Now!"

Simon tossed the gun onto the porch. It bounced on the floorboard, then skidded to rest against one of the posts.

"Your turn." Victor addressed Metwater.

Metwater fired, at the same time Andi brought her foot down hard on Victor's instep, driving the stiletto heel of her boot into the top of his foot. With a roar of rage, he grappled to hold her, but she lunged free.

Simon dove for his gun and came up firing. But Victor had already retreated behind the SUV. Andi had disappeared—Simon hoped somewhere well out of the range of gunfire. He had taken cover behind a large pine tree, halfway between the cabin and the SUV. He was safe for now, but trapped between his two opponents. He leaned against the tree, trying to catch his breath, the cold seeping through his clothes as he listened for sounds of movement from Metwater or Victor.

It was too quiet. Simon worried one of the men—or both—had left and gone after Andi. He focused on the side of the cabin where Metwater had been, unable to detect any movement in the dim light. Somewhere nearby, an engine roared to life. Lights flared on, and a vehicle pulled from the trees farther up the driveway.

"My car!" Victor shouted. He climbed into the SUV and started the engine. Simon aimed for the vehicle, but he only managed a single shot before Victor sped down the driveway.

The rumble of engines and crunch of tires on gravel and snow faded, leaving a ringing silence. Simon stepped out from behind the tree. "Andi!" he shouted.

"I'm right here." She emerged from behind the outhouse.

Simon ran to her and she fell into his arms. He held her tightly for a long moment, unable to speak.

"What happened?" she asked after a long moment.

"They came in two separate cars. Victor left his parked up by the road—probably with the keys in it so he could make a quick getaway if he had to. Metwater's SUV was in the driveway. He took Victor's car and now Victor has his."

Andi frowned. "Did they come here together?"

"I don't know. I'm beginning to think not." Reluctantly, he released her. "Come on," he said. "We have to get out of here."

"Yes, we need to leave," she responded.

"I don't think they'll come back, but they might," he said.

"I'm not worried about that," Andi said. "We need to leave because I think I'm going into labor."

Simon stopped and stared at her. "Are you sure?"

She rubbed her belly. "I've been having pains for a while now," she said. "Then, just now, my water broke." She opened the coat to reveal her soaked gown. "Ready or not, I think I'm going to have this baby."

Chapter Sixteen

Don't be afraid, Andi told herself as another pain rocked her as soon as she and Simon stepped into the cabin. When he looked at her, she forced a smile. "I'm sure we have plenty of time," she said.

"I'll get the luggage," he said. "You wait here."

As soon as he was out of sight, she steadied herself with one hand on the back of a chair. Should she insist they stay here in the cabin, with the fire and bed and shelter? Did cops know anything about delivering babies? Was that part of their training?

But the thought of having her baby out here all alone terrified her. She wanted doctors and nurses and bright lights, sterile sheets and painkillers if necessary.

Simon emerged from the bedroom, suitcases in hand. He wore his coat now, and when she hugged him, she felt the reassuring hardness of the bulletproof vest. "I'll bring the cruiser around," he said. "You wait here."

Waiting. It seemed that was all she had been doing lately. She leaned back against the porch post and closed her eyes. Had it really only been eight months ago that she had discovered she was pregnant? At the time, she had been nervous but happy, looking forward to building a family with the man she loved—of making a new life of her own that wasn't dependent on her father's wealth or his plans for her future.

But her lover hadn't been so happy, and she had been horrified to learn that he was married, with two other children she had had no idea existed. Her father had been equally unsupportive, offering to pay for an abortion, more concerned with keeping the scandal a secret than worrying about his daughter's feelings.

So she had run away. She hadn't called it that, of course. She had been "moving on" and "striking out on her own," but all she had done was retreat into the wilderness, change her name and become involved with a handsome, charismatic man who was as false as all the other men she had met in her life.

"Lean on me." Simon's arm encircled her and she opened her eyes and looked into his weary, concerned face. She saw strength in his eyes, not scorn or impatience or any of the other emotions she had too often seen in other men's eyes. "Watch your step," he said. "It's icy."

"Bet you're glad I wore these silly boots now," she said as he helped her to the car.

He squeezed her arms. "Don't ever let anyone tell you you don't have guts," he said.

He shut the passenger door, then returned to the cabin to retrieve the bags and load them in the back. Seconds later, he was guiding the cruiser down the snowy driveway.

"Where are we going?" she asked. "I have no idea where the nearest hospital is."

"It's probably in Breckenridge," Simon said. "But all we need is to get back in cell phone range, and we can call for an ambulance."

"Good." She spoke through clenched teeth as another burst of pain rocked through her.

Simon reached over and took her hand. "You okay?" he asked.

She nodded. "I'll be fine. Just...let's get out of here."

He hunched over the steering wheel, gaze shifting back and forth, searching, she realized, for any sign of Daniel or Victor. "You don't think they're waiting for us, do you?" she asked, anxiously searching the woods closing in on both sides of the road.

"Their tire tracks are headed the same direction we are." Simon indicated the crisp tire tread imprints in the snow on the road. "I think Victor is chasing Metwater."

"I think Victor would have killed me and not thought twice about it," she said. "Daniel wouldn't have cared, either. I'm nothing to them." The knowledge sent a wave of nausea through her.

"They don't have the capacity to care about anyone but themselves," Simon said.

She wanted to ask him if he cared, if he would ever abandon her that way, but the words stuck in her throat. Protecting her was his job, one he was good at. He had admitted he had feelings for her, but clearly duty came first to him. How could she ever fit into his rigid, law-and-order world?

Another pain hit and she was unable to stifle a cry.

The car swerved, then righted once more. "Are you all right?" Simon asked.

"Stop asking me that! I don't know if I'm all right. I'm having a baby."

"How far apart are the pains?"

"I don't know."

He glanced at the clock on the dash. "Tell me when the next one hits."

"Okay." She scooted to the edge of the seat, the safety belt straining across her torso, and they both waited in tense silence. She gripped the dash as another pain tore at her. "Now," she gasped.

The lines between Simon's eyes deepened. "About four minutes," he said. He pulled out his phone and frowned at the screen.

"Do you have a signal?" she asked, fighting a wave of panic. What if they didn't make it in time?

He shook his head. "But we'll be in range soon. We'll get an ambulance."

She closed her eyes and clenched her teeth, every sense focused on her body, on the tension and the pain and the child shifting inside her. This was really happening. And she wasn't ready.

The sound of the tires changed as they turned onto pavement, and she opened her eyes again. The highway stretched out in front of them, empty and snow covered, wind stirring up eddies of snow that rose and swirled at headlight level like dancing ghosts.

Simon pulled to the shoulder of the road and took out his phone. "This is Agent Simon Woolridge with the Ranger Brigade, and I'm on highway 285 south of

Fairplay," he said. "The woman with me is in labor. Her pains are four minutes apart."

Andi couldn't hear the voice on the other end of the line. She closed her eyes again and pressed her forehead to the passenger window, the iciness of the glass sending a shiver through her. Wind rocked the vehicle as Simon waited for someone on the other end of the line.

"We're at mile marker... I can't see a mile marker," he said. "But we're just past the turnoff for County Road Twenty-Four... Yes, her water has broken... Yes... No... How long do you think it will be?... No... I'll call you back if I need to."

He ended the call and tossed the phone onto the console, his mouth twisted in an expression of frustration. "What did they say?" Andi asked. "Are they sending an ambulance?"

"They said it will be forty minutes, maybe an hour," he said. "A major pileup on I-70 has diverted all the local transport, and it will be that long before they can get to us."

She fought down a wave of panic as a hard gust of wind rocked the vehicle. "What were all those questions that you were answering yes and no to?"

He kneaded the bridge of his nose. "They asked if I had ever delivered a baby before."

"Have you?"

"Not exactly." He opened the driver's door and put one foot out. "I'm going to get the first aid kit and some blankets from the back of the cruiser," he said. "I think you should move into the back seat, where you'll have more room."

"What do you mean, not exactly?" she called after him, but he had already shut the door and was walking around to the back of the cruiser.

Icy wind whipped through the vehicle when he opened up the back hatch. Andi turned away from him, wanting to insist that he keep driving—all the way to Breckenridge if he had to. But she knew they didn't have time. The increasingly urgent need to push told her this baby was going to be born, whether she was ready or not.

Simon came around to the passenger side and opened the door, his arms full of blankets. "I'll spread one of these on the seat for you to lie on," he said. "I've got a couple of clean towels, too, and some bottled water."

He reached to help her out and she gripped his hand. "Have you ever delivered a baby?" she asked again, staring hard until he met her gaze.

Before he could answer, another contraction rocked her. She let out a low groan, and Simon massaged her shoulder.

When the pain passed, she let him help her move to the rear seat and scoot back, legs stretched out toward him. A cold wind swirled around the vehicle, hard granules of snow splatting against the open doors and gathering on the floorboards. His eyes met hers once more. If he was afraid, he was doing a good job of hiding it. "I once watched my uncle deliver a baby at a clinic in Mexico," he said. "I was seventeen and I was helping out there for the summer. When they brought the woman in, I think everyone had forgotten I was in the room. I didn't do anything—I stood in the corner and watched."

"What did you think?" she asked.

"I was terrified and fascinated." He made a face. "I remember there was a lot of yelling, and a lot of blood—two things I wasn't used to back then."

"And you are now?"

"Let's just say I've seen more of both over the years. They don't shake me as much now."

"I hope you remember some of what you saw," she said.

He held up a paperback book. "I have some instructions here that should help. But really, there's not a lot I can do. Yours is the hard part."

Another pain rocked her, this one more intense. She tried to stifle her scream by biting her lip, but Simon grabbed her hand and squeezed. "Go ahead and make all the noise you want," he said. "There's no one else out here to hear us anyway."

ANDI'S SCREAMS CUT through Simon like razors. With shaking hands, he tore one of the clean towels into strips, as instructed by the book he had wedged open on the floorboard of the backseat. *Get a grip*, he told himself. *Time to man up and do your job.*

He tried to remember everything his uncle had done when he had delivered that baby in his clinic all those years ago, but he had been so young then, fighting a mixture of horror and embarrassment. There was no room for any of those feelings now.

He glanced up and into Andi's wide, frightened eyes,

and tried to force a smile. She was counting on him to get her through this. Her baby was depending on him too. He squeezed her hand. "You're doing great," he said.

"What does the book say?" she asked.

He glanced down at the open pages. "We should see the head at the entrance of the birth canal," he said. "That's called crowning. A couple more strong pushes after that, and the baby will be born. I have to clear any mucous from the baby's mouth and nose and make sure it's breathing, then tie off the cord and keep it warm, and deliver the afterbirth."

"So much to do," she said, before another cry of pain choked off her words.

Following the instructions in the first aid manual, he laid out a clean towel, water, scissors, first aid tape and alcohol wipes. "Something's happening!" Andi cried.

"I can see the head." Simon dropped to his knees, ignoring the snow and dirt, bracing himself to support the baby when it emerged. He barely registered the crunch of tires on snow, and glanced to his left to see a vehicle pulling in behind him, the grille almost touching the back bumper. Then another cry from Andi forced his attention back to her.

"Another push or two, I think," he said.

"It hurts so much!" she screamed through her tears.

"You can do this." And then he was holding the baby, a writhing, sticky bundle pulsing with life. He stared at it, overwhelmed by such a feeling of awe that he was glad he was already on his knees. The infant was so tiny and perfect, so alive… He shook his head, forcing himself out of his reverie, and consulted the first aid manual. Following the instructions illustrated on the page, he carefully wiped the baby's mouth and nose, then gently turned it over. "It's a girl," he said, surprised at the tears choking his voice.

"Let me see her." Andi struggled to sit up, tears streaming down her face. The baby let out a lusty cry and the sound made Simon laugh. He laid the baby on Andi's stomach, and she spread her hand protectively over the baby's back.

A shadow loomed over him, and something hard pressed against his temple. "How does it feel to bring a new life into the world?" Victor asked. "When you're about to lose yours?"

"Go away!" Andi screamed. "Don't touch my baby!" Ignoring the pain it cost her, she leaned forward, trying to cover the infant's body with her own.

"I don't care about your brat." Victor kept the gun pressed to Simon's temple, but he was focused on mother and child. "Give me the key."

"The key?" Andi asked.

"Don't be stupid. I know you have the key that belonged to Metwater. Give it to me."

"He hid it in this necklace." She grasped the pendant and tugged, trying to tear it from her neck, but the gold chain refused to budge.

"Give it to me!" Victor roared. Snow swirled around him, collecting in his blond hair and on the shoulders of his wind-whipped coat. He looked like some demon out of a horror novel.

"I'm trying," she cried.

"I need to tie off the umbilical cord," Simon said, his voice eerily calm in the midst of chaos.

"Shut up," Victor said. "If you don't give me the necklace I'll kill him now."

Sobbing, Andi wrenched the necklace free, and hurled it at him. It sailed over Simon's head and landed in the snow. Victor dove for it as Simon rose, his gun drawn, but it was not his bullet that struck Victor in the shoulder and sent him spinning to the side.

Daniel Metwater stepped forward, his foot crunching the necklace into the snow. Victor looked up from where he lay sprawled in the snow, blood dripping from his blasted shoulder, and all the color drained from his face. "You!"

The gun fired again, and red blossomed in the calf of Victor's right leg. His keening wail echoed around them. Andi folded herself more securely over the baby, who cried softly and nestled against her stomach. "I want the key," Metwater demanded. "Tell me where it is or I'll shoot again. The other leg this time."

"The necklace," Victor gasped. "The key is in the necklace."

Keeping his eyes and the pistol fixed on Victor, Metwater bent and scooped the necklace from the snow and dropped it in the pocket of his ski jacket. Then he stood over Victor, who bowed his head and buried his face in the snow.

Andi looked away, sure Daniel would kill the Russian now. But instead of the explosion of gunfire, she heard the sound of tearing fabric, as Simon worked to tie off her baby's umbilical cord. "I was paid to kill you once before, David," Victor said. "A fee I was never able to collect."

Metwater leveled the gun at Victor's head. "My name is Daniel. David was my brother."

"No, you're David," Victor said. "You knew we were closing in on you so you came up with a plan—a smart, perfect plan. You went to your brother Daniel. The good brother who always came through for you, who always got you out of trouble. You invited him to dinner at your place. You drugged him. Then you paid a tattoo artist a lot of money to duplicate your infamous lion tattoo on his arm. Then you shot him and dumped his body in the river, and you stepped into his life. You identified his water-ravaged corpse and arranged for a hasty cremation. With David presumed dead, you didn't have to worry about the *Bratva* coming after you as payback for all the money and drugs you stole from us. But just to be safe, you went into hiding. You became a prophet in the wilderness."

Andi stared at the two men. "That's why you didn't want anyone to see the tattoo," she said.

Metwater's eyes met hers. "You were the only one who knew," he said. "Once you and your cop friend are dead, I'll be safe."

She clutched at her baby, determined to protect the child. She hadn't come this far to die out here in the snow. "Simon," she whispered.

He glanced up at her and gave a small shake of his head, then reached for the scissors to cut the cord.

"You forgot that the *Bratva* never forgives those who

betray them," Victor said. "You were supposed to deliver a million dollars as a favor to us. Instead, you stole the money."

"Lies!" Metwater screamed. "You can't prove any of it."

"I found the tattoo artist," Victor said. "That was a mistake, leaving him alive. Or maybe you did come after him, but too late. He took the money you paid him and ran—it took us quite a while to track him down."

The distant wail of a siren rose over the whine of the wind. Andi's eyes met Simon's once more. He had risen and was standing between her and the two men. His gun was drawn, but he held it low at his side.

"It's too late for you now," Victor said, his voice strained. "The police are coming for you."

The words were scarcely out of his mouth before Metwater fired again. Andi screamed as the Russian slumped to the ground. Metwater pivoted toward Simon, and Andi screamed again. "No!"

Chapter Seventeen

Simon dropped to a crouch, his hands slippery with the blood of Andi's baby, the gun cold in his hand. Metwater stood with his gun still smoking, calmly taking aim, ready to kill without emotion or regret. He had been cold-blooded enough to kill his own brother, so what were Andi and a cop to him now? He looked on his targets not as adversaries, but prey. He had every tactical advantage over Simon.

Except that Simon was determined to live. He wouldn't leave Andi and her child defenseless. He wouldn't let this killer win.

With a roar of rage, he sprang up and charged at Metwater, striking him full on, even as a bullet whistled past his head. Metwater landed hard on his back, the gun still in his hand. Simon struck out viciously with a karate chop to Metwater's wrist that sent the gun skittering into a snowbank.

The two men grappled, rolling around on the shoulder of the road, coming to rest against the tires of the ambulance that skidded to a stop beside them. Metwater shoved Simon away from him, scrambled to his feet and lurched to his car. By the time Simon had risen, he was driving away.

Simon searched the snow for his weapon and found it near his cruiser. He wiped it on his jacket and re-holstered it, then made his way to where one of the EMTs knelt beside Victor. "He's dead," the EMT said. He stood. "What happened here?"

"It's a long story," Simon said.

"They usually are," the EMT said.

"He's not your patient." Simon led the way to the cruiser and looked in at Andi. She had pulled the fur coat over her and the baby, whom she still cradled on her stomach. She looked pale and frightened.

"Simon!" she said. "I was so afraid."

"Ma'am, let's just have a look here." The two EMTs shouldered Simon aside. While one examined Andi, the other began radioing in particulars, starting with a call for police assistance.

Simon walked to the back of the cruiser and leaned against the bumper, feeling shaky as the adrenaline left him. Cold seeped through his shirt and vest. He should put on his coat, but he was too exhausted to move. Victor's still figure lay a few feet away, facedown in the bloody snow. Wind ruffled his hair and tugged at his jacket.

So Daniel was really David, a man who had killed his own brother, sacrificing the one person he had been closest to, letting him take the fall for the crimes he had committed. He had played the role of the innocent brother for months, and might even have gotten away with it, if not for his own greed. Somehow he had come to the *Bratva*'s attention, and they had figured out his scam.

Andi had seen the damning tattoo, so he had had to come after her. Her millions had been just an added bonus. He might have gotten away long before now, if he hadn't been determined to help himself not only to the stolen million dollars, but to Andi's wealth as well.

Simon turned to stare in the direction Metwater had driven. He was running out of places to hide now. He was getting more desperate, and more reckless. As soon as Simon had Andi settled, he would go after the man who had tried to kill her. He wouldn't stop until he had Metwater in custody.

The EMTs wheeled a gurney across the snow to the side of the cruiser and transferred Andi and her baby to it. Simon moved around the cruiser to stand beside her. "How are you doing?" he asked. The EMTs had cleaned her and the baby up some, and cut the cord so that she could cradle the now-swaddled newborn to her breast.

"I can't believe what just happened," she said. "Do you think it's true—that Daniel is really David?"

"He didn't deny it," Simon said. He brushed her hair from her eyes, the strands silken against his fingers. "Are you sure you're okay?"

"I'm fine. And the baby is fine—thanks to you. Everything is going to be all right now."

"I forgot to tell you happy birthday earlier," he said.

She gave a weak laugh. "It's been an eventful day." She looked down at the infant at her breast. "I think I already have the best present ever."

"I have some loose ends to tie up here," Simon said. "But I'll be at the hospital to see you as soon as I can."

She nodded and he started to turn away, but she reached out and clutched his hand. "Wait."

He turned back to her. "What is it?"

"They key Daniel—David—was looking for—"

"You did the right thing, giving it up to him. It wasn't worth your life to argue with him."

"No—it wasn't in the necklace. I took it out."

He frowned. "When did you do that?"

"In the cabin. I knew he and probably Victor too, wanted it, and I was afraid of what they would do to me. I thought it would be better if I didn't keep it on me. So I took it out and hid it in the cabin. It's in my uncle's toolbox, under the sink in the kitchen."

"All right. Thanks for letting me know."

"I still can't believe he murdered his own brother," she said. "The brother who had always helped him. His twin. How could anyone do something like that?"

"I don't know. Maybe sometimes something gets broken in a person that makes it easier for them to do horrible things."

"We need to go now," one of the EMTs said. "We need to get mom and baby out of the cold."

Simon hesitated, then bent and kissed Andi, a brief buss on the lips. "I'll be by to see you soon." She would be safe in a hospital, surrounded by other people. He needed to find Metwater, and make sure he didn't come after her again.

"I love you," she said. "Don't ever forget that."

"I love you too. And I won't forget." The words were

easier to say than almost anything he had ever said, akin to a miracle, considering how hard and messy he usually found emotions to be. It was as if he had built up a callus over his heart and this beautiful, trusting and strong woman had lifted it off, making him at once more vulnerable and more free.

As the ambulance, lights flashing but no siren, pulled onto the highway, two Colorado State Patrol vehicles pulled in front of Simon's cruiser. "Agent Woolridge?" A silver-haired man in a heavy black coat stepped out of the first vehicle and addressed Simon.

"Yes." Simon straightened and offered his hand.

"Sergeant Nick Schwartz." The older man looked down at Simon's hand, but didn't take it. "Are you all right, sir?"

Simon realized his hands were still covered in blood. He wiped them on his uniform, but it was almost as soiled. "I was delivering a baby," he said, by way of explanation.

Schwartz nodded toward Victor's body. "What happened to him?"

"He's a fugitive I've been pursuing. Victor Krayev, a Russian hit man."

"You take him out?"

"No. He was killed by a man who goes by the name of Daniel Metwater." The real story was too complicated to go into now. "I need you to put a guard on Ms. Matheson at the hospital. She could still be in danger from Metwater."

Schwartz and his partner exchanged looks. "We can do that," Schwartz said. "But we'd like a few more details."

"It's a long story," Simon said.

"This is a story I want to hear," the other man, a trim Hispanic with black-rimmed glasses, said.

"It'll have to wait," Simon said. "I have some things I have to do right now."

"Sir, we'll need you to make a statement," Schwartz said.

But Simon was already in his cruiser with the engine running. "I'll be in touch," he said, and drove away.

He waited to make sure no one had come after him, then pulled out his phone and dialed Ranger Headquarters. Carmen Redhorse answered. "Simon! What's going on? We were expecting you hours ago."

"I ran into a little trouble. I need to speak with the commander."

"Simon." Graham Ellison's voice held more warmth than Simon had expected. "Are you all right?" the commander asked. "Is Andi all right?"

"She's doing okay. She had her baby—a little girl." He looked down at his hands. "I delivered it." The idea filled him with wonder.

"Good job. Where are you now?"

"I'm still near Fairplay. She and the baby are on their way to Breckenridge in an ambulance."

"Why didn't you go with them?"

"They'll be okay. Victor Krayev is dead, and the local police agreed to put a guard on her."

"Did you kill Victor?"

"No. Metwater did. Victor was sent by the *Bratva* to kill him and to retrieve a key to a safe-deposit box that apparently contains money the Russians think belongs to them."

"So Daniel Metwater shot him?" Graham asked.

"Not Daniel—David. Apparently David Metwater killed Daniel and assumed his brother's identity in an attempt to get away from the Russians. But they learned the truth and came after him anyway."

"You're saying the man who died in Chicago wasn't David, he was Daniel?" Graham asked. "Back up and start over. Slower this time."

So Simon told him the story of the two brothers, one who stole a million dollars from the Russian mob and tried to get away with it by switching identities with his straight-arrow brother. "Apparently, the body was so deteriorated from a week in the water that the chief means of identification was the distinctive tattoo," Simon said. "David, as next of kin, essentially identified the body as himself."

"How did he get around having an autopsy performed, since the body was that of a murder victim?" Ellison asked.

"Maybe he bribed someone?" Simon said. "I don't know. But he somehow convinced authorities to take his identification as final proof of identity, then he had the body cremated."

"And he declared himself so transformed by his brother's death that he turned his back on his old life and hid out in the wilderness with a bunch of followers," Ellison said.

"Except the leopard couldn't completely change his spots," Simon said. "He got greedy. He wanted Andi

Metwater's money, and he wanted the million dollars he had hidden away in a safe-deposit box. The *Bratva* hadn't forgotten about that money either though. And they figured out the truth about which brother had really died."

"How did they do that?" Graham asked.

"I don't know. But they found the guy David paid to give his brother the tattoo. Once they knew the truth, they sent Victor to retrieve the key to the safe-deposit box where David had stashed the money, and to exact revenge for trying to double-cross them."

"But Metwater killed him first. And he got away?"

"He would have killed Andi and me if the police hadn't arrived. He got away, and he has the locket that belonged to Michelle's sister. He hid the key to the safe-deposit box in it, though he'll soon find out the key isn't in it now. Andi was afraid to carry it around, once she knew its significance, so she hid it in her uncle's cabin."

"When Metwater finds out, he'll come after Andi again," Graham said.

"Maybe. The local police have agreed to put a guard on her at the hospital. But Metwater strikes me as a smart guy—good at figuring out puzzles. I have a feeling he'll check the cabin first, so I'm headed there now."

"You should wait for backup."

"I should, but if I do that, he'll get away. And I don't want to risk him coming after Andi again. I want this to end now."

"I can't authorize a solo pursuit," Graham said.

"I'm not asking permission, sir. I'm only advising you of what I'm doing."

"Simon."

"He tried to kill the woman I love, and her baby. I'm not going to give him a second chance."

The commander was silent for a long moment. Simon was getting used to those silences—it meant Graham was thinking, coming up with a plan. "I'm going to contact state patrol when I get off the phone and send them after you," he said. "If they get to you before you find Metwater, they'll be under orders to take you with them."

"Fair enough, sir. But tell them not to hurry. I want a piece of this guy."

"Good luck, Simon. But remember that luck will take you only so far."

"I'll remember, sir. And thank you."

He hung up the phone, and gripped the steering wheel with both hands. He wasn't nervous or afraid. His instincts told him he was doing the right thing. Metwater was going to be at the cabin. And Simon was going to be there, too, to take him down.

The Prophet might have thought he had gotten away with murder, but Simon was determined to prove him wrong.

SIMON FOLLOWED THE TRACKS of Metwater's tires all the way down the forest service road that led to the cabin. The snow had stopped and the sun had come out, glinting off ice crystals so that the whole world looked as if it were coated in white sugar.

He passed the turnoff for the cabin and drove a half mile farther, then parked on the side of the road. The tracks he had been following had turned off at the cabin.

Either Metwater hadn't expected anyone to follow him or he was so focused on the key—and the million dollars it led to—that he didn't care.

Simon cleaned his hands and drank some water, then began working his way toward the cabin. He would approach it from the back and try to catch Metwater by surprise. The Prophet wouldn't give up without a fight, so Simon would have to use every advantage.

He hadn't gone very far before he was wet to the knees, melting snow soaking into his clothes. Branches caught and tugged at his coat and a crow cawed indignantly overhead. Simon ignored the bird and the wet and kept going, gun drawn, carefully placing each step, yet moving as swiftly as possible.

He heard Metwater before he saw him. The thud of something being dropped was followed by the crash of breaking glass. More thuds and crashes. Once, the Rangers had been called to deal with a bear that had become trapped inside an RV. The bear had destroyed the interior of the trailer before the Rangers succeeded in freeing him. Metwater sounded as if he was wreaking the same kind of havoc. Good. The noise would help cover Simon's approach.

At the edge of the trees behind the cabin, he paused. He detected no movement outside, though the crashing sounds continued inside. He counted to ten, deliberately slowing his breath, then darted forward, to a position to the left of the big back window.

The glass of the window was shattered, a slight breeze stirring the curtains. Simon remembered that Victor had entered the cabin this way when he had tried to kidnap Andi. He waited, listening to the muffled slamming doors and clatter of items falling.

Simon leaned over and looked inside. The mattress was half off the bed, the covers on the floor. All the drawers had been removed from the dresser, the contents scattered. No sign of Metwater—though Simon could hear him in the front of the house.

He climbed in the window and moved toward the source of the commotion, stepping around mounds of winter clothing and tumbled stacks of magazines. At the door to the bedroom, he paused, peering around the jamb.

Metwater was crouched in front of the kitchen sink. He pulled out a small metal toolbox, the red paint scratched, rust showing in spots. He opened the lid and began pawing through the contents, then, with a growl of frustration, upended the whole thing on the floor. Wrenches and screwdrivers bounced across the wood floor, and nails and screws rolled in every direction.

"Ah!" he exclaimed, and picked up something from the floor. The small brass key glinted in the sunlight as he held it aloft.

Simon stepped from the bedroom and leveled his gun at the other man. "David Metwater, you're under arrest," he said.

Metwater froze, then turned slowly toward him, the key still in his hand, his gun tucked into the waistband of his trousers. "It was a mistake to come after me," he said. "You should have quit when you had the chance."

"Lay your gun on the floor and stand up with your hands where I can see them," Simon said.

"Do you know what this key is?" Metwater asked.

"Your gun," Simon said. "Drop it."

"This is the key to a safe-deposit box that contains a million dollars. Money I took from the *Bratva*. Can you imagine the audacity? No one steals from them and gets away with it. But I did."

"I'm arresting you for the murders of Daniel Metwater and Victor Krayev," Simon said. "You have the right to remain silent."

Metwater sneered. "You don't think I'll come quietly, do you?" he asked. "Not after all I've been through to get here. I'm going to kill you, and then I'm going to find Asteria and kill her. Then no one will know I'm not really Daniel Metwater, the prophet who was persecuted by the authorities."

"Plenty of people know the truth now," Simon said. "Put down your weapon and keep your hands where I can see them."

"Have you ever seen a million dollars?" Metwater asked. "Stacks and stacks of bills. More money than many people will see in a lifetime."

"You are entitled to consult an attorney," Simon said. "If you cannot afford one, one will be appointed for you by the court."

"Shut up." Metwater shifted his focus from the key to Simon. "I know my rights. I have been arrested before—or rather, David was arrested. Daniel has a clean record. But we don't have to do this. We can come to an agreement that will satisfy us both."

"I'll only be satisfied when you're behind bars," Simon said.

"Hear me out." Metwater held up the key again. "Let me go and I will give you half of the contents of this box. Half a million dollars. Think of that."

"Your words are worthless to me," Simon said.

"You think I will cheat you, but no. Half a million dollars, Officer. Cops don't get paid that much, do they? Think of what you could do with half a million dollars."

Half a million would build a new wing on the orphanage his aunt managed on the border. It would buy supplies and medicine for the clinic his uncle ran. It could fund a scholarship in memory of his father and mother.

"Put down your gun," Simon said.

"Of course." Metwater drew the gun from his waistband, extended it in front of him, and fired.

Simon dove for the floor, the bullet thudding into the wall behind him. His own shot caught Metwater square in the chest. He fired a second time, and a third, until Metwater dropped his weapon and sank to the floor. The brass key clattered on the wood and came to rest in a beam of sunlight by the table.

Sirens whined in the distance, moving closer. Simon rose to his knees, heart pounding, his breathing coming hard. He was still sitting that way when the state patrol officers burst in, guns drawn. Simon laid his pistol aside.

"He's dead," he said. "It's over."

ANDI SMILED DOWN at the baby in her arms, who looked up at her with wonder in her eyes. The nurses had dressed her in a pink onesie and a little pink hat, and wrapped her in a flowered flannel blanket. All the trauma surrounding her birth hadn't harmed her. The doctors had pronounced mother and baby both healthy, and free to go home as soon as all the paperwork had been processed.

Home. Andi had no idea where that was now. With the Prophet still on the loose, would she need to go to the safe house? And then what? Her twenty-fifth birthday had passed, so she supposed she was a rich woman. She could buy a house—one with a sunny room for a nursery, and a backyard where her little girl could play when she was older. But the idea didn't excite her. A house by herself sounded so lonely. Empty.

A knock on the door interrupted her contemplation. She looked up and Simon stepped into the room. Her heart beat wildly at the sight of him. He was back in uniform, his hair neatly combed, his face close shaven—this was the Simon she remembered from all his visits to the Family's compound in the woods. Except that this time he carried a bouquet of flowers—red daisies and orange mums and purple lilies spilling from a twist of green tissue. He wasn't smiling as he walked toward the bed, his eyes focused first on the baby, then on her. Dark eyes that made her melt a little inside. But right now they also made her want to cry. She was afraid of what he would say to her—and what he wouldn't say.

She spoke first, rushing to get the words out. "I'm so glad you're okay," she said. "I've been worried." As the hours passed when he didn't come to see her, she had imagined everything from him being killed to him deciding he never wanted to see her again.

"You didn't have to worry about me," he said.

"What happened?" she asked. "The Prophet?"

"He's dead. He won't have a chance to hurt you again."

His face was grim, and she wondered if he had been the one to kill Metwater. But she wouldn't ask. She didn't want that kind of ugliness in this room—not now.

Simon stared again at the baby. "Is she okay?" he asked. "Are you okay?"

"We're both doing great. Would you like to hold her?"

She half expected him to say no, but instead, he laid the bouquet at the foot of the bed and carefully took the baby in his arms. She looked impossibly tiny there— and so right. Andi's eyes stung and she swallowed past a lump in her throat.

"She's beautiful," he said, and looked up at her.

"I named her Caroline, after my mother."

"It's a beautiful name." He looked down at the baby, who stared back up at him, as if trying to figure him out. "She's so tiny," he said.

"You look just right, holding her," she said.

"I don't know anything about babies," he said.

"Neither do I." *We can learn together*, she thought, but was afraid to say it.

"I should tell you what happened after I left you," he said, his eyes still on the baby.

"You don't have to," she said.

"I want to." He hesitated, then added, "I think I need to."

"All right."

"I went back to your uncle's cabin. I figured once Metwater discovered the key was no longer in the locket, he would go there to look."

"Was he there?"

"Yes. He had found the key. He tried to bribe me, offering me half of the money if I would let him go."

"But you turned him down."

"Yes." He folded the blanket back from little Caroline's face. "He tried to shoot me and I shot back. He's dead now."

"Oh." Was it wrong that the news made her feel relieved? "What will happen to the money now?"

"That will be up to the authorities in Chicago. They'll have to figure out which bank issued that key and where the box is located. The money will probably end up going back to the government."

"I'm so glad you're all right," she said again. "I can't thank you enough for everything you've done. If you hadn't been there when I went into labor, I don't know what I would have done."

"Don't thank me. I didn't do anything special."

"I wouldn't have made it without you. Caroline wouldn't have made it."

"Don't look at me like I'm a saint," he said, his expression angry. "I'm not. I'm not going to save you or be as good as you want me to be. I know good people— truly good people. My aunt is a nun who runs an orphanage on the border. My uncle is a doctor who gives away thousands of dollars' worth of medical care every week. Both my parents died because they stood up to help others. I'm nothing compared to them."

"Stop it!" It was her turn to be angry now. "I know you think I'm a naive, starry-eyed girl," she said. "And I was that once. But I've done a lot of growing up in the last few weeks—mostly in the last few days with you. I know you're not perfect—you're grumpy and reticent and impatient and you snore. But those things don't matter to me. Because I see beneath all that stuff you use to keep other people from getting too close. I see it because I used to be that way too."

"You were never grumpy, and you don't snore."

"No, but I know how to keep people at a distance by remaining aloof. They think it's because you believe you're better than them, but I know it's because you think you'll never be good enough. You can't let anyone get close enough to find that out." She leaned toward him. "But we let each other get close, Simon. We couldn't help it. And what I found out is that we're a lot more alike than you give us credit for."

His gaze met hers, pinning her in place. "All I want to know is, did you mean it when you said you love me?"

"Yes. Too much."

"You can't love someone too much," he said.

"It feels like it, when even the idea of you being taken from me rips me in half."

"I'm not going anywhere." He leaned toward her, the baby between them, and his lips met hers, a kiss of such sweet tenderness that she felt tears well once more.

She opened her eyes and found him looking at her. "I'm not going to let you go," he said.

"Good. Because I'm not going anywhere. Except home with you, if you'll have me."

"I'm not an easy person to live with."

"I'm not expecting easy. Just someone I can count on." She didn't need a man with all the answers, just one who wouldn't let her down. Simon had proved he was that person—not a prophet or a politician or a celebrity, but a good man who would do his best for her, and made her want to do her best for him.

"Let's go home," he said. "We have a new life to get started on."

"I can't wait," she said. "This is going to be the best one yet."

* * * * *

LAWMAN FROM HER PAST

DELORES FOSSEN

Chapter One

Someone was watching him. Deputy Cameron Doran was certain of it.

He slid his hand over the gun in his waist holster and hoped he was wrong about the bad feeling that was snaking down his spine. Hoped he was wrong about the being watched part, too.

But he knew he wasn't.

He'd worn a badge for eleven years, and paying attention to that bad feeling had saved him a time or two.

With his gun ready to draw, Cameron glanced around his backyard. Such that it was. Since his house was on the backside of the sprawling Blue River Ranch, his yard was just a smear of grass with the thick woods only about fifteen feet away. There were plenty of trees and underbrush. The edge of the river, as well. However, there were also trails that someone could use to make their way to his house.

Someone like a killer.

You'll all die soon.

That was what the latest threatening letter had said. The one that Cameron had gotten just two days ago. Not exactly words anyone wanted to read when they opened their mail, but he'd gotten so many now that they no longer held the emotional punch of the first one he'd gotten a couple of months ago. Still, he wasn't about to dismiss it.

Cameron had another look around, trying to pick through the thick clusters of trees, but when he didn't see anyone, he finished off his morning coffee and went inside. Normally, he would have made a beeline to the nursery so he could say goodbye to his nephew, Isaac, before heading off to work at the Blue River Sheriff's Office, but this morning he went to the window over the sink and kept watch.

From the other side of the house, he could hear Isaac fussing, probably because the nanny, Merilee, was changing his diaper. Isaac was only a year old, but he got up raring to go. He objected to the couple of minutes delay that the diapering caused.

Just when Cameron was about to decide that the bad feeling had been wrong after all, he saw it. Someone moving around. Since those particular trees butted right up against an old ranch trail, the movement got his complete attention.

"Merilee," he called out to the nanny. "Keep Isaac in the nursery a little while longer. And stay away from the windows."

Cameron knew it would alarm the woman, but there was nothing he could do about that now. If this turned out to be a false alarm, then he could smooth things over with her. But for now, Isaac's and her safety had to come first.

He drew his gun, and as soon as he opened the door a couple of inches, Cameron spotted more movement. And the person who was doing the moving.

A woman peered out from one of the trees, and even

though she was still pretty far from him, he caught a good enough glimpse of her face.

Lauren Beckett.

She stepped out in full view of him so he got an even better look. Yeah, it was Lauren, all right. She still had the same brunette hair that she'd pulled back into a ponytail. The same willowy build. The last time he'd seen her she'd been a teenager, barely eighteen, but the years hadn't changed her much.

If he'd ventured a guess of who might have been lurking around his place, he would have never figured it would be her. Especially since he'd built his house on Beckett land. *Her* family's land. Of course, Lauren hadn't considered her siblings actually family—or him a friend—in nearly a decade.

Cameron felt the punch of old emotions. Ones he didn't want to feel. He and Lauren had parted ways long ago, and he hated that the tug in his body was still there for her.

He looked at her hands. At her wedding ring. She was still wearing it though he knew her husband had died from cancer a year and a half ago when Lauren had been pregnant. Of course, she might still be wearing the ring because she and her late husband had a child together. A son, if he remembered correctly.

Who was he kidding? He remembered, all right. Little details about Lauren just stuck in his head whether he wanted them there or not.

"What are you doing back there?" he asked.

He started to reholster his gun but then stopped when she fired glances all around her. Lauren had her teeth clamped over her bottom lip, and she motioned for him to come to her.

Hell.

He'd been right about that bad feeling. Something was wrong.

"What happened?" he demanded, but she just kept motioning.

Cursing under his breath, Cameron stepped out and locked the door behind him. Judging from Lauren's nervous gestures, someone else could be out there, and he didn't want that person getting into the house. Keeping watch around him, Cameron gripped his gun with two hands and started toward her.

More memories and emotions came. It'd been ten years since he had seen her. Since he'd kissed her. Ten years since their worlds had turned on a dime. Her mother and father had been murdered. Butchered, really, and even though their killer had been convicted and was behind bars, Lauren hadn't thought justice had been fully served.

Because she also blamed Cameron for not doing enough to save her folks.

That was okay because Cameron blamed himself, too.

All of those thoughts vanished for a moment, though, when he made it to her and stopped about two feet away. Still close enough to catch her scent and see those intense blue eyes. She didn't say anything. Lauren just stood there, staring at him, but he could tell from the tight muscles in her face that this wasn't a social visit.

Not that he thought it would be.

No. Lauren had said her final goodbye to him a decade ago, so it must have taken something pretty bad to come to him this way. Unless…maybe she wasn't here for him.

"Your brothers probably haven't left for work yet and are still home," he told her. They didn't live far, either. "Gabriel lives in his old place, and Jameson has a cabin about a half mile from here."

She didn't seem the least bit surprised about that, which meant maybe Lauren had kept up with her family, after all. Good. Because Cameron wasn't the only one who thought of Lauren often. So did her brothers and her sister, Ivy.

"I can't go to them." Her voice was raw and strained.

"Because you broke off ties with them," Cameron commented. "Don't worry about that. You're still their sister, and they'll help you. They love you," he added, hoping that would ease the tension he could practically feel radiating off her.

Lauren blinked, shook her head. "No. Because their houses are on the main road and someone might see me." She turned, glancing around again, and that was when Cameron spotted the gun tucked in the back waist of her jeans.

He cursed again. "What's wrong?"

A weary sigh left her mouth. The kind of reaction a person had when there was so much wrong that she didn't know where to start. But Cameron figured he knew what this was about.

"We've all been getting threatening letters and emails," he volunteered. "I'm guessing you got one, too?"

She nodded and dismissed it with a shake of her head. "You're raising your sister's child?"

Again, she'd managed to stun him. First with her arrival and now with the question. It didn't seem the right thing to ask since this wasn't a "catching up" kind of conversation.

"Gilly's son, Isaac," Cameron clarified. It had been a year since his kid sister's death, and he still couldn't say her name without it feeling as if someone had put a meaty fist around his heart. "What about him?"

Lauren didn't jump to answer that. With her forehead bunched up, she glanced behind her again. "Is he…okay?"

Isaac was fine. Better than fine, actually. His nephew was healthy and happy. That wasn't what he said to Lauren, though. "Why are you asking?"

"I need to see him. I need to see Gilly's son."

That definitely wasn't an answer.

Cameron didn't bother cursing again, but he did give her a flat look. "I'll want to know a lot more about what's going on. Start talking. Why are you here, and if you're in some kind of trouble, why didn't you call your brothers? Because I think you and I both know I'm the last person on earth you'd come to for help."

She didn't disagree with that, but another sound left her mouth. A hoarse sob. And that was when tears sprang to her eyes. "Please, let me see him."

He wasn't immune to those tears, and it gave him a tug of a different kind, one he didn't want. "Tell me what's going on," Cameron repeated.

Lauren frantically shook her head. "There isn't time."

Cameron huffed in frustration. "Then make time. Is someone after you? And what does that have to do with Gilly's son?"

She stared at him, her mouth trembling now, and those tears still watering her eyes. "Someone tried to kill me."

That put him on full alert, and he automatically caught on to her arm and pulled her behind him. Cameron positioned himself in between her and the area where she kept glancing.

"Keep talking," he insisted. He didn't see anyone out there, but the woods were fairly thick here. "When and where did this happen?"

Again, no fast answer. Which it should have been. After all, a murder attempt should have been fresh enough in her mind that Lauren could have rattled off the details.

"Last night," she finally said. "Two armed men broke into my house in Dallas and shot me."

The profanity flew out of his mouth before Cameron could stop it, and he whirled around just as she pulled back the collar of her dark blue button-up shirt. There was a bandage there. A bandage covering what had to be a sensitive wound judging by the way Lauren winced when she moved her shoulder.

"I'm okay," she added. "Well, physically anyway. The bullet only clipped me, and I was able to get away from them."

Good. But that didn't cause Cameron to feel any relief. "What about your son? Was he hurt?"

"No. There was a panic room in the house, and I had his nanny take him there right after the burglar alarm went off. I didn't manage to get in there in time before they got to me." She paused, choked back a sob. "I heard them say they had orders to kill me. And it wasn't a case of mistaken identity or anything. They said my name."

That did it. He took hold of her hand. "Come on. I'm taking you to Gabriel right now."

But Lauren pulled away from him. "No. Not yet anyway. Not until I know it's safe. I also heard the men say they were cops."

Cameron stared at her. "Cops? Maybe. Criminals don't always tell the truth, but even if they had, your brother's not dirty."

Even though she didn't come out and say it, she'd once suspected Cameron of being just that—dirty. He hadn't been, but Lauren had deemed him guilty by association. Because he'd been friends with the family of the man who'd murdered her parents. If that friendship hadn't existed, then her mom and dad might still be alive.

Somehow, Cameron had never learned to live with that.

"Gabriel and Jameson aren't behind this," she said. "Whatever *this* is," Lauren added in a mumble. "But if those men were really cops and they know all about me, then they must figure I'd go to my lawmen brothers." Another pause, and she dodged his gaze. "This is the last place they'd expect me to come."

True. It wasn't exactly a secret about Lauren's hatred for him. But that wasn't hatred he was seeing in her eyes now. It was fear. Cameron was certain he was feeling some of that, as well. Fear for her. But there were still some very weird things going on.

"Where's your son now?" he asked.

That was concern number one. Once Lauren and the child were safe, then he could work out the rest with her. The *rest* would include bringing in her brothers on this. No way would Gabriel and Jameson want to be left out when someone was gunning for their kid sister, and it didn't matter if they were estranged from Lauren.

She fluttered her fingers in the direction of the trail. "He's in the car with the nanny. That's why I can't stay. I have to get back to him."

Yeah, she did, and Cameron would go with her. "Take me to him, and I can bring all three of you inside while we work this out."

She did more of that frantic head-shaking. "Not yet. Not until I know. Not until I'm sure I can trust you."

Cameron pulled back his shoulders. Trust had indeed been an issue between them in the past. Her trust for him anyway. But from what he could see in the depths of her eyes, this went beyond their past.

"If you didn't trust me, why come here?" he snapped. And he hated how much it stung that this bad blood was still between them.

"I didn't have a choice." Her voice cracked. "I need to see Isaac."

There it was again—something else she'd said that didn't make sense. Or maybe it did. Cameron hadn't been with Gilly when she'd died from a blood clot less than twenty-four hours after giving birth. He'd still been on the road trying to get to her in Dallas. Lauren had been there, though. Maybe had even spoken to her since Lauren and his sister had remained friends. Not only that, they'd lived in the same city.

"Did Gilly tell you something before she died?" It was the same tone he used to interrogate a suspect. Not an especially friendly one, but he wanted answers, and Lauren was going to give them to him now.

Lauren's mouth opened a little to let him know the question had surprised her. Well, welcome to the club. He'd been surprised by a lot of what Lauren had said.

"No," she answered after several long moments. "This isn't about Gilly. This is about her son. Does he look like her or like his father?"

Now it was Cameron's turn to take a moment before

he responded. "I never met his father, Trace Waters. Never wanted to meet him."

She made a sound of agreement, which meant Lauren knew that Trace had been abusive. Something that Gilly hadn't told Cameron until it was too late for him to go to Dallas and beat the living daylights out of the moron for laying a hand on his kid sister. By the time Cameron had heard, Trace had disappeared. Then, several weeks after Gilly had died, someone else had taken it beyond the beating stage and had killed Trace in a drug deal gone wrong.

"Trace's mother, Evelyn, came to the ranch once," Cameron explained. "She pulled a gun on me and demanded her son's baby." He felt his mouth tighten. "I don't like it when people pull guns on me so I had her arrested. The moment she made bail I slapped her with a restraining order."

"And that worked? Evelyn stayed away?"

He shook his head. "She tried to get on the grounds a couple of times, but the hands spotted her and stopped her. After the third time, she ended up in jail, where she's spent the last four months."

Cameron hoped the woman would do something behind bars that would keep her there. He wasn't concerned about losing custody to her. Gilly had made it clear to the hospital staff that she'd wanted Cameron to raise her son. But he didn't want Evelyn to be a free woman so she could try something else stupid.

"Does Isaac look like Gilly?" Lauren pressed. "Or anyone else in your family?"

Cameron nearly said no, but Lauren wasn't getting answers until he had some from her. "Let's get your baby and the nanny into the house, and we can talk."

"He doesn't look like Gilly," she said like gospel. "Or Trace."

Cameron lifted his shoulder. "Lots of kids don't look like their parents. Plus, he's a baby. Only thirteen months old." He huffed, scrubbing his hand over his forehead. "Look, I don't know where this is going, but I can have Gabriel come out—"

Only because he wasn't expecting it, Cameron didn't see Lauren pull that gun from the back of her jeans.

And she pointed it at him.

His heart slammed against his ribs. Damn. He should have been able to stop this before it'd even started, but Cameron fought the instinct to lunge at her and snatch that gun from her hand. He sure as hell wasn't pleased about this, though.

"What do you think you're doing?" he demanded once he got his teeth unclenched.

"I'm saving my son." Lauren used the barrel of the weapon to motion toward the house. "And you'll take me to him. I want to see Isaac now."

Chapter Two

Lauren saw exactly what she'd expected to see in Cameron's eyes.

Anger.

There was plenty of it, too, along with the shock of having her pull a gun on him. This certainly wasn't the way Lauren had wanted all of this to play out, but she hadn't exactly had a lot of options. The seconds were ticking away.

"Move," she ordered Cameron in the strongest voice she could manage. Which wasn't much. She didn't feel strong at all. Just terrified.

This couldn't be happening.

Over the past decade, she'd accepted that she could be in danger from the lunatic who kept sending those threatening letters, but she couldn't accept that two innocent babies could now be in harm's way.

"Put down the gun," Cameron warned her. And it was indeed a warning. Unlike her, he had managed the strong tone, and it had a dark edge to it. An edge that reminded her that she was holding a cop—an experienced one—at gunpoint.

"I can't." She tried to make that sound like an apology and failed at it, too. "I need to see Isaac."

Of course, Cameron would want to know why, and Lauren would tell him. First, though, she had to see the baby.

"Can't?" he repeated, that edge in his voice going up a notch. It went up in his smoke-gray eyes, too.

When she'd been a teenager, the girls had called them bedroom eyes because he was so hot. Still was. With that dark blond hair and natural tan, he'd always had rock-star looks. Those looks were still there in spades, but there wasn't a trace of his bedroom smile.

"Please," Lauren tried. "Just let me see him, and I might be able to clear all of this up."

"You'll clear it up now." Again, it was a warning. "And if you don't, you won't get anywhere near my nephew. However, you will get to see the inside of a jail cell."

She had no idea if that was a threat or not. He certainly had grounds to arrest her, and the fact that they'd once been lovers might not be enough leverage to stop this situation from snowballing.

Cameron still had hold of his gun, but he used his left hand to reach for his pocket. For his phone, she realized. He was going to call one or both of her brothers, and she didn't want them involved in this yet. Not until she could at least try to make things safe.

"No!" she said.

It was the only thing she managed to get out of her mouth, though, because Cameron didn't take out his phone. He lunged at her. Fast. Before Lauren could even react and get out of his way, he rammed into her and sent them both to the ground. While they were still falling, he knocked her gun from her hand.

"Start talking right now," Cameron growled, and he

pinned her hands to the ground so she couldn't reach for her gun. He pinned her, too, with his body since he was on top of her.

Lauren's heart was racing. Along with that, she got a new hit of adrenaline. Something she definitely didn't need since her nerves were already firing in every inch of her.

She looked at Cameron, their gazes colliding, and for a moment she remembered what had once been between them. The intimacy.

The love.

Yes, once she'd loved him, and she thought maybe he'd felt the same way about her, but it was obvious those emotions were long gone. Well, maybe not the heat that had first drawn them together, but he definitely wasn't having any warm and fuzzy feelings about her now.

Lauren struggled, trying to force him off her, but when it was obvious this was a losing battle, she knew she had to say something.

And that something was going to shatter the life Cameron had built here.

"Did I hurt you?" he asked, the question surprising her.

Only then did she remember the wound on her shoulder. That part of her hadn't hit the ground, thank goodness, and since it was a constant throbbing pain, it had become a sort of white noise. Something she was trying to push aside so it wouldn't cause her to lose focus.

"No. I'm not hurt." But in hindsight, she probably should have lied. Maybe then, Cameron would have let her go.

"Talk to me," he snapped. Obviously, he was over his

concern for her injury. Of course, she couldn't blame him when there were so many other things for them to discuss.

"We're in danger," she started. Lauren had to clear her throat and repeat it so it'd have some sound. "Those men who tried to kill me got away, and I believe they'll be looking for me. Maybe for you, too."

Because he was right in her face, it wasn't hard to see the doubt go through his eyes. Despite the doubts, though, he still had a look around them. A cop's look. Good. Lauren didn't want anyone sneaking up on them. Or worse—trying to sneak into the house.

"What do those men have to do with me?" he snarled.

"Maybe everything."

She tried to gather her breath. Couldn't. Cameron wasn't overly muscled, but he wasn't a lightweight, either, and with his chest pressing against her, she couldn't get enough air. He must have realized that, but he didn't move. Probably because he thought she would go for her gun again.

Which she would.

Since there was no easy way to say this, Lauren just blurted it out. "I believe someone swapped my baby with Gilly's."

She gave him a moment to let that sink in, but she couldn't give him the time he needed. She also continued to keep watch as best she could. Hard to do that, though, while on the ground.

He shook his head. "Why would anyone do that?"

"I'm not sure. Please, let's just check on Isaac, and then we can go over all of this."

Cameron didn't answer. Not with words anyway. But his cold, hard stare told her that wasn't going to happen.

"Someone started following me days ago. Two men in a dark car," she added. "I believe those were the same men who broke into my house."

"The men who tried to kill you." Cameron said it as if he didn't believe her. She couldn't blame him. She'd had hours to try to come to grips with it, and part of her still wasn't ready to accept it.

She nodded. "Before they found me, I heard them talking to someone on a communicator, and that's when they said they were cops."

"They could have lied," he reminded her again.

"True. But they still broke in for a reason. And that reason was my son, Patrick. They wanted to kill me and take him." She huffed in frustration because his skeptical look was only getting worse, and she wasn't explaining this well at all. "Just please move off me so we can both keep watch."

She saw him debate that for several moments. Lauren had lost track of how long she'd been out here with him, but Dara, the nanny, would be getting even more worried than she already was.

"If you try anything else stupid, I will put you right back on the ground," Cameron growled.

He finally shifted his body to the side, rolling off her. He also snatched up her gun as he stood. Lauren didn't like not being armed, but at least when she got up, she was able to better keep an eye on the trail behind them.

"Does your nephew look like your sister?" she came out and asked.

He stopped glancing around long enough to shoot her a glare. "That proves nothing. He could have inherited genes from generations ago."

Lauren hesitated a moment. "Does he look like me?"

His quick glare intensified, but what he didn't do was deny it. "First, you have to convince me that a swap even took place before I'll start speculating about who my nephew does or doesn't resemble."

Fair enough. Or at least it would have been fair if time was on their side. She instinctively knew it wasn't.

"I was telling the truth when I said I can't be sure a swap took place, but the men said once they had Patrick, they could do a DNA test and go from there. Go from there," she emphasized. "I believe that means they'll come here next."

Cameron cursed, and it wasn't tame. "That's a big leap to assume the men were talking about Isaac."

"A leap except that I'd already started to get suspicious. Patrick doesn't look like me or my late husband." She swallowed hard. "He looks like you."

She could tell from his slight flinch that Cameron reacted to that. Maybe because he saw something of her face in Isaac's?

"Gilly could have arranged the swap," Lauren went on. "She was afraid of Trace, and if she knew she was dying, this might have been her way of preventing Trace from getting his hands on their child."

Though it sickened her to think that Gilly, a woman she considered her friend, would have intentionally done something like this since it could have put Lauren's own precious son in danger.

"Gilly wouldn't do that," Cameron insisted. "If she was worried about her baby's safety, she would have gotten word to me."

"Maybe. But Gilly was dying. Scared. And they'd had trouble getting in touch with you."

He flinched again, and she knew why. Cameron had

gotten caught up in a lockdown at the prison, where he'd gone to interview a potential witness. He'd been trapped there for hours with no way to leave and get to his sister even though she'd gone into labor.

"But Gilly might not have done this," Lauren added a moment later.

Mercy, she wished she'd rehearsed this or something because it was hard for her to put her line of thinking into words. Equally hard for her to imagine it had happened. "My late husband was Alden Lange, and his business partner or his sister could be the one responsible. They both hate me. Or at least they hate that I have control over Alden's estate."

The flat look Cameron gave her told her he wasn't buying that. And she hoped she was wrong. Because both Alden's sister, Julia, and his partner, Duane Tulley, could be very dangerous. They might have seen this as some sick mind game to watch her suffer. Of course, her suffering could also be profitable for them if it led to one or both of them getting their hands on Alden's money.

"How would Trace or any of these other people have gotten into the hospital nursery to switch babies?" he asked.

Lauren didn't have the answer to that, either. "It must have been an inside job since the babies wear bracelets with security chips that would trigger an alarm if they were carried out of the hospital. I'd just started checking out the medical staff when I was attacked."

He made a sound, a rumble deep in his throat. "And why did you do that? What made you suspicious?"

"I kept thinking it was strange that I would look at my son and see you." She waved that off before he could say anything about it. She didn't want to talk about why the image of Cameron's face was still so clear in her head after all these years and after all the bad stuff that'd gone on between them.

"I had a DNA test done," she went on. "So I could compare Patrick's DNA to mine. I'm supposed to get the results back any day now, but I made the mistake of asking the housekeeper if there was anything still around with Alden's DNA on it." She'd cursed herself for doing that. "I wanted to have the complete DNA results, but I think the housekeeper told Alden's sister what I'd asked for."

At least Cameron hadn't simply dismissed her. He tipped his head to the trail. "We'll get your son and sort this out." Lauren was about to blow out a breath of relief, but then Cameron added, "For the record, I don't believe there was a swap. Isaac is my nephew. But if Duane and Julia are bad news like you think they are, then they could have been the ones behind your attack."

He took her by the arm again to get her moving, but Lauren dug in her heels. "I can't risk bringing my brothers into this yet. Those thugs who attacked me could have connections to Duane and Julia, and they could find out I'm here."

This huff was even louder than his last one. "Look, Gabriel is the sheriff, and my boss. As well as your brother. No way would he risk putting you in danger. I'll just go inside, call him on his personal line and have him come out here."

"No." She couldn't say that fast enough. "I heard those men say if my family got in the way, they would have to kill them."

She hated when his skeptical look returned. Because

she had the same skepticism. "I know those thugs could have wanted me to hear what they were saying, that they could have been feeding me information. But why would they have done that, then shoot me and try to take Patrick?"

"That's what we'll find out—as soon as I call Gabriel." He tightened his grip on her arm and managed to drag her a few steps.

"They could be watching the front of your house from the road. They could be watching Gabriel's and Jameson's places, too. That's why I used the trail. Only the locals know it's there, and it's not easy to spot unless you're looking for it."

Cameron couldn't argue with that, not the last part anyway, even though it looked as if he wanted to dispute something. *Anything.* "We'll go in through the back of my house. Even hired guns won't be suspicious if they see the sheriff dropping by to visit with one of his deputies."

Lauren wasn't so sure of that at all. Anything out of the ordinary might trigger those men to shoot again. And this time, Isaac and anyone else who happened to be around could get hurt. If the gunmen were truly out there, they could be looking for any sign she was there, and Gabriel's visit might give her away.

"I shouldn't have come here," Lauren said under her breath. She lifted her head, making direct eye contact with Cameron. "But I just had to know if Isaac's really my son. Don't get me wrong. I love Patrick with all my heart, but I had to find out the truth."

Cameron hesitated, volleying glances at the house, the woods and her. Just when she thought he was about to give in and let her go inside, she heard something.

Footsteps. Cameron heard them, too, because he pushed her behind him and aimed his gun in the direction of the sound.

Someone was running toward them.

Oh, God. Had something happened to Patrick?

Nothing could have kept Lauren behind Cameron. She snatched her gun from his left hand and would have taken off toward her car, but she finally saw something.

Something that stopped her cold.

Dara. The nanny had Patrick clutched to her chest, and she was running—fast. Probably as fast as she could go.

"They found us," Dara shouted. "Run!"

Chapter Three

Cameron hadn't been sure of what he was going to do, but there was no time left to debate it now. All of his lawman's instincts told him that the stark fear in the woman's voice was real.

So was that baby she had gripped in her arms.

A little blond-haired boy who was about the same size as Isaac.

Cameron forced himself not to think that everything Lauren had told him was real. If this was truly his nephew, anything he felt about that would have to wait. Right now he had to get them to safety.

"Get inside the house," Cameron told Lauren.

She didn't listen, of course. Neither would he if that'd been his child out there. Lauren started to run toward the nanny, but Cameron hurried in front of her. The moment he got to the woman and child, he hooked his arm around them, maneuvering them in front of him, and he got them running again.

"Keep watch around us," Cameron told Lauren.

Maybe that would stop the panic he saw rising in her eyes. It was also something that needed to be done. Because if those two armed thugs were on their tail, then they had to get inside—fast—but they also needed to make sure they weren't about to be gunned down. If necessary, they would have to take cover before they even reached the house.

The little boy wasn't out and out crying, but he was whimpering. Probably because he'd picked up on their fear and because the running was jostling him. Cameron tried to ignore the sounds he was making, and he got them on the porch. He had to fumble in his pocket to get his keys to unlock the door, but the moment he did that, he pushed them inside.

"Get on the floor," he ordered.

Cameron relocked the door, set the security alarm and went to the window to keep watch. He also fired off a text to Gabriel, asking him to come over. Lauren's brother didn't live far and could be there in minutes if he hadn't already left for work. If so, then Gabriel would have to drive back.

A lot could happen in those extra minutes it would take Gabriel to do that.

Cameron still had a much too clear image of the bandage on Lauren's shoulder where she'd been shot. Those goons could be returning now to finish her off.

Lauren scrambled to the nanny, taking Patrick into her arms and pulling him close. There were tears in her eyes again, and she was trembling. The nanny wasn't faring much better. Hell, neither was he. Cameron wasn't trembling the way they were, but he was worried because they had two babies in the house, and he might not be able to protect them if those gunmen started shooting.

"I saw an SUV coming up the trail," the nanny said. Her breath was gusting so hard that it was difficult to understand her. "I couldn't drive off since there were trees blocking the way so I got out and started running with Patrick."

Yeah, there were downed trees back there. Probably shrubs, too, since it wasn't a trail that was often used.

"It could turn out to be nothing," the nanny added in a hoarse whisper. "They might not be the men who were after us."

Judging from her tone, she didn't think that was true. Neither did Cameron. It was too much of a coincidence for someone to show up on that trail so soon after Lauren had been shot.

"Did you get a glimpse of anyone in the SUV?" he asked the woman.

"Barely. I could just make out the outline of the driver behind the tinted glass. I think there was another man in the passenger seat."

Maybe the same two who had attacked Lauren in Dallas. If so, they'd come a long way. And they had probably had some inside help since Lauren had been right about the trail. Not many people outside the area knew it existed. Of course, a police officer might know because they could have tapped into the area maps that were in the database at San Antonio PD.

Hell, he hoped they weren't dealing with dirty cops.

"Is everything okay?" someone called out from the other side of the house. Merilee.

That tightened the knot in his stomach. He could tell Merilee was terrified, as well. She'd been Isaac's nanny right from the start, and since there'd already been two attacks on the ranch, she knew something was wrong.

"Just stay put in the nursery," Cameron settled for saying. He didn't want to unnecessarily alarm the woman even though she was probably well past the alarm stage already.

Cameron also had a second reason for keeping Merilee and Isaac where they were. This way, Lauren wouldn't see Isaac. Of course, she would see him soon enough, but right now he needed her to focus. If Lauren saw him and truly believed he was her son, then she might fall apart.

"Hand Patrick to Dara," Cameron told Lauren. "I need you to keep watch at the window on the side of the house."

He hated to ask her to do that, but right now she was their best bet. Besides, he knew Lauren could shoot since he'd been the one to teach her.

She gave a shaky nod, passed the baby back to the nanny and with a tight grip on her gun, she went to the window near the breakfast table. He didn't have to remind her to stay back. She did. Lauren positioned herself against the side of the glass so she could still peer out.

"Nothing," she relayed to him.

It was the same from his view. That didn't mean the men weren't out there, though. Lauren had been out there for a while before he'd spotted her. Plus, it was possible the men were regrouping, maybe calling for their own backup so they could storm the place and take the baby.

But why?

That was something he intended to find out once they were out of any immediate danger.

Behind him, Patrick started fussing, and he made the mistake of glancing back at the boy. Cameron hadn't been able to see his face earlier when the nanny was running toward them. He saw it now, though.

Oh, man.

It felt like someone had knocked the breath right out of him. The kid had blond hair, and those were definitely the Doran gray eyes. In fact, the resemblance was close enough that Patrick could have been mistaken for Cameron's own son. He wasn't.

But the boy was his nephew.

Cameron silently cursed. This was not what he wanted in his head right now, but it was a fight to keep the thoughts at bay. What the hell was he going to do?

He forced his attention back to the window just as the sound shot through the room. Clearly, everyone was on edge because both Lauren and the nanny gasped. But it wasn't a shot being fired. It was just his phone ringing, and Cameron saw Gabriel's name on the screen. Good. Maybe that meant the sheriff was there.

Cameron put the call on speaker, laying his phone on the counter so his hands would be free in case there was an attack.

"What the hell is going on?" Gabriel demanded the moment he came onto the line.

Since he wasn't going to have time to get into everything, Cameron went with the short version. "Lauren's here, and some men are after her. They tried to kill her."

Gabriel cursed, but he quickly reined it in, no doubt because he realized his kid sister was listening. "Any reason she came to you and not me?"

Gabriel didn't rein in his emotions on that question. Cameron heard the anger come through loud and clear. The emotion was in Lauren's expression, too. Her forehead was bunched up, and she had her still-trembling bottom lip clamped between her teeth. With everything else she was facing, she probably didn't want a showdown with her brother, as well, but it was going to be on the agenda whether she wanted it or not.

"I'll explain it all later," Cameron told him, but he had to raise his voice to speak over Patrick. The baby was fussing even louder now. "The men who are after Lauren will be in an SUV," he added to Gabriel. "It's possible they're on the trail behind my house."

"They're not. I just spotted a black SUV coming up from the back of my folks' old place."

Cameron bit back a groan. The trails coiled all around the ranch, and the men had obviously found a way out of the woods. That meant they could be trying to escape so they could regroup and come at Lauren again. As much as Cameron hated the notion of that, at least it would give him a chance to get the babies, nannies and her to a safe place.

"The SUV isn't moving," Gabriel went on, "and I can't tell if anyone is still inside it. They could have already gotten out and slipped onto the ranch grounds."

Not exactly a comforting thought, but Gabriel was right. Cameron didn't know how long it'd taken the nanny to get to Lauren and him, but the thugs could have driven off the moment she started running. If so, that would have given them plenty of time to get to the old Beckett house, and then the chance to escape.

Or sneak up on Cameron's house.

"I've stopped on the road and am waiting for Jameson," Gabriel continued a moment later. "Once he's here, we can go closer. Why do they want Lauren?" he tacked onto that.

"She's not sure yet." But it gnawed away at him to

think it could be because of his sister's scummy dead boyfriend. "Just give me a heads-up if you see these clowns."

"Will do. Is that Isaac crying?"

"No. It's… Lauren's son." Cameron hadn't meant to hesitate, but it'd just seemed to stick in his throat.

Gabriel's silence let Cameron know it hadn't been easy for him to hear. That was probably because Lauren hadn't bothered to introduce her son to the rest of her family. Even though things had been strained between Lauren and him since their parents' murders, it still had to cut Gabriel to the core. For him, it was all about family, and he'd worked damn hard to bring his siblings back to their birthplace.

Cameron ended the call, and he went to the back door to look out the small windows there. The angle was better for giving him a view of the opposite side of the yard that Lauren was watching. The SUV was the other direction, but it didn't mean the thugs couldn't have brought some help along.

"I think I see something," Lauren said.

That sent Cameron running to her, and he followed her pointing finger in the direction of the far side of his barn. Since the barn was closer to the old Beckett house than Cameron's, it would be a likely place for someone to hide.

But he didn't see anything.

"I'm obviously on edge," Lauren admitted. "It could have been my imagination."

She looked up at him at the exact moment he looked down at her, and it seemed as if there was something else she wanted to say to him. An apology, maybe, but the silence said it all. Because she'd been giving him the silent treatment for the past decade. No reason for this to be any different.

He kept watch, but even though he didn't see anything, it didn't mean someone wasn't out there. Which made him rethink their position. There were way too many windows in this part of the house. Plus, it was hard to hear anything with Patrick crying.

"Stay low," Cameron instructed the nanny, "but take the baby to the nursery. It's the first room off the hall." He tipped his head in that direction. "Go with them," he added to Lauren.

But she shook her head. "You need me to help you keep watch. I don't want those men getting in the house."

Neither did he, but Cameron had figured she'd want to be with her baby. And she probably did. However, like him, Lauren almost certainly knew things could turn on a dime.

"Merilee?" he called out. "A woman and little boy are joining you in the nursery. Once they're in there, lock the door, and all of you get down on the floor."

"What's happening?" Merilee asked. "Are you okay?"

"I'm fine. Lauren is here," he said after a pause.

Merilee would remember Lauren since she'd been the Beckett housekeeper all the way up until the time of the murders. Lauren's mom was a former cop who also worked the ranch, and Merilee had been a pseudo-nanny to Lauren and her siblings.

He nearly asked about Isaac, to make sure his nephew was all right, but right now Cameron only wanted to focus on what was going on outside. Besides, if something had been wrong in the nursery, Merilee would have let him know.

"Thank you," Lauren whispered.

Cameron was about to tell her not to thank him yet, but the movement stopped him cold. This time he saw what Lauren had almost certainly spotted by the barn.

A man.

He only got a glimpse of him, but the guy was wearing camo. Definitely not a ranch hand.

"He's got a gun," Lauren relayed to Cameron.

Yeah, he'd seen it, too. Again, just a glimpse, but it appeared to be a rifle. Not good because it gave the intruder a longer range that he could use to shoot into the house.

Without taking his attention off the man, Cameron pressed redial on his phone, and Gabriel answered on the first ring.

"Jameson's here," Gabriel explained. "We're going to the SUV now."

"Don't. One of the shooters is here at my place by the side of my barn. I figure he's not alone."

Gabriel made a sound of agreement followed by some profanity. "Okay, we're on the way to your place. I'll also get some of the hands over there."

"Tell them to be careful. The guy is armed, and he's in position to pick off anyone who comes up the road to my house."

And that was probably the reason he was there. Which made that bad feeling inside him go up a significant notch. If these goons knew the trail, maybe they'd watched the place. Perhaps his house. It wouldn't have been hard to do. On any given day there were at least two dozen hands working the ranch along with deliveries and the normal traffic that came with a place this size.

There could be gunmen waiting to ambush Gabriel, Jameson and anyone else who came this way.

Because if their ultimate goal was to get the baby, then it wouldn't matter how many people they killed.

He hated to put something else on Lauren's shoulders, but he needed an extra pair of eyes at the front of the house. That meant he'd have to stay to keep watch of the thug by the barn. Cameron was about to give her instructions as to what to do, but the blur of motion stopped him.

There was a second gunman at the back of the barn.

Unlike his partner, this one didn't immediately duck back behind cover. He lifted his rifle and fired. The shot crashed through the window right where Cameron was standing.

Chapter Four

Lauren shouted for Cameron to get down, but it was already too late. The gunman had fired the shot, the bullet blasting through the window.

In the blink of an eye, she saw a piece of glass slice across Cameron's arm. He was wearing a shirt, and she could immediately see the blood start to spread across the sleeve.

She ran to him, but Lauren wasn't quite able to reach his arm. That was because Cameron took hold of her and dragged her to the floor. But he didn't stay there. He got right back up and took aim out the now gaping hole in the window.

"You're hurt," she said, her breath gusting so hard that Lauren had trouble speaking.

"I'm okay," he grumbled.

But she had no idea if that was true. She couldn't tell if the glass was still in his arm or not because of all the blood.

From the other side of the house, Lauren heard a sound she didn't want to hear. Patrick was crying. Probably because the noise from the gunshot had frightened him. She considered going to him, but she didn't want to leave Cameron alone. She got confirmation that would be a bad idea when two more shots came through the window. These slammed into the side of the fridge.

"Merilee!" Cameron called out to the nanny. "All of you need to get down on the floor and stay there." He glanced at her then, letting Lauren know that applied to her, too.

However, she shook her head. "If I go to the side window, I might have a clear shot and be able to stop the gunman."

"Yeah, and he might have a shot to stop you. Stay down," he repeated, this time through clenched teeth. She couldn't tell if the tight expression was for her or because he was grimacing in pain.

Lauren huffed. She'd forgotten just how stubborn Cameron could be, but this brought it all back. Worse, he didn't stay out of the line of fire. He leaned away from the wall, took aim out the window and pulled the trigger.

The blast echoed through the room. Through the entire house. And Lauren heard both babies cry. She prayed the nannies could keep the boys as calm as possible, but better yet, she just wanted the women to protect them so that none of the bullets could make it to them.

Her son was in danger.

Both her sons.

Because Isaac might be hers by blood, but Patrick was also hers in every way that mattered. Now the babies were at huge risk, and she didn't even know why. That was what cut away at her right now. That, and the bullets that continued to tear into the house.

She thought of what Cameron had said earlier. About Trace's mother, Evelyn, pulling a gun on him. And Lauren wondered if she was behind this. But she couldn't be. For one thing, the woman was in jail, and for another, she wanted custody of her grandson and almost certainly wouldn't put him at risk like this.

But Julia or Duane were capable of that.

They wouldn't have nearly the level of concern for Patrick or any other child that Evelyn likely would. In fact, it would make things easier for Julia or Duane if Lauren and her son were out of the way.

That certainly didn't help her raw nerves.

However, there was a third player in all of this. The idiot who was sending those threatening messages to her and her family. If so, they didn't have a clue who they were dealing with, and that person might not care if everyone inside the house died in a gunfight.

Cameron fired another shot, and he followed it with some profanity. "He's ducked back behind the barn."

Probably because Cameron's shots were getting too close to him. Lauren doubted, though, that the man was retreating. No. He was probably regrouping or else contacting his comrade so he could come at them from a different angle.

Cameron ran to the side of the room where Lauren had been earlier, but the moment he made it to that window, the gunman sent more bullets their way. That created yet another spray of glass over the room and caused Cameron to scramble back. Thankfully, he didn't get cut this time, and the bleeding on his arm seemed to be slowing down. Still, he needed medical attention. That wasn't going to happen, though, until those gunmen were stopped. No way could an ambulance risk coming to the house, since they would drive right into gunfire.

Cameron's phone rang, the sound somehow making it through the deafening blasts. He glanced at the screen and tossed it to her. "It's Gabriel. Let him know what's going on and find out his location."

Lauren cursed her trembling hands because it took her precious seconds to hit the answer button, and she put it on speaker so that Cameron could hear.

"Is everyone okay?" Gabriel asked right off.

"No. Cameron's hurt. His arm is bleeding—"

"I'm fine," Cameron snarled. "I've got a shooter by the barn and another out by the road."

That sped up her heartbeat even more because her brothers would be coming up that road to get to them. She prayed they didn't get hurt, or worse.

"Yeah, I've already spotted the one on the road," Gabriel answered. "That's why Jameson and I stopped. The guy's in the ditch. If he lifts his head enough, Jameson can take him out."

Good. Except that would mean Jameson would have to take a huge risk to do that. Lauren had no idea if that guy was firing at her brothers or not. It was hard to tell with all the bullets flying.

"What about you?" Gabriel continued. "Can you shoot the one by the barn?"

"Haven't managed it so far, but I can't keep letting him fire bullets into the house."

No, they couldn't. Each one was a huge risk to the babies. And that meant she needed to push aside her fears and do something. She was the daughter and sister of a sheriff and had had firearms training. While she certainly didn't have experience in finishing off hired guns, she had plenty of motivation to put an end to this.

"Are there only two of them?" Gabriel asked a moment later.

Good question, and she could tell from Cameron's

frustrated sigh that he didn't know the answer. "Two men attacked your sister last night and shot her in the arm so I'm guessing it's the same pair."

Gabriel cursed again, and Lauren recognized that tone after all these years. He was furious, and that fury wasn't limited to only these men, either. As her brother and the sheriff, he would have expected her to come to him with this. Later, she'd need to explain why she hadn't done that. But that would have to wait.

"I can try to distract the shooter by firing out the kitchen window," Lauren offered. "That way Cameron can try to get him from the front of the house."

That offer didn't please Cameron. It earned her a scowl, but she gave him one right back. "As you said, we can't let him keep firing shots."

She could see the debate Cameron was having with himself about that, but before he could say anything, his phone beeped, indicating he had another call coming in.

"It's from an unknown number," she relayed to him.

"Answer your phone, Deputy," the gunman shouted from outside. The shots also stopped. "We gotta talk."

"The thug by the barn is calling me," Cameron told Gabriel. "While I see what he wants, try to do something about the guy in the ditch. I don't want him getting any closer to the house."

"We'll do what we can," Gabriel assured him.

Lauren pressed the button to take the second call, and she crawled even closer to Cameron so he wouldn't miss a word of what this snake had to say.

"Are you ready to put an end to this?" the gunman asked without any hesitation. "Because I've got a solution that'll make sure your nephew and that other little boy don't get hurt."

"Who are you?" Cameron snapped.

"You don't need to know my name to listen to what I got to say."

"No, but I do need to know who hired you so I can put his or her butt in jail for multiple accounts of attempted murder."

The guy chuckled. "Let's just say that's not gonna happen and move on. You want me to stop shooting up your house, then here's what you have to do. Put Lauren on the phone so the two of us can talk this out."

A chill slid through her. Of course the goon knew she was there, but it was still stomach-twisting to hear him say her name. She opened her mouth to tell him she was listening, but Cameron shook his head and shot her a warning glance.

"Anything you think you need to say to Lauren, you can say to me," Cameron told the gunman.

"I don't think so. Something tells me you're not gonna be nearly as easy to reason with as she'll be." Considering his casual tone, he could have been discussing the weather, but Lauren knew there was nothing casual about any of this.

"You want money, is that it?" she asked.

That didn't please Cameron. No surprise there. He mumbled some profanity and hurried to the other side of the window—probably hoping he could get off a shot while the gunman was talking.

"Money?" the gunman repeated as if it was a joke. "No, sugar. Money ain't gonna fix this."

She hated his flippant attitude and wished she could be the one to silence him. But Lauren wanted that silence only after they'd learned who had hired this monster. Then him, his partner and his boss could be arrested.

"What, then?" she demanded, and Lauren hoped she sounded less shaky than she felt.

"I want you, sugar."

For just a handful of words, they packed a punch along with making her skin crawl. She wasn't sure if he'd meant for it to sound sexual or not.

"All you have to do is walk out the back door," the gunman continued. "Of course, I'm gonna want your hands in the air so I can make sure you don't have a gun. And I'll also want you to tell the deputy that he's out of the picture right now."

"You're not going out there," Cameron told her before the gunman had even finished.

"Figured you'd feel that way, but just think about those little kids. Do I hear them crying? Bet they're real scared, but they're gonna get a lot more scared when I start shooting again. Because once I start, I won't stop until I've ripped your place to shreds. You got thirty seconds, or the bullets start up again."

Lauren sucked in her breath so hard that she nearly choked, and she managed to get to her feet.

"No." Cameron hurried toward her, catching on to her and pulling her down against the fridge. He also took his phone from her and hit the end call button. "He'll gun you down the moment you step outside."

She shook her head, not disputing that since she figured that was exactly what would happen. Someone wanted her dead.

"But if I don't go out there, he'll shoot into the house," she reminded Cameron, though she was certain he hadn't forgotten that.

"He'll do it anyway." He took hold of her chin, lifting it and forcing eye contact. Brief eye contact, just enough for her to see the determination in his eyes before he went back to the window to keep watch. "Think it through. He'll have to kill me, too, so he can escape. In fact, this plan could be about me. A way to draw me out while using you. Because that snake knows I won't let you go to your death."

That last part was definitely true. Cameron wasn't a coward, and he was married to that badge he had clipped to his holster. He would put his own life ahead of hers or anyone else's that he needed to protect.

She tried to figure out if that was indeed what the gunman had in mind, but the thoughts were flying through her head, making it hard to think. The only thing that was coming through loud and clear was that she had to do something, anything, to save the babies.

Cameron glanced around, too, as if trying to sort out what to do, and he finally tipped his head to the front of the house. "Take your gun and go to the window in there. Stay to the side, but if you get a shot, take it."

She didn't thank him. In fact, Lauren didn't say anything for fear he would change his mind. As she was leaving, she heard him make a quick call to Gabriel to tell him to do something to eliminate the guy in the ditch.

Lauren's pulse was thudding so hard now that it was hard to hear, and her feet felt heavy, as if she was trudging through mud. Still, she moved as fast as she could and tried to ignore the sounds of the babies crying. She had to focus, had to do her part to make this right. Then she could deal with the fallout of the baby swap and everything else that her homecoming would cause.

There were three windows in the living room. A huge one that faced the front and two side ones that had a view of the barn. She went to the one that she hoped would give her the best vantage point.

It did.

She immediately caught a glimpse of the gunman, and he was lifting his rifle, pointing it right at the house. That put her heart in her throat. She hadn't needed anything to add to the urgency of their situation, but that did it anyway.

Lauren didn't waste even a second. She broke the glass with the barrel of her gun and took aim. The gunman shifted his position, trying to turn his weapon at her. But it was too late.

She fired.

And she was right on target. The bullet slammed into the guy's chest. He stayed there, frozen and crouched, his rifle ready, but neither he nor his gun moved. So, Lauren shot him again.

He finally dropped like a stone.

Despite the fact that she'd probably just killed a man, she only felt relief and not the emotion of having just taken a life. That was because if he'd been given the chance, he would have killed them all.

She heard the footsteps, hurrying toward her. Cameron. From his angle in the kitchen, he probably hadn't been able to see the fall, but he certainly saw it now. There was no relief on his face, though, because they heard something else.

Another shot.

This one hadn't come from the barn. It had come from the front of the house, and it wasn't a single shot, either. Three more quickly followed.

There was no trace of relief now for Lauren. Because she knew her brothers were in the general direction of that fresh round of bullets. Maybe the gunman's partner had figured out what had gone on by the barn and was now trying to take out anyone that he could.

Lauren turned to run to the front window, but Cameron moved in front of her. "Watch the guy you shot and make sure he doesn't get up."

She was about to tell him that she doubted that could happen, but there was more gunfire. Then Cameron cursed when he looked out the front window.

"Change of plans," he said. "Get down now."

There was more than enough urgency in his voice for Lauren to drop to the floor, but she'd barely had time to do that when Cameron threw open the front door. The security system started to beep, indicating the alarm was about to go off. He ignored that, though, aimed his gun and fired. He got off four rounds before he stopped pulling the trigger.

Lauren waited, praying and afraid to ask what had happened. Several moments later she heard something she actually wanted to hear.

Gabriel's voice.

"Is everyone okay?" her brother called out.

Since the babies were still fussing, Lauren knew they were alive, but she got up to hurry to the nursery to make sure. But she stopped when she saw the chaos in front of Cameron's house.

Two men dressed in camo were sprawled out by the ditch. The one nearest the house was clearly dead, but the other one was still moving around. Both Jameson and Gabriel had their weapons drawn and were closing in on him.

Her stomach sank. Lauren hadn't even known about the third gunman. He could have attacked them from the front while the thug by the barn was keeping them occupied. Thank God Cameron and her brothers had spotted him and stopped him from doing any more harm.

"I had to shoot him," Cameron said. He pressed in the numbers on the security key pad to stop the beeping. "I didn't have a choice."

It took her a moment to realize why that sounded like an apology. It was because two of their attackers were dead, and the third one was injured. Maybe even dying. Dead men wouldn't be able to tell them the person or the reason behind what had just happened.

"Stay inside," Cameron added. "But keep watch to make sure there aren't others."

Lauren hadn't exactly relaxed, but that put her back on high alert again. So did the fact that Cameron hurried outside. Where he could be gunned down like her brothers if there were other thugs hiding.

Even though Cameron had told her to stay inside, Lauren got her gun ready and stepped into the doorway so she'd have a better view of the yard and road. Her brothers were already by the injured man by the time Cameron reached them. She could see them talking, but she couldn't hear what they were saying.

But she had no trouble seeing the alarm on Cameron's face.

Whatever the man had said to him had caused Cameron's shoulders to snap back. Her brothers had similar reactions, and Gabriel took out his phone as he made his way to the house. Cameron and Jameson were right behind him. That was when Lauren realized the injured man was no longer moving.

Gabriel made eye contact with her, and while he continued his phone conversation, he caught on to her arm and maneuvered her back inside the house.

"What about the man?" she asked.

"He's dead," Cameron told her the moment he reached the porch.

The sickening feeling of dread went through her. "Did he say anything?" But Lauren fully expected that answer to be no.

It wasn't.

Cameron nodded. "He gave us the name of the person who hired him." His mouth tightened when he made eye contact with Lauren. "The gunman said it was *you*."

Chapter Five

"I didn't hire those men," Lauren repeated.

It wasn't necessary for her to keep saying that. Cameron hadn't believed it from the moment the thug had tossed out that stupid accusation. Those men had been firing real bullets into the house as well as at Lauren and him, and there was no way she would have put her son in danger that way.

Either son.

Because Cameron was also certain she was already thinking of both boys as hers. They weren't. But that was something they would have to sort out later.

For now, they needed to get to the bottom of why the attack had happened. Gabriel and Jameson were already on that. Lauren's brothers were outside with the medical examiner and the CSIs. The ambulance, too. There'd been no need for medical assistance for the gunmen—they were all dead. But the medics were apparently there for Lauren and him.

Whether they wanted them there or not.

Cameron certainly didn't. He wanted to be outside with the other lawmen, trying to get answers, but instead he was on the sofa in his living room while a medic stitched up his arm. Another medic was checking out Lauren's gunshot wound, as well.

"This isn't necessary," Lauren insisted. It was yet something else she'd been repeating.

Cameron didn't bother to voice his complaint since Gabriel had told him he wouldn't be returning to work until the medic gave him the okay. So far, the guy wasn't okaying anything. He was causing Cameron plenty of pain with each stitch. Of course, that was a small price to pay considering they were all alive and, for the most part, well.

"Is it okay if we come out now?" Merilee called out.

It had been well over a half hour since the attack had ended. If the thugs had brought any other hired guns with them, those guys would probably be long gone. But it still seemed too big of a risk to take.

"Let's call this finished," Cameron told the medic, and even though the guy gave him a hard look, he put in the last stitch and slapped on a bandage.

"Stay put. I'll come to the nursery," Cameron added to Merilee.

That got Lauren moving, too, and despite the fact that the medic was still dabbing something on her arm, she jerked away from him, following Cameron when he started out of the living room and up the hall. Both medics grumbled something that Cameron didn't bother to hear. He needed to see Isaac to make sure for himself that both boys were all right.

Lauren was right on his heels when Cameron knocked on the door. Merilee must have been right there waiting because she opened up right away. She didn't have Isaac in her arms, but Cameron spotted him. He was on the floor, playing with Patrick. Dara was next to both of them.

Cameron felt the punch of relief. Yes, he'd known the boys hadn't been harmed. He'd gotten that reassurance minutes after the attack when he'd been able to talk to Merilee. So had Lauren. But she also must have needed more because she hurried to the boys, kissing them both.

Kisses that got Merilee's attention.

The nanny looked at him, her eyebrow raised. "I'll explain later," Cameron whispered to her. "Thanks for keeping them safe."

"Is it actually safe?" Merilee questioned before Cameron could step away.

"No," he admitted after a pause. "We don't know who hired those men."

And he needed to figure out what to do about that. His house was in too vulnerable of a spot on the ranch since it was backed up against the woods and those trails. Added to that, there were now broken windows, so he would need to move Lauren, the boys and the nannies. First, though, he needed to see Isaac.

The boys were no longer fussing. In fact, they were looking a little confused—Isaac, especially—at the long hug that Lauren was giving them. When Cameron sank down on the edge of one of the chairs, Isaac scooted out of her grip and immediately went to him.

"Nunk," Isaac babbled. It was his attempt at uncle, and it always made Cameron smile. Even more. And while he hugged Isaac often, this hug was especially needed.

Of course, Isaac didn't let the hug go on for long. He was a kid always on the go, and the moment Cameron stood him on the floor, Isaac toddled his way back to Patrick. He dropped down next to him, where there was a huge pile of toy cars and horses.

Seeing them side by side put a knot in Cameron's stomach. If he'd had any doubts about the baby swap, he didn't have them now. He could see his sister, and himself, in Patrick's face, while Isaac was a Beckett. Cameron hadn't seen it before because he hadn't been looking for it.

Hell.

What was he going to do now?

Lauren looked up at him at the exact moment that Cameron looked at her. She didn't say anything, but she seemed to be waiting for something. Maybe for him to offer some perfect solution to fix all of this. But at the moment he was drawing a blank because the one thing he wasn't going to do was give up the little boy he'd been raising for over a year. He couldn't have loved his own son more than he loved Isaac.

Cameron automatically reached for his gun again when he heard someone coming up the hall. He stood, stepping in front of the others, but it wasn't a threat this time. It was Gabriel and Jameson.

Lauren stood, slowly, and she rubbed her hands along the sides of her jeans. Her brothers didn't exactly run to her, either, and Cameron figured they needed some time to hash this out. After all, Lauren had basically abandoned them, but again, that was something that would have to wait.

"Cameron told us about the possible baby switch," Gabriel said, his voice not exactly warm and fuzzy.

She looked at Cameron, probably wondering when he'd had a chance to do that. It'd been in the yard when he'd managed to have a very short conversation with Gabriel while they were waiting for the medics to arrive. And Cameron had indeed added that word—*possible*. But Gabriel and Jameson were no doubt seeing what Cameron had—Patrick's resemblance to them.

Jameson huffed, went to Lauren and pulled her into his arms. "You shouldn't have stayed away," he whispered to her, but since the room was suddenly quiet, Cameron had no trouble hearing.

"I couldn't," she answered. When Lauren pulled back, she was blinking back tears. "Not after what happened to Mom and Dad. I just couldn't stay."

Gabriel didn't argue with that. Not with his voice anyway. But that wasn't exactly a forgiving look in his eyes.

Of course, Cameron hadn't expected there to be. Like Gabriel and Jameson, he'd stayed in Blue River. He'd dealt with the aftermath, had helped put a killer behind bars and then had tried to pick up the pieces and use them to build a new life. Lauren hadn't done that, and it'd cut Gabriel to the core that he hadn't been able to keep the family together.

"Uh, should Dara and I take the boys to one of the other rooms?" Merilee asked after glancing at Gabriel's expression.

"No," Lauren answered without hesitation. Cameron agreed. He didn't want the babies out of his sight for now. If Lauren's brothers were going to have words with her, they'd have to keep it G-rated.

Lauren kissed Jameson on the cheek, and she went to Gabriel. Her steps were tentative and so was the kiss on the cheek she gave him.

"I don't expect you to understand what I did," she

said, her voice a little shaky now. "And I'm sorry for bringing this danger to the ranch."

Gabriel stared at her, the muscles in his jaw battling each other. He seemed to be ready to start that tirade that was bubbling inside him, but he reached out, pulled Lauren to him and kissed the top of her head. It would have been a perfect moment if Lauren hadn't winced. It wasn't from the kiss, though. It was because of the pressure the hug was putting on her injured arm.

She stepped back, both her and Gabriel's gazes going to the fresh bandage, and Cameron figured Gabriel would have cursed if it hadn't been for the little ears in the room.

"You should have come to me when the trouble started," Gabriel insisted.

Lauren shook her head. "I thought the men who did this were cops."

"They weren't," Gabriel said without hesitation. "And I don't need ID's on them to know that."

Jameson made a sound of agreement, went to the babies and sank down on the floor next to them. "The one who accused you of hiring him had a prison tat on his neck. Plus, this wasn't the kind of attack a cop would do. Not a smart cop anyway. If they'd been the real deal, they could have gone to your house, flashed their badges and gained entry that way. You're the daughter and sister of cops, and you would have let them in."

Now it was Lauren who made a sound of agreement after making a soft moan. "I panicked. I didn't want them to get to Patrick."

Gabriel nodded. "Panicking is exactly what they wanted you to do because it caused you to run."

Her brother hadn't come out and said it, but he likely

believed that it'd caused Lauren to run to the wrong man—Cameron. In Gabriel's way of thinking, she should have gone to him, immediately, and that way he could have perhaps prevented this attack.

"So, how did this baby swap happen?" Jameson asked.

It was the question that had been repeating through Cameron's mind. "Gilly maybe orchestrated it," he admitted.

Gabriel looked ready to mumble some more profanity, but he bit it off when he glanced at the boys. "To protect her son from Evelyn and that scumbag boyfriend of hers."

Cameron hated that his sister had been in a position like that, and he also hated he hadn't been there to give her another option.

"We need to start from the beginning," Gabriel continued a moment later. "We'll need DNA tests on the boys—"

"I've already done one on Patrick," Lauren volunteered. "I'm waiting on the results now."

"Good. But we have to do Isaac's, as well, and we should repeat Patrick's, too, and compare it to Cameron's." Gabriel looked at Cameron as if questioning to see if he was opposed to that. He wasn't. What Cameron was opposed to, though, was the fallout.

"I love Isaac," Cameron admitted. He hadn't intended to say that aloud. It was stating the obvious, and that *obvious* was true for Lauren, too. She loved Patrick.

Gabriel didn't need for them to spell out where this would eventually lead. To some kind of custody issues. Maybe a huge legal battle if Lauren tried to go after both boys.

"If the DNA results prove there was a switch," Gabriel went on, "then the next step will be to get hospital surveillance footage to see if we can spot who's responsible. In the meantime, I can get someone to the jail to question Evelyn."

"I can do that," Jameson volunteered, and he stood, taking his cell from his pocket. He was about to make a call, but the ringing shot through the room. Not Jameson's phone, though, but Lauren's.

She looked at her phone screen as if steeling herself up for what she might see there. Probably because she thought this could be another attacker. But she didn't look afraid. She groaned, a sound of frustration.

"It's Julia," she explained. "My late husband's sister."

Good. While it was obvious Lauren didn't want to talk to the woman, Cameron wanted to hear what she had to say. Especially since Julia could be a suspect in this. Of course, the most obvious person was Evelyn, and it didn't matter if she was locked up. People could do all sorts of bad things from behind bars.

"She calls you often?" Cameron asked.

"Rarely. And it's never a pleasant conversation. We talk mainly through our lawyers these days."

Lauren stepped out of the room, but Cameron followed her. Anything that happened right now could be related to the investigation, and he wanted to hear what Lauren's sister-in-law had to say. Lauren obliged by putting the call on speaker. She also moved as far up the hall as she could go.

"What the hell is going on?" Julia immediately demanded. No wonder Lauren had been dreading this. The woman was clearly hostile.

"I was about to ask you the same thing," Lauren countered without even pausing. "Someone tried to kill me, and I need to know if you had anything to do with that?"

"What? You'd better not be accusing me of something like that."

Cameron considered holding his tongue but then decided against it. "Lauren is fine, by the way. Good of you to ask."

"I don't care if she's fine," Julia spat out. "And who the hell are you anyway?"

"Deputy Cameron Doran," Lauren answered. If she was bothered by Cameron inserting himself into this conversation, she didn't show it. She just gave another weary sigh.

"Your old boyfriend." Julia said that as if Cameron were some kind of disease. "Yes, I know about you. I know everything about Lauren. She moaned out your name when she was under anesthesia after having an emergency appendectomy. *Cameron, Cameron*, she kept saying, so I did an internet search and found out you were a deputy in that hick town she comes from."

Cameron wasn't sure how to respond to that especially since the color began to rise in Lauren's cheeks. Maybe she hadn't wanted him to know that she'd thought about him over the years. It didn't mean anything, though. People in pain said all sorts of things that just happened to fall from their memories.

"Well, Deputy, are you the reason I had two cops at my house last night?" Julia demanded.

Cameron glanced at Lauren to see if she knew anything about that, but she only shook her head. "What cops?" Cameron pressed.

"How the heck should I know? Guys with badges. I saw them on the security camera outside my house and didn't answer the door. That's because I figured Lauren had sent them."

Lauren huffed. "And why would I do that?"

"To upset me. To try to intimidate me into backing off from the lawsuit. But guess what? I'm not backing off. *Ever.* My brother and I built his company—together. You didn't have anything to do with that. And it should be mine."

"Obviously Alden didn't agree with that because he left the company to Patrick."

Julia cursed, and it was pretty raw. "Because he didn't have time to change his will before he died. You saw to that, I'm sure. Always bad-mouthing me to him."

"I didn't need to bad-mouth you." Unlike Julia, Lauren's voice was practically calm. "Alden knew what you were."

Julia's profanity got even worse. The woman had a temper, and even though Cameron didn't need any more incentive for her to be a suspect, that only made him realize he needed to start digging into Julia's financials.

"Alden was stupid," Julia went on. "You had him eating right out of your hand. Hell, the kid doesn't even look like him, and yet he was willing to hand over a fortune to him."

Everything inside Cameron went still, and he reached out and muted the call for a moment. "Does Julia know about the baby swap?"

"No." But then Lauren shook her head again. "At least she's never given me any indication that she knew."

Well, that comment was definitely some kind of *indication*.

Cameron unmuted the phone. "Did you hire gunmen to come after Lauren?" he came out and asked the woman.

"I'm not going to dignify that with a response. Just tell her to quit sending cops to my house."

"I didn't send them," Lauren insisted, but she was talking to the air because Julia launched into another verbal tirade.

"No one else would have had a reason to send them. It had to be you."

"They might not have been cops," Cameron interrupted. "The men who tried to kill Lauren pretended to be police officers. Your visitors could have come to your house to kill you."

Julia gasped. "Why?"

"I don't know," Cameron answered. "Maybe for the same reason they attacked Lauren. You said you saw the men on your security camera. Do you have footage we can study to see if we can try to identify them?"

"Maybe. I'll look." But she made it sound as if it'd be some big inconvenience. "Have you asked Duane if he has footage?"

Again, Lauren looked puzzled enough by Julia's comment that Cameron knew she was hearing this for the first time.

"Duane?" he questioned. Of course, Cameron had already heard the man's name. He was Alden's business partner, but he wasn't sure how the guy fit into this. Or even if he did fit.

"Duane Tulley," Julia snapped. "He called me about a half hour ago and said cops came to his house, too. He wasn't there. He was staying overnight with his girlfriend, but he has a remote security system and saw the men on the camera."

"Was it the same men who came to your place?" Cameron asked.

"Who knows. Maybe. Lauren, so help me, you'd better not be behind this."

"I'm not—" But that was all Lauren managed to say before Julia continued.

"Just keep me out of your problems. The lawsuit is going before a judge next month, and I don't want you playing games to try to sway this to your side."

Cameron was certain he looked just as puzzled as Lauren did. "You think I'd fake an attack to get sympathy from a judge?"

"Yes, I do." And with that, Julia ended the call.

Lauren stared at the phone for a moment before she gave a heavy sigh and slid it back into her pocket. "Now you know why I thought Julia could be behind this. My sister-in-law hates me."

No way could Cameron argue with that. "Just how much money is at stake in Alden's estate?"

"At least twenty million."

Well, hell. That was plenty of motive for Julia to do all sorts of things. Including hiring someone to murder Lauren. That would definitely get Lauren out of the way and would give Julia control not just of the money but Patrick, as well.

Or rather, Isaac.

It twisted his insides to think of that woman having any kind of claim on the baby Cameron loved.

"I'll have to speak to Duane," Cameron told her. "I not only need the security tapes but I'll also need to question him." Julia, too, of course. "I'm guessing Duane has motive for wanting you dead?"

Lauren nodded, pushed her hair from her face. "It

all goes back to the money. But if he could get Julia, Patrick and me out of the picture, Duane would inherit everything."

Cameron could see how that might play out. And that was playing out in a very bad way. "Duane could have hired those men to kill you with plans to set up Julia. Then he could use DNA proof to verify that Patrick isn't Alden's son."

He watched as Lauren processed that and saw the exact moment she followed that through to what could happen next.

Duane would need to make Isaac disappear.

Because Isaac could indeed be Alden's rightful heir.

Hell, he needed to bring Duane in ASAP, too. But first he had to work on making sure Lauren and the babies were safe.

"I'm sorry," Lauren said, drawing his attention back to her.

The apology irritated him since this wasn't her fault. Well, for the most part anyway. Gabriel was right that she should have gone to him when this had first started, but she certainly didn't need to be feeling any regret about that.

She blinked hard, obviously still fighting those tears, and Cameron had to do some fighting of his own. He wanted to pull her into his arms, to try to reassure her that all would be well. But it was best not to break down the barriers Lauren had put up when she'd left town. Besides, he wasn't ready to forgive himself, either, for letting Travis walk that night of the murders.

"Yes," she said as if she knew exactly what he was thinking.

Lauren touched his arm, rubbed gently and then

headed back toward the nursery. However, she didn't make it far before they spotted Jameson coming out of the room. He had a troubled look on his face.

Hell. What now?

"There could be a problem, and you both need to come back to the nursery," Jameson told them.

That got Lauren and Cameron moving plenty fast, but when they hurried into the room, the babies were fine. They were still playing on the floor, and the nannies were there with them. It looked like nothing was wrong.

Until he made eye contact with Merilee.

Cameron saw the fear again. The concern in Gabriel's expression, too.

"Evelyn's out of jail," Gabriel said. "And one of the hands just spotted her on the road that leads to your house."

Chapter Six

If someone had told Lauren two days ago that she'd be back at Gabriel's, she wouldn't have believed them. Yet, here she was. And not only was she dealing with the old memories of the murders, but she also had some new nightmares to add to the mix.

How was she going to keep the babies safe?

Gabriel had certainly done his part to make sure that happened. They'd moved both boys, the nannies, Cameron and her to his place. He'd assured her that he had a solid security system and that the hands would be patrolling the grounds. But Lauren wasn't sure that would be enough.

Especially with Evelyn out of jail.

Even though one of the hands had seen her near the ranch, she hadn't come to Cameron's or Gabriel's. Maybe because there had been cops and CSIs to scare her off. If she'd been the one behind the attack, she might not have realized all her hired guns had been killed, and she had possibly come with the hopes of snatching Isaac. Thankfully, that hadn't happened, but before Gabriel could get out to the road, the woman hadn't been there, either.

In fact, they didn't know where Evelyn was.

And that only added to Lauren's nightmarish thoughts.

She heard the footsteps outside the makeshift nursery that Gabriel and his wife, Jodi, had set up, and she reached for her gun. Which she no longer had. She'd put it on the top of the fridge because she didn't like the idea of having it on her when she was around the babies. But there was no reason for a gun anyway.

Because it was Cameron.

Like her, he'd spent most of the past two hours in the nursery, only stepping out to take calls. Lauren figured she should be making calls, as well, but she hadn't been able to tear herself away.

"They're still sleeping," Cameron whispered when his attention landed on the quilt where both boys were sacked out.

Hopefully, Dara was getting some rest in one of the guest rooms, as well. Merilee certainly was. She was napping on the daybed not far from the boys. With the high-stress day that they'd all had, Lauren figured the women were having a serious adrenaline crash. She certainly was and felt dead on her feet.

Cameron looked as exhausted as she did, and like her, he was probably having some pain. They'd declined the meds the medics had left for them, though. No way did she want her mind clouded any more than it already was.

"Anything on Evelyn?" She, too, kept her voice at a whisper even though the boys hadn't stirred even when there'd been other noises in the house.

He kept his attention fixed on the boys but shook his head. "But she's definitely out of jail. She was released on parole two days ago, and the board didn't bother to contact me to let me know."

Two days. Enough time to orchestrate all of this. But something about that wasn't right.

"If Evelyn was behind this, why come after Patrick and me?" Lauren asked.

"Maybe because she found out about the baby switch." Cameron answered so quickly that it meant he'd given this some thought. "If she knew Patrick was her grandson, she'd do anything to get him."

Yes. But Lauren was still having trouble thinking of Patrick as anything but her child. He wasn't. He was Gilly's biological son, and that meant Evelyn could have some kind of legal claim to him.

That thought nearly brought her to her knees.

Lauren staggered a little, catching on to the door frame to steady herself. Cameron also caught on to her by slipping his arm around her.

"You can't let this get to you," he said, maybe figuring out what she'd just realized. "Evelyn has a police record. No judge is going to give her custody."

"No clean judge. But Evelyn certainly has the money to pay one off. And hire as many fake cops and thugs as she wants."

The woman was a millionaire many times over, and that was probably why she hadn't spent much time in jail for pulling a gun on a cop. Still…

"If Evelyn wants her grandson so much, then why would she have put Patrick in danger like that?" she pressed.

He lifted his shoulder, and because he still had hold of her, it meant his arm slid against the side of her breast. He noticed, too, mumbled an apology and then eased away from her.

Lauren immediately felt the loss of no longer having him to support her. But it was a loss she shouldn't be feeling. She couldn't take that kind of comfort from Cameron. Not with this fire still simmering between them. A fire he was feeling, as well, she realized when their gazes connected.

He looked away from her, mumbled some profanity and then scrubbed his hand over his face. "Did you ever meet Evelyn?"

It was a good question, but she suspected he was asking to make sure they got their minds off that fire and back where it belonged—on figuring out who was behind the attacks.

"I met her once," Lauren answered. "It was at Gilly's apartment. I was there visiting your sister, and Evelyn showed up. Gilly wasn't pleased, and it wasn't a pleasant conversation. She wanted Gilly to have an amniocentesis done to prove the baby was her grandchild. Gilly refused. The test has risks, and there was no doubt in Gilly's mind that the baby was Trace's."

That gave her another jolt. Because the baby Gilly had been carrying had been Patrick.

"How did Gilly and you reconnect after you left Blue River?" he asked.

Lauren didn't have to think hard to remember that. "Gilly just rang my doorbell one day. She said she'd found me through an internet search and that she was moving to Dallas. We were both pregnant at the time, and she'd heard about my husband dying." Lauren paused. "Did Gilly tell you she'd moved near me?"

"No." His jaw tightened a little. "In fact, she didn't mention you at all. I knew you were in Dallas. That came up once when Gabriel was trying to get in touch with you."

Yes, Gabriel had tried many times. And early on after she'd left, Gabriel had come to see her every other month or so. There'd been nothing recent, though. Maybe he'd given up on ever bringing her back to the ranch. Ironic that it was danger and not family that had caused her to return.

"You knew Gilly was afraid of Trace?" Cameron continued a moment later.

She nodded. "I think Gilly might have moved to Dallas because it was far away from Trace but close to me. I don't believe she wanted to go through the pregnancy alone, and before my parents' murders, Gilly and I had been close."

Not that she needed to tell Cameron about that. He knew she'd been best friends with his sister because Lauren had spent plenty of time at their house. His folks were no longer around, though. His mom had died when Cameron was only six, and his dad had left shortly after Cameron became a deputy. It hadn't been a huge loss for Cameron or Gilly since their father had spent more time drinking than being a dad. Lauren supposed his father felt Gilly would be in good hands so Cameron had ended up raising his sister.

And now he was raising her son.

Or so Cameron had thought.

Lauren took a deep breath, ready to bring up the subject of what they were going to do, but from the corner of her eye, she spotted Jameson making his way toward them. He was sporting the same serious expression that he'd had since her arrival.

"You have a visitor," Jameson said, motioning toward the front of the house. "Duane Tully. He says it's important."

Cameron groaned. "He's not inside, is he?"

Jameson lifted his eyebrow in a "no-way" expression. "He's parked in the driveway with two hands watching him to make sure he stays put. I told him if it's really that important, he should head straight to the sheriff's office. He's still one of our suspects, right?"

"He has motive to kill me," Lauren verified. "Why does he want to see me?"

"He won't say. That makes me want to arrest him and haul him to jail."

Lauren wouldn't mind the man being in jail, but right now Duane seemed the "safest" of their suspects. As far as she knew, he'd never been in jail, never pulled a gun on a cop and wasn't brimming with venom the way Julia was.

"Gabriel was going to question Duane anyway," Cameron pointed out. "And I'd want to listen to what he has to say. I'd rather not have to leave Lauren and the boys right now to do that. So maybe Gabriel can question him here? After Duane is searched for weapons, that is."

Lauren didn't like the idea of being under the same roof as the man, but it was better than the alternative. Plus, they needed to ask him about the so-called cops that'd come to his house.

"Merilee," Cameron said the moment Jameson gave them the go-ahead nod.

The nanny's eyes immediately flew open, and she sprang to a sitting position. "What's wrong?"

"Maybe nothing," Cameron assured her. "I just need you to watch the babies while Lauren and I have a chat with someone."

Cameron waited until Merilee had gotten to her feet

before he shut the door. Good. Isaac would probably nap for at least another half hour, and he would be cranky if he didn't get those extra minutes.

They went downstairs where Gabriel was waiting in the foyer. "You're seeing him?" he asked right off.

Lauren nodded.

Gabriel huffed. The kind of huff to indicate he wasn't sure this was the right thing to do. Lauren wasn't sure of that, either. But she did want to hear what Duane had to say. Besides, the house was as safe as the sheriff's office would be. Lauren could see armed ranch hands outside, and Jodi was at the front window—her gun drawn. She would no doubt watch to make sure Duane hadn't brought any hired guns with him, and since Jodi was a security specialist, she had nearly as much training as Gabriel.

"I'll frisk him," Gabriel grumbled. He glanced at his wife, a stay-safe warning passing between them, before he headed out.

When Gabriel opened the door, Cameron automatically pulled Lauren behind him, and Jameson stepped in front of her, as well. Again, they were risking their lives for her, and she hated that it'd come down to that. However, despite their quick maneuvering, she still managed to get a glimpse of Duane.

And he got a glimpse of her, too. Duane looked weary and not at all there to do battle with her. That was something, at least. Considering he'd filed a lawsuit against her for Alden's estate, she didn't expect him to be friendly, but maybe he could give them something to help with the investigation.

"Ivy called a little while ago," Jameson told her as they waited for Gabriel.

Ivy, her sister. Like plenty of other things about being at the ranch, her sister's name brought back more of those old memories. Mostly good. Once, Ivy and she had been close. But like Lauren, Ivy hadn't stayed in Blue River, either. She'd left shortly after the murders and had only recently come home.

"Ivy wants to see you," Jameson went on. "Theo and she are down in Houston clearing out her place there, but I told them that for now they should stay put."

Good. Lauren wanted to see her sister, as well, but it was too risky for Ivy to be here since she also had a son. There were already enough people in danger at the ranch.

"I'm sure you remember Theo," Jameson added. "Well, Ivy and he are engaged now."

That created some sudden tension in the foyer. Not because Ivy and Theo were back together. That didn't surprise Lauren. The two had always been in love. But Theo's father, Travis, was in jail for murdering Lauren's parents. Obviously, her sister had gotten past that if she was planning to marry Theo.

Lauren hadn't quite managed to do that, though. And that lack of getting over it involved Cameron. He didn't say anything—he didn't need to—but it was always there. Because he was the lone person who'd had the chance to stop Travis that horrible night, and he hadn't done it. One day Lauren would ask her sister how she'd put that all behind her, and then maybe she could do the same.

Jameson adjusted his stance again, and both Cameron and he slid their hands over their guns as Gabriel approached the house. He had his hand clamped around Duane's arm as if arresting the man.

"Lauren," Duane greeted. The moment he was inside, Gabriel shut the door and armed the security alarm.

Yes, the stress was definitely there, etched around Duane's eyes, and he wasn't the polished businessman that he usually was. He was wearing jeans and a casual shirt rather than the pricey suits that he favored.

"I heard about the attack from Julia," Duane said to her. "I came as soon as I could."

Lauren shook her head. "How'd you get here so fast?" His house was hours away in Dallas.

"I was already on my way. I wanted to talk to you after those cops showed up at my house last night. Julia said you sent them to harass me, but I figured there was more to it than that."

"I didn't send them," Lauren insisted. "And I have reason to believe they could have been hired killers."

"Yes, the sheriff mentioned that to me. You really think someone would want me dead?"

"I don't know," she answered honestly. "I also don't know who hired the men or why they came after me. But you should take precautions just in case."

Duane looked at all three lawmen, maybe to see if they agreed with that, and even though Cameron, Gabriel and Jameson didn't speak, Duane must have seen something on their faces to make him nod.

"I'll look into hiring a bodyguard." He took a piece of paper from his pocket and handed it to Gabriel. "That's the code to access the online storage for the footage from my security system. Maybe you can compare the faces of the men who came to my door to the ones who were killed here at the ranch."

Lauren hoped she was wrong, but the way Duane had said that last part almost made it seem as if he was sympathetic about the thugs who'd attacked them and been shot in the process.

"What about Julia?" Cameron asked Gabriel. "Has she turned over her footage?"

"Not yet." Gabriel looked at the paper and then went into the adjoining living room to use a laptop that was on the coffee table. Jodi stayed at the window, keeping watch.

"Don't expect Julia to just cooperate," Duane muttered. He made a sound of frustration. "Julia's the reason I wanted to come and talk to you face-to-face," he added to Lauren. But he didn't say anything else. He just stood there, glancing around as if trying to figure out what to do.

"Did Julia do something I should know about?" Lauren came out and asked. "Did she hire those men?"

"I honestly don't have any idea about that." Duane paused again. "But I do know she's getting desperate. Did you know she's practically broke?"

Lauren hadn't thought Duane could say anything that would surprise her, but she'd obviously been wrong. "No. And that doesn't sound right. Both Alden and Julia inherited huge trust funds—"

"Julia drained hers to pay off some bad investments," Duane interrupted. "She doesn't want anyone to know," he quickly added, "but a PI I hired learned about it when I had him looking into some background stuff for the lawsuit."

Since Duane had filed that lawsuit against Lauren, she very much wanted to hear this—and especially why he'd included Julia in it.

"How and what did the PI learn?" Cameron asked, taking the words right out of Lauren's mouth.

Duane glanced away from her again. Not a good sign.

"I was looking for something to prove you cheated on Alden," the man finally said. "Yes, I know it's a stretch, but I can't just hand over the company that I helped build."

"You're not handing it over. You still own twenty-five percent. As does Julia."

"And Patrick owns the rest, the majority share," Duane spelled out for her. "You know that Alden wanted me to run the company."

"I know no such thing," Lauren argued. "In fact, at the time of Alden's death, you two were at odds with each other. He didn't approve of some of the investments you'd made. Were they bad investments like Julia's?"

"No," Duane snapped, and he repeated it. "It was just a difference of opinion, something Alden and I would have worked out if he'd lived."

He stared at her as if waiting for her to say something. Maybe something about giving in to him and handing over Patrick's shares. But they weren't hers to give.

Heck, they weren't even Patrick's.

They were Isaac's.

If Duane knew that, he might be trying to get rid of the baby so he'd have a better shot at getting the company. Of course, Julia had an equal motive since she wanted her hands on the money from Alden's estate.

"Alden was my best friend," Duane went on, "and while you and I never really got along, I don't want to see his son harmed."

Lauren pulled back her shoulders so fast that it caused her stitches to pull, and the pain rippled through her. Cameron noticed, too, because he leaned in and made brief eye contact with her before his attention slashed to Duane.

"Explain that," Cameron demanded. "Who would want to harm his son?"

"Julia." This time Duane didn't hesitate. "The PI I hired not only learned she was nearly broke, but he also found out she's in debt to a loan shark. I think she's past being desperate and would do anything to get her hands on her brother's money.

"And the only way Julia could do that would be to kill Patrick and her. If Julia knew there was a possibility of a baby swap, then that could send her after Isaac, too.

"I know about the DNA test you had done on your son," Duane added. "Yes, I know it's snooping, but I'm desperate, too. Not like Julia, but I want to hang on to my company."

Cameron glanced at her, no doubt to see if she was aware that Duane knew about the test, and she wasn't.

"What DNA test?" Lauren asked. Yes, it was a lie for her to pretend she didn't know what he was talking about, but she didn't intend to confirm anything to Duane.

"The PI had someone follow you," Duane admitted. "He saw you go to the lab. He went in after you when the receptionist was logging in the information."

Sweet heaven. If the PI had found out about that, then Julia could have, too. In fact, it was possible that Julia had had someone watching her, as well.

"The DNA test was for me," Lauren said. Again, it was a lie. "There were rumors my mother had had an affair, and I wanted to be sure that Sherman Beckett was really my father."

Duane couldn't have possibly looked more skeptical. Probably because Jameson and she were side by side, and the resemblance was definitely there. However, Duane hadn't known her folks so maybe he would think they resembled their mother.

"I'll have to send the footage to the crime lab for confirmation," Gabriel said, coming back into the foyer. "But I'm pretty sure the men who paid you a visit are the same ones who tried to kill us."

Some of the color drained from Duane's face. "Julia," he said through clenched teeth. "You have to stop her. Arrest her. Get her to confess."

"Give us everything your PI found out about her," Cameron fired back, "and maybe that'll be enough to get a warrant."

Maybe. Without proof, it would be just hearsay, but it was possible the PI had found something else.

Duane turned as if to leave, but he stopped and made eye contact with Lauren again. "The best way to stop Julia might be to settle the lawsuit with her. That could give her the money to pay the loan shark, and she might back off."

That was true if Julia was the one behind this. But Alden hadn't wanted his sister to have the money, and again, it wasn't Lauren's to give away. Still, it was something to consider if it would keep the babies out of danger.

"I suppose you want Lauren to settle the lawsuit with you, too," Cameron commented to Duane.

Duane shrugged, the answer obvious. "All I'm asking for is enough of the shares so I'll be majority holder. Her son can keep the rest. And it's only fair since it's my company."

That set her teeth on edge because it wasn't only

his. And again, she didn't want to barter off Isaac's birthright. One day he might want to run his father's company. It would be easier for Lauren to give up the money since she had plenty of her own that she could pass onto her children, but if she gave Duane the company, she would never be able to get it back.

"I'll think about that and let you know what I decide," she settled for saying.

She expected Duane to look at least slightly optimistic about that. He didn't. He studied her expression as if trying to figure out if she would truly consider it, and then he mumbled something she didn't catch. Lauren didn't believe it was a compliment, though.

With a scowl on his face, Duane motioned for Gabriel to disarm the security system. Her brother did, and he closed the door behind the man. Gabriel also stood at the side windows, no doubt to make sure Duane left.

"Lawsuits?" Jameson repeated.

Lauren nodded. "Both Julia and Duane are suing me. Well, suing Patrick anyway." She paused. "If I can prove a baby swap, then the lawsuits will have to be refiled. That'll cause delays that neither Duane nor Julia will like."

"No," Cameron agreed.

Cameron didn't spell it out, but Lauren figured they were thinking the same thing. That it would be easier for Julia or Duane to eliminate Isaac. Or maybe even both boys.

"You believe what Duane said about Julia owing money to a loan shark?" Gabriel asked.

Lauren had to shrug. "I suppose it could be true. Alden always claimed Julia was irresponsible with money. That's one of the main reasons he didn't want to turn over any part of his estate to her. That, and he wanted Patrick…his son…to have it."

But if it was true about Julia's debts, then that made her even more dangerous.

"I'll get Julia in for questioning," Gabriel assured her.

She was about to tell Cameron and her brothers that they needed to do more to beef up security and they had to make sure neither Duane nor Julia got anywhere near the babies, but Cameron's phone rang before she could speak.

"It's Jace Morrelli," Cameron relayed when he looked at the screen.

Since Jace was another of Gabriel's deputies, that immediately snagged her attention. He could have updates on the investigation, and thankfully Cameron put the call on speaker so she could listen.

"Evelyn Waters just showed up here at the sheriff's office," Jace said without a greeting. "She's demanding to see Lauren and you."

"Is she armed?" Gabriel asked right off. "If she is, arrest her because it'll be a violation of her parole."

"I searched her. No weapons. But she's talking crazy. That's why I called you." It sounded as if Jace blew out a long breath. "She's claiming that Lauren swapped her baby with Gilly's, and Evelyn insists she can prove it."

Chapter Seven

Cameron wasn't sure if this was the right thing to do—bringing Lauren to the sheriff's office. But he'd figured since Evelyn was there and making wild accusations, then Gabriel and he might as well do an interview with not only her but Julia, as well.

Neither conversation would be pleasant.

Still, they were necessary. What wasn't necessary was for Lauren to be there, but she had insisted. Well, she had after Gabriel had assigned two deputies to guard the babies. With Jameson, Jodi and the hands there, as well, Cameron hoped it was enough protection so that hired thugs couldn't get to them.

"You can't go into the interview room," Cameron reminded Lauren when Gabriel pulled to a stop in front of the sheriff's office.

"I'm still going to talk to Evelyn," she insisted. "I want to know how she found out about the baby swap. And why she thinks I'm responsible for it."

Cameron could only sigh. She wanted to confront the woman—he got that—but Lauren had already been through hell and back, and Evelyn wasn't going to make this situation better. Even with that, Cameron doubted he could have stopped Lauren if he'd tried. If he'd been in her shoes, he would have wanted the same thing.

He opened the cruiser door, taking hold of Lauren's hand so he could get her inside as fast as possible. Gabriel did the same. Cameron had hoped they'd have a moment before they had to face the storm, but the "storm" was right there. Evelyn was in the squad room, seated next to Jace's desk, and she stood the moment she laid eyes on them.

Cameron hadn't thought that jail time would ease the hatred Evelyn had for him, and it hadn't. He could see plenty of it in her eyes, but this time the hatred wasn't just for him. No. The woman was aiming some of it at Lauren, too.

"You swapped the babies, didn't you?" Evelyn said, the emotion causing her voice to tremble.

Lauren shook her head. "I don't know what you mean. What swap?"

"You know. You damn well know," Evelyn snapped.

"Uh, you want me to hang around or should I get the interview room ready?" Gabriel asked.

"Definitely get the room ready," Cameron assured him. "Evelyn obviously has a lot to say." Maybe she'd say the wrong thing and implicate herself in the attacks.

Mumbling some profanity under his breath, Gabriel went toward the hall, where there were a pair of interview rooms and his office.

"I do have plenty to say," Evelyn verified. "Plenty to tell you about my grandson being swapped with Lauren's baby."

"Why would I do something like that?" Lauren fired right back at her.

"To keep Trace's son from me, that's why." She

shifted her attention to Cameron. "How long have you known and why didn't you tell me?" Evelyn's voice had gotten louder with each word.

"A reminder," Cameron warned her. "You're on probation. Keep your temper in check, or I will put you back in jail."

She stood there as if daring him to try that, and part of him wanted her to push this so he could lock her back up. Then she might not be a threat to the boys. But first he wanted Evelyn to explain some things.

"Why do you believe someone switched the babies?" Cameron asked.

Evelyn huffed as if the answer was obvious. And maybe it was. Maybe she'd seen a picture of Patrick. The boy didn't look like Trace, but he did resemble the Dorans.

"I got a phone call two days ago," Evelyn said. "The person didn't identify himself, but he said Lauren had done a DNA test on her baby, and the reason she'd done that was because he wasn't hers. He was Trace's."

Now it was Lauren's turn to sigh because she hadn't missed the timing of this. It was when the PI Duane hired had followed Lauren to the lab. Apparently, Cameron needed to have another chat with the man to find out why he'd involved Evelyn in this.

"The DNA test was for me," Lauren said, repeating the lie she'd told Duane. "There was some question about whether or not Sherman Beckett was actually my father."

Like Duane, Evelyn didn't seem to buy that, either. "After I got that call," Evelyn went on, "I did some digging. I found the names of the staff who were working for those three days that both boys were in the hospital nursery."

Since the other deputies were working on the same thing, that piqued Cameron's interest. "And?"

"Dr. Gina Boyer," Evelyn said without hesitation. "I don't have the proof yet, but it all points to her."

Cameron looked at Lauren to see if she recognized the name, and she nodded. "She was an OB resident."

"And in debt up to her eyeballs," Evelyn provided. "She transferred to another hospital less than a week after the babies were born."

Cameron took a notepad from Jace's desk, jotted down the doctor's name and handed it to his fellow deputy. "Find out everything you can about her."

Jace nodded and got right on that, and Cameron turned back to Evelyn. "Did you contact this doctor?"

"I tried. She wouldn't take my calls. Wouldn't see me, either. That alone is suspicious."

"Maybe." Cameron shrugged. "Or maybe she's just busy and didn't want to talk to a stranger."

Evelyn's mouth tightened. "She wouldn't talk to me because she knows I'm onto her. She knows that I found out Lauren paid her to switch the babies."

A weary sigh left Lauren's mouth. "Again, why would I possibly do that?"

"Because of that barracuda of a sister-in-law, Julia. You must have known it would make your boy a target so you decided to make my grandson a target instead."

Since Cameron's arm was against hers, he felt her muscles tense. "I would have never done that," Lauren insisted, but her voice was now a tight whisper.

"No?" It didn't sound as if Evelyn was buying that, either. "Then who switched them?"

"I don't have any proof anyone did," Lauren answered. "And apparently neither do you. Now I have a question for you—did you hire thugs to attack me?"

Evelyn huffed. "Right. Go ahead. Try to wiggle out of this by putting the blame on me."

"You have a history of violent behavior," Cameron reminded the woman. A reminder that earned him a glare.

"I pulled a gun on you because I was desperate." She had to say that through clenched teeth. "Because you wouldn't let me see my grandson. Now I find out he wasn't my blood, after all."

"Does that mean you're about to accuse me of swapping the boys?" he pressed when the woman didn't continue.

Evelyn's eyes narrowed as if she might be considering that, but she shook her head. "I don't think you knew. But she did." She tipped her head to Lauren. "And now that psycho sister-in-law is coming after her."

Cameron's hands went on his hips. "That's your second reference to Julia. How do you know her?"

"I don't. Never met the woman. But I don't have to know her to have her investigated. After I got that phone call about the DNA test, I had my staff drop everything they were doing and start looking into things."

Since Evelyn owned a large public relations firm, she probably did have the manpower to dig up plenty of dirt, but it made him wonder if all of this was meant to cast blame on Julia or even Lauren so the blame wouldn't be squarely on her own shoulders. Yes, Julia and Duane had motives. But so did Evelyn.

Gabriel reappeared in the hall and motioned for Evelyn to follow him. She did. And Cameron and Lauren were about to do the same, but Jace stopped them. He had the landline phone pressed to his ear and was holding his hand over the speaker part.

"I have Dr. Boyer on the line," Jace said once Evelyn was out of earshot. "You want to talk to her now?"

Cameron couldn't take the phone fast enough, and he put it on speaker for Lauren. "Dr. Boyer, I'm Deputy Cameron Doran from the Blue River Sheriff's Office, and I have Lauren Lange with—"

"Yes, this is about that woman, Evelyn Waters," the doctor interrupted. "She's left more than a dozen messages on my work phone, and I believe she has someone following me."

Cameron didn't doubt that, and since it appeared the doctor knew what this was all about, he launched right into his question. "Evelyn believes you might have taken part in a baby swap that happened a year ago. Did you?"

"No," she answered.

He didn't like the doctor's hesitation or the fact that she didn't even add anything to that. In his experience, innocent people tended to protest a lot when accused of a crime. "Did you have contact with Gilly Doran's and Lauren's newborn sons?"

"Of course. I was working at the hospital when they were born. I was one of your sister's doctors and was with her when she died." Another hesitation. "She's the reason I left and went to another hospital. Gilly was one of my first patients. The first one I ever lost," Dr. Boyer added.

So, maybe she wasn't covering up anything and this was just a difficult conversation for her. It was certainly difficult for him. This doctor had been there with his sister, but he hadn't been. That was a wound that was never going to fully heal. Now he had to do what was right by Gilly and make sure her son was safe.

"Dr. Boyer, this is Lauren," she said. "I've had some trouble. Someone's been trying to kill me."

It sounded as if the doctor gasped. "You don't think that has anything to do with something that happened at the hospital?"

"I don't know. That's what we're trying to find out. My son and Gilly's son could be in danger, and you might be able to help."

The doctor certainly didn't jump to offer anything. Finally, though, she asked, "How?"

"Just think back to those two days that our babies were in the hospital nursery at the same time," Lauren continued. "Did Gilly say anything about her son being in danger? Or maybe you saw someone suspicious?"

"You mean someone like Evelyn Waters?"

Cameron saw Lauren go stiff. "Yes. Did you see her?"

"I can't be sure," the doctor said after a long pause. "It's possible. That was over a year ago, and I wasn't getting a lot of sleep. There were so many people in and out, and I didn't really even know the other staff yet."

That sounded like a perfect storm for someone wanting to do a baby swap. But if it'd been Evelyn, why hadn't she just tried to take the child?

If that was indeed her plan, that is.

There was another angle to this.

"Did my sister tell you about her abusive ex, the man who was the father of her child?" Cameron asked.

"Yes." The doc didn't sound so eager to admit to that. "She showed me a picture of him and begged me not to let him get near the baby."

Cameron was thankful for that, but he needed to know if the doctor had taken it past the stage of merely looking out for Trace.

"Did Gilly ever mention anything about swapping the babies to keep them from her ex?" Cameron pressed.

Silence.

The moments crawled by, causing Cameron to curse under his breath.

"No," Dr. Boyer finally answered. "Look, Deputy Doran, I have to go. A patient here needs me."

Before Cameron could say anything else, the doctor ended the call. Cameron stood there, staring at the phone and debating if he should try to call her back. But he doubted she would answer. Besides, he should do a background check on her and see what they were dealing with. First, though, he wanted to hear if Evelyn would give Gabriel anything they could use.

"I don't think Gilly could have done the swap on her own," Lauren said as they walked toward the observation room next to where the interview was taking place.

"If she was desperate enough, she could have figured out a way." Cameron silently cursed that, too. His sister had been so desperate because he hadn't been there to help her.

"Don't put this on yourself." Lauren touched his arm and rubbed it gently.

Cameron didn't like that her touch gave him some comfort—her words, too—but it did. The comfort felt, well, nice, but he needed to focus on what Evelyn was saying. Except she wasn't saying what he wanted to hear.

"I think it's time I brought in my lawyer," he heard

Evelyn say once Lauren and he were in the observation room.

Lauren groaned, and Gabriel looked as if he wanted to do the same. Cameron wasn't sure what'd caused the woman to play the lawyer card, but it meant this interview was over. Or at least it would be until Evelyn's attorney arrived. Thankfully, she took out her phone and made the call that would hopefully get him or her out here ASAP.

"And I'd like some coffee while I wait," Evelyn added when Gabriel stood.

Gabriel didn't agree to get her any, but he left the interview and came into the observation room with them.

"What happened?" Lauren immediately asked.

"I asked her if she had anything to do with those dead gunmen."

It was a question that needed to be asked so Cameron couldn't fault Gabriel for it. Still, this was a frustrating delay. "Did Evelyn say anything before she pulled the plug on the interview?"

"Not really. Just a rehash of what she said in the squad room."

Too bad. And Cameron wasn't going to be able to add anything in the good news department. "Lauren and I talked to Dr. Boyer. I think she's hiding something, so we need to get her in for questioning."

Gabriel gave a weary sigh, nodded and glanced at Evelyn through the mirror. The woman was taking out her phone. "I've got some calls to make so keep an eye on her. She might pitch a fit if she figures out I've locked the door, but I don't like a parolee being able to walk around in the place. Not with Lauren here anyway."

Cameron agreed. Evelyn herself wasn't that formidable, but she could be calling in another round of hired thugs. What they needed was to be able to find a money trail that linked Evelyn to the dead guys. Or to one of their other suspects. Right now all they had were a bunch of pieces and no way to put them together to tell them who was guilty.

"I hate to even bring it up," Lauren continued after Gabriel had left, "but is there any chance Travis Canton could be behind this?"

"You mean because of the threats we've all been getting," Cameron finished for her. "I doubt it." Now, this was something *he* hated to bring up. "Travis hasn't exactly been hostile to me, and he actually liked Gilly. I can't imagine him doing anything to put her boy in danger."

Of course, the man had been convicted of a double homicide so that meant he was pretty much capable of anything. "I'll check with the prison and make sure he hasn't had any unusual visitors," Cameron offered.

Lauren made a soft sound, part frustration, part groan. "This is why I hate being here in Blue River. It always comes back." She squeezed her eyes shut for a moment, and Cameron thought maybe she was fighting back tears again.

He was fighting back some regret. Not just for what he hadn't prevented that night ten years ago but for what he was about to do now. Even though he knew it wasn't a smart idea, Cameron glanced at Evelyn to make sure she had stayed put—she had—then he slipped his arm around Lauren and pulled her to him.

Just like that, time vanished, and they were suddenly lovers again. And it was something his body wasn't going to let him forget.

She leaned back, staying in his arms, but Lauren looked up at him. Yep, he'd been right about those tears. Her eyes were filled with them, and they were threatening to spill down her cheeks. He brushed his mouth over one when it fell.

Not a smart idea, either. But then he seemed to be going for broke in the "making huge mistakes" department. He cupped her chin, using his thumb to catch another tear. Of course, that meant touching her while the air was electric between them. Added to that, Lauren was definitely in vulnerable mode right now. That was probably why she didn't move away from him.

Cameron, however, couldn't explain why he didn't move away from her.

His feet seemed nailed to the floor. So he stood there, volleying glances at the mirror while waiting for either Lauren or him to put icing on this by going in for a kiss. He wanted that. Badly. Judging from the uneven rhythm of Lauren's breath, so did she. And for a couple of moments Cameron had no trouble remembering how her mouth would feel against his. How she would taste.

Since it was obvious neither of them had any sense left to do the right thing, fate got involved and helped them out. The sound of the footsteps, followed by someone clearing their throat, finally got them apart. Lauren practically scampered away from him. That probably had something to do with the fact that Gabriel was in the doorway, and he was scowling at them.

Cameron and he were friends, but that didn't mean Gabriel wanted him to get involved with Lauren again. Especially at a dangerous time like this. Added to that, Cameron really did need to keep his focus on the investigation.

"I just got off the phone with the lab," Gabriel said, his scowl still in place. "The one that Lauren used to do Patrick's DNA."

Cameron felt his stomach tighten, and Lauren caught on to his arm as if to steady herself.

"It's not good," Gabriel added. "Someone stole the test results."

Chapter Eight

Lauren rocked Patrick in the chair in the nursery. Across from her, Merilee was doing the same thing to Isaac in another rocker that Cameron had brought over from his house.

Cameron wasn't in the room, though. Since they'd returned from the sheriff's office hours earlier, he was in the kitchen making calls and working the case. Something Lauren wanted to be doing, as well, but she didn't even know what else she could do. She'd called the lab immediately after Gabriel had told her the test results had been stolen, but she hadn't gotten much of an explanation.

Simply put, the lab tech didn't know what'd happened. According to him, he'd run the test, but when Gabriel had called to press him for the results, it wasn't there. Someone had deleted it from the computer log. Now Cameron was trying to figure out who'd done that since the same person was likely responsible for the attacks.

But why would someone want the results hidden?

Lauren didn't have an answer for that—though part of her wished there was some way for both boys to be biologically hers. Then she would have a claim on them. Of course, Cameron was perhaps wishing the same thing.

Eventually, they would have test results, though, since Gabriel had taken DNA not only from the boys but also from Cameron and her. Soon they would have confirmation of what Lauren already knew. No. It was more than that. She felt it all the way to her bones.

"It's funny how the boys are on the same schedule," Merilee whispered. She smiled down at Isaac. "They eat, nap and wake up around the same time." She got up and eased Isaac into the crib.

Lauren made a sound of agreement, and since Patrick was completely sacked out for his nap, she put him in the crib next to Isaac. Despite the nightmare that was going on, it soothed her to see them so peaceful like this.

"I'll be in the kitchen helping Dara with dinner," Merilee added. "Wouldn't be a good idea to rely on Cameron or Jodi to fix anything."

So Lauren had heard. Apparently, sandwich-making was the limit to their culinary skills. Lauren still had some baby food in the diaper bag she'd brought with her, but Dara had insisted on cooking something from scratch. Now the nanny was making the rest of them dinner.

Since the boys would likely sleep through the night, Lauren took the baby monitor so she could find a quiet place to start making some calls to friends who might have heard something, anything, about Julia or Duane. Then she planned on sleeping in the nursery. It wouldn't be as comfortable as the guest room that Jodi had fixed up for her, but she didn't want to be far from the boys.

In case more of those hired guns tried to come after them again.

Gabriel probably wouldn't like it, but Lauren wanted to hire some extra security. Maybe some bodyguards. And that was going to be the first call she made. However, she'd barely had time to go into the hall when she saw Cameron making his way toward her.

He glanced in at the boys, then at the monitor she was holding before he motioned for her to follow him. He didn't go far, just into the foyer. The overhead light was on there. Unlike the nursery, where all the blinds and curtains had been closed all afternoon. Lauren had realized it was already dark outside.

When Cameron stopped and turned to her, he opened his mouth. Closed it. As if he'd changed his mind about what to say.

"Are you okay?" he asked.

Lauren didn't want to know how bad she looked for him to say that. Probably about as bad as she felt. "Just tired and frustrated."

"Yeah." She heard the frustration in his voice, too. But that wasn't only frustration in his eyes.

Maybe Cameron was remembering the near kiss that'd happened at the sheriff's office. Lauren hadn't thought for a minute that she was fully over Cameron, and that moment between them had proven it.

He glanced away as if knowing what she was thinking. "You want the good news or the bad news first?" he asked.

Lauren sighed. "The good." Since she wasn't ready for anything else bad, she figured she needed something—anything—positive first. And this attraction between them definitely didn't fall into the positive category.

"I found out more about Dr. Boyer," Cameron explained. "No red flags whatsoever. She left the hospital where the babies were born so she could move to Austin to be near her family. Her mom has late-stage cancer."

So the doctor hadn't fled after doing a baby switch. "But why did she sound, well, suspicious when she was talking to you?"

He lifted his shoulder. "My guess is that she got too close to Gilly, and she blamed herself in some way for Gilly's death."

The doctor shouldn't do that because Gilly had died from a blood clot. It wasn't common, but it did happen, and in Gilly's case, there was nothing anyone could have done to stop it.

Lauren took a deep breath and tried to steel herself up. "What's the bad news? And please don't tell me we're about to be attacked again."

"No attack. The hands are guarding the road and checking anyone coming in and out of the ranch. Jameson even has a couple of his Ranger friends helping."

Good. But she still wasn't nixing the idea of bodyguards just yet.

"Evelyn is making waves," Cameron said a moment later. "As soon as she left the sheriff's office, she had her team of lawyers petition a judge for custody of Patrick."

Lauren shook her head. "But she doesn't even have proof that Patrick is her son's baby."

"Oh, she's petitioning to get DNA results, too." He rubbed his hand over the back of his neck. "The thing is—Evelyn stands no chance of getting custody unless she can prove in some way that you or I hid her grand-son from her. She'll want to make the judge believe we obstructed justice in some way."

Well, it definitely wasn't good news, but Lauren wasn't sure it was enough of a threat to put that trou-bled expression on Cameron's face. "There's no proof because we didn't do anything like that."

But then it hit her.

"While we're being investigated, a judge could put the babies in foster care." Just saying it aloud caused Lauren to stagger back, and she caught on to the wall.

"Isaac would be fine, probably," Cameron added. "Because a judge would likely give temporary custody of him to one of your siblings. But Evelyn and I are the only living relatives that Patrick has."

That nearly knocked the breath out of her and made Lauren even more unsteady. Cameron noticed, too, be-cause he slid his arm around her. "They can't take Pat-rick. I won't let them."

"Neither will I," he assured her.

Cameron said that with such confidence that she looked up at him to make sure he wasn't lying. He wasn't. "He's my nephew, and I'll hide him if I have to."

He'd break the law—which no doubt would cut him to the core. But the cut would be even deeper if Patrick was taken away from her. She'd break plenty of laws to keep him. Of course, Evelyn and the law weren't her only threats.

Cameron was, too.

"What are we going to do?" Lauren came out and asked. "What are *you* going to do?" she amended.

He didn't ask her to clarify, but he did look as if he

wanted to repeat the question to her. "I wish there was an easy fix for this."

So did she. But there wasn't, and it was breaking her heart. Cameron must have seen that, as well, because he said some profanity under his breath and pulled her to him. Lauren didn't resist. Nor did she stop herself from looking up at him. It was a mistake, of course, because they were already too close to each other. Especially their mouths. And that was never a good thing when it came to Cameron and her.

"I should go back into the kitchen," he said.

But he didn't, and Lauren didn't let go of him, either, so he could do that. Instead, she slipped her arm around his waist, drawing him even closer than he already was.

Cameron said more of that profanity before his mouth came to hers. The jolt was instant, a reminder of all those feelings and memories she'd been battling since she'd come back to the ranch. It was almost too much, and in some ways, it wasn't nearly enough.

Because it made her want more of him.

Cameron must have known that because he deepened the kiss, sliding his hand around the back of her neck and angling her so that she got an even stronger dose of those old feelings. New ones, as well. Cameron had always known how to set her body on fire, and he clearly hadn't forgotten that. But there was something different, too. The kind of intensity between two people who were no longer kids.

The stakes were sky-high, and that seemed to make the kiss even better. And worse. Worse because it was so good and made her wish that it wouldn't end with just a kiss.

However, it did end.

Cameron snapped away from her, and in the same motion, he pushed her behind him and drew his gun. Because the kiss had clouded her mind, it took Lauren a moment to realize why he'd done that. Because someone was out on the porch.

"It's one of the hands," Gabriel said.

Lauren also hadn't known that her brother was so close, and she wondered if he'd seen that kiss. If so, she was certain she would catch some flack about it later.

Lauren quickly looked out the window so she could see the ranch hand. She recognized him. Allen Colley. He'd started working for her family when she was a kid.

"Two San Antonio cops just showed up," Gabriel added. "Not alone, either. They have Julia with them."

Lauren immediately looked at her brother for an explanation, but Gabriel didn't give her one. "Step to the side," he instructed.

Lauren didn't want to do that. She wanted to see what was going on, but she did move into the adjoining living room. She wasn't in the direct line of the door, but she could still see from the window.

"The babies," she said, glancing down at the monitor.

"They'll be fine," Gabriel assured her. "These guys don't have a court order or search warrant so they're not getting in the house."

Good. But if they didn't have those things, then she wondered why Gabriel had allowed them onto the ranch.

Her brother disarmed the security system and opened the door. That was when Lauren spotted the SAPD cruiser parked in front of Gabriel's house. The two uniformed officers were already out of their vehicle, and Julia was between them.

"What do they want?" Cameron asked.

"Julia supposedly has some info that's critical to our investigation." Gabriel slid his hand over his gun, and that was when Lauren realized this could all be some kind of hoax. More fake cops. Ones that Julia herself could have hired.

"I checked with SAPD," Allen said, not looking any more comfortable about this than Gabriel, Cameron and she were. "The lieutenant confirmed these guys were his and that he'd sent them out here."

Lauren still wasn't breathing easier just yet because the lieutenant could be dirty, too. She hated that she could no longer trust everyone with a badge, but it was too risky to let down her guard.

"I'm Sergeant Terry Welker," the officer on the right greeted them. He was yet someone else who didn't look especially pleased about this visit. He tipped his head to the other cop. "This is Detective Miguel Rodriguez. I'm pretty sure you know Ms. Lange."

"They know me, all right, and they're trying to smear my name," Julia promptly snapped.

Cameron reholstered his gun and huffed. "It's not a smear if it's the truth. You're desperate for cash because you're in debt to a loan shark." He shifted his attention to the sergeant. "Did she tell you that?"

Julia certainly didn't jump to deny it, which meant she probably thought they had some kind of proof. They didn't. Well, other than Duane's accusations, but since he was a suspect, too, Lauren wasn't about to accept everything he'd told them. But in this case, it appeared Duane had been right.

Lauren moved back to the edge of the foyer, coming into Julia's view. The woman aimed a scowl at her, but Lauren gave the woman one right back. Because owing money to a loan shark was plenty of motive for the attacks. It sickened Lauren to think the babies could be in danger because of money.

"This visit doesn't have anything to do with that," Julia insisted. "Believe it or not, I've come to help you. Not for your sakes. But so you'll leave me the hell alone."

Cameron didn't ask how she'd come to help. Instead, he looked at the sergeant for answers. "She demanded we escort her out here. Said you might shoot her if she just showed up."

"Not if she'd shown up at the sheriff's office. This is my home," Gabriel reminded them, and it wasn't a friendly reminder, either. Her brother obviously didn't want Julia anywhere near the ranch.

"We went there first," the detective answered. "When neither you nor Deputy Doran were there, Ms. Lange wanted us to bring her here so she could give you something. She's not armed—we checked—and she wouldn't give the info to us."

"Because I don't want this to fall into the wrong hands."

Lauren had no idea what Julia had, or rather what the woman claimed to have, but she shook her head. "You couldn't force her to turn it over to you?"

The sergeant grunted as if he wished he could have done that. "Ms. Lange's not under arrest." He shot Julia a hard glance. "That was before we knew about the loan shark, though. I'll be looking into that."

Good. Lauren hoped SAPD dug until they got to the truth.

"Anyway," the sergeant went on, "your brother-in-law, Theo Canton, and I are old friends, and I thought

I'd bring her here as a favor to him. I know he's worried about what's going on with the trouble you had here, and he'd like to put a stop to it. I figured if Ms. Lange could help in any way, that it'd be worth the drive."

Maybe it would be. If not, Lauren was certain that Cameron and Gabriel would put a quick end to this little visit.

Julia gave Cameron a piece of paper that she took from her purse. Lauren looked at it from over his shoulder, but it appeared to be some sort of code.

"That's the password for the computer files," Julia explained. "Files for Alden's business."

Lauren had a closer look, but she didn't recognize the site for the online storage, the password or the files. "I manage my late husband's company," Lauren said to the cops. "These aren't my files, and—"

"No, they're Duane's," Julia interrupted. "He's been keeping secret books from you. No good reason I can think of for doing that, but if you go through those files, you can see there's money missing. Enough to pay some thugs to kill you so he can get the company he believes he should have had all along."

Lauren felt her breath go thin. Of course she'd known Duane could be behind this, but it put an icy chill through her to hear it spelled out like that.

"How did you get this?" Cameron asked her.

Julia pulled back her shoulders. "I was looking for any kind of files or notes my brother might have left before he died."

Translation—Julia wanted to find something she could use for her lawsuit to get Alden's money.

"You hacked into Duane's files," Lauren concluded.

"Company files," Julia corrected. She pointed to the

paper. "And I got you something that'll not only clear my name, but you can also use to arrest Duane."

The sergeant turned to Gabriel. "Since the company is in Dallas and the computer hacking happened there, that's out of our jurisdiction. You want to call in your brother Jameson to handle this?"

Since Jameson was a Texas Ranger, he didn't have a set jurisdiction. He could basically do whatever local law enforcement asked him to do.

Gabriel nodded. "I'll have Jameson check it out. If he finds anything, he'll let you know. And if there's nothing else, I'd like for you to get Ms. Lange off Beckett land."

The cops made sounds of agreement. The detective started back to the cruiser with Julia, but Sergeant Welker stayed behind. However, he didn't look at Gabriel but rather Cameron.

"I made some calls on the way over here," the sergeant said. "Just so I could figure out what the devil was going on with Ms. Lange. Anyway, I discovered Evelyn Waters was out of jail. I remembered all the trouble you had with her a few months back."

"Yeah," Cameron verified, "she's out on probation."

"I heard." The sergeant huffed. "I thought you might want to know that she got out early thanks to Judge Wendell Olsen. They're old friends—belong to the same country club and such. Anyway, the only reason I'm bringing it up is because Evelyn's looking to have her record expunged. Then it'll be as if she never even committed the crime."

"Can she do that?" Lauren immediately asked.

"Not without friends in high places," the sergeant answered. "This might not amount to anything, but I heard that Evelyn plans to have Judge Olsen help her get custody of her grandson. Just thought you'd want to know," he added before he walked away.

The chill inside her got even colder. So cold that it caused Lauren to shudder. "I won't let that woman have Patrick or Isaac."

"No," Cameron quietly agreed.

Gabriel shut the door, reactivated the security system and went to the window to watch—making certain that Julia did indeed leave. Lauren headed straight to the nursery, and even though she was moving pretty fast, Cameron caught up with her.

"It's time for us to hide the boys," she insisted. Yes, she was panicking, and she couldn't make herself stop.

Cameron took hold of her arm and stepped in front of her. "Not yet. But there is something we need to do."

"What? Because I'll do anything to keep them safe."

"So will I." Cameron looked her straight in the eyes when he continued. "And that's why you and I need to get married."

Chapter Nine

Cameron hadn't been sure what Lauren's reaction would be when he proposed to her. Or rather when he had *insisted* they get married. He had figured she would be shocked.

And she was.

He had also expected her to need some time to think about it.

And she had.

But what he hadn't counted on was that her thinking time would last through the night. She hadn't even brought it up when Patrick had awakened around two in the morning, and Cameron and she had ended up in the nursery together. Lauren had rocked the baby back to sleep while she hummed to him. What she hadn't done was given Cameron an answer. Or for that matter, she hadn't even talked that much to him. Granted it was an ungodly hour, but still he'd expected something—including a flat-out no answer.

Now it was causing his own round of thinking time as he sat in the family room with his third cup of coffee and went through the latest emails about the investigation. Cameron had been certain that Lauren would jump on the idea since it might be necessary to stop

Evelyn's claim to custody. Even a dirty judge would have trouble explaining why he would deny custody to a married couple and then hand the baby over to a grandmother with a criminal record.

Of course, nothing they did might be enough to stop Evelyn, who seemed hell-bent on raising her grandson. Since she'd done such a bad job raising Trace, Cameron didn't want the woman to have a second chance to screw up another child's life. Especially when that child was Gilly's son.

He downloaded the next round of emails, scowling at the one that caught his eye. It was from Sergeant Welker, SAPD. It was an account by an informant that Welker identified only as a "credible source," who basically repeated what Welker had already told them. Evelyn was gearing up for a fight. Maybe that wouldn't include another attack, but just in case Evelyn did have that on her agenda, Cameron had added even more to their security measures.

Gabriel and he had posted hands on the old trails that coiled around the ranch. It wasn't foolproof since gunmen could still go through the woods to get to them, but there was no way they could watch every acre of land. Cameron could only hope that if thugs did get near the house, then the other hands and reserve deputies would see them and stop them.

The next email didn't cause Cameron's scowl to fade. It was from Jameson, who was now handling the so-called evidence Julia had given them. The Rangers' computer guys had gotten into the files without a hitch, and it did indeed appear that Duane was keeping a second set of books, but it could be something that Julia had set up to incriminate the man. It was going to take time to unravel everything, and time wasn't something that was on their side.

Cameron had a bad feeling in the pit of his stomach.

The feeling eased up a lot, though, when he heard the chatter. Baby talk. He'd seen both boys when they'd gotten up about an hour earlier, but Lauren, Jodi and the nannies had whisked them away for baths and breakfast. That was probably like therapy for them and a good way to get their minds off the danger that seemed to be skulking right up to their doorsteps. That potential danger was the reason Gabriel was working in his home office. Jameson would be returning soon, too, after he finished up some things in Dallas.

The chatter got louder, and Cameron expected to see all the women, including Lauren, come into the room. But it was only Lauren. She had a baby on each hip, and she was smiling. *Really* smiling.

Her happiness faded some, though, when her attention landed on his face. Probably because of his somber expression after reading those emails. Cameron quickly tried to fix that, though. He put his laptop and coffee aside and got to his feet.

"Nothing new on the investigation," Cameron told her right off, and he went to them.

They were a welcome sight, that was for sure. Both boys had obviously had their baths and been fed because they looked ready to do some serious playing. They were squirming to get down—probably because there were some plastic toy blocks on the coffee table.

However, the squirming shifted to a different direction when Isaac reached out for Cameron. He took the boy, brushing a kiss on the top of his head, but Patrick must have wanted a part of that because he reached for

Cameron, too. Cameron quickly found his arms filled with babies. Patrick gave him a sloppy kiss on the cheek while Isaac bopped Cameron on the nose.

Lauren laughed.

It was silky and soft, but it faded, though, just as the smile had done.

Lauren picked up two of the blocks and handed both of the boys one. Of course they went straight in their mouths, but it would keep them occupied for a couple of seconds while he chatted with Lauren.

"In case you missed it last night, I did bring up the subject of marriage," Cameron reminded her.

She nodded, then dodged his gaze. On a heavy sigh, Lauren dropped down into the chair next to the sofa. "When I was a teenager, I used to plan our wedding," she said. "You knew that, of course."

He did. He'd heard her talking to Ivy about it. It'd scared the heck out of him, too, because Lauren had been just seventeen. If her father had caught wind of it, he probably would have fired Cameron, punched him or both. Back then, marriage hadn't even been on his radar, but he had been attracted to Lauren. Wisely, he'd held back on the attraction, though, until she had turned eighteen. They'd had just a couple of short weeks together before the night that changed everything.

"Old water, old bridge," she added in a mumble.

Cameron wished that hadn't felt like a slap. Or a lie. It might be old baggage, but the attraction was still just as strong and new as it had been when she'd discussed marrying him with her sister.

As he'd predicted, the boys started to squirm, and he stood them on the floor next to the coffee table so they could reach the rest of the blocks.

"I just thought it would be easier to fight Evelyn if we had a united front," Cameron told her.

Lauren didn't argue with that. In fact, she didn't say anything for several long moments. "I agree. We should get married."

Cameron snapped toward Lauren and stared at her. She didn't look convinced this was the right thing to do, but then, Cameron wasn't so sure it would work, either. Right now they didn't have a lot of ammunition to fight custody with anyone. Not with the DNA results not in yet, and he wasn't going to allow either boy to be placed into foster care.

"I talked this over with Gabriel," Lauren added.

Cameron hadn't figured anything else she could say would surprise him, but that sure did. "And?"

Lauren lifted her shoulder, and without missing a beat, she caught Isaac when he wobbled and nearly fell. She steadied the baby before she looked at Cameron. "He understands."

Yeah, but that was a whole different thing than approving of it. He was reasonably sure that Gabriel no longer held any resentment for Cameron's screwup ten years ago, but he would still want to protect his sister. Lauren's husband had only been dead a year and a half, and Gabriel probably thought it was too soon for her to get married.

And it might be.

But their options were limited here.

"Anyway, I can get started," she went on. She stood, rubbing her hands along the sides of her jeans. "I mean, I can call the courthouse and see about putting a rush on a license."

"I've already done that. Just in case you said yes. I

know the clerks who work there, and one of them can bring it over this morning. The justice of the peace can come out, as well, and marry us."

She dragged in a long breath, nodded again. "You've been busy."

"I wanted to save time. My guess is that Evelyn will be visiting her judge friend today if she hasn't already."

Cameron hadn't expected this to be a romantic moment. After all, they were devising a plan to save the children they both loved, but Lauren looked as if she was bracing herself for a huge disaster. Not exactly a way to stroke his ego. Especially after that hot kiss that'd happened just yesterday.

Lauren finally looked him straight in the eyes. "If this marriage arrangement goes south," she said, "please promise me that you won't try to keep either of the boys from me."

"Of course. You'll make the same promise to me?"

"Yes." She stood and fluttered her fingers to the back of the house. "I'll tell the others. Any idea how soon you can get the clerk and justice of the peace out here?"

He took out his phone. "ASAP."

"Good." She took another of those long breaths and repeated it before she scooped up the babies.

Cameron was about to tell her to leave them while she did whatever it was she needed to do, but his phone rang before he could do that. When he saw the name on the screen, he decided it was a call he should take.

Duane.

He showed her the screen, and Lauren put the boys back on the floor. No doubt so she could listen.

"Duane knows the accusations Julia made against him?" she asked.

"He knows. Jameson called him last night." Which meant this probably wasn't going to be a pleasant conversation. Still, Cameron wanted to know what the man had to say about those files.

He didn't put the call on speaker in case Duane started cursing. Even though the boys were too young to understand it, Cameron still didn't want them hearing it. However, he held out the phone between Lauren and him so that she could lean in and listen. She moved to the sofa next to him.

"Why did you have the Texas Rangers come after me?" Duane said without a greeting. Unlike his other conversation with Cameron and Julia, this one did not have a respectful tone to it. "You know anything Julia said about me would be a lie."

"She had computer files," Cameron reminded the man.

"Files that she concocted to make me look guilty." And yes, Duane peppered that with some profanity. "If she gets me out of the way, she has an easier path to getting her brother's company. I can't believe she convinced you that what she found was real."

"She didn't convince us," Lauren said. "But it had to be investigated. That's why Jameson was called in. If the files are bogus, then he'll figure that out."

Duane made a sharp sound of disagreement. "Innocent people get railroaded all the time. In fact, there are plenty who believe Travis Canton was wrongfully convicted of murdering your parents."

That caused the skin to crawl on the back of Cameron's neck, and Lauren didn't seem to fare much better. She clamped her teeth over her bottom lip for a moment, as if trying to keep her composure. Despite the sudden bad turn of mood in the air, the boys thankfully didn't seem to pick up on it. They continued to play with the blocks, banging them against the hardwood floor.

"Why would you bring up Travis?" Cameron demanded from Duane.

"Because it's true. Travis never confessed. Heck, he doesn't even remember if he's guilty. You didn't lock him up that night when you found him drunk, and that made him an easy patsy for someone who needed a scapegoat."

All of that had been in the newspapers, so it wasn't surprising that Duane would know those details. What Cameron wanted to know was why this man was even interested in the old murders.

"How long ago did you file the lawsuit against Lauren and Patrick?" Cameron asked.

Duane hesitated, maybe because he realized he'd just spilled something he shouldn't. "Are you accusing me of something?"

"Just asking a very simple question."

Of course, it wasn't that simple. Cameron wanted to know if the lawsuit was somehow tied to the threatening letters they'd been receiving. Lauren, included. Maybe Duane was trying to intimidate her or send her running by making her believe her parents' "real" killer was going to come after Patrick and her.

"About six months ago," Duane finally answered. Definitely not a trace of friendliness in his voice. "Why?"

"Because shortly after that, Lauren started getting death threats. Did you have something to do with that?"

"No!" No hesitation that time. "Hell, I called you to

try to clear up the lies Julia told, and now you accuse me of this?"

"I'm not accusing. Again, I'm just asking a simple question."

"No," Duane repeated, though it sounded as if he'd spoken through clenched teeth. "I didn't threaten Lauren. And I didn't do any creative bookkeeping so I could steal money from the company. I sure as hell didn't hire any gunmen to go after Lauren."

Well, Cameron had gotten his answers, but he wasn't sure if they were the truth or not. There was no way Duane would just confess his wrongdoing, since it could land him in jail. Especially if Jameson could connect any missing funds to the bank accounts of those hired thugs who'd been killed at the ranch. That would be a charge of conspiracy to commit murder and would give Duane plenty of time behind bars.

"Why did you really call?" Cameron pressed.

He expected Duane to shout out his innocence again. He didn't. "Evelyn Waters called me first thing this morning."

Judging from the way Lauren's eyes widened, that surprised her as much as it did Cameron. "What did she want?"

"To invest in my legal fund to fight Lauren. In exchange, she'll want a piece of the company once I reclaim it."

Hell. Evelyn was really on the offensive, and Cameron thought he knew why she'd gone about it at this angle. Maybe Evelyn thought she could cause Lauren to go broke with a long legal battle. Or maybe just wear Lauren down. It wasn't going to work. Cameron didn't come from money, but Lauren did. And the Becketts would join forces to make sure she had whatever funds she needed. Plus, she could always tap into her trust fund.

"A word of advice about Evelyn," Cameron warned the man. "She could be looking to use you as a patsy. If she breaks the law again, and it sounds as if she's very close to doing that, then she'll want someone to take the fall for her. She could have you in her sights for that."

"I'm not worried about Evelyn," Duane insisted the moment Cameron had finished. "Julia's the snake in all of this. You'd better hope she doesn't team up with Evelyn. With Evelyn's seemingly unlimited supply of cash and Julia's desperation, it could be an unholy alliance."

Yeah, one that could have already happened. Evelyn could have given Julia the cash to pay those gunmen. That way, if Evelyn managed to kill both Lauren and him, she'd have a better shot at getting her hands on the baby.

"If Julia's the snake you think she is," Lauren said, "then we need proof to stop her. Do you have anything we can use? Something more than just her owing money to a loan shark."

"That should be enough," Duane snapped. But then he huffed. "I'll look and see what I can find. I have some incentive now that Julia's set the dogs on me with those fake files."

Cameron jumped right on that. "If they're truly fake, then figure out a way to prove that. The Rangers are looking into it, of course, but they could use your help."

He wasn't so sure of that. In fact, Jameson might not want any interference from a suspect, but it could keep Duane busy. Of course, if Duane was behind the attacks, then this was all just a ruse anyway. The man could have called them just to keep the focus on those files rather than the fact that someone was trying to kill them.

"Find something to put Julia behind bars," Cameron repeated to Duane, and he ended the call.

During the conversation, Cameron had glanced at Lauren a few times while also keeping an eye on the boys, but he really looked at her now. There were no tears in her eyes, but he saw that this was taking a serious toll on her. It was the same for him, too.

"Marrying you might not help," she said, her voice a whisper.

"It might not." Cameron had thought about all angles of this, and there was one angle that he needed to mention. "If we're married and one of us dies, then the other one would have a legal claim to the boys. We'd need to do guardianship paperwork, of course. And wills."

Hell, that caused Lauren to go way too pale, and he reached for her, pulling her into his arms. The embrace didn't last, though. Isaac lost his balance again, and Lauren bolted from the sofa. This time she didn't get to him in time, and the baby fell. He didn't hit hard, but it was enough to cause him to start crying. The commotion must have upset Patrick because he started to cry, as well.

Lauren scooped up both boys, kissing them, and Cameron went to her to help. He didn't get far, though, because his phone rang again. The sound of it only caused the babies to cry even louder. Lauren motioned for him to take the call while she took the babies in the direction of the kitchen.

Cameron figured this might be Duane calling back, but it wasn't a name or number he recognized. He pushed the answer button and hoped it wasn't someone from the press wanting a story. There'd already been a couple of those calls, and he didn't want another. Especially since he had "wedding" arrangements to make.

"Deputy Doran," he answered.

But the caller didn't say anything, and it put a knot in his stomach. Was this another hired gun?

"What do you want?" Cameron snapped.

"Uh, I'm Maria Black," the caller finally said.

He mentally repeated the name, and it rang a bell, but Cameron couldn't make the connection of why it seemed familiar.

"I was a nurse at the hospital where your sister, Gilly Doran, had her son," the woman added several moments later.

Bingo. Now he remembered. He'd spoken to her briefly after learning Gilly was dead. Other than her name, Cameron couldn't recall anything else about her. But just the fact that she had gotten in touch with him piqued his interest.

"Is something wrong?" he asked. Because it was possible that Evelyn was harassing her in some way.

"Yes." Her voice cracked, and it sounded as if she was crying. "I think someone's trying to kill me."

That was not what Cameron wanted to hear. "You need to go to the cops now. Where are you?"

"I'm on my way to the Blue River Sheriff's Office right now, and I need to see you. Lauren, too. God, I'm so sorry, Deputy Doran."

The knot in his stomach got worse. "Sorry for what?"

The sound of her sob was loud and clear. "I wouldn't

have done it, but your sister begged me to help her. She was dying, and she begged me to do it. Please forgive me. I'm the one who switched the babies."

Chapter Ten

Lauren sat in the back of the cruiser, staring out the window but not really seeing anything. She felt numb. Of course, she'd known in her heart that the boys had been switched, but she hadn't prepared herself to hear the proof of that.

If it was the truth, that is.

She hadn't gotten a chance to speak to the woman who'd called Cameron, but there had indeed been a nurse named Maria Black who had worked at the hospital where Lauren and Gilly had had their sons. And while it wouldn't have been easy, Maria would have been in a position to make the switch. That didn't mean she had, though.

"Evelyn could have put the nurse up to doing this," Lauren said to Cameron and Gabriel. Her brother was behind the wheel of the cruiser, and Cameron was in the backseat with her.

Judging from their quick sound of approval, the two had already come to that conclusion. "Do you remember Gilly ever mentioning this nurse?" Cameron asked.

"No. But she was on the ward where we were. And Gilly was desperate to keep her baby from Trace. He was still alive then, and she was terrified of him."

That caused a muscle to flicker in Cameron's jaw. It was obviously a sore subject that his kid sister had been in an abusive relationship. One that he hadn't been able to stop. But then, Gilly had kept a lot from him because she'd been worried that Cameron might kill Trace if he learned that Trace made a habit of beating her up.

"When we get to the sheriff's office, I'll ask Maria to take a polygraph," Gabriel said. "It's not conclusive, but if she's lying, it might spur her into telling the truth." He paused. "You do know I'll have to arrest her, right?"

Lauren nodded. She was torn between hating the woman and wanting to thank her for trying to keep Gilly's child safe. Of course, by doing that, Maria had put their lives in a tailspin.

"I can't think of a reason why Julia or Duane would do a baby switch," Lauren tossed out there.

"They could have hoped to prove Patrick wasn't Alden's child," he reminded her. "That might help Julia's lawsuit to get her brother's estate. It might help Duane's cause, too."

True, but that seemed a stretch. Not for Evelyn, though. She might have thought it would be easier for her to kidnap Patrick since Lauren wouldn't have been on the lookout for the woman. Still, it might not have been anything that complicated. Because Maria could be telling the truth.

"I'm guessing you two will go through with this marriage while you're here?" Gabriel asked.

Lauren hadn't been expecting his question. Though she should have. She knew that Cameron had told Gabriel about their plan to wed. She also knew her brother didn't approve. To him it probably seemed like a knee-jerk reaction, one that Cameron and she might regret later. And they might. But doing something—anything—felt better than just spinning her wheels.

"What the hell?" Gabriel mumbled, and he slowed the cruiser.

Since they were still a good mile from town, that put Lauren's heart in her throat, but it took her a moment to figure out what had caused her brother to say that. There was a car just ahead, parked on the shoulder. The driver's door was wide-open.

"You recognize the car?" she asked.

"No," Gabriel and Cameron answered together.

Definitely not good. This wasn't a heavily traveled section of the farm road. In fact, the only traffic was usually from people who lived nearby, but there was a way to access the road from the interstate so occasionally people would take the wrong exit and then look for a turnaround.

"Get down on the seat," Cameron told her.

Lauren had already felt the surge of adrenaline, and that caused her to feel even more. Her breathing was already too fast. Her heart was throbbing in her ears. She did start to move lower but not before she got a glimpse of someone slumped behind the wheel of the car.

A woman.

One Lauren thought she recognized.

"I think that's Maria Black," she managed to say before Cameron pushed her down on the seat.

"There's blood," Gabriel grumbled.

That sent her heartbeat up another notch, and Lauren immediately thought the worst. Easy to do since Maria had said someone might be trying to kill her. Mercy, had some hired thugs gotten to her before she could make it into town?

After Gabriel called for an ambulance, he stopped directly next to Maria's car, and Lauren had another look just to make sure it was indeed the woman. It was.

And, yes, there was blood.

It was on the side of her head. Maria's face was turned toward them with her head resting on the steering wheel. Lauren was about to ask if she was dead, but then she saw the woman move.

"Stay in the cruiser with Lauren," Gabriel told Cameron.

Lauren could tell he didn't want to do that. Cameron wanted to be out there helping his boss, but he stayed put. However, he did open the door a fraction and drew his gun.

Because the person who'd injured Maria could still be around.

Keeping low, Lauren glanced around, trying to spot anyone else in the area. There weren't many trees on this stretch of land, only pasture, so it would be hard for someone to hide. But then she remembered one of the goons at the ranch who'd hidden in the ditch outside Cameron's house. There were plenty of ditches, including one that was just to the right of Maria's car.

"Be careful," she warned her brother.

Gabriel also drew his gun and went to Maria. Lauren couldn't hear what he said to her or vice versa, but she did see the woman's lips move. Maria didn't seem strong enough, though, to lift her head, and she didn't open her eyes. Lauren couldn't tell if that was because the woman was dazed or if she was dying. Yes, there was blood, but it didn't seem like there was enough to indicate she was bleeding out. It was possible she'd had to slam on her brakes and hadn't been wearing her seat belt. Her head could have hit the steering wheel. She certainly had seemed frantic when she'd called them, and people in a panic made mistakes.

"Maybe it won't take long for the ambulance to get here," Lauren muttered. And while she was hoping, Lauren added that whatever Maria was saying to Gabriel, that it would help them figure out what the heck was going on.

Gabriel took Maria's hand and had her press it to her side. Maybe that meant she was injured there, as well, and her brother had done that to make sure the wound didn't bleed too much. After Gabriel had done that, he came by the side of the cruiser.

"She says someone rammed into the rear end of her car," Gabriel explained. He wasn't looking at them, though. Like Cameron, he was keeping watch around them. "A big bulky guy got out of the other vehicle, came up to her and shot her at point-blank range."

Oh, mercy. Lauren had to put her hand to her chest to try to steady her heart. "How is she still alive then?"

"My guess is she won't be for long. The bullet appears to have grazed her head, but she was shot in the chest, too."

Cameron cursed. "What did Maria say to you?"

"She only said one word, and she kept repeating it." Gabriel paused. "Julia."

The air was suddenly so still that it felt as if everything was holding its breath. Everything including Lauren.

"Julia's behind this," Lauren heard herself whisper.

"Or someone wanted Maria to believe she was," Cameron quickly pointed out.

Yes, that was possible. Julia had perhaps tried to set

up Duane, and now he could be doing the same to her. But why would he, or Julia for that matter, hire someone to murder Maria?

Gabriel's head whipped up, his attention going in the direction of the road behind him, where she heard the sounds of someone slamming on their brakes. Lauren hoped it was just someone who belonged out here, someone who was stopping to see if they could help.

But judging from Gabriel's expression, he didn't think that.

Neither did Cameron. He pushed Lauren all the way down on the seat, and Gabriel ran back to the cruiser. However, before her brother could get back in, Lauren heard another sound.

Someone fired a shot.

CAMERON DIDN'T HAVE much time to react. In the blink of an eye, the shooter leaned out from the SUV, sent a bullet slamming into the cruiser and ducked back behind the heavily tinted glass. Almost immediately, the driver sped up, and Cameron knew they were about to slam into them.

He didn't have to tell Gabriel to hurry. He was. But Cameron did have to warn Lauren again to keep down. She was obviously terrified for her brother. And she should be. Gabriel was literally out in the open, and another shot could kill him.

However, the gunman didn't fire again. That was because the SUV did plow right into them, jolting them forward.

Cameron's shoulder smacked into the back of the seat, the impact so hard that the pain jackknifed through him. But that was the least of his worries. The impact also caused the cruiser to collide right into Gabriel. Lauren shouted out to him as he fell to the ground.

Now more shots came. Three of them, and Cameron had to fight to regain not only his balance but his aim, too. Hell, he was hurting, but he pushed that aside and threw open the door that had slammed shut during the collision. He had to return fire. Had to keep these thugs from killing Gabriel.

Cameron leaned out of the cruiser, took aim at the SUV's front windshield and started firing. The glass was obviously bulletproof, but his shots were doing some damage. They were causing the glass to crack, and maybe that would be enough to obstruct the driver's view.

It wasn't enough for the gunman, though.

The thug's hand came out from the passenger-side window, and he fired at Cameron. Cameron had to scramble back, and in the same motion, he pushed Lauren onto the floor in case the glass on the cruiser gave way.

"My brother," she said on a rise of breath.

He couldn't see Gabriel, which meant he was probably pinned down in front of the cruiser. He couldn't stay there because Cameron needed him back in so they could get the heck out of there. That meant trying to get Maria into the cruiser, as well.

Cameron took out his backup weapon from the side holster in his jeans and handed it to Lauren. "This doesn't mean I want you getting up and returning fire," he warned her. "I want you to have it just in case."

What he meant was in case all else failed and those goons made it to her. If that happened, it would mean they would have already shot Gabriel and him.

"What are you going to do?" Her voice was shaking like the rest of her.

Something that wouldn't be particularly safe, but then, nothing was safe right now. He gave her his phone, as well. "Make sure we have some backup on the way out here."

That wasn't just busywork, either. Cameron wasn't sure if Gabriel had requested assistance when he'd called the ambulance, and if he hadn't, Cameron needed more deputies on the way now.

"They're coming," Lauren relayed to him a few seconds later. "But the ambulance can't get in here as long as shots are being fired."

Yeah, he'd known that would be the case, but he had to try.

"Don't get up," he told Lauren one last time.

He threw his door all the way open, using it for cover. Not just for him but for Gabriel, too.

"We need to get Maria," Cameron said to Gabriel.

Cameron didn't shout it because he didn't want to telegraph his moves to the gunmen, but they likely couldn't have heard anyway because the bullets were slamming nonstop into the cruiser. It wasn't only the passenger firing, either. The driver had gotten in on the shooting.

Gabriel came around the side of the cruiser. He didn't appear hurt—thank God—and he opened the front door. Cameron didn't lean out far enough to make himself a target, but he fired some shots at the gunmen, hoping he would get lucky and hit one of them. He didn't, but at least it caused them to pull their hands back into the SUV. That gave Gabriel and him a few precious seconds to rescue Maria.

Even though Gabriel had said the nurse probably wasn't going to make it, Cameron couldn't leave her there to die. The thugs would likely just shoot her again, and this time, they would finish her off.

Cameron and Gabriel both took hold of Maria, dragging her out of her car and into the front of the cruiser. Gabriel climbed over her, getting behind the wheel, and Cameron scrambled to get in the backseat. He almost made it, too.

But the SUV slammed into them again.

Cameron heard Lauren call out to him. He heard Gabriel curse, too, but he couldn't respond. That was because the impact caused the still open back door to smack against his head. His arm and shoulder were still hurting, but this was a whole new level of pain. Worse, it dazed him enough so that it blurred his vision.

The shots started coming at him again, the bullets tearing through the metal in the door. Cameron groped around, trying to orient himself, but he was pretty sure he was failing. Until someone caught on to his arm and pulled him onto the backseat of the cruiser. He landed against the seat and came up, ready to fire.

But Lauren fired first.

That was when he realized one of the thugs was right there. Just a few feet away from him. The guy had obviously gotten out of the SUV with plans to get close enough to kill him. And that was exactly what he would have done if Lauren hadn't put a bullet in his head.

The shooter dropped to the ground.

Seeing his partner fall must have enraged the driver because he slammed the SUV into them again.

"Hold on," Gabriel warned them a split second before he gunned the engine and sped off.

The jolt tossed Cameron and Lauren around again, and it didn't help that the SUV managed to ram them one more time.

Cameron got his door shut, and he pivoted in the seat to try to figure out what he could do. Not much. The front of the SUV had almost certainly been reinforced, but there wasn't much damage to it. That meant the driver had no trouble coming at them again. Gabriel pushed the accelerator even more, trying to get them out of there.

Despite the ringing in his ears, Cameron heard a welcome sound. Sirens. Backup had arrived. But the thug in the SUV no doubt heard them, as well, because he slammed on his brakes. The road wasn't that wide, but he managed to get turned around in just a few seconds.

And he drove off.

Cameron wanted to go after the SOB and beat the truth out of him. He wanted to find out who'd hired him and his dead partner to try to kill them. But it was too risky to do that. Instead, Gabriel instructed the backup to go after the SUV while he continued to drive toward town. It didn't take long for the SUV to disappear from sight.

Lauren's hands were shaking hard, but she was able to use his phone to call the ranch. "The SUV might go there," she said.

That upped his concern a couple of notches. Even though he knew there were plenty of security measures in place, Cameron didn't release the breath he'd been holding until he heard Jameson tell Lauren that all was well at the ranch. The babies were fine.

Two cruisers went flying past them, heading in the same direction as the SUV. Cameron only hoped they could catch up with him and bring the snake in alive for questioning.

Gabriel kept volleying glances in the rearview mirror and at Maria, but he also made a call to the sheriff's office.

"Are you okay?" Cameron asked Lauren.

She nodded. "But you're not. Your head is bleeding."

"I'm fine." That was possibly the truth, and even if it wasn't, Cameron had no plans to do anything about it.

He cupped Lauren's face, checking for any injuries but didn't see any. However, there was a new level of fear in her eyes. Of course, she had just killed a man. Her second one in two days. It would only add to the other nightmares she already had.

"How about you?" he asked Gabriel. "Are you hurt?"

"Just some bruises." He tipped his head to Maria. "She can't say the same, though."

No. Now that the woman was in the cruiser, Cameron had no trouble seeing that the front of her dress was drenched in blood. Cameron pulled off his shirt and held it to her chest wound. It wasn't much, but maybe it would help until they could get her to the hospital.

"What about the ambulance?" Lauren asked. "How soon can it get here now that the shots have stopped?"

"It's just about a half mile up," Gabriel answered. "I talked to Jace at the office, and he said they're waiting for us."

Good. That would mean Maria would soon get the medical attention she needed.

"Julia," Cameron heard Maria mumble. Her voice was too weak, and he wasn't sure if she could manage more than just that one word, but Cameron had to try.

"Did Julia hire the men who did this to you?" Cameron asked.

Maria opened her eyes, and it was as if she was surprised he was there. "Deputy Doran," she said. Her gaze drifted to Lauren. "I'm so sorry."

"The apology can wait." Cameron hated to sound harsh, but hearing that wasn't going to help them. "Why do you keep saying Julia's name?"

Maria dragged in a shallow breath. "She came to see me."

Probably not a good thing especially since Julia was desperate for money. "You told her about the baby swap?"

Maria nodded, and her eyes drifted down. "Be careful."

It was definitely a warning, but Cameron didn't get a chance to press her for more. That was because Gabriel hit the brakes again. This time, though, it was for the ambulance. He pulled to a quick stop right next to it, and the medics rushed out to take Maria.

"I'll ride with her to the hospital," Cameron insisted.

With the seconds ticking away, he figured he only had a few minutes at most to get what he needed from Maria. The truth. And then maybe he could finally put an end to this once and for all.

Chapter Eleven

Lauren sat at Gabriel's desk and waited. Something she'd been doing since they'd arrived at the sheriff's office over an hour ago. There wasn't much else she could do until Cameron called with news from the hospital.

Maybe the news would be good. Maybe Maria would survive surgery and be able to tell them what was going on. Until then, Cameron had no plans to leave.

At least the boys weren't anywhere near the danger and the aftermath. Lauren hadn't been able to stop herself from calling Dara three times to make sure all was well there. It was. And now she had to pray it stayed that way.

She heard the footsteps heading toward her, and Lauren practically jumped to her feet. But it wasn't Cameron. It was Gabriel. He had a foam box in one hand, a bottle of water in the other, and he was sporting a very concerned look.

"A sandwich from the diner," he said, putting the box and water on the desk in front of her. "You need to eat."

Yes, she probably did, but she wasn't hungry. In fact, her stomach was churning. Still, she would try to keep something down. It wouldn't do any of them any good if she got light-headed.

"Anything from Cameron?" she asked, but she already knew the answer. If there had been, Cameron would have texted her. He knew she was on pins and needles while she waited.

He shook his head and opened the foam box when she didn't touch it. Lauren sat down and took a small bite of the BLT. There wasn't just one sandwich, though, but two. Gabriel must have thought she was starved. Or just eager to sample something she hadn't had in a long time.

"You remembered this was my favorite," she said. He'd even gotten a bag of her favorite chips to go with it.

"Of course I remembered. You're my sister."

There was some emotion that went with that comment, and Lauren knew they were talking about a lot more than just the sandwich.

She looked up at him, their eyes connecting. "I can't apologize for leaving Blue River. I *had* to go."

If he agreed with that, he didn't show any signs of it. "Now you're back." He paused, a muscle flickering in his jaw. "With plans to marry Cameron."

There was definitely no hint of agreement for that, either. "We don't want any chance of the boys being sent to foster care."

Gabriel nodded. Finally, they'd found some common ground. "And then what? What do you do when we stop the person behind the attacks?"

At least he'd said *when* and not *if.* This had to stop. They couldn't keep going on like this.

"I don't know," she answered honestly. "When the DNA tests prove there's been a swap—"

"There was," Gabriel interrupted. "I just got the results back. I texted Cameron, too, so he knows."

Obviously, Lauren had known the swap had taken place, but it still felt like a shock. A violation, really. Someone—Maria, probably—had swapped the babies, and in doing so had robbed Lauren of being with her son for the first year of his life. She'd done the same to Cameron.

"I love Patrick just as much as I do Isaac," she said, pushing the sandwich aside. No way could she take another bite.

"I know. Cameron feels the same way."

He did. Lauren had no doubts about that, either. "That's another reason for the marriage. Neither of us can give up the babies we've been raising."

Gabriel stayed quiet for a moment. "So you…what? Try to make a real go of it?" He didn't wait for an answer. "Because if you're not, then that's not right for Cameron or you. Especially Cameron. You've had a marriage, a real one, but Cameron's never had that. He deserves it."

Lauren was already reeling from the DNA news and everything else that'd happened, but that only added to the feeling. She hadn't expected her brother to have that objection.

But he was right.

Cameron did deserve better. He deserved a real wife who loved him and wanted to build a family with him. Lauren could give him the family—that was already in place—but she wasn't sure she could handle the rest. A real marriage to Cameron would mean her staying in Blue River. It would mean forgetting her past. And she wasn't sure she could do that just yet.

"What are you suggesting?" she came out and asked.

"That you hold off on saying I do at least for a day or so until you've had time to give it more thought."

Good advice. But it wasn't advice she could take. "It would crush me if the boys were taken away. In fact, I couldn't let that happen, and that means Cameron and I could end up breaking the law."

Gabriel gave her a snarled look that only a lawman big brother could manage, and he made a suit-yourself sound. Since she'd obviously ruffled his feathers, Lauren went to him and brushed a kiss on his cheek. She hadn't expected it to help and was surprised when it did. It soothed his expression a bit anyway.

"I love you," he said. "I only want the best for you. For Jameson, Cameron and Ivy, too."

She knew that. So did they. But there were no easy ways for her to get "the best." Right now she'd just settle for keeping the babies and the rest of them safe.

"I love you, too," Lauren answered.

They had a nice moment, one that felt like old times before Gabriel tipped his head to the sandwich. "You should finish eating. You're going to need your strength. Duane and Julia are on their way here now."

That wouldn't be fun, but it was necessary. "They agreed to come?"

Gabriel gave her a flat look. "I didn't exactly ask. I told them I'd put out warrants for their arrests if they didn't show up. I want to question Julia especially."

Yes, because Maria had kept repeating the woman's name.

"I thought if I had Julia and Duane here together, that one of them might blurt out something when they started arguing with each other," Gabriel went on.

"There seems to be enough bad blood between them that it brings out the fangs."

It did. And the two had had no trouble incriminating each other in their other conversations. Too bad nothing had panned out on those so Gabriel could make an arrest. There'd been no proof that Julia had hired those gunmen, and the Rangers hadn't had any luck confirming that the files Julia gave them were real and not some attempt to set up Duane.

"And Evelyn?" she asked. "Are you bringing her in, too?"

Gabriel got that hard look again. "She's not answering her phone, and according to her housekeeper, she didn't come home last night."

Lauren thought about that for a moment. "Could she be with her *friend*, Judge Olsen?"

Gabriel shook his head. "I called him. He didn't know where she was, either. I pressed him for some info about his relationship with Evelyn." He put relationship in air quotes. "But he got huffy and reminded me that I was a small-town cop who had no right to question him."

"That sounds like something a guilty man would say. Please tell me there's something that proves Evelyn has bought off Judge Olsen?"

"Nothing. So far," he quickly added. "I'm hoping either Julia or Duane will have something to say about that, too. All three—Duane, Julia and Evelyn—seemed to be coiled around each other like a family of snakes."

They did. And that was unsettling. It was bad enough if only one of them was behind this, but if they'd teamed up…well, Lauren didn't want to go there.

She heard more footsteps, and Lauren hurried to get

past Gabriel so she could peer out into the hall. Gabriel didn't let her get far, though. He stepped in front of her, probably because he thought it was one of their suspects. It wasn't.

It was Cameron.

He was wearing a bandage on the side of his head near his right temple, but even seeing that didn't diminish the relief she felt. It flooded through her, and Lauren practically ran to him. She hadn't intended to do it, but she put her arms around him and kissed him.

Cameron's muscles tensed, probably because he hadn't been expecting it. And because Gabriel was almost certainly watching them. Still, Cameron didn't push her away. He let the kiss linger until Lauren eased back.

And that was when she saw the weariness in his eyes. Lauren was pretty sure she knew what it meant, too.

"Maria's dead?" she asked.

He nodded and brushed a kiss on her cheek. Not a kiss of relief as hers had been. Also not one of passion. That had been meant to comfort her, and much to her surprise, it worked.

She'd been right about Gabriel watching them. He was in the doorway, but he walked out, stopping directly in front of them. "Did Maria say anything else?"

"No." Cameron scrubbed his hand over his face and blew out a long, frustrated breath. "She was unconscious by the time she went into surgery, and she died on the operating table."

Lauren reminded herself that the woman's chances of surviving hadn't been that good, but it was still a blow. Not just because they wouldn't be able to get answers from her but also because a woman was dead.

Maria hadn't exactly been innocent since she was the one who'd switched the babies, but she didn't deserve to die because of what she'd done.

"Whoever's behind this can now be charged with murder," Gabriel said.

He was right, but the trick would be to catch the person.

As if waiting for something, Gabriel glanced at both Cameron and her. Maybe he wanted to discuss the marriage, but he didn't get a chance to do that. That was because his phone rang. When he glanced at the screen, he mumbled something about having to take the call, and he went into the squad room.

"Make sure she eats," Gabriel told Cameron from over his shoulder. "Her lunch is on my desk."

Cameron immediately took her back into her brother's office, and she was about to remind him that he needed to eat, too, but he sat across from her and helped himself to some of the chips. She handed him half the sandwich, and he started in on that, as well.

"You know about Duane, Julia and Evelyn?" she asked.

He nodded, then drank some of her water, too. It seemed…intimate or something. Which her body thought was good. Of course, her body often had thoughts like that around Cameron.

"SAPD is looking for Evelyn," he explained, which meant Cameron had been keeping up with the case even when he'd been at the hospital. "The justice of the peace will be here soon, too."

He took something from his shirt pocket and handed it to her. A marriage license.

"I had the clerk bring it to the hospital," Cameron added. He ate more of the chips and stared at her. "Having second thoughts? Or did Gabriel talk you out of doing this?"

"He tried," she admitted. And paused. "FYI. You deserve better, though. Better than a marriage of convenience."

The corner of his mouth kicked up in a slight smile, and he leaned across the desk to drop a kiss on her cheek. "Lauren, there's nothing convenient about you," he drawled.

There it was. The heat that always went to flames. It set off red flags in her head. Because the heat could lead her to do things that shouldn't be happening. At least not now anyway. Cameron and she had too much without adding sex to the mix.

The heat faded considerably when she heard the voices in the squad room. Julia and Duane had arrived. And they'd brought their lawyers from the sound of it. Someone—a man —was talking about this being harassment.

"I haven't started to harass you yet," Gabriel growled, his voice low and dangerous as only Gabriel could manage. "Trust me, you'll know when I've started."

Cameron and she stepped into the hall just as she saw Gabriel motioning for Duane and Julia to follow him. Lauren had been right about the lawyers. There was a man and woman, both wearing business clothes, and they fell in step behind Gabriel as he led them toward the interview room.

Julia stopped to give Lauren a glare.

Lauren glared back and hoped she wouldn't lose her temper and punch the woman. Julia had been a thorn in her side for years, and Lauren had reached her limit. So that her brother wouldn't have to arrest her for assault, she stayed just slightly behind Cameron when they went into the interview room with the others.

"They're going to stay for this?" the female lawyer balked.

"Yes," Gabriel said without hesitation. "And rein in your attitude. Just a short while ago, the three of us had thugs shoot a lot of bullets at us. They killed a woman. And before that woman died, she said one thing—the name of your client. I think Cameron, Lauren and I deserve a few answers about that."

"What?" Julia had just sat down, but that brought her right back to her feet. "That nurse said I did this?"

Obviously, Julia knew plenty about this situation, and judging from her lawyer's scowl, she didn't like that her client had just admitted as much.

Gabriel put his hands on the metal table and leaned in, his face getting very close to Julia's. "Tell me everything you know about *that nurse*."

Duane huffed. "I don't know why I got called in for this. Obviously, this is Julia up to her old tricks again." He got up to leave, too, but Cameron shot him a glare that could have frozen Texas in August.

"Sit," Cameron said through clenched teeth.

Duane sat, but his lawyer—the bald guy in a gray suit—rattled off a legal protest. He didn't mention the word *harassment*, though.

"Your client has the means, motive and opportunity to be behind that attack," Gabriel reminded the lawyer. "That's why he's here. And that's why he's staying here until I get answers. Don't," he added when the lawyer opened his mouth. "I have enough to arrest your client, and I'm in a bad enough mood to do it. Just let Deputy

Doran and me ask the questions, and we might be able to get to the bottom of this."

Maybe it was the badass looks on Cameron's and her brother's faces, but the lawyers, Duane and Julia didn't say anything.

Gabriel waited a couple of seconds, and he turned back to Julia. *"That nurse,"* he repeated. "Start talking."

Julia didn't do that right away. She took a deep breath first. "I went to see her. You already knew I was suspicious about Patrick. Because he doesn't look like Alden or me. Or Lauren, for that matter. I'd hoped Lauren had cheated on my brother, that the baby was someone else's. Like *his*." She motioned toward Cameron. "It's obvious Lauren still has feelings for him."

It probably was obvious. Lauren sighed. This old attraction was hard to hide.

"Anyway, Maria didn't admit it at first," Julia went on, "but she finally said she'd switched the babies. She claims she did that because of his sister, Gilly." She pointed to Cameron again. "Gilly was afraid of her baby's father, Trace Waters. Well, I thought that was a stupid reason to do the switch because Trace could have gone after the wrong kid. He could have gone after my nephew."

Julia probably wanted them to think that she cared if that happened or not. She didn't. It would make Julia's lawsuit a little easier if Alden's son wasn't around to be his rightful heir.

"Did Maria happen to say how she did the switch?" Cameron asked.

"I didn't ask about that, but Maria claimed she never intended to put my nephew in danger. She said Gilly had told Trace that the baby wasn't his, and that she would prove it with a DNA test. She had Maria do a test on Alden's son and was having the results sent to Trace. That way, he wouldn't try to take the baby."

That helped soothe Lauren's nerves a bit. At least Gilly had had a plan to protect Isaac. And if Trace had insisted on repeating the DNA test, he would have assumed Gilly had been telling the truth about the boy not being his. Still, there was something not right about this.

"Why didn't Maria tell us what she'd done after Gilly's boyfriend was killed?" Lauren pressed.

"How should I know?" Julia snarled. "I only saw the woman once."

"Yet she kept repeating your name when she was dying." Gabriel stared at her, clearly waiting for an explanation about that.

But an explanation didn't come from Julia. It came from Duane.

"Julia met with Maria more than once," Duane said. Julia opened her mouth as if to shout out a denial, but Duane added, "I have proof."

"You can't possibly have proof—" But Julia stopped, her eyes narrowing. "You had me followed."

"I did," Duane readily admitted. "I wish I'd had you watched 24/7 because that way you wouldn't have had the chance to set up those fake books to try to get me in hot water."

"You had no right," Julia spat out as if she was completely innocent in all of this, and she looked ready to launch herself at Duane.

Cameron got in between them. He pointed to Julia. "How about telling us the truth? Not just about Maria but everything else."

"I have told the truth," she insisted. She paused.

"Other than the number of times I met with Maria. What does it matter if I met with her once or three times? It doesn't," she quickly concluded.

Cameron huffed. "It matters because you lied. Now, I want to know why."

Julia made a sound of outrage, and she pushed away her lawyer when she tried to whisper something to Julia.

"I didn't see the point in Maria telling Lauren and you what happened," Julia finally explained. "I mean, you were both raising the babies, and it would only send things into a tailspin."

It didn't take long for Lauren to figure out what Julia had done. And what she'd intended to do. "You paid Maria hush money. Or you could have silenced her by threatening to turn her in to the cops. Of course, you didn't plan to keep it a secret. My guess is you were going to spring the DNA results during the lawsuit. That way, it would negate Patrick's claim to Alden's money."

"Bingo," Duane agreed. "And the reason Julia didn't spill the news sooner was because she didn't want to give you time to figure out what was going on. She was counting on you being stunned enough to just hand over the money to her."

"And it might have worked," Lauren said over the profanity Julia was aiming at Duane. "Except I also got suspicious and had a DNA test done. I would have known the results and had time to figure out what they meant long before the lawsuit."

"That's why Julia hired the gunmen." Duane, again.

Julia went after Duane, this time slamming into Cameron. Her lawyer caught on to her, and between Cameron and her, they managed to get Julia back in her seat.

"My client shouldn't have to sit here and listen to these allegations," the lawyer snapped.

"They're not allegations," Duane responded without hesitating. "Julia came to me months ago and wanted us to team up against Lauren. She thought there was something I could do to drive Lauren back into Cameron's bed. That way, Lauren might decide the lawsuits weren't worth fighting. I mean, it's not like Lauren needs the money or anything."

Gabriel glanced at Lauren, and even though he didn't come out and say it, this was probably what he'd had in mind when he wanted them all in the room together. Obviously, Duane and Julia had been trying to figure out how to get their hands on Alden's money and company.

Julia was glaring. Not just at Duane, either. She shared that glare with Cameron and Lauren. "You have no proof I've done something wrong."

"But we do," Cameron assured her. "You met with a criminal suspect—Maria. You knew she'd committed a crime, and you didn't tell the cops. That definitely falls into the 'done something wrong' category."

Julia sputtered out some angry sounds and slid back her chair, scraping the metal legs against the floor. She got to her feet. "Duane doctored the company books, and I don't see you harassing him like you're doing to me."

"Oh, I'll get to him," Gabriel said. His phone dinged with a text message, and he glanced at the screen before returning his attention to Julia. "Duane knew about Maria's crime, too, and didn't report it. That means both of you are going to stay for a while as my deputies take your statements. I'll have a little chat with the DA to see if he wants me to go ahead and arrest you."

That started more protests from Julia, Duane and their attorneys. They were all so loud that it was nearly impossible to hear what any of them were saying. Gabriel ignored them all and turned to Cameron and her.

"Wait here," Gabriel added to Julia and Duane, and he motioned for Cameron and Lauren to follow him into the hall. Her brother didn't say anything, though, until he'd shut the interview room door. "Maybe they won't kill each other before I get Jace in there to take their statements." He tipped his head to the squad room. "By the way, you two have a visitor."

So that was what the text had been about. And Lauren soon saw who the visitor was. Henry McCoy. He'd been the justice of the peace for as long as Lauren could remember.

Cameron looked at her. The kind of look that implied he was trying to figure out what she was thinking. Was she still up for this? Or was she having second thoughts?

The answer to both questions was yes. Lauren wasn't sure this was the right thing to do, but she was going through with it. She gave Cameron a nod. Her brother must have known what that meant because he huffed. However, Gabriel didn't try to talk her out of it. He walked on ahead of them, making his way to Jace's desk. No doubt to tell the deputy to get started with those statements.

"Thank you for coming," Cameron told Henry. He went to the man and shook his hand.

"Cameron, Lauren," Henry greeted. The man was in his early seventies now, and he seemed frail in a suit that practically hung off him. His smile seemed genuine, though. "Always figured you two would tie the knot." His smile faded. "I hate that it's under these circumstances, though."

It didn't surprise Lauren that Henry knew about the attacks. Or that Cameron and she had once had a thing for each other. Heck, he might even know about the baby swap.

Henry looked around. "You want to say the vows out here or in one of the offices? Oh, and you don't need a witness, but maybe you'd like Gabriel to be there."

Lauren wasn't so sure Gabriel would want to do that, but she turned to ask him. Before she could do that, though, Cameron's phone rang, and she saw Jodi's name on the screen. It gave her another jolt of adrenaline, and it must have done the same to Cameron because he quickly answered it and put the call on speaker.

"Cam, you need to get back to the ranch ASAP. There's been some trouble." Jodi paused. "Evelyn's here."

Chapter Twelve

Cameron hated that he was having to rush Lauren out of the sheriff's office. When they were in a panic, it was hard to think straight, and with a mind-set like that, it could make them easy targets for those hired guns who were still out there. Still, Cameron didn't have a choice.

He couldn't let Evelyn get anywhere near the babies.

"Where's Evelyn now?" Cameron asked Jodi.

"I'm holding her at gunpoint. I had Jameson stay inside with the boys."

Good. Even though Gabriel had plenty of work to do, he must have heard what Jodi said because he grabbed the keys for the cruiser that was parked right out front. He motioned for them to go with him.

"How the hell did Evelyn get on the ranch?" Cameron hurried Lauren into the vehicle, and the moment they were in, Gabriel took off.

"We think she came in on that trail at the back of your house."

The one that Lauren had used. Lauren shook her head, maybe to let him know that she hadn't told the woman about the trail, but her headshake wasn't necessary. Cameron knew she wouldn't do that.

"Here's the thing, though," Jodi continued a moment later. "There's no vehicle on the trail. The hands checked. When they found Evelyn, she was in your yard. She looks dazed or something. I think someone might have drugged her."

Well, hell. Cameron certainly hadn't expected that. "Was she armed?"

"No. And she has some cuts and scratches on her hands. They look like defensive wounds to me."

Cameron looked at Lauren to see if she was making sense of this, but she seemed just as baffled as he was. Maybe, though, this was some kind of ruse.

Or trap.

That put his heart in his throat. "Are you outside with her?" he asked Jodi. Cameron met Gabriel's gaze in the rearview mirror and saw the concern in his eyes.

"Yes. The hands brought her here, but I didn't want her in the house."

Neither did Cameron. But he didn't want Gabriel's wife being gunned down. "Move her to the porch." It wasn't ideal, but at least it would give Jodi a little cover, and she wouldn't be so out in the open.

"Make sure the hands keep watch," Gabriel added. "We're already on the road and will be there soon."

"Hurry," Jodi said. "I got a bad feeling about this."

Since Lauren, Gabriel and he had been attacked just hours earlier, Cameron wasn't feeling so easy, either. Of course, Evelyn usually brought trouble with her wherever she went.

Cameron ended the call so he could keep watch around them. After all, they were going to have to drive right past the place where Maria had been shot.

And where Lauren had killed a man.

It wouldn't be a good thing for her to see—since

she'd be reliving that latest nightmare—but it was the shortest route to the ranch, and they would have to take it. The minutes counted now, and he wanted to get to Jodi so that she wouldn't have to be in harm's way. Judging from the way Gabriel was speeding, he felt the same.

"Why would Evelyn have done this?" Lauren said, but she seemed to be talking more to herself than to him.

"Maybe she's desperate." Or worse. She could have gone off the deep end.

Cameron's phone rang, the sound causing Lauren to gasp. It got Gabriel's attention, too. Probably because he thought it was his wife calling back with bad news. But it wasn't a number that Cameron recognized.

That bad feeling skyrocketed. Because this could be one of the gunmen. Cameron answered it, putting it on speaker, but he didn't say anything.

"Deputy Doran?" the caller asked. "I'm Judge Wendell Olsen. I'm a friend of Evelyn—"

"I know who you are," Cameron interrupted. "Did you put her up to trespassing onto the Beckett Ranch?"

The judge made a slight gasping sound. "Trespassing? No, Evelyn wouldn't do that."

Cameron didn't groan, but that was what he wanted to do. "Yes, she would, and she's there now."

"Not by choice. Something must have happened."

Either that or the judge didn't know just how loony his friend could be. "Why are you calling?" Cameron didn't bother to make his tone sound even marginally pleasant because he didn't like this clueless clown distracting him.

"I was worried about Evelyn. And her housekeeper just called. SAPD found Evelyn's car in a parking lot at a bar in south San Antonio. It's not an area where Evelyn would go. I think she was kidnapped."

That would mesh with the defensive wounds that Jodi thought the woman might have. Still, Cameron wasn't buying this. Evelyn could have something up her sleeve.

"Why would a kidnapper take Evelyn to the ranch?" Cameron came out and asked the judge.

"To make her look guilty of violating her restraining order. And you're the person who'd gain the most from that." The judge also wasn't tossing out any friendly vibes.

It took Cameron a moment to get his jaw unclenched. "You just accused me of a felony. Want to rethink that?"

Silence. For a long time. "I don't want you railroading a woman who simply wants to see her grandson."

"Evelyn doesn't want to *see* him," Cameron corrected. "She wants custody of him. Big difference, and from what I'm hearing, you think you're going to try to make that happen."

More silence from the judge. Then he said, "I'll get Evelyn's lawyer and the San Antonio cops out to the ranch."

"SAPD has no jurisdiction in Blue River," Cameron reminded him.

"Then I'll get the Rangers."

Olsen really wasn't going to like this. "No need. There's already one at the ranch. Jameson Beckett. I suppose you'll threaten us with the FBI next, but they have to be invited to an investigation. I'm not inviting them. Not for this anyway. However, I wonder what they would think about a judge pressuring local law enforcement to do his bidding because his friend with a criminal record just committed another crime."

Cameron figured that put a scowl on the judge's face. "I just want to make sure Evelyn's treated fairly." And with that, he ended the call.

Great. Now he had a meddling judge added to this mix. It made Cameron rethink the idea of staying at the ranch. It was time for him to look into a safe house for Lauren and the babies.

Gabriel took the turn to the ranch so fast that Cameron was surprised he didn't lose control of the cruiser. He grappled with the steering wheel, keeping it on the road, and he sped toward his house.

The hands were definitely out and about. Cameron spotted six of them, and one of them had to open the cattle gate so that Gabriel could drive through. The moment the house came into view, he saw the reserve deputy, Mark Clayton, in the front yard. And he also saw Jodi. She was indeed on the porch by the front door and was holding a gun. She had it aimed right at Evelyn, who was sitting on the top step a good eight feet away from Jodi.

Gabriel braked to a stop and threw open the door. In the same motion, he drew his gun. "Go inside," he told Jodi.

Cameron rarely heard that kind of emotion in his boss's voice, but it was definitely there now. Gabriel loved Jodi, and it was obvious he'd been worried about her. Cameron was, too, but he was just as concerned for Lauren and the others in the house.

"I told Jodi I'd keep an eye on the woman," Mark said, "but she insisted on doing it herself."

That didn't surprise Cameron. He'd known Jodi his whole life, and her stubborn streak was just as big as her heart. Since she was a security specialist, she had the training to hold someone at gunpoint. The training to protect herself, too, but Gabriel almost certainly hadn't wanted the woman he loved in danger.

"Wait inside with Jodi," Cameron told Lauren.

She hesitated, then shook her head. "I don't want Gabriel and you out here. It's too dangerous."

Lauren was right. A good sniper might be able to pick them off. That was why he had to hurry this along. He brushed a kiss on her cheek and gave her a nudge to get her moving. He gave her a different kind of nudge when he whispered, "Check on the boys. Make sure they're not near the windows."

Her eyes widened, and she practically ran inside. One down, one to go. Plus, he really did want to make sure the boys were in the safest place possible. Lauren would see to it that they were.

Gabriel, however, didn't go in. He went onto the porch, blocking the door with his body. Probably in case Evelyn tried to bolt inside.

"Your wife said she would shoot me if I moved," Evelyn told Gabriel.

"She would have. And if you move, I'll shoot you if Cameron doesn't beat me to it first."

It was an empty threat. Well, the shooting part was anyway. Jodi had told them that Evelyn wasn't armed, so they couldn't use deadly force on her, but Cameron would stop her if she tried to get in the house.

"Start talking," Cameron demanded. "Why are you here?"

Evelyn looked him straight in the eyes. "Because you set me up."

Cameron huffed and tried to rein in his temper. "Let's deal in reality and not fairy tales. I haven't had time to set you up. I've been too busy dodging bullets from hired guns. And if I did want to frame you for something, the ranch is the last place I'd bring you."

She kept staring at him as if trying to figure out if he was telling the truth. She must have decided he was because Evelyn finally looked away and touched her fingers to her mouth. The gesture muffled a sob. For the most part anyway. Cameron still heard it. Normally, he had a soft spot for a crying woman, but he wasn't feeling anything more than wariness when it came to Evelyn.

"Start from the beginning," Gabriel said. "Tell us what happened."

Since this could go on for a while and he was still in the yard, Cameron joined Gabriel by the door.

"I was leaving my office to go home when a cop pulled me over," Evelyn explained. "It wasn't a cop car, but he had a blue flashing light. And a badge. He showed me his badge." She pressed her fingers to her mouth again. "I lowered the window to ask him why he'd pulled me over, and he pulled a stun gun out. I fought him, but he hit me with it."

Evelyn turned, showing them her neck. There were indeed two wounds there that looked like the kind of marks a stun gun would make.

"Did you get the cop's name?" Gabriel asked.

"No. In fact, I don't remember much after the stun gun. I think he must have drugged me. When I woke up, I was out in the middle of nowhere. The woods," she clarified. "My car wasn't there. Neither was my phone or purse. So I started walking on a path. I ended up in your backyard."

"Convenient," Cameron mumbled.

She lifted her head, the anger flashing through her

eyes. "No, it wasn't. I was attacked by a cop and brought here."

"By a fake cop," Cameron corrected. "Lauren, Duane and Julia all had fake police officers go to their homes. In Lauren's case, the guy shot her in the arm."

Evelyn gasped. "Was my grandson there when that happened?"

Cameron nodded. "He was in the house."

And he carefully watched Evelyn's expression. The color drained from her face, and she seemed horrified. But Cameron didn't know if that expression was because her grandson had been in danger or because Evelyn had hired those thugs and they'd gone against her order to make sure the baby was safe.

It took several moments before Evelyn regained her composure. "May I see him? May I see Patrick?"

Cameron didn't even have to think about this. "No. Not as long as you're a suspect in these attacks."

Even though that was a serious accusation he'd just made, Evelyn didn't lash out. "But you'd let me see him if there was no chance of his being in danger, if the fake cops and hired guns were caught?"

Now he had to think about it. "I'd consider it if I knew beyond a shadow of a doubt that you had no part in any of this. That includes Maria Black's murder."

Her mouth dropped open, and she got to her feet. "Maria's dead?"

Cameron wasn't going to get into how she knew the nurse. Apparently, everyone connected to this had known her.

"She's dead," Gabriel verified. "A gunshot wound to the chest at point-blank range. My guess is a fake cop who someone hired did that to her."

Evelyn shook her head and looked genuinely distressed about that. She glanced around as if trying to figure out what to do. Cameron hoped she didn't try to run because he didn't want to have to go after her.

"Will you be taking me to the sheriff's office?" she asked Gabriel.

Gabriel tipped his head to Mark. "No, he will be." He motioned toward Allen Colley, one of the hands who was close to the house. "And he'll go with you, too. I'll be there later when I've made sure things are okay here."

Both Cameron and Gabriel waited on the porch until Mark, Allen and Evelyn were in the cruiser and Mark had driven away.

"You believe her?" Gabriel asked him as they went inside.

"No." But then Cameron had to shrug. "Maybe she's telling the truth. Julia or Duane could have set her up because they needed a patsy." And Evelyn would have made a great patsy because of her police record.

Lauren and Jodi were right there waiting in the foyer for them. Gabriel reset the security system, hooked his arm around Jodi and moved her away from the door. They went toward Gabriel's office.

"I heard most of what Evelyn said," Lauren volunteered. "First, though, I checked on the boys. They're okay."

Cameron didn't doubt that, but he wanted to see for himself so he made his way to the nursery. The relief came when he spotted them napping on a quilt on the floor. The disappointment, too, because he'd wanted to hold them. He certainly needed something to ease the tension he was feeling.

Lauren helped with that when she gave his hand a gentle squeeze.

Both Dara and Merilee were in the room, sitting on the floor next to the boys. The curtains were drawn, and the lights were off.

"Everything should be all right now," Cameron told them, and he hoped that was true.

Merilee gave a shaky nod and made her way to a chair where she picked up her e-reader. Dara said something about getting a snack and headed to the kitchen. He doubted she'd be eating, though, since she didn't look very steady.

Cameron hated what this was doing to Dara and Merilee. Hated what it was doing to all of them. Thankfully, the only ones who didn't seem to be aware of the danger were Patrick and Isaac.

He looked at Lauren, taking her back into the hall so their conversation wouldn't wake the boys. But Lauren spoke before he had a chance to say anything.

"We're leaving the ranch?" she asked.

They were obviously on the same wavelength. He nodded. "It'll take me a while to set up a safe house, but I should have it ready by tomorrow."

She didn't question that. Didn't argue. But then, Lauren knew full well that the hired guns were still at large, and another attack could happen despite all their security measures.

"We'll also need to postpone the marriage plans," Cameron continued. "I don't want to take you back into town, and I don't think it's a smart idea to have the justice of the peace come here."

Lauren made a sound of agreement. "The thugs could maybe use him to get to us."

Yep. Heck, the thugs could use anyone, and that was why it was best if they were away from here. Every minute they stayed at the ranch, they put Lauren's family and the ranch hands in danger.

Cameron was about to find a quiet place to work so he could start on making the arrangements for the safe house, but he heard footsteps, and a moment later Jameson came into the hall. He looked in on the boys before he motioned for them to follow him into the foyer.

"I got some news on the loan shark Julia owes," Jameson explained. "The guy's name is Artie Tisdale, and he's bad news. He wouldn't say much to me on the phone. I think he was afraid I was recording it, but one of the other Rangers is headed over there now to talk to him."

It didn't surprise Cameron one bit that the guy was wary of talking to law enforcement. He probably wouldn't say much to the other Ranger, either, but they had to try.

"Did he admit Julia owed him money?" Lauren asked her brother.

"He chose his words carefully, said that he'd *helped Julia out* when she was short of cash, but of course he didn't admit to being a loan shark. He also didn't say anything about what he would do if Julia didn't pay back the cash soon."

Cameron thought about that. "Tisdale could have paid for the hired guns. Heck, they could be on his payroll. Is there anything to link Tisdale to the dead gunmen?"

"There's no money trail, but yeah, I could see Tisdale doing that to protect his investment. If Julia gets her brother's estate, then she could pay back Tisdale's loan along with all his other expenses."

Lauren shuddered, rubbing her hands along the sides of her arms. She winced a little, too. A reminder of her injury. Cameron wanted to kick himself for not having a medic check her out when they'd been at the sheriff's office.

"I'll let you know if the Ranger gets anything more from Tisdale," Jameson went on. "In the meantime, I'll look for any connection between Tisdale and the thugs. Something might turn up."

Cameron wanted that to happen, but a loan shark had probably covered his tracks.

Jameson turned to walk away, but Gabriel came hurrying into the foyer. One look at his face, and Cameron knew something was wrong.

"Please tell me there aren't gunmen on the ranch," Lauren said.

Gabriel shook his head. "No, but gunmen just attacked Allen and Mark. And they took Evelyn."

Chapter Thirteen

Lauren stared out the window of the guest room. She wasn't standing directly in front of it, though. Cameron's orders. He'd also told her to keep the curtains shut, which she had, but she could still look out through the small gap on the side where the curtains met the wall. She could see part of the ranch and her parents' old house.

It was a view she'd seen a lot as a kid since Gabriel's place had once belonged to their grandparents.

She'd come here plenty of times and stayed in the rambling big house. Had actually stayed in this very room even though in those days it had been her gran's sewing room. But this was a first for her to stand at the window and keep watch for hired guns.

And Evelyn.

Everyone was on the lookout for the woman. For the thugs, too. But the ranch had over a thousand acres. That made it nearly impossible to watch every part of it. The gunmen could take advantage of that. Maybe Evelyn, too.

Since that only caused Lauren to feel more depressed, she turned her attention to the makeshift bed on the floor where the boys were sleeping. Dara and

Merilee had volunteered to sleep in the nursery with them, but Lauren had thought it was safer for them to be on the second floor. Plus, she hadn't wanted them near her. That way, if something went wrong, she could grab them and try to escape.

At least Mark and Allen hadn't been hurt when the gunmen had attacked the cruiser. In fact, Mark had said the men hadn't even seemed interested in them. The goons had rammed into the cruiser, running it off the road. When that happened, they'd opened the door, dragged out Evelyn and put the woman in their SUV before they sped away.

Lauren had no idea if Evelyn was still alive or if this had been some ruse to make it look as if she'd been taken. Either was possible. Heck, the judge could have even helped her do this so she could escape.

Lauren sank down on the floor not far from the boys, and she leaned the back of her head against the bed. Her body needed sleep, but her mind was still racing too much for that to happen. Maybe, though, she'd be able to get in a nap since they would likely be moving to the safe house in the morning. That would bring a whole new set of worries since they'd have to take the boys out in the open, but maybe once they were in place, there'd be some peace of mind, too.

All of their suspects and the hired guns knew the location of the ranch. They almost certainly knew Cameron, the boys and she were in Gabriel's house. That was why they had to move, and Lauren only wished they didn't have to go through the long night before that happened.

She'd left the door open, so she had no trouble hearing someone walking toward the bedroom. It was Cameron. Not a surprise. He'd been checking on them and giving her updates every half hour or so. Since he'd been keeping his footsteps light—hard to do with cowboy boots on a wood floor—he probably hoped that he would find her asleep. At least the boys were, and that was enough for now.

Even though the lights were all off, there was still enough illumination coming from downstairs that she could see his weary expression. Of course, that weary expression was on a very hot face, so she saw that, as well. As she usually did when she had eyes on Cameron, she felt that tug in her belly. Felt it lower, too. But she figured they were both way too tired for tugs or kisses.

"Anything on Evelyn?" she whispered. Best to get her mind on something else other than Cameron's face.

He shook his head, went to her and sank down next to her on the floor. Not touching her exactly, but he sat close enough for her to catch his scent. He'd showered, probably because he'd had blood on his shirt from the earlier attack. Now he was not only wearing clean clothes, he also smelled like soap and the leather from his boots.

That didn't help the tug.

Normally, she wouldn't have considered those scents a turn-on, but her body suddenly seemed very interested in that combination.

"There's been no ransom demand," Cameron said. "And she hasn't turned up dead. Judge Olsen thinks we're behind it, of course. I think Evelyn wants to play the victim card because she thinks it might stop her from being arrested. It won't," Cameron assured her.

Good. Well, maybe good. If Evelyn was guilty, Lauren definitely wanted her in jail, but the truth was, the woman could be a pawn in all of this. A pawn who could now be in grave danger if those thugs weren't actually working for her.

"Gabriel did find out more on the cooked books that Julia claims she found," Cameron went on. "There's definitely some money missing from the accounts. Not a lot, considering the company has over ten million in assets." He turned to her. "Did you know it was worth that much?"

She nodded. "Isaac is the heir to all of that."

He stayed quiet a moment, a muscle flexing in his cheek. "I'd give away every penny to keep him safe."

So would she—along with every cent in her own personal accounts. But even that wouldn't ensure he was safe. Those thugs could still come after them.

"How much money was missing?" she asked.

"About thirty grand. Enough to fund the attacks and then some."

Yes, it was. "I'm guessing Duane is saying he's innocent, that he didn't take it?"

He nodded, but his forehead bunched up when he looked down at her. Not her face. But her shoulder. Cameron mumbled some profanity, reached out and unbuttoned her shirt. Since this didn't seem to be his version of hasty foreplay, Lauren figured he was checking her wound.

"I meant to change the bandage for you," he said, peeling it back and having a look at it.

She'd already had a look, and while the sight of it turned her stomach, it wasn't serious. "I changed it after my shower," she told him. "Jodi gave me some antibiotic cream to use on it."

He made a sound, sort of a disapproving grunt. Maybe because the wound turned his stomach, too. Or maybe he thought the home doctoring wasn't nearly enough.

Since he was examining her, Lauren did the same to him. She eased back the bandage on his forehead and had a look. It was clean but would probably leave a scar. It would just give him some more character on his face.

As if Cameron needed more of that.

"You're scowling," he pointed out. "Does the cut look that bad?"

She lowered her gaze, making eye contact with him, and Lauren wasn't sure what he saw, but the corner of his mouth lifted for a moment. "Oh, *that*," he said.

Yes, that. She looked away, but it didn't help. She was already caught up in the moment. Lauren would have liked to blame it on spent adrenaline and the fact that she didn't know if she was going to live long enough to see another day. Realizing something like that had a way of making every moment seem as if it might be her last. But she couldn't lie to herself. What she was feeling had to do with the attraction and nothing else.

"I kissed you in this room once," he said, glancing around.

He had, and she was a little surprised he remembered. She'd been seventeen then. Her grandparents had already passed away and Gabriel had moved in. Lauren had come to get her gran's sewing machine so she could mend the seam on her favorite shirt. Cameron had walked with her there so he could help her carry it back to her house.

"Apparently, a chore like that was fuel for a kiss back then," she joked.

"Breathing was fuel for a kiss," he joked back.

Except it was the truth. Still was. And that caused Lauren to sigh.

She should just get up, move away from him and keep watch again. There were so many reasons for her not to be with him. She didn't want it to cloud her mind. She shouldn't jump into that kind of intimacy until she was certain of her feelings for him. Plus, the boys were in the room.

But those good reasons turned to dust when Cameron leaned in and kissed her.

Despite his being so close, she hadn't seen the kiss coming, but Lauren had no trouble feeling it. One touch from his mouth, and the heat trickled through her. Head to toe.

He lingered a moment, deepening the kiss, before he pulled back and looked at her. Maybe to gauge her reaction. It must have gauged well because it caused him to give that hot half smile again.

"I guess breathing is still a fuel," he said, his voice low. Husky. A Texas drawl that pulled her right in.

Lauren figured either walking out or staying would be the wrong thing to do. Staying would lead to sex. Walking out would no doubt give her plenty of regrets. That was why she slid her hand around the back of Cameron's neck and pulled him to her for another kiss.

And she made sure it was plenty long and deep.

Enough to rid them of the breath that was apparently fueling some of this. Of course, the kiss did its own share of fueling, too.

"Give yourself some time. Think about it before you do anything," she said.

Cameron looked up at her, and she had no trouble seeing the surprise on his face. Lauren figured that surprise increased a lot more when she got to her feet and headed for the door.

CAMERON WASN'T SURE what was going on in Lauren's head, but he sure as heck knew what was going on in the rest of her. That'd been heat he'd seen in her eyes. Plenty of it. And the heat had been in her kiss, too.

So why was she leaving?

The simple answer to that was she wasn't, and he would make certain of that. He got up as fast as he could and hurried to her. She'd already made it into the hall by the time he caught up with her, but she was just standing there—as if trying to figure out what to do.

"Is this about having second thoughts?" he asked.

A soft breath left her mouth. "No. Second thoughts happened hours ago. I'm on third and fourth thoughts now."

Yeah, he'd been there, done that. And all those doubts hadn't solved a thing. He still wanted Lauren, and she felt the same way about him. Cameron proved that in a really stupid way. He hooked his arm around her waist, hauled her to him and kissed her.

Obviously, if Lauren needed some thinking time, this was not the way to go about it. So he didn't kiss her for long. Just enough to rid her of more of her breath. And he stepped back. Cameron figured she was either about to chew him out or—

She went with the *or*.

She took hold of the front of his shirt, gathering it

up in her hand as she pulled him closer. Lauren kissed him, and this time it wasn't a kiss to prove anything. It was scalding hot and meant to send them straight to bed.

Cameron responded, all right. He put his arms around her, dragging her right against him. Not that it took much effort. Lauren was already headed in that direction. Her breasts landed on his chest while the kiss raged on.

Cameron did his own version of raging. He slid his hand beneath her top, touching the bare skin on her stomach. It was hard to think, but he forced himself to remember the gunshot wound on her shoulder. He didn't want to hurt her.

If the injury was bothering her, Lauren showed no signs of it. She also showed no signs of the timid teenager who'd become his lover over ten years ago. No. This was a woman's kiss. A woman's touch. And this woman apparently knew exactly what she wanted.

She wanted him.

Lauren turned him, putting his back to the wall, holding him in place while she made the kiss even deeper. Cameron did more touching, too, sliding his hands into the cups of her bra. She must have liked that because she made a sound of pleasure. It wasn't loud, but it gave him another reminder.

They were in the hall of her brother's house. Gabriel or the others could come walking up at any second.

Cameron silently cursed and started maneuvering her back into the bedroom so he could shut the door. Of course, there was a problem here, too. The babies. Yeah, they were asleep, but if much more moaning and grappling went on, Lauren and he could wake them.

When he stopped kissing her, Lauren looked to see

what'd caught his attention. She glanced at the boys. Then, back at Cameron. All the while she was nibbling on her bottom lip. Maybe she was realizing the logistics of having sex wasn't going to be easy.

But it wasn't impossible.

Cameron looped his arm around her and got her moving. He grabbed the baby monitor along the way but put it on the counter as soon as they were in the adjoining bathroom. Lauren was the one who shut the door, and she immediately launched into another kiss.

The overhead light was off, and Cameron kept it that way, though there was a night-light by the sink. It was just enough for him to see the heat and the determined look in her eyes.

He was still having doubts about whether this should happen or not, but the longer the kiss went on, the more the doubts faded. Soon, he quit thinking and went with it. He pulled Lauren back to him, and this time he had more than kissing on his mind. Well, more than just kissing her mouth anyway.

She made another of those pleasure sounds when Cameron pushed up her top and kissed her breasts through the lace cups of her bra. It was good, but it got a whole lot better when he opened the front clip. That way, he could kiss her without the thin layer of fabric between them. She must have liked that, as well, because she fisted her hand in his hair and held on.

As he went lower.

Cameron got in some kisses to her stomach. Got her unzipped, as well, but Lauren seemed to want to kick up the pace. She achieved that by sliding her hand down into the waist of his jeans.

Yeah, she was kicking this up, all right.

He got rock-hard. And desperate to have her. Not exactly a good combination when he needed to make sure he didn't hurt her while he also listened to the baby monitor.

"Please tell me you have a condom," she said.

"Wallet, back pocket," he managed to answer.

She went after it, doing some clever touching along the way. It felt more like foreplay than looking for something they needed for safe sex. Of course, there were a lot of other "unsafe" things about this, but Cameron chose not to think about that right now. That probably had plenty to do with Lauren unzipping him.

Since there wasn't exactly anywhere else to go, Cameron lowered her to the floor. His back landed on the hard tile, but he barely noticed.

That was because Lauren landed on him.

Straddling him, she took out the condom and tossed his wallet aside.

Cameron did a little tossing, too. Even though he liked seeing Lauren on top of him, he had to move her to get her out of those jeans. Not easy to do. The bathroom wasn't that big, and Lauren wasn't making things easier because she was fighting to get his jeans off, too.

Everything suddenly felt way too urgent, and it was taking an eternity to rid them of their clothes. Cameron finally managed it, and Lauren moved back on top again. It was the best position so that her shoulder didn't get hurt, though he certainly didn't see any trace of pain on her face.

But he did see the pleasure.

Cameron was certain there was plenty of that on his face, too, because he was feeling a whole lot of it in his body. The feeling went up significantly when she got the condom on him and took him inside her.

Lauren went still, as if savoring this for a moment, and in the milky light, she made eye contact with him. It was as if the past ten years just vanished. They were young lovers again before the tragedy that had torn them apart. The ache came. The reminder of just how much he'd lost that night.

And then it was gone.

Because Lauren started to move. That rid him of the ache but created a different kind of one. His need to pleasure her. The need for release.

He caught on to her hips, guiding the movement that was taking him in and out of her. Not that she needed any guidance. Lauren was doing just fine on her own. Better than fine, actually. She was taking them both to the only place that either of them wanted to go.

She put her hands on his chest, anchoring herself while she leaned down and kissed him. Her mouth was still on his when she pushed against him one last time and shattered. That was all Cameron needed, and with the taste of her roaring through him, he gave in to the release and went with her.

Chapter Fourteen

The sound woke Lauren, and she jackknifed in the bed. It was a loud boom. And for several heart-stopping moments, she thought they were under attack, that one of those hired thugs had made it onto the ranch and fired a shot at them.

"A storm moved in," Cameron said. He was close to the bed. Very close. Right by the nightstand just a couple of inches from her. "It's thunder."

She heard the words, but it took a while for them to register. It was indeed storming. Lauren could hear the rain hitting against the windows and the tin roof. There was even a crack of lightning. But she wasn't sure how she'd managed to sleep through that or Cameron getting out of the bed.

Actually, she wasn't sure how she'd managed to sleep at all.

She had, though. She had apparently fallen asleep after Cameron carried her to the bed, and now it was morning. *Late* morning. Well, late for her anyway. It was seven thirty.

"I took the boys downstairs when they woke up about a half hour ago," Cameron said as he made an adjustment to his shoulder holster. "Dara and Merilee changed them and are feeding them breakfast."

Good grief. She'd slept through the babies getting up, as well. Obviously, sex with Cameron was an amazing stress reliever for her to be able to do that. She hadn't slept through the night since she'd become a mother.

"You should have gotten me up sooner," she grumbled.

He shrugged. "I had some things I had to work out. Things to do with the investigation," he added. "Besides, I wanted you to get some rest."

She wanted him to have some rest, too, but she was betting he hadn't gotten much. They'd gotten in bed together, but before she'd fallen into a deep sleep, she'd remembered him getting up to go to the window to look out. Keeping watch to make sure those thugs didn't come back for another round.

She threw back the covers, only to remember that she was stark naked. Cameron noticed, too, and he gave her one of those lazy smiles that reminded her of why she'd landed on the bathroom floor with him in the first place.

"We need to talk, so you should probably get dressed."

"Talk?" she questioned.

"About the safe house. About some other things." He was obviously keeping it vague, and she might have pressed for more, but he leaned down, brushing a kiss on her mouth. Coming from any other man, it would have qualified as a peck, but even a brief kiss was potent when it came from Cameron.

"I'll meet you in the kitchen," he added and headed for the door. But then he stopped and looked back at her. "By the way, Gabriel knows we were together last night. He came to the room at around five to check on you."

Lauren groaned. She didn't mind Gabriel knowing, but it wasn't something she wanted to discuss with him. Gabriel wouldn't feel the same way, though. She'd get another big-brother lecture from him about guarding her heart.

And it was a lecture she needed to hear.

She should do some heart-guarding, but considering she'd had sex with Cameron—amazing sex at that—that ship had already sailed.

The moment Cameron was out of the room and had shut the door, Lauren hurried from the bed and to the shower. She didn't even wait for the water to reach the right temperature. She just rushed through it and tried not to think of what could go wrong with the move to the safe house. They'd already been through so much, and she didn't want anything else bad to happen.

Lauren changed her bandage, got dressed and was ready to rush out of the room when she spotted something on the floor to the side of the vanity. Cameron's wallet. She'd tossed it there after she'd taken out the condom, and Cameron must not have seen it. She picked it up, the wallet falling open. And that was when she saw it.

The edge of the photo.

It was tucked in one of the slots normally used for credit cards. Without thinking, she lifted it out and got a shock. It was a picture of Cameron and her. They were smiling, and he had his arm slung over her shoulders.

She instantly remembered when it'd been taken. They'd been outside the barn at her house, and Ivy had just walked in on them making out. They'd been fully clothed, thank goodness, but Ivy had insisted on snapping the shot with her phone. Her sister had sent them both the picture, but Cameron must have had his printed out.

Strange that he would have kept it all these years. It seemed like something a man would do when he was in love, and Cameron had never come close to saying the L-word to her. Of course, maybe he'd put the photo there way back then and had forgotten about it.

Lauren headed downstairs, hoping to find Cameron alone so that she could give him the wallet without anyone noticing. No such luck. He was in the kitchen and so was everyone else who was staying in the house.

Like all the other rooms, the curtains and blinds were drawn here. Merilee and Dara were at the table eating breakfast. Jameson was holding Patrick, and Cameron had Isaac. Jodi was at the back window, peering out the side of the blinds. And Cameron and Gabriel were going over a map that was on the laptop computer screen.

They all stopped what they were doing and looked at her.

Gabriel's eyebrow lifted, and since it seemed as if everyone in the room knew what had happened in the guest room bath, she went to Cameron, kissed his cheek and handed him his wallet. What he didn't do was smile or kiss her back. For a moment she thought that was because Gabriel was standing there, but everyone else was looking somber, as well.

"What happened?" Lauren immediately asked.

Cameron put his wallet in his pocket and touched the map. That was when Lauren realized it wasn't an ordinary map. It was the ranch. It showed not only some of the trails but also the nearby roads.

"About two hours ago, one of the hands spotted a suspicious vehicle here. A black SUV." Cameron tapped the road that was only about a quarter of a mile from Gabriel's house. "The hands were down by the cattle gate and used binoculars to read the license plate." He paused. "It was bogus. There's no vehicle registered with those plate numbers."

Well, there went any trace of that dreamy morning-after feel from sex. Lauren glanced at the others and realized they'd already learned this bad news. And it was bad. That vehicle had been way too close to the house. Obviously, this is what Cameron had meant by needing to talk to her, but Lauren had figured it was going to be a discussion about arrangements for the safe house.

"Two hours," she repeated. "Why didn't you come up and wake me?"

"I woke Cameron instead," Gabriel said, looking straight at her.

Good grief. She wasn't normally such a sound sleeper, but that did explain why they'd had the time to come up with this plan. They'd probably been talking about it for the past two hours, and that meant Cameron hadn't just rolled out of bed when she'd awakened. He'd probably come up just so he could have her get dressed.

There was a loud boom of thunder, and Patrick started to fuss. Lauren took him, cuddling him close to her and hoping he didn't pick up on the fear that was starting to crawl through her.

"The SUV was gone by the time I made it to the road," Jameson said, obviously taking up where Cameron had left off. "I looked around but didn't see it."

What he didn't say was that didn't mean it was gone. The SUV could be on one of the trails or a side road.

"I have a reserve deputy posted here." Gabriel tapped the road that led from town to the ranch. "About an hour ago he saw a black SUV. It had different license plates from the one that was near here. But the plates were fake, too. The deputy went in pursuit, but the vehicle got onto the main highway before he could reach it."

If there were hired thugs in the second SUV, they could have doubled back. Or while the deputy was out chasing them, more hired guns could have gotten in place to launch an attack. That spelled out the bottom line for Lauren.

"It's too risky to take the babies out on the road," she said. "We can't take them to a safe house."

Gabriel, Jodi and Jameson all made sounds of agreement. Cameron groaned. "That doesn't mean they'll be safe here, either. You saw how easily Evelyn got through the trails. So could these guys."

That panic and fear weren't just crawling now. Both emotions were at a full sprint. Their situation sounded hopeless, but it couldn't be. They couldn't just stand by waiting for another attack.

"We need to do something." Lauren knew she sounded desperate because she was.

Cameron nodded, then paused. He looked as if he wanted to curse. "I don't like even asking you to do this, but I can't think of another way. Our first priority has to be to keep the babies safe."

"I agree," Lauren said without hesitation. "What do we need to do?"

Cameron looked her straight in the eyes. "We're going to have to force the gunmen to come after us. We'll have to make ourselves bait."

"FOR THE RECORD, I don't like this plan," Gabriel spat out.

Neither did Cameron, but he couldn't stomach the

thought of the babies being caught up in another attack. Apparently, neither could Lauren.

"So, how do we do this?" she asked. Again, no hesitation. "How soon can we make it happen?"

She probably had doubts, just as Cameron and Gabriel did, but Cameron knew something that was much worse than doubts and fear, and that was having the babies they loved in danger.

"The cruiser is already parked out front," Cameron explained. "You and I will pretend to get into it with the babies. What we'll be carrying are blankets that will hopefully look as if we have the boys. Since it's pouring rain, it shouldn't seem suspicious that we'd have them covered up like that."

"Where will the babies be?" Lauren asked him. Patrick was still fussing a little so she rocked him gently, brushing a kiss on the top of his head.

"Patrick and Isaac will stay here at the house with Gabriel, Jodi, the nannies and Mark, the reserve deputy. Jameson and Jace will come with you and me."

Cameron took a deep breath before he continued. Here was the part that was going to make Lauren very uneasy. "The gunmen probably have the place under surveillance, so we need to make them believe the babies are truly gone from the ranch. That means sending the hands back to the bunkhouse and to the barns. We need them out of sight."

She shook her head. "But what if gunmen come here after we leave?"

That was a question that had bothered Cameron right after he'd learned about the SUV being in the area. "The ranch hands will be close enough to respond." Not immediately, though. And that in itself was a risk.

"Merilee and Dara will be in the hall bathroom with the boys," Gabriel added. "It's the safest place in the house since there are no windows. Jodi, Mark and I will stand guard. If there's a sign of trouble, we'll sound the alarm and get all of you back here."

And there was the other concern that was eating away at Cameron. If there was trouble, then Lauren and he could be right in the line of fire. That was better than having the babies at risk, but it was nowhere near ideal.

Simply put, Lauren could be hurt.

Heck, Jace and Jameson could be, too.

"If we see the SUV once we're on the road," Cameron continued, "then it'll almost certainly follow us. We'll lead them here." He pointed to one of the larger trails that was about five miles from Gabriel's house. "Or here." Cameron moved his finger to another trail. "It's far enough away from the ranch—"

"Wait," Lauren interrupted. "Why lead them there? There are woods. The river, even."

"There'll be some hands, reserve deputies and even Rangers hidden on those trails." He checked his watch. "They'll be in place by now."

And with some luck, the hired guns hadn't spotted them. If they had...well, Cameron didn't want to go there.

"We also recorded this shortly before you came downstairs." Jameson hit a button on his phone to play the sound of the baby whimpering. It was almost identical to what Patrick had been doing just moments earlier, but this had come from Isaac when Merilee had stopped him from spilling his sippy cup of milk.

"Why would you need that?" she asked, turning first to Jameson and then to Cameron.

"In case the attackers call us." Cameron patted his phone. "They have my number because they've called me before. This way, they'll hear the recording and believe the babies are with us."

Lauren stood there, her forehead bunched up. She was obviously processing all of this, and Cameron wished he could give her more time, but he couldn't.

"If you can think of a safer way to do this," Cameron said to her, "I'd love to hear it."

Lauren rocked Patrick some more and shook her head. "Would we leave now?"

Cameron nodded. "The sooner the better. We need to put some distance between the boys and us."

She blew out a breath, kissed Patrick again and then did the same to Isaac. Lauren handed Patrick to Dara. "Please take care of them," she whispered, and she included Gabriel and Jodi in the glances she gave the nannies.

"I'll get the blankets ready," Jodi said, passing Isaac to Merilee. She headed out of the room.

Gabriel handed Lauren a gun that he took from the top of the fridge, and she tucked it in the back waistband of her jeans. "I've already given Cameron some extra ammo," Gabriel explained. "And make sure your phone is with you. Just in case."

Yeah, in case this plan went south and those goons tried to kill them. If that happened, then Lauren would be the one who'd probably have to make the call since Jameson, Jace and he would be returning fire.

Lauren checked to make sure, and she already had her phone in her front pocket. That meant they were as ready as they could be.

Jameson certainly didn't seem so eager to get out

the door. He huffed and grabbed two Kevlar vests that he'd gotten from Gabriel's home office. "My advice is to lay this on top of the blankets. So it looks as if you're protecting the babies. Then, once you're in the cruiser, put them on." He tapped his chest. "Jace and I are already wearing ours."

That was something Jace and Jameson had done because they'd thought they would be taking the babies to the safe house. Now they would be doing backup for Lauren and him, and the vests might come in handy.

It didn't take Jodi long to return with the blankets, and she'd already rolled them up in such a way that it did look like bundled babies. She handed one to each of them, and while Lauren took it, holding it against her shoulder as she'd done to Patrick, she also gave both boys another kiss.

Cameron kissed them, too, and he draped the vests over the blanket bundles, but he didn't linger. "Go ahead and take them to the bathroom," Cameron instructed the nannies.

No need to stretch out this goodbye. For one thing, it wasn't the safe thing to do, and besides, there were tears in Lauren's eyes. Best not to have her break down. Not until they were in the cruiser, at least.

Cameron waited until he heard the bathroom door shut with the nannies and the boys inside, and Jameson, Lauren and he headed to the front door where Jace was waiting.

"Move fast," Gabriel instructed.

Lauren probably hadn't needed anything else to put more alarm in her eyes, but that did it. Because it was a reminder that there could be snipers.

Gabriel turned off the security system so they could

get out the door, but Cameron was certain he would reset it. There wasn't anyone else he trusted more to protect Patrick and Isaac, but Cameron prayed it would be enough.

The rain seemed to be coming down harder now, and the lightning was close. So close that the thunder boomed almost immediately after the strikes. Definitely not a good time to be out driving, but they couldn't wait it out. The storm was supposed to last most of the day.

Cameron took hold of Lauren's arm to help her down the slippery steps, and Jace and Jameson ran ahead of them to open the doors. The moment they were inside, Jace drove away.

Lauren looked back at the house, tears watering her eyes, and even though Cameron doubted it would help, he kissed her. Her gaze came to his then, and even though she didn't say anything, he knew her heart was breaking.

She'd been through way too much in the past couple of days, and he certainly hadn't helped matters by having sex with her. Yeah, it'd felt necessary at the time, but it had caused them both to lose focus. Had been confusing, as well. But that was something he could dwell on another time.

"Go ahead and put on the vest," Cameron instructed.

He lay the blankets on the seat next to her and helped her into the Kevlar before she put on her seat belt. Cameron got on both his jacket and his seat belt, and then he immediately drew his gun. That didn't help with the alarm in Lauren's eyes, either.

"It's just a precaution," he told her. A necessary one.

As they'd discussed, Jace drove away from town and in the direction of one of the trails. It was hard to see much of anything because of the rain sheeting over the windows. Still, Cameron kept watch. So did Jameson and Jace from the front seat.

"So what's put Gabriel in a snit?" Jameson asked. He glanced back at his sister. "And it's not a snit because of the danger. I'm pretty sure this one's more personal."

Lauren frowned. "Gabriel found me with Cameron."

Jameson laughed. "Like old times. I seem to remember him not approving of you two way back when."

He hadn't. Gabriel had thought Cameron was too old for Lauren. And he had been. But that age difference no longer seemed like an obstacle. A good thing, too, because they had plenty of other obstacles to get in their way.

"Want my advice?" Jameson said, but he didn't wait for Lauren to answer. "Just let Gabriel know you're in love with Cameron, and he'll back off. Love cures a lot of ill will between siblings."

Lauren made a sound of surprise that was borderline outrage. That meant she didn't love him. Not that he thought she did. Lauren had fallen out of love with him years ago, and heck, it probably hadn't even been real love then. He'd been her crush.

A thought that made him frown.

Was that all it'd been?

The attraction had definitely been there, now and then. But maybe her feelings for him hadn't gone beyond basic lust.

"You were more than a crush to me," Cameron mumbled under his breath, but it was obviously loud enough for Lauren to hear because she practically snapped toward him.

However, she didn't blurt out anything to reassure

him that he'd just babbled the truth. "You have a picture of us in your wallet," she said.

Now she was the one who looked alarmed at saying something she hadn't meant to say. He nodded, admitting that he did indeed have a picture. One she must have seen when he'd left his wallet on the bathroom floor. But Cameron didn't get a chance to add anything to his nod. That was because Jameson spoke first.

"A black SUV just pulled out of the side road behind us." Jameson drew his gun and turned in the seat. "And it's following us."

Chapter Fifteen

The plan was working. Now Lauren had to hope that was a good thing and that they could truly lead these thugs away from the ranch.

"Speed up," Cameron instructed Jace. "They'd expect us to do that if we actually had the babies in the car."

Cameron gave an uneasy glance behind them at the SUV, followed by an equally uneasy one at the sky. Going fast on these roads wasn't a safe idea, but he was right. They needed to make this as realistic as possible. That meant taking risks.

More than the ones they'd already taken.

She prayed that whatever they would do, it would make Patrick and Isaac safe. Lauren didn't want these goons anywhere near the boys. Still, it was a chance that could happen. While Cameron and she were luring the gunmen, the gunmen could be playing a cat-and-mouse game to get them away from the house.

"They're speeding up, too," Jace relayed.

Lauren got a glimpse of that, and yes, the SUV was much closer now, but Cameron took hold of her arm and lowered her to the seat. "Pick up the blankets," he instructed. "Hold them as if you'd be holding the boys.

The cruiser windows are tinted, but they still might be able to see inside."

True, and again they had to make this look believable. Lauren gathered up the blankets in her arms, making sure they stayed rolled up.

"How much farther is the trail where we'll be turning?" she asked.

Cameron didn't jump to answer, and she saw the renewed alarm on his face. "Hold on," he warned her. "They're going to hit us."

It wasn't a second too soon because the jolt came. So hard that even with her seat belt on, it slung her forward. The strap caught her wounded shoulder in the wrong place and caused the pain to shoot through her. She made a sharp gasp that she tried to muffle, but she failed because Cameron looked at her. But he didn't look for long.

That was because the SUV rammed into them again.

The cruiser went into a skid on the wet pavement, and she could see Jace fighting with the steering wheel to keep control. The cruiser tires clipped the gravel area just off the asphalt and sent a spray of rocks banging against the doors and undercarriage. It sounded like gunfire.

"Hold on," Cameron repeated, and this time he took hold of her.

The SUV rammed into them again. And again. Obviously, the front end of the vehicle had been reinforced because the engine was still roaring behind them.

"Let me see if I can do something about this," Cameron said when Jace finally got the cruiser back on the road surface.

He lowered his window, the rain immediately dampening the backseat. Despite the summer temperatures, the spray of water was cold, and Lauren started to shiver. Part of the shivering, however, was because Cameron was about to make himself an easy target for those hired killers.

Cameron leaned out enough so he could take aim, and he sent two shots in the direction of the SUV. Since Lauren was down on the seat, she couldn't tell if he hit anything, but at least the SUV didn't ram into them.

But the gunmen did something worse.

They returned fire. The shots slammed into the roof of the cruiser. The bullets didn't tear through it, but Lauren could hear them slice across the metal.

"Why would they be shooting with the babies inside?" she asked, the question meant more for herself than the others. "Why would they risk that?" It didn't make sense if they wanted the boys alive.

If.

"They're not firing kill shots," Cameron answered. "If they were, they'd be shooting into the window. I think they're just trying to run us off the road."

Yes, but even that could hurt Patrick and Isaac. Maybe that meant these thugs didn't care if the babies were harmed or not. Or they could have figured out the boys weren't in the cruiser.

That thought didn't make her breathe any easier.

Lauren tried not to panic, but it was hard to rein in the fear. Not only were their precious babies in danger, but these goons could end up killing Cameron and her in a car wreck, too. Of course, that could be what the person behind this wanted. If it was Julia or Duane, they wanted her dead. Evelyn probably felt the same way about Cameron. She didn't want to think of what would happen to Patrick and Isaac if these thugs succeeded in carrying out whatever orders they had.

"How long before we get to the trail?" Lauren repeated.

"A minute, maybe." Jace was volleying glances between the road and the rearview mirror.

The SUV rammed into them once more, but this time Jace managed to keep control. There was no other traffic, thank goodness, so Jace swerved into the oncoming lane to stop them from being hit again.

"Let me try to hold them off." Jameson lowered his window as Cameron had done, and he sent three shots at the SUV.

Maybe those shots would buy them some seconds until they could get to the trail. Of course, the SUV would follow them. That was the plan, after all. The driver could still ram into them. But they wouldn't be going at such a high speed on the trail, and there'd be an ambush waiting for the thugs. Maybe they'd be able to capture at least one of them alive so they could get some answers.

"Everyone hold on," Jace said. "The turn is just ahead."

Lauren pulled in her breath and held it. There were wide ditches on each side of the trail, and if the SUV hit them again, they could land in one of those. They were filled with water and mud, and the cruiser would likely get stuck.

There was another thing that could go wrong, too. Simply put, the gunmen might not follow them. They might recognize this could be a trap and just speed away so they could regroup and come after them again.

Jace had to hit the brakes to slow down for the turn,

but he was still going pretty fast when he took it. The trail was a mixture of gravel, dirt and grass, and judging from the way Jace had gripped the steering wheel, he must have expected them to go into another slide.

And they did.

The back of the cruiser fishtailed, slinging them around again, but Jace got them back on course. He didn't speed up right away, though, and Lauren knew why. He was waiting for the gunmen.

She lifted her head to look out the back window. It seemed to take an eternity, but it was only a few seconds before she finally saw what she needed to see. The SUV made the turn, as well, and came after them. Jace hit the accelerator again.

"The reserve deputies and the Ranger should be about a half mile up," Jameson explained. He kept his eyes on the SUV but motioned for Lauren to get back down on the seat.

She did. But she hated she was being protected like this when all three of the men were high enough in the seats that they could be shot. Of course, the gunman's bullets would have to get through the glass first.

That thought had barely crossed her mind when there were more shots fired. These slammed into the trunk of the cruiser. Definitely not as "safe" as those on the roof since the trunk was right next to the backseat.

"What the hell?" Jace mumbled.

That put her heart right in her throat, and Lauren lifted her head again so she could see what'd caused his reaction. There was a motorcycle, and it was parked just beneath some trees just off the left side of the trail.

"Is that the Ranger?" Jace asked.

Jameson shook his head. "Maybe it's one of the reserve deputies. I'll ask Gabriel."

He took out his phone, no doubt to call their brother, but Jameson didn't get a chance to do that.

Because there was a blast.

It was deafening. Lauren couldn't be sure, but she thought maybe it'd come from the direction of the motorcycle. She was sure of something else, though. It hadn't been the sound of a bullet. No, this was something much, much bigger. And whatever it was, it hit them.

Hard.

Jace still had hold of the steering wheel, but it didn't seem to do any good. That was because whatever had hit them exploded into the front end of the cruiser. There were ditches here, too. Ones almost as wide as those on the road. And that was exactly where the blast sent them.

CAMERON DIDN'T KNOW what the guy by the motorcycle had shot at him. He'd barely had time to spot the man before he'd fired something. Not a grenade. The blast hadn't been big enough for that, but it'd been some kind of explosive device.

Jace cursed when the cruiser pitched to the left, and the deputy had no control when the tires on that side went into the ditch. Because of the rain, it was more of a small stream, and they instantly went into the bog.

Trapping them.

They were much too close to the motorcycle guy, since he was on the same side of the trail.

Cameron glanced down at Lauren to make sure she hadn't been hurt in the impact. She hadn't been, but she'd already pulled her gun and was about to sit up. He pushed her right back down.

Behind them, the SUV came to a stop. Not a fast one, either, which meant they'd slowed down enough, probably because the driver had known this was going to happen. And what had happened was the worst-case scenario for this plan. Because now they were trapped.

"I'll call the backup," Jameson said. He, too, still had his weapon drawn, and he was looking all around them.

Cameron was looking, too, but he could no longer see the man by the motorcycle. He'd likely slipped into the woods, and there were plenty of hiding places for him. The trees and underbrush were thick here.

"How far away is backup?" Lauren asked. She was shaking some, but not nearly as much as Cameron had expected her to be doing. Good. Because he might need her to help him shoot their way out of this.

He hated that she was in this position. Hated even more that he was the reason she was here. But Lauren and he were of a like mind on this. They'd wanted to do whatever it took to protect Patrick and Isaac.

And maybe that could still happen.

Cameron had to hold on to that hope. Unless the thugs had brought an army with them, then they might not be able to get to them in the cruiser. Added to that, backup was almost certainly on the way here, and they shouldn't be that far away.

"Backup's coming," Jameson verified when he finished his call.

Cameron looked back at the SUV again. No movement there. The men were staying inside. There was also no movement from anywhere in the woods, but he was dead certain more men were out there.

Hell.

"This could be a trap for the backup," Cameron told Jameson.

Jameson cursed, too, and made another call. Of course, backup would have anticipated that the thugs would be on the lookout for them, but they probably thought they'd be coming to a gunfight. There hadn't been a shot fired, though, since the blast that'd disabled them. That didn't mean, however, that more shots wouldn't come soon.

Cameron's phone rang, the sound knifing through the silence. Lauren gasped, and then she groaned when she saw *Unknown Caller* on the screen. It was almost certainly their attackers. Cameron answered and put it on speaker, but he didn't say a word.

"Deputy Doran," the caller said. "Looks like you and your woman are in a tight spot. I think this is what folks mean by sitting duck."

The thug was stating the obvious, but it still put a knot in Cameron's gut to hear it. "What do you want?" Cameron snapped, and he motioned to Jameson to play the recording on his phone. Within seconds, there was the sound of Isaac fussing.

"I want you and your woman, of course. Those kids, too," the thug said. "Good to know the little fellas weren't hurt during the blast."

"What if they had been?" Lauren snarled. "You could have hurt them. Is that what your boss wants you to do—hurt babies?"

There was plenty of anger in her voice, but Cameron figured it was also a stall tactic. The longer they kept him talking, the more time backup would have to arrive.

"Don't have a clue what my *boss* wants to do to them,

and it falls under the heading of I don't care. I just want my money. And no, don't bother to start offering me a payoff. I'm more or less committed to this, you see."

Which meant he could be being blackmailed or coerced in some way. So Cameron tried a different angle. "If you want immunity, you've got it." That was a lie. As a deputy he couldn't make an offer like that unless he cleared it with the DA. "All you have to do is tell us who hired you."

"No more talk about that," the gunman growled. "Just shut up and listen." He sounded impatient now. Probably because he knew they would have already requested backup, and that time was running out for him. "You and your woman need to get out of the cop car."

"And the babies?" Cameron asked. "Which one do we bring?" Because that would narrow down the identity of the person responsible for this. If the man said to bring Isaac, then it was either Duane or Julia. But Evelyn would want Patrick since he was her grandson.

"I would say just bring one of them, but since I don't know which one," the gunman snarled, "I'll be needing you to step out with both of them. And I'm not gonna do a countdown or anything. You come out with them now."

Cameron doubted the man would want to hear this, but he didn't have a choice. He couldn't take Lauren out there for her to be gunned down. "It's too risky for the babies."

"Hell, it's too risky for you!" the goon practically shouted. "Now, move. I'd better see that door opening right now."

Cameron looked at Jameson and Jace to see if they were ready for whatever was about to happen. They were. Jameson had turned off the recording, put his phone back in his pocket and he had a firm grip on his gun. So did Jace.

And Lauren.

"They'll come to the cruiser after us, won't they?" she asked.

As a minimum. And they didn't have to wait long for that minimum, either.

"Time's up," the gunman said, but the words had hardly left his mouth when Cameron saw something he didn't want to see. It was the guy who'd been by the motorcycle. This probably wasn't the one they'd been talking to since this man didn't have a phone.

However, he did have some kind of launcher.

And he aimed it at the cruiser.

Before Cameron could even react, another explosive came their way. It crashed into what was left of the front end of the cruiser, tearing the metal and engine apart. It also knocked out the front windshield. They had to shelter their eyes from the flying glass and debris.

"Still not convinced you should get out?" the goon on the phone said. "The next one goes right into the cop car where y'all are sitting."

It was a bluff. Possibly. But Cameron couldn't call him on that bluff, and he didn't have time to come up with a plan. They were going to have to run for it, and there was only one direction to go. To the right, away from the thug with the launcher. That meant they'd have to run directly in front of the SUV.

Cameron looked at Lauren, who'd just followed his gaze out the window. Judging from her expression she knew what was about to happen.

"Take both blankets, one in each arm," he instructed. That might save her from being gunned down.

Lauren gave a shaky nod and gathered them up. "When do we start running?" she asked.

"Now."

Cameron threw open the door and started shooting.

Chapter Sixteen

Lauren hadn't had nearly enough time to steel herself up for this, but maybe there was no chance of that happening anyway. Not with the strong possibility that they were all about to die.

Cameron got out ahead of her, took aim at the man by the motorcycle and sent several shots his way. Lauren didn't look back to see if that had pinned down the guy or sent him scrambling. She just ran as fast as she could while trying to keep hold of the blankets. Despite the rain and the slick, muddy surface, she raced across the narrow trail, went several yards into the woods and dropped behind a tree.

She had her gun. She was holding it in a death grip beneath the blankets. But no way did she have a clean shot. That was because Cameron, Jameson and Jace were in between the motorcycle thug and her.

"Run!" she called out to them.

They did, but they weren't hurrying as much as she'd done, and they were volleying their attention between the motorcycle and the SUV. Good thing, too, because it was only a handful of seconds before both SUV doors opened, and the armed men leaned out. They stayed in the SUV and behind the doors, using them for cover.

While they sent round after round of bullets at Cameron and the others.

Lauren didn't have a clean shot of them, either, so she could only pray that they reached safety.

Cameron and Jameson did. They ran toward her, but they only made it a few feet off the trail and ducked behind the first tree they reached. It was still much too close to the SUV, but at least they were no longer in a direct line of fire.

Unlike Jace.

He wasn't nearly as lucky.

Lauren watched in horror as a bullet slammed into Jace's arm.

She heard him make a sharp sound of pain, and he scurried to the front of the cruiser. It was a wreck, but at least he was out of the path of the men in the SUV. Not from the motorcycle guy, though, or anyone else who happened to be out here in these woods. That was why Lauren tried to keep watch for him.

Soon, very soon, Jace would need an ambulance, but there was little chance of getting one out here unless they stopped these hired guns. That meant killing them, since she figured they hadn't come out here with plans to surrender.

The thugs from the SUV continued to fire at Cameron and Jameson, forcing them to stay put, though Cameron did look in her direction. Just a glimpse. And she saw the same worry on his face that was no doubt on hers.

She caught some movement from the corner of her eye. It wasn't by the motorcycle, where she'd last seen the guy with the launcher. It was a good fifteen feet past that. But it was the same man, all right. He was behind some dense shrubs, and he lifted something. Not a launcher this time. But rather a gun.

And he aimed it at Jace.

"Look out, Jace!" she yelled.

But Lauren did more than just shout out a warning. She dumped the blankets on the ground and shot at the guy. She missed. Cursed herself for doing that because the man dropped back out of sight. She had no doubt, though, that he was still there, waiting for a shot where he could finish off Jace.

Her phone dinged with a text message, and while Lauren hated to take her eyes off her surroundings, she knew this could be important. It was. It was from Cameron.

Stay put and keep holding the blankets, he texted. Backup can't get to us right away.

Lauren did pick up the blankets, but her breath froze. The fear wedged there in her throat that'd clamped shut.

No.

That wasn't what she'd wanted to hear.

They needed backup. Worse, it could mean the Ranger and reserve deputies had been hurt or killed. Obviously, these hired guns had known they were trying to lead them to a trap. If they'd spotted the lawmen, then they could have taken them out before Jace had even driven onto the trail.

She forced herself to breathe. To think. Hard to do with the bullets still flying all around, not just from the SUV shooter but also from Cameron and Jameson.

Plus, she had to watch for the man with the launcher. He could send another one of those explosives at Jace. Or at Cameron and Jameson, for that matter. Lauren didn't think he would aim at her, though. Not as long as he thought she had the babies in her arms. It didn't make her feel better to know that she was safe while Cameron, Jace and her brother weren't.

Lauren adjusted her gun, holding it beneath the blankets, and she continued to keep watch. The gunman who'd had the launcher finally leaned out from cover again. Like before, he took aim at Jace. But this time, Jace must have seen him because he fired first. Unlike her shot, Jace's didn't miss, and the guy fell to the ground.

Good, one down and at least two to go.

It wasn't safe for Jace to try to make his way across the trail to her, but he did drop lower to the ground. She could see that he was grimacing in pain. However, he was also looking around to make sure there weren't others who could pick him off.

Even over the noise of the gunfire, Lauren heard another sound. A car engine. Someone was coming up the trail and would soon be behind the SUV. She hoped it was Gabriel or another cop, but she couldn't count on that. She had to do something to help.

Now that Jace was out of immediate danger, Lauren started moving. She stayed crouched as low as she could manage while still carrying the blankets, and she began to make her way to Cameron.

Jameson and he had almost certainly heard the car and knew that it could mean more trouble. If they had to fend off more gunmen, she wanted to be in a position to help.

Lauren kept moving. Kept checking her, too, to make sure Jace was all right. He was still in the same spot, and she didn't see any other hired thugs trying to get to him.

"Stay down," Cameron snapped when he spotted her. "Don't come any closer."

"I can help you return fire."

He didn't answer her, not with words, but he gave her a stern look while he continued to trade shots with the gunmen. Lauren did get down, but she went several more feet first and then took cover behind a tree. All in all, it wasn't a bad position because she had line of sight of Cameron and Jameson as well as Jace.

There was blood on his shirt.

The rain was soaking him, but the blood continued to flow. She saw him grimace again, and he pressed his hand over it. Probably to try to slow the bleeding.

In the distance she heard something else to let her know that things had gone wrong. More gunfire. It seemed to be coming from two areas—both up the trail and back by the road. The gunfire was probably why the backup couldn't get to them.

She kept her attention on their surroundings, but Lauren took out her phone again so she could try to text Gabriel. He almost certainly knew what was going on, but she wanted to make sure the babies were all right. Before she could press his number, though, her phone rang.

Unknown Caller.

Her heart thudded against her chest. Because the gunman was calling her. Maybe because Cameron was too busy shooting to answer. But it did make her wonder how he'd gotten her number.

She hit the answer button, but as Cameron had done earlier, Lauren didn't say anything. It didn't take long, though, before she heard the voice.

"Lauren," the caller said. "There's only one way for

your brother and Cameron to get out of this alive. And that's for you to bring me the babies now."

CAMERON HAD HEARD Lauren's phone ring, and he'd hoped it was Gabriel calling to reassure her that he had a plan to rescue her. But after one look at her face, Cameron knew it wasn't that.

Something was wrong.

Of course, the worst possible scenario came to mind. That something bad had happened at the ranch; that they were under attack. There were plenty of people at Gabriel's to protect Patrick and Isaac, but that didn't mean one of the boys couldn't have been hurt.

He wasn't close enough to Lauren to hear what she was saying, but she was definitely responding to something the caller had said. Not a good response, either. Lauren cursed the caller, and then her gaze flew to him.

Yeah, something was definitely wrong, but he didn't think it was fear that he saw. Cameron thought she was angry. So angry that every visible muscle was tight.

Even though Cameron had insisted that she stay put, Lauren started toward him. She didn't exactly stay down, either. She hurried, but at least she was continuing to hold the blankets to her chest. Unfortunately, they no longer looked much like babies because the rain had soaked the blankets. It had soaked Lauren, too. The rain was dripping off her face.

When she was still several feet away, Cameron ran to her, pulling her behind the tree with Jameson and him. He was about to ask her what'd happened, but she just handed him the phone. Her hand was shaking. *She* was shaking. But her eyes were narrowed almost to slits.

"It's Julia," she said.

Cameron doubted the woman was calling to check on them or declare her innocence for the umpteenth time. No. She was the person behind this. Probably the person in the car that'd just come to a stop in back of the SUV. Hell.

Of course, she was one of their main suspects, but it sickened him to think of this witch putting Lauren and everyone else in danger. And he figured Julia was doing that because she needed money. Now Cameron could feel his own surge of anger, and he hoped he got a chance to settle the score with this woman.

"What do you want?" Cameron snapped when he finally spoke to her. Jameson moved closer so he could hear over the drone of the rain.

"Lauren and Isaac," Julia said without hesitation. "Have them come to my car, and you, Patrick and anybody else you brought with you will be safe. You can even get an ambulance out here for your deputy friend."

Cameron wanted the ambulance for Jace, but that was too big of a price to pay. Jace would feel the same way about it, too.

"You really think I'll just allow Lauren and Isaac to go to you?" Cameron asked. "You'll kill them."

Now Julia hesitated. "No. I'm not about to kill my brother's son. Lauren and Isaac will be taken to an undisclosed location, and once I have the money from Alden's estate, I'll release them."

"Right." And he didn't bother to take the skepticism out of his voice.

Lauren was plenty skeptical, as well, and he didn't think her trembling was all from the cold rain. It was also from the rage she was feeling right now. Cameron had to make sure that rage didn't cause Lauren to do something stupid. Like try to go after Julia.

"You don't believe me," Julia remarked. She sounded so calm she could have been discussing the weather, but Cameron figured the woman was also feeling loads of emotion. Fear being one of them. Julia had to know that so many things could go wrong now.

That applied to Lauren and him, as well.

"You should believe me," Julia went on. "I'll disappear after I have the money and settle my debts. I plan to move overseas. A place where I can't be extradited back here."

There were many countries that didn't have extradition treaties with the US, but Cameron still wasn't convinced.

"I figure you'll stay put, right here in Texas," Cameron said. "And you'll probably set up Duane or Evelyn to take the fall for this."

Silence. Which meant he was probably spot-on with his theory. No way would Julia take the blame for any of this.

"You need to hurry," Julia warned him, her voice crisp now. "Don't count on help from your lawmen friends, either, because my men are holding them off on the road."

Cameron didn't like the sound of that, and he hoped none of them had been hurt. The injury to Jace was enough. "You've hired an awful lot of thugs for someone who's flat broke."

"Funded with money from Alden's company," she admitted. "And a little help from the person who loaned me money."

So the thugs belonged to the loan shark. That was

why none of them had been willing to negotiate a deal with Cameron. Their boss wouldn't have killed them. And this way, the loan shark ensured that he'd get not only the money Julia owed him but then some, too. Heck, the loan shark might end up taking most of the entire estate. Along with killing Julia. But the woman probably hadn't realized that.

"Your deputy might have managed to take out the person who was manning the launcher," Julia went on. "But there's someone else out there who can do the same job. He has orders to fire if Lauren doesn't come to me with Isaac. You've got a minute to send her out here."

"I'll go," Lauren whispered.

Cameron cursed and muted the call. Even though Lauren already knew this, he thought it was worth repeating. "She wants you dead."

"Yes, but when I get to the car, she'll want to take a look at Isaac, to make sure I've brought the right baby. When she does that, I can escape."

There were way too many things that could go wrong—especially since Julia would have at least one hired gun in the car with her. Still, they didn't have a lot of options here. If the guy with the launcher fired at them, then they'd all die.

Cameron forced himself to think, and there was no completely safe way to handle this. But maybe he could do something to ensure that Lauren made it out of this alive.

"Make sure there's not another launcher," Cameron told Jameson.

Jameson nodded, and he started moving. Unlike Lauren had done, he kept low. Obviously trying to stay out of sight while he made his way closer to the cruiser and the area where they'd last seen the launcher.

"Give me thirty seconds before you start walking out to Julia," Cameron added to Lauren. "I'll try to get as close to Julia's car as possible so I can be in place to help you escape."

He gave one of the blankets an adjustment and gave her a quick kiss. Cameron wished there was time to say more. Exactly what, he didn't know. But he hated to think that these might be his last moments with her.

"Thirty seconds," he repeated, and Cameron started moving.

Thankfully, there was plenty of underbrush so he could keep hidden, but Julia had probably figured he'd be trying to do something exactly like this.

He counted off the seconds in his head, and once he was close to that thirty-second mark, Cameron stopped and got ready to fire. He considered just shooting into the windshield of Julia's car with the hopes he'd hit her or her goons. But then the guy with the launcher would no doubt retaliate.

Cameron felt the punch of dread go through him when Lauren stepped out. Right out in the open. Of course, that'd been the plan, but still, he hated that she had to be in harm's way like this.

"I'm coming," Lauren called out to Julia.

She had a bundled blanket in the crook of her right arm. And she also had her gun. It wasn't hidden nearly enough, but there was no way Cameron could warn her now. Lauren was walking directly to the car.

The car doors opened. Both on the driver's and front passenger's side, and even though no one got out, Cameron figured these were the hired goons. Julia was probably in the backseat, but he couldn't see her.

"You'll want to drop that gun," one of the thugs told Lauren.

Lauren stopped, hesitating, and she let go of it so that it fell to the ground. She started walking again. Only making it a few steps.

Before the shot blasted through the air.

LAUREN HEARD THE sound and braced herself for the bullet to hit her. The old saying was true. Her life did flash before her eyes. The pain and the happiness. She'd known that Cameron had been a big reason for a lot of her happiness, and she regretted that she had never told him that.

But the bullet didn't hit her.

Stunned, she stood there a moment before she realized the guy on the driver's side of Julia's car had fired the shot at Cameron. Lauren's stomach went to her knees, and she called out for him.

No response.

The anger came, quickly replacing the stunned fear, and Lauren charged toward the gunman.

"Don't shoot her," Julia yelled. "Not until we have the kid."

Lauren had figured all along that Julia had no plans to let her live, and Julia had just confirmed that. Since holding the baby gave Lauren some protection, she kept running. Except she didn't go to the driver. She ran to the other side of the vehicle, where she hoped to get her hands on Julia.

Behind her, she heard the explosion. Mercy, that was where Jameson had been going, and she prayed he hadn't been hurt. Maybe he'd managed to get out of the path before that blast went his way, but she couldn't risk even glancing over her shoulder to check on him.

There was another shot.

The bullet slammed into the driver, and it'd come from Cameron's direction. She prayed that meant he hadn't been hurt and added the same prayer for her brother.

The thug on the passenger's side took aim at Cameron, and he started shooting. One shot right after the other. And Cameron wasn't returning fire.

Lauren kept moving, pushing aside all the gunfire and the possibility that the gunman would turn his weapon on her. In case he tried that, she held the blanket even higher so that it would make it harder for her to kill him.

When Lauren reached the car, the thug stopped shooting at Cameron, and he reached out to grab her. She didn't give him a chance to do that, though. She used the entire weight of her body to ram into the car door, which, in turn, rammed into him. He cursed her and howled out in pain. But Lauren ignored him and threw open the back door.

Julia.

The woman sat there, alone on the backseat, and she had a gun aimed right at Lauren.

"Give me the kid," Julia snarled.

Her sister-in-law had never been friendly to her, but now Lauren saw the pure hatred in the woman's eyes. She was certain there was hatred in her own eyes, too. Hatred that she aimed at Julia.

Yelling at the top of her lungs, Lauren tossed the blanket at her. She caught just a glimpse of Julia's stunned look before Lauren launched herself at the woman. Pinpointing all of her rage into her fist, she punched Julia right in the face.

Julia didn't just sit there and take that, though. She let out her own feral yell, and she came at Lauren, grabbing her by the hair and shoving her back. They fell out of the car and onto the ground. Unfortunately, Julia landed on top of Lauren, and she whacked her gun across Lauren's jaw.

The pain slammed through Lauren so hard and nearly robbed her of her breath. Still, that didn't stop her from fighting back. Nor did the shots that she heard being fired all around them. Cameron and maybe Jameson were in a fight for their lives, but Lauren was in her own fight. One that she had to win so that she could help Cameron and the others.

Lauren managed to catch on to Julia's wrist to stop the woman from hitting her with the gun again, but Julia only punched her with her left hand. That one wasn't nearly as hard as the first one had been, but it still dazed her for a moment.

"You should have just brought the kid!" Julia shouted. "They'll kill me now, but first I'll make sure you're dead."

Lauren had no intention of just letting her do that. While she still had a grip on Julia's wrist, Lauren shoved up her hand—and Julia's gun slammed into the woman's chin. Julia cursed her again.

And pulled the trigger.

The gun was close to Lauren's ear. Too close. Because the blast from the bullet was so loud that it deafened her. But she had no trouble feeling, and even though Julia's shot had missed her, that didn't stop her from head-butting Lauren.

Enough of this. Lauren wasn't just going to lie there while Julia beat her into unconsciousness. Then she'd be an easy kill. She didn't intend to make any of this easy for Julia.

Lauren mustered as much energy as she could, and she threw Julia off her. She moved fast to pin the woman's hands to the ground by throwing her body over Julia's.

"Kill Cameron," Julia shouted out to her hired thug. "Kill him now." And the thug fired some shots.

That was not the right thing for Julia to say, and it caused a new wave of anger to wash through Lauren. She slammed her forearm into Julia's face, causing the woman's head to flop back. Lauren took full advantage of that. She ripped the gun from Julia's hand, turned toward the thug.

Lauren fired.

But her shot wasn't necessary. The thug was already in the process of falling to the ground. That was when she saw Cameron. Alive, thank God. And with his gun aimed right at the fallen man.

Beneath her, she felt Julia's body tense. The woman was probably about to gear up for another round of the fight. She didn't get a chance to do that, though. Cameron raced toward them, and he pointed his gun at Julia.

"Please move so I can shoot you," he said through clenched teeth.

Julia went limp, her hands dropping to her sides. Lauren didn't relax, though. She got up and took aim at the woman, as well.

Lauren risked a glance at Cameron to make sure he

was okay. He seemed to be. No blood anyway. She was certain she was bleeding, though, from the punches she'd taken from Julia.

The sound of running footsteps sent Cameron snapping in the direction of the cruiser. Lauren looked there, too, and saw a welcome sight.

Jameson.

Her brother seemed fine, too.

"The guy with the launcher's dead," Jameson said. "I don't see any other hired guns around, but we need to get out of here." He glanced down at Julia. "We can get that piece of slime behind bars."

Julia had a strange reaction to that. She looked up at Lauren and laughed. "It's not over," the woman said. "I had a backup plan in case something went wrong. In case you didn't bring the babies with you, after all."

"What do you mean?" Lauren asked, and she reminded herself that anything that came out of the woman's mouth could be a lie.

But this didn't feel like a lie.

Not with that sick smile on Julia's face.

"Evelyn didn't want any part of the violence," Julia continued. "She didn't want to get her hands dirty. But she's at the ranch now to get her grandson. And I sent enough hired guns with her to do just that."

Chapter Seventeen

Cameron couldn't get to his phone fast enough, and he prayed that Julia's threat was all just a bluff. But he also knew Evelyn. Knew that she was desperate to get her hands on Patrick, so she might indeed have fallen for something like this.

"Hurry," Lauren said. She was firing glances all around, no doubt looking for a way to get to the ranch ASAP.

"I'm calling Gabriel," he told her, and he pressed the number. It rang and then went to voice mail.

Hell.

That was not what Cameron wanted to hear. Apparently, neither did Lauren, because she hurried to Julia's car. "The keys are in the ignition."

If they took it they could leave immediately, especially since the cruiser had been disabled. "Jace..." Cameron mumbled.

"Go," Jameson insisted. "I'll stay with him and see if I can get the ambulance out here. If not, I can take the gunmen's SUV."

Cameron figured there were some concerns about the plan, but his bigger concern was getting to the boys. He ran to the car, motioning for Lauren to get in, but she had by the time he got behind the wheel.

There was no place to turn around, so he threw the car into Reverse. "Look for any kind of tracking devices," he added to Lauren.

He figured Julia wouldn't have put anything like that on the vehicle, but it was possible the loan shark had. That was just one possible obstacle. The next one was the hired guns that Julia said were at the end of the trail—the very place they needed to go to get back on the road to the ranch.

"I don't see anything," Lauren said. She shook her head, the panic in both her expression and her voice. "But if it's small enough, it could be hidden underneath something."

Yeah, and it probably wouldn't be that small. Still, it wasn't something he could worry about right now, especially since there was the biggest worry of all— possible gunmen at the ranch. And Gabriel was short some hands and deputies because they'd been at the sites where they were supposed to trap the gunmen.

They'd failed at that.

But Cameron couldn't fail at getting to Isaac and Patrick.

"Try calling Gabriel again," Cameron told her.

She did, all the while she was mumbling something. A prayer from the sound of it. Cameron said a few himself.

"Voice mail," Lauren relayed to him, and she groaned. Not an ordinary one but the kind that sounded as if she was about to cry.

"Keep trying," he pressed. "And get down on the seat."

He knew that was only going to cause her more alarm, but there was nothing he could do about it. They were approaching the end of the trail, and while he didn't hear any gunfire, that didn't mean the shooters weren't there. Added to that, the car probably wasn't bullet resistant like the cruiser.

While she kept redialing Gabriel's number, Lauren did sink lower in the seat, but she kept her head high enough to keep watch. Cameron was watching, too, and that was why he had no trouble spotting the three vehicles at the intersection of the trail and the road. One was a black SUV, identical to what the other hired guns had driven. There was also a cruiser and a truck that he knew belonged to one of the ranch hands.

"I don't see any gunmen," Lauren said on a rise of breath.

Other than Allen, the ranch hand, neither did he. He had the butt of a rifle resting against his hip. There was a Texas Ranger next to him and a reserve deputy on the other side of the trail. Cameron slowed down and lowered his window.

"The gunmen are dead," Allen said to Cameron. He tipped his head to the trail. "How about up there?"

"Dead. There could be trouble at the ranch. Lauren and I are headed there now, but you should go check on Jameson and Jace. Jace will need an ambulance. Is the road clear?" he asked without pausing.

"As far as I know. I'll follow you," Allen volunteered.

Cameron thanked him but didn't wait for the man. He backed out onto the road, and now that there was room to turn around, that was exactly what he did. Fast. And he sped toward the ranch.

The rain had slowed some, but there was still plenty of water on the road. It was a risk, but Cameron didn't slow down. Everything inside him was yelling for him to get to the boys as fast as he could.

"Gabriel," Lauren said.

Finally. But Cameron didn't breathe easier just yet. "Put the call on speaker. Are the boys okay?" Cameron asked the moment Lauren did that. "Julia said there could be gunmen at the ranch."

"Yeah to both. The boys are fine, but we've definitely got some armed thugs."

The panic slammed through Cameron. Through Lauren, too, because he heard her make a hoarse sob.

"That's why I couldn't answer your call," Gabriel continued. "I'm out by the barn where I just took out two of them."

Two. But Cameron was betting there were more than that. Heck, Julia could have sent a dozen of them.

"Julia sent them," Cameron explained. "And Evelyn will be with them."

"We have Evelyn in handcuffs, facedown on the porch, but we haven't managed to round up a final gunman yet. He's somewhere near the front of the ranch. Maybe by the road. If I thought it would do any good, I'd tell you two to wait until—"

"We'll be there in about a minute," Cameron interrupted.

"I figured you'd say that. Just be careful because this guy has a rifle with a scope." Gabriel ended the call, probably because he had his hands full making sure the house was safe. Which was exactly what Cameron wanted him to do.

"I'm not staying down on the seat this time," Lauren said. "I want to stop this guy."

Like Gabriel, Cameron knew he didn't stand a chance of winning that argument with her. Besides, he might need her. Lauren had proven herself to be a good shot, and he wanted all the backup he could get. No way did he want this guy firing anywhere near Gabriel's house.

Cameron slowed when they approached the turn for the ranch, and he drew his gun, keeping it in his hand, but he didn't see anyone. Well, no one that he didn't recognize anyway. There were two ranch hands, both armed, and they were in a truck parked on the side of the road. He pulled to a stop next to them and lowered his window again.

"We lost sight of the guy," the hand said. "But he came this way, and he's wearing all black."

That wasn't an especially good camouflage color, but he could be hiding in the trees that were nearby. Of course, that would be the first place someone would look for him. And maybe this man knew that.

"Check the ditch on your side," Cameron told Lauren.

He kept his window down and moved the car up so the hands' truck wouldn't be obstructing his view. He angled his head to get a better look. Like the ditches on the trail, these were filled with water. Water that was almost black under the iron-gray sky and rain.

Cameron crept along at a snail's pace, searching, while Lauren did the same on the other side. He was a good twenty yards from the ranch hands before he spotted something.

The gunman.

The guy was squatting chest-deep in the water. And yes, he had a rifle. One that he immediately started turning toward Cameron.

Cameron didn't even bother telling Lauren to watch out. There wasn't time. He just took aim and fired. Not one shot but three. The bullets slammed into the guy's chest, and they must have killed him instantly because the thug didn't even get the chance to pull the trigger.

Lauren sat there, frozen for a moment. She'd seen way too much death in the past couple of days, but she didn't leave her attention on the dead gunman for long. She looked at Gabriel's house. She didn't need to tell Cameron to hurry there now. He did. Because they both had to see for themselves that the boys were truly okay.

"Cameron shot the gunman," she said to Gabriel when she called him. "Yes, he's dead. Was anyone hurt at the ranch?"

Since she hadn't put this call on speaker and because his heartbeat was drumming in his ears, Cameron didn't hear what Gabriel said. However, the news must have been good because Lauren released the breath she'd been holding.

"No one's hurt," she relayed to Cameron when she ended the call.

Cameron was glad for that, but he wasn't feeling any relief yet and wouldn't until they were inside.

He went too fast again, the tires shimmying over the slick surface, but he managed to get them to Gabriel's. Before he'd even brought the car to a full stop, Lauren was out and running to the porch. Cameron was right behind her. There was no sign of Evelyn, thank goodness.

When Cameron went through the front door, he expected Lauren to already be on her way to the bathroom or wherever they'd moved the boys. But she wasn't. She was in the foyer with Jodi.

"Where's Evelyn?" Cameron asked, hoping the woman wasn't in the house.

"One of the Rangers took her into town to lock her

up," Jodi answered. "I'm thinking this will pretty much put an end to any challenge she might have for custody."

Yes, it would. That was the silver lining in this. The other silver lining was Lauren.

Lauren whirled around to Cameron when he shut the door, and before he even saw it coming, she was in his arms. She kissed him. Not one of those passion-laced kisses that'd led to sex. This one seemed to be from pure relief.

"You saved my life," she said, her voice cracking.

There were tears in her eyes. And bruises and small cuts on her face from where Julia had punched her. It made him want to go back and throttle the woman. But Cameron didn't want to give Julia another moment of his time.

"And you saved mine," he answered.

Lauren nodded, managed a half smile and brushed another kiss on his mouth. "Good. Because I'm in love with you. Now, wipe the blood off your chin so we can see Isaac and Patrick."

He automatically reached to take care of the blood, but then her words sank in. It was too late, though, for him to respond because Lauren took off running toward the hall bathroom.

Jodi just shrugged. "I think the only person surprised by that I-love-you is *you*."

What? Cameron shook his head. That certainly wasn't common knowledge.

Was it?

Again, there was no time to dwell on it because he hurried after Lauren. And he found her, all right. She was on the bathroom floor and had both boys in her arms. She was showering them with kisses. Isaac liked it because he was giggling, but Patrick was fussing and trying to get away from her so he could get to his toy horse.

Cameron scooped up both the boy and the horse in his arms, and Patrick rewarded him with a sloppy kiss on the cheek. That kiss went a long way to soothing the adrenaline that was still surging through him.

"Is it okay for us to leave the bathroom?" Merilee asked. "Because it seems as if Lauren and you should have some family time with the boys." Dara added a sound of agreement.

Family time. That made it sound as if their marriage—a real marriage—was a done deal.

Cameron nodded. "Just stay inside and don't go near any windows," Cameron instructed. He needed to go out and check on Gabriel, to make sure the danger had passed before things could start getting back to normal.

Well, his new normal anyway. Whatever that would be.

He sank down on the floor next to Lauren, and Patrick and Isaac must have taken that as playtime because both boys went to the stash of toys that was all over the bathroom floor and started bringing them to Lauren and him.

Lauren turned to Cameron, and she eked out another smile. "Everything considered, you don't look shell-shocked."

Then he was covering it well, because he was. Shell-shocked about the attack, about how close they'd come to dying and Julia's obsessive greed. But what Lauren had told him was at the top of that list of surprising things.

I'm in love with you.

Cameron was about to ask her if it was true, but she leaned in, and with that smile still in place she kissed him. It wasn't a relief kiss this time. No, this one had some heat to it. When she finally broke away, his breath was a little thin, but he was ready to launch into the conversation they needed to have.

But the footsteps stopped him.

Since the boys were right there, Cameron drew his gun and pivoted in the direction of the doorway. However, it wasn't a gunman. It was Gabriel. He glanced at all of them before his attention settled on his sister.

"Are you okay?" he asked.

Lauren nodded. She touched a bruise on her cheek that had obviously gotten Gabriel's attention. "Trust me, Julia looks worse. I got in some punches, too."

Gabriel winced a little, probably because he hated having to hear about his kid sister being in a fistfight with a would-be killer. It would certainly give Cameron some nightmares for years to come. They'd gotten damn lucky that Julia's shot had missed.

"Jameson has Julia on the way to jail," Gabriel continued. "And I think we got all the hired guns, not just here at the ranch but also the ones on the trails," Gabriel added to Cameron. "But everyone should stay in for a while until we've searched the grounds."

Good. Cameron didn't want to take any more risks with Lauren or the babies. "Has Julia said anything else?"

Gabriel shook his head. "She just yammered about wanting her lawyer. She'll want a plea deal but won't get one. I'll make sure of that. And we have enough from what Julia said to arrest the loan shark."

"That would hopefully keep the guy off the streets for the rest of his life. After all, he'd supplied the hired guns who'd killed Maria."

Lauren shook her head. "I still don't know why Julia sent those men to my house. She knew about the swap so why didn't she just try to take Isaac?"

"Because I think she wanted concrete proof of the swap," Gabriel answered. "If she'd managed to get you out of the picture, she would want to be able to prove that she had Alden's son in her custody."

True, but Cameron seriously doubted Julia would have kept Isaac around any longer than necessary. Only until she'd gotten her hands on the money.

Gabriel hitched his thumb to the front of the house. "I need to go out and check on the hands."

"I can help," Cameron volunteered.

"No," Gabriel said without hesitation. "You should stay here and work things out with Lauren." He paused and lifted an eyebrow when Cameron just stared at him. "Jodi mentioned what she'd heard in the foyer."

Great. Now Gabriel might want to punch him. Except he didn't make any move to do that. However, Gabriel did glare at him some.

"Just make Lauren happy," Gabriel growled. "Because if you don't, you'll have to answer to me."

Lauren huffed. "Let Cameron get his footing first before you go all alpha on him." Then she added a wink to her brother.

It seemed, well, such a light moment, considering they were only minutes out of an attack. But then it was hard to stay gloom and doom with the boys crawling all over them. Even Gabriel was smiling when he strolled away.

"My footing?" Cameron asked.

"Yes. I figured you'd need some time to come to terms with me telling you I love you."

He opened his mouth, closed it and tried to come up with a good answer to that. "You meant it?"

Her eyebrow came up. "Of course I did. You thought it was some heat of the moment thing?"

"I didn't know," he admitted. "I thought maybe you said that because of the boys."

She didn't say, "What?" but that expression was all over her face.

"You know, because you want us to have a life together with the boys," he clarified. And he was obviously not gaining any ground here. She was frowning now.

Lauren huffed again, slipped her hand around the back of his neck and kissed him. Really kissed him. This one had much too high of a heat level considering they weren't alone.

"Do you know now?" She kept her mouth right next to his as if ready to convince him again.

Cameron didn't need convincing, but he kissed her anyway. There it was. More than the heat. More than this insane attraction that had been brewing for years. It was deeper than that, and now Cameron could finally tell her.

"I love you," he said, taking Lauren into his arms. "Not because of the boys, either—though they're a sweet bonus. I love you because of us. Because of you and me."

That was the right thing to say because Lauren smiled and pulled him to her for another kiss.

* * * * *

LET'S TALK
Romance

For exclusive extracts, competitions
and special offers, find us online: